A PUFFIN BOOK
PROPERTY OF
D0682896

Henry Treece was an English poet and historical novelist. Born in 1911 in Wednesbury, Staffordshire, he went to the local high school and then to Birmingham University where he studied English, History and Spanish. After he graduated he became a schoolteacher, and later served in the RAF Bomber Command during World War II.

When the war was over, he returned to teaching and writing. One of his earliest books for children was *Legions of the Eagle*, published in 1954. He went on to write many tales of the Vikings, Romans and Celts.

Henry Treece died in 1966 and *The Dream-Time*, his last novel for children, was published after his death in 1967 with a postscript by renowned children's historical fiction writer, Rosemary Sutcliff.

HENRY TREECE

THE VIKING SAGA

Illustrated by Christine Price

PUFFIN BOOKS

UK | USA | Canada | Ireland | Australia
India | New Zealand | South Africa

Puffin Books is part of the Penguin Random House group of companies whose addresses can be found at global.penguinrandomhouse.com.

www.penguin.co.uk
www.puffin.co.uk
www.ladybird.co.uk

Viking's Dawn first published by The Bodley Head 1955
Published in Puffin Books 1967
The Road to Miklagard first published by The Bodley Head 1957
Published in Puffin Books 1967
Viking's Sunset first published by The Bodley Head 1960
Published in Puffin Books 1967
This collection published as *The Viking Saga* in Puffin Books 1985
Reissued in this edition 2016
004

Set in 10.5/14.5 pt Sabon LT Std
Typeset by Jouve (UK), Milton Keynes
Printed and bound in Great Britain by Clays Ltd, Elcograf S.p.A.

A CIP catalogue record for this book is available from the British Library

ISBN: 978-0-141-36865-8

All correspondence to:
Puffin Books
Penguin Random House Children's
80 Strand, London WC2R 0RL

Contents

Viking's Dawn

Contents

About this Book

This is the story of a voyage made by a shipload of Northmen about the year AD 780, before the regular Viking invasions on Britain began. In this book the word 'Viking' means 'a sea-traveller,' though it can also be taken to imply 'a dweller along the wicks', or fjords. 'To go a-viking', therefore, is to go on a voyage.

Who were the Northmen? It is perhaps wrong of us to think of them as being definitely Norsemen or Danes or Swedes or Finns or Lapps. At this stage in their history they had not fully developed those differences in nationality which they have today. Though, of course, there was some similarity, especially in their folk tales and myths. Horic's wind-tying, and his trick with the beetle, both belong to Lapp folklore; while Thorkell's tale about the Vikings who discussed the afterlife while waiting to be beheaded comes from a Norse saga.

What manner of men were these Northmen? They are often described as being bloodthirsty pirates and nothing else. Yet it is worth noting that when they had settled in this country they became some of its most law-abiding inhabitants. Moreover, their wonderful sagas show that their literature was a highly cultivated one; the splendid construction of their longships demonstrates their intelligence and ingenuity. No doubt they *were* fierce and reckless; yet it must be remembered that they had to face equally fierce and reckless enemies. Had the Vikings not possessed such qualities, they would not have left their enduring name on the pages of history as they have done.

But why did the Northmen suddenly decide to go a-viking, after centuries of quiet living? Historians have a number of answers to this question. Some say that the Scandinavian countries were becoming overpopulated and that the Vikings sought new homes. Yet it is a strange thing that, in the early stages at least, after making their raids, they then returned to their own homes. Other scholars say that the Vikings were some of the most independent Northmen, who wished to get away from the new centralized governments that were being set up at home. Still others put forward the theory that the Northmen were carrying on a great battle against Christianity, which was at last threatening to engulf them. Such experts see the Viking invasions as being 'the last great effort of Odin to limit the dominion of Christ'. Yet, once again, it is worth noting that when they became Christians, the Vikings were only too anxious to spread their new faith, even to the extent of chopping off the heads of those who would not forsake Odin!

It is all a great enigma. Perhaps those historians who say that the Vikings sailed simply because the herring on which they fed had moved to other places are as near as anyone else in solving the problem. But what we do know without any doubt is that they *did* sail and, in sailing, created a great sea tradition which we British have inherited from them; for the blood of Aun and Harald and Thorkell runs in our veins too.

This book sets out to tell the story of one of the earliest voyages, not one of the great journeys, for it happens before the sea-rovers had a very clear idea of the broader world about them. Yet it was a pioneer voyage, and so full of unforeseen dangers. It is the tale of one longship, on one voyage.

In our world, when we are used to big aircraft making their daily trips across the Atlantic, month in and month out, we perhaps forget those early pioneers who flew ten miles – and then no more. We admire those prairie schooners that passed over the wide spaces, from one side of America to the other; but do we ever give a thought to those wagons – small worlds of wood and canvas to their occupants, like our longship – whose wheels and shafts lay, bleached like bones among the cactus in the cruel sunlight, after the Indians had fired them?

Nowadays, perhaps too many of us long for immediate glory. We ignore, and even despise, those who do not quite 'make the grade'. Yet they are often the pioneers, because of whose hard efforts later adventurers find an easier success. Someone must set the ball rolling, whoever scores with it afterwards!

Have you ever seen the painting which shows an incident in the boyhood of Raleigh? In it an old sea dog is telling the boy about the adventures to be met with on the high seas. Young Raleigh sits, cross-legged and wide-eyed. The old sailorman passes on his experience to one who will make a more glorious use of it one day. But *who* was that old man?

Perhaps, when you have read this, you may see the importance of Thorkell and the many others who went to Valhalla. And perhaps you will understand Harald better. I hope so.

HENRY TREECE

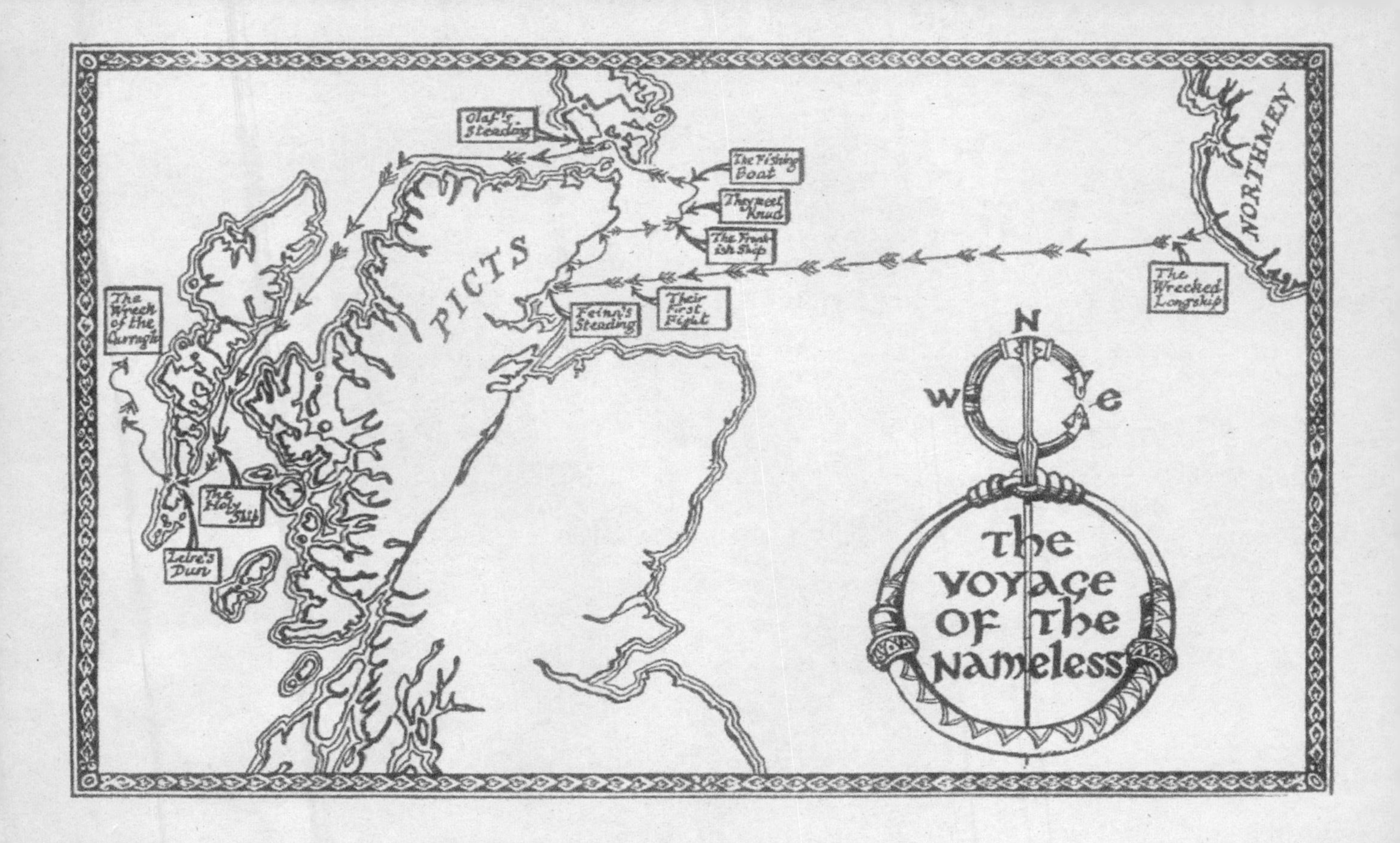
The Voyage of the Nameless
N
W
E
NORTHMEN
PICTS
The Wrecked Longship
The Fishing Boat
They meet Knud
The Frankish Ship
Their First Fight
Feinn's Steading
Olaf's Steading
The Wreck of the Curragh
The Holy Isle
Lelre's Dun

1. The Hall by the Tarn

TWO FIGURES stood in the darkness, a man and a boy. Behind them the pine woods sighed, as though overcome by a great and unnameable sadness, the melancholy sound made by all ancient forests. As the round moon came from behind a bank of cloud, throwing its silver light over the rough and rocky land below, the two figures peered down into the valley beneath them, their heavy cloaks sweeping away from them in the night wind that blew towards them from the woods. A great white seabird circled above their heads, crying harshly and pitifully in the moonlight. They shuddered at the sound, looking up in dread. The man's bearded lips moved silently, as though he spoke a charm against the witches of the night. The moon slowly withdrew behind the straggling cloudbank, and for a moment there was utter darkness once more.

Then suddenly, from the valley, came a surge of flame, a great red and orange spurting-up of light. A thick cloud of oily smoke rose above it, into the night air. A flock of birds flew, twittering up from the valley, to the woods. The two

watchers drew in their breath as the many wings beat above them in the darkness.

Now the fire-glow spread and its angry light flared out over a black tarn nearby, so that the man and boy saw reflected in the sombre water every shape and hue of the flames.

The man licked his lips and said, 'His hall burns well, son. When we laid the logs for him, I did not think we should see such a sending-off fire.'

The boy said, 'Such a king as he does not deserve a funeral fire like that. A king who has no ship to take him to Odin is not worth following. Better a man should go a-viking for himself.'

The man looked angry for a space. Then he smiled and said, 'It would go hard with us old ones if you young cocks ruled the world! Gudröd could not help being a poor man. There are too many kings in the land, lad; and not all of them can be rich men. My choice fell out badly, to pledge myself to a poor man, that is all. Yet, no doubt, Odin will receive Gudröd in Valhalla no less courteously because he sails there in a burning house than if he came in a longship!'

The boy frowned and said, 'You served him too faithfully, Father. We should have left him before the famine came. When his corn failed, we should have gone to the coastwise Norse and lived off fish. The herring never fail.'

Now the fire had reached its height and began to slacken. The air about the two was filled with the smell of acrid smoke. Small burnt particles and ashes fell about them. The man wiped his hand across his forehead. His gold arm-ring flashed in the glow. He said, 'Who is to know? One day the herring might go away. Then what will the fishers do? They will have neither corn nor fish, Harald. How shall a Norseman live then, think you?'

'He will live on his wits, as Odin meant him to, Father,' said the boy. 'There are other lands and other folk who have plenty. The Danes have plenty, so have the English. Or a man could voyage overland and take his bread from the Romans. There is no need to starve, Father.'

Now the blaze below them was sinking to a dull glow and the birds were flying back from the wood towards the tarn's dark waters.

The man said, 'Life is never sure, Harald. Whichever way a man turns, he thinks he might have done better to take the other path.'

The boy frowned and shut his eyes tight, as though squeezing the sudden tears from them. 'If we had left Gudröd sooner, my mother and brothers might still be alive with us. They would not have died in the famine.'

The man made an impatient movement under his cloak, almost as though his hand would strike the boy, but he answered calmly, 'Only Odin knows whether that is true, son. We might have lost them in a village-burning if we had gone to the coast. They might have been chosen as sacrifices when the fishing went badly. We do not know. At least, old Gudröd did not call for sacrifices. That much can be said for him.'

The boy's voice was bitter. 'No, he knew which side his bread was buttered. He had so few followers left that he could not afford to lay any of them on the stones. He might have had to do a hand's turn himself, if he had done.'

The man turned away from him, impatiently. 'Come, Harald,' he said. 'We will make the best of a bad job and find another lord to follow.'

They made their way towards the dark woods, and only once did they turn back to glance at the dying embers of Gudröd's great hall. As the pine trees enfolded them the man said, 'This way lies the fjord, if the beasts of the forest will let us pass.'

The boy said, 'Better to become the bear's supper than to remain the cow's slave.'

The man smiled grimly, 'Who shall say that but one who has found himself on the bear's dish?'

They spoke no more as they pushed past the overhanging boughs and went into the deep darkness of the forest.

2. Thorkell Fairhair

THE FJORD was full of the noise of busy men. The very air seemed to vibrate as in a great open-air smithy. The clanging of anvil-blows, the hammering of planks, the buzzing of long two-handed saws echoed and re-echoed across the enclosed blue water. And all these sounds seemed to glance like flat stones over the surface of the sea-valley, to lose themselves up the farther rocky slopes and then in the great dim forests that crowned the rim of the inlet and stretched far away into the mountains, into the unknown frightening spaces of trolls and witches.

The little thatch and wooden settlement that straggled along the shore of the fjord throbbed with activity. Black-faced men in leather aprons worked the great ox-skin bellows to fan the flames of many outdoor furnaces; others beat out long iron nails on anvils that were gripped between their padded knees; yet others walked backwards down long rope-walks, twisting the harsh fibres in their raw hands. The women worked busily stitching, with thick waxed thread, or at the shuttles of their looms, which were set up outside the hovel doors so as to make the most of the new and welcome spring light. Children scurried back and forth, fetching and carrying for their sweating elders, sometimes a hammer, or a pail of ice-cold water to temper the iron, sometimes a roughly-cut hunk of barley bread or a pannikin of corn-wine.

All worked in that place, even the very old and the crippled. The ship they were building was not the toy of one man; it was the property of them all. And it was almost finished. Another day at the most would see it ready for the painters. Even the oldest ones, plaiting thongs, horny-handed in the shadow, saw new dreams of gold taking shape before their dim eyes. 'Share and share alike,' thought they. 'To each his portion, and may she speed well and return laden before I make my greetings to Odin.' This longship had been built by the whole village. Those who were skilled in shipbuilding had worked day by day, with an adze on the planks or walking backwards along the rope-walks. Those who had no such skill, or were too old to wield an axe or to ply a needle, had contributed in other ways, either by supplying food and drink to their more active neighbours, or by paying good money to shipwrights to come from afar ... And all this, so that the ship should bring back profit to the village. These men did not think of glory, or even of adventure. They were practical men – as most northerners are – who wanted a good return for their labour or money. And the ship which they were creating would bring back those good returns, they hoped. This village had heard of the rich court of the Franks. They had seen the fine silks and the painted pictures that had come from Miklagard. And such English noblemen as had crossed the northern seas to them had worn gold about their necks and arms ... The rest of the world must be very rich, they thought.

And so they built this longship, to relieve the rest of the world of some of its surplus riches. The village on the fjord could do with a little gold, and some silks. It would not even object to a few pictures – provided, of course, that the artist had used real gold leaf in painting them!

Among all these fjord folk, the longship lay on her runway like a royal thing, a proud princess whose slaves attended to her every want. A longship that would brave the harsh buffeting of the open seas, or out-trick the subtlest of rivers. A handsome shell in which a warrior king would feel proud to drift out on an ebb tide, the death-flames licking round him as he lay among his furs and his weapons and his hounds, on that last long journey to Odin's feast hall.

Of clean and fresh-smelling oak, the longship was almost eighty feet long, from stem to stern, and sixteen feet broad at her middle. Standing over seven feet high from keel-bottom to gunwales, she dwarfed the many busy men who toiled about her on the stocks, even though as yet her forty-foot mast had not been stepped into its socket in the keel. They smiled at each other, satisfied with their work. If the good weather held, they would step the mast tomorrow, so that it would fall backwards quickly and easily when the forestay was eased off. And tomorrow, by the help of all the gods in the groves, they would fit the other ropes, the stays to prow and stern, those that braced the long yardarm, those that ran on pulleys to raise and lower the sail . . .

The foreman of the shipwrights wiped a rough and work-soiled hand over his red face. He turned to the apprentice lad who caulked the smart clinker-built planking of the sides.

'Never was maiden more comely,' he said. 'Trust a horse before a hound, a hound before a lass – and a longship before them all!' The boy grinned back at him. 'Maybe you are right, Master Björn,' he said. 'But women can be useful at times! My aunt and my sisters have woven the sail for her, and a fine thing it is – all red and blue and green, in great stripes the thickness of a pine-trunk.'

'Ay, and your mother has embroidered the pennant, hasn't she, lad?' said Björn, smiling.

The boy looked down, as though he knew not what to say. 'Well, Master,' he ventured at last, 'she has edged it and put on its long golden fringe, but no one has told her what emblem to work on the white silk. It rests as unmarked as the snows on the Bear Mountain. We know not what name she shall carry.'

He glanced at Björn craftily, as though expecting his master to give him the answer. But Björn only whistled and bent to examine a row of rivets and their great square washers that held the long oak planks fast together.

'Ay, ay,' he said, in a whisper, 'who knows what she will be named!'

The boy was suddenly conscious of a hush about him. He stopped working and bent towards Björn. 'Here is the one, Master, who will know, if anyone does.'

Björn turned and then pulled his forelock, and, like all the other workmen, stood silent and waiting. And among the huts by the blue water a name was whispered that fetched the young maids to the doorways, and put a smile on the faces of the older women.

'Thorkell Fairhair! Thorkell Fairhair!'

In the shadow of one hut an old man sat, patiently mending a fishnet. His hands were gnarled and twisted with rheumatism, but he forced them on and on, to tie the knots in the tarry twine. A long sword-cut had once ploughed the length of his cheek and had taken away the teeth on one side of his jaw. He heard the name, this old warrior, and a shiver seemed to pass over his face like a little cloud before the sun. His battle-scarred face wrinkled along its war-cuts in a strange, ironic smile.

'Ay, Thorkell Fairhair, the maids call him, knowing but his beauty! Thorkell Skullsplitter is his name in other parts.'

He shrugged and went on mending the net, his head shaking a little with a palsy brought on by the bitter wind that blew along the fjord for the greater part of the year.

The young man, Thorkell, stood among the silent folk. He was but of medium height, and slimly made. As yet he wore no moustaches or beard, and his blue eyes looked out of his smooth face as mildly as a girl's. Only there was something in the thin twist of his lips that took away from the gentleness. Something in the lean twitching of his jaws that spoke of tireless nervous energy. Something in the quick catlike tread that told its own tale of sudden action. Those who noted only the long corn-golden hair that hung, unplaited down his back, down the gilded mail shirt, would have been deceived, thought Björn.

Those who noted only the many glittering rings that circled his long slim fingers, the thick armbands that clasped his arms, the gold gorget at his throat, would have been deceived, thought the apprentice lad, with a secret grin. This was no maid; this was Thorkell, call him by whatever name you cared or dared, but Thorkell.

And when Thorkell came to the village, men were silent until he gave the word to speak. Even the old warriors, men who had killed bears in the high summer on the mountain tops. Some said he was the son of an outlawed king; some said he was a king himself, of another land beyond Ultima Thule; some, the oldest ones who had lost their grip on the life of ordinary men, whispered that Odin had sent him down among the Northmen to see what they were up to and to report back when he had seen. But when one too-daring young warrior in his cups had called him 'Thorkell Odinson' to his face, he had kicked the fool's feet from under him and had come near to throttling him with those same slim, ring-laden fingers ... So no one really knew what to think. And now Thorkell Whoever-he-was stood looking at the longship, looking and smiling faintly, out of those cold blue eyes, that seemed to see beyond the hull, beyond the ice blue fjord, beyond the farther hills and forests, and on and on, beyond the very rim of the world herself ...

Behind him stood another one. His sacking cloak hung as limply as the rough red hair that he had plaited loosely and had braided with leather shoelaces; a tall thin man, with the nose of a hawk and the quick eyes of a ferret. A man who was constantly scratching his side or poking a bony finger into his great red ears. This was a different sort of man. He wore no mail shirt, but a long leather jerkin, plated here and there with strips of iron to act as armour of a sort. About his thin waist he wore a rusting chain – not a gilt-studded belt, like Thorkell's. But from that chain hung something more terrifying than the red-sheathed longsword that Thorkell bore; a mace of bog oak, into which a score of sharp flints had been sunk, each one jutting horribly forth, its sharpest point outward. This was a weapon to fear in all truth. The sword is deadly, but its work is done in a minute. Such a thing as this man wore might bring the torments of the damned upon a man before Odin smiled down on him and gave him some relief.

The villagers saw the mace, saw the strange, sad, sheeplike face of the man as he scratched his thin hair or shuffled his high shoulders as though the nibbling-ants were at him. 'Wolf Water-hater,' they said. 'Wolf who has never washed in his life and vows to stay like that until his time comes!'

And even the children giggled and pushed closer to see this Wolf, who had sailed on every sea man knew, yet hated the very thought of water touching his tender skin!

Then the long silence was broken. Thorkell turned his head towards the tall man. 'Is she fair?' he asked, laconically.

Wolf stepped forward so pompously that even the apprentice lad smiled. He went onwards, his pale eyebrows raising and lowering themselves, and seemed to look at the longship as though he had never seen one before.

He stopped and poked his red finger into one of the sixteen oar-ports that ran along each side of the ship in the third strake from the top. They were not round holes, but long narrow ones. Wolf ran his finger along them for a while, then turned and said, 'Cut off the shipmaster's thumbs; he is too lazy to carve a circle.'

There was a stir among the folk. Björn was a true Norseman and did not wait for anyone to ask where he was. He stepped down from his plank and nodded to Thorkell. Then he waited for the other to speak. Thorkell said, 'Shall we cut them off with your own knife or with mine?' He drew a long thin blade from his girdle. The haft was set with coral, noted Björn. The village folk drew in their breath. The children were secretly cuffed into silence. The old man mending the net shrugged his shoulders and licked his forefinger to twist another knot, as though he had heard it all before and thought it little worth the noting.

Björn said, 'Yours, Thorkell. Mine is too tarry from the ropes.' He held out his hand for Thorkell's knife. It was a pretty one and Björn was curious to see how it was made. Thorkell handed it to him and the shipmaster examined it carefully and then returned it with a smile. 'Not much good against a wolf, I should say,' he said.

Thorkell said, 'You are wrong, Björn. If you were to keep your thumbs, I would bet you a horse against a yard of rope that this knife is just the thing to probe beneath a spring bear's fat.'

He went towards Björn to illustrate what he was saying. 'Look, the blade is thin and keen. You just slip it under his arm as he grasps, and you roll sideways, like this, and then he falls, but you must be ready to jump back for he weighs heavier than a chariot! He would crunch your leg like a winter stick!'

As he said this he made the movements of the hunter, while Björn pretended to be the bear waked from his hibernation. The folk stood stock-still, sucking in their breath with expectation, for they were simple northern folk who readily gave themselves to a tale.

Thorkell thrust with his thin knife, and the strong-armed Björn watched and twisted sideways as the hunter twisted. And the bear held the knife clasped firm beneath his armpit. Thorkell was trapped!

So long the two held this lock that a child said, 'Mother, the men are silly with the new sun. I want my milk, mother! Milk, mother!'

Then Thorkell let his knife fall on the pebbled shore of the fjord. He straightened up and smiled. Björn straightened up and smiled too. Then Björn stooped and picked up Thorkell's knife and gave it back to him.

'Here are my thumbs,' he said.

Thorkell said, 'Wolf, you are a fool. You should go back to the Caledonians and say that you are a fool. Björn is a sensible man. He has bear's blood in him, like all proper Northmen. Björn will tell you why the oar-holes are not round.'

Björn said, 'Master Thorkell, saving your presence, Wolf is a fairly sensible man for a Pict, but he is hasty. That is all. The oar-holes are not round because my lad here has sense. In truth, he has never sailed farther across the water than this fjord, but he has sense. This is his idea. "When you have the sail up," says he, "you do not need the oars, Master." I spoke him fair and agreed with him. "All right," says he. "When you pull in the oar, what have you left?" "A hole," says I. "Right," says he, "then make your hole flat and straight, so that an oar can come into the ship by it, allowing for the blade. Then make a little shutter over the flat hole, and you have got rid of the fear of water!" All this said the boy, and like a fool I followed him, for the idea seemed a good one to me. And I put little shutters, as he had said, over the oar-holes, so that the ship would be safe from the waves.'

Björn moved across to the longship and pointed to the securely-bolted pieces of wood.

Thorkell watched him. Then he turned his pale blue eyes upon Wolf, slowly, steadily, with a sidelong motion of the head. And the smile on his lips was not pleasant to see. The old man in the shadows lowered his war-torn face and said, 'Aiee, Aiee, Wolf should not speak so fast!'

Thorkell said, 'Wolf, come you here, you dolt of dolts.'

Wolf shambled back from the longship as readily as he had gone to it, a smile on his thin red face, his thin red hand still scratching under his leather jerkin.

'Kneel before the shipmaster and beg his pardon,' said Thorkell, looking down at him.

The villagers stared as the thin man knelt.

'Not with his knife,' said Wolf, pleasantly. 'I would prefer yours, Thorkell. Every man can make a mistake, but that is no reason why he should suffer more than a twelvemonth.'

Björn said, 'Must he take my punishment, Thorkell?'

Thorkell said, 'Who talks of punishment among a free folk such as this? A man may have a joke, may he not, without spoiling the hand of a good tradesman?'

Wolf looked down at his red scarred hands. 'What trade can these follow, Thorkell?' he said, smiling quietly.

Thorkell kicked him gently in the side and rolled him over on to the pebbles. Then Wolf rose, rubbing his long finger below his nose, with a comical expression on his face, and Thorkell put his arm about his shoulders.

'Come, sideman,' he said, 'let us drink a horn of mead in this place and think about a name for the ship.' Then as an afterthought, he said, 'Come you, shipmaster, and let us drink together, for you seem a sharp fellow.'

Björn said, 'Not I, Thorkell, but my apprentice.'

'Bring him, too,' said Thorkell. 'A lad who has thoughts about oar-holes like that should make a Viking one day.'

3. The Crew-Choosing

NOW SHE lay ready, the proud longship of the fjord. In the three days since Thorkell Fairhair had returned to the village, the master painters had been at work on her, using their bright hues to transform the smooth-planed oak to a picture of magnificent colour. Each strake of her sides was painted a different colour, red and blue and ochre. Her gunwales were gilded. Each shutter over the oar-ports was painted a deep black. Her tall mast stood silver in the sunlight. The high-flung bows and stern shone richly under a thick layer of gold leaf, varnished with an Eastern resin to withstand the salty ravages of any deep and distant ocean. Even the platforms, fore and aft, were coloured leaf green, with an especially durable pigment whose secret was known only to these travelling craftsmen who journeyed here and there along the fjords at this time, selling their skill to any community that had such a venture in hand.

Thorkell Fairhair and his henchman Wolf sat at a rough table on the edge of the village, at the spot where the shore first started to run down to the fjord. On the board before them lay a heap of white knucklebones, perhaps four score in all. Thorkell's long sword lay beside them in its sheath, its hilt turned away from his hand so that he might only draw it at a disadvantage.

Behind the table stood the villagers, in many rows, old men, women and the children. Dogs and grunting pigs wandered here and there, some of them even stopping to rub against the trestles, or to push beneath the stools of the seated men.

Before the table stood a long line of men, some of them villagers, even men who had wielded the heavy adze on the oaken planks or dragged the giant spokeshave along the tall mast; others were men from farther away, who had heard the news of the venture and were anxious to share the excitements of the voyage. Yet others came from beyond the fjord, from far away where different kings ruled and different gods haunted a man's dreams. Yet all were welcome to Thorkell Fairhair, whatever strange tongue they spoke, whatever the colour of their skin.

For Thorkell must gather about him forty sailors before his new longship might set her face towards the farthermost seas. Forty men who feared nothing and who used a weapon as readily as they pulled at an oar. It was not always easy to find so many men of such qualities from one small community. And now men stood before him, saying their names, and the name of their weapon, laying their hands palm upwards on the tabletop so that Thorkell could judge whether they were callused enough to pull at an oar for days on end ... Those he rejected with a grim smile and a nod of his golden head smiled back as grimly and walked away, taking the path they had come, to find another village where a good ship was being pushed out into the fjord – for at this time a great restlessness was sweeping across the countries and men everywhere woke up with the itch to be moving . . . Those he chose were given a pair of the knucklebones to keep, as sign that they were under contract to Thorkell. They must keep these bones safely, until such time as they wished to break with him and leave the ship. Then, all they had to do was to hand them both back, putting one in his right hand and one in his left, with the words: 'The snow leaves the hills, the leaf leaves the trees, the bird leaves the nest – and I leave you.' Once the bones were given and the words spoken, neither man was under any obligation to the other, and might even kill each other should they feel the need to do so. But while the man had the bones and the words had not been said, he was bound to serve and to obey; nor might either harm the other even in the slightest degree, without becoming liable under the law of the folk-meeting to severe penalties. And these laws were strictly adhered to, even among men who might be called thieves and murderers by the rest of the world – the Christian world of the Franks and the English . . .

'I am Rolf Wryneck, steersman, and my dagger is named Battlefang,' said a thin man who carried his head on one side and seemed to sniff with a perpetual cold.

Thorkell turned back to Wolf and both laughed. 'This man should serve us well,' said Thorkell, 'for he will be able to see round the corners before we get there! Here are the bones, Rolf Wryneck, and may you steer us well!'

'I am Gnorre Nithing, from Finland, and my sword is Grunter,' said the next man, so stooping and round-shouldered that he almost looked deformed.

Wolf said, 'Nithing is a strange name, man. It is only given to one who has broken the law and whose life is any man's to take.'

Thorkell looked at him searchingly. 'What did you do, Nithing?' he asked sternly. 'No outlaw can sail with me.'

The Finn looked piteously at Thorkell. 'Master,' he stammered, 'I killed a man. Only that.'

'Only that!' echoed Thorkell, gazing at the Finn's bent back and stooping posture. 'What was he, a straw man in the spring festival?'

The villagers began to laugh and the Finn's face went red. He stammered and could not answer. His coarse hands trembled as he laid them on the table.

'Come man, speak up,' said Wolf, half jeering.

Then the man behind the Finn pushed forward. In height and breadth he was the biggest man the village had ever

seen. His harsh black hair hung down unkempt beneath his iron, horned helmet. About his massive chest he wore an untanned bearskin, pulled in to his thick waist with a length of rawhide. A double-bladed axe swung down to the ground from the strap.

'The Nithing asks for work,' he said to Thorkell, without any sign of respect. 'He does not ask to be tried by the folk-meeting here. He killed a man who had killed his brother. But that man was a king in Finland, and so Gnorre became a Nithing. I would have killed him. Would not you?' He fixed his red-rimmed eyes on Wolf and his great black beard jutted out towards Thorkell's henchman.

There were many about the table at that moment who edged away a little and took a firmer grip on their weapons, for it was at such moments as these that a deadly fight might begin.

Wolf scratched the side of his nose calmly and came round the table. He stood within an axe-stroke of the great man and said pleasantly, 'It is peaceful up there in the woods, among the trees. Here a man can hardly move for folk. And always there are women under his feet screaming that he will wake the baby.'

The big man smiled back grimly and said, 'I am of the woods. I get my clothes from the woods as you see. I am at home there. I know nothing of women and babies, but I will go with you to the woods.'

Now all about the table sucked in their breath for they knew what these calm words meant. Only Thorkell seemed unmoved. He said, 'Who are you to come here boasting of your prowess over bears? We have each killed a bear and do not go about parading his skin like a young man who is anxious for the girls to think him brave.'

The big man stopped smiling and said, 'I wish to call you Master, or I should answer you another way. I am Aun Doorback and this is Peacegiver.' He rattled the great axe on the tabletop. 'I speak now for Gnorre Nithing because he is not a man to speak for himself. He is a warrior and a Viking, not a talker about firesides.'

Thorkell smiled up at him gently, 'What right have you to speak for another man, Aun Doorback?' he said.

'The best right of all, Master Goldhair,' said Aun. 'It was my brother that Gnorre killed.'

There was a murmur among the villagers.

'Did you not wish to kill Gnorre, then?' asked Thorkell.

'No, Master,' said Aun. 'If Gnorre had not killed him, I should have done, for my brother was an evil man.'

'Should you not be king in his place, then?' asked Thorkell.

Aun said, 'Yes, but when the folk-meeting judged Gnorre to be an outlaw, I could not stay and rule such a stupid people. I chose to go with Gnorre and keep men from striking him down unjustly.'

Thorkell said, 'Take you two pairs of bones, Aun. One for yourself and one for Gnorre. You may be a good man.'

But Aun would not go from the table. He turned now to Wolf. 'Have we a debt to settle?' he said.

Wolf said, 'Let me feel the weight of your axe.'

He took the great weapon and made the motion of raising it. The veins in his arms stood out and his face was red. He smiled ruefully and said, 'I pity the bear on whose skull that falls.'

He handed back the great axe.

'I will fight you with knives or not at all,' he said.

Aun burst into a great laugh and said, 'I have never used a knife but to cut my meat. I should not be able to do more than scratch at you.'

Wolf said, 'That would suit me, friend! As for me, I should burst a blood vessel if I swung an axe big enough to match that tree trunk.'

They looked long at each other. Then Aun held out his hand and said, 'You are too brave a man to feed the ravens. I will not send you to your death, Redhead.'

Wolf took his hand and said, 'It would be a pity to spoil such a great mound of a man with my wicked little knife.'

Thus they were friends and Wolf went back behind the table, while Aun and Gnorre drew to one side to let the next man come forward.

And so the names were given, of man and weapon: Hasting and his axe Dream-maker; Gryffi and his sword Yell-stick; Kragge and his knife Homegetter; Ivar and his axe Pretty One, and so on, along the line of men, until at last there was only one man left. Yet Thorkell still had six knucklebones upon the table, enough for three men.

The last man sat silently, away from the others. He seemed to be crouching upon the pebbles, as though he were busy with something that held his attention. He had forgotten where he was. All eyes turned towards him and many men laughed to see him. He was very small and his face was the yellow colour of parchment. His black hair was shaven from the sides of his head and his one long plait was wound round and round on top of his skull and held up with bone pins. His eyes were narrow and his cheekbones high.

Thorkell called to him a time or two and at last he heard and came towards the table. Then they laughed. He wore a long heavy cloak of sheepskin and trousers of reindeer hide, but they hung too low between the legs so that his appearance was that of an ape rather than a man. He walked with his toes turned in and his long arms hanging at his sides.

When he got to the table he smiled, ignoring the laughter, and stood silent. Thorkell said, 'Are you a man?'

He did not understand the question and said thickly, 'No, I think not.' All the village roared, even the children, who crowded round to see what that funny man was like.

'Look at the beads sewn on to his skin tunic,' said one child.

'Yes, but look at the great bone rings on his wrists and arms. No bear has bones big enough to make such rings. He must be a Lapp wizard,' said another.

Thorkell heard the child. 'Are you from Lapland?' he asked.

The little man smiled even more broadly and shook his head so violently that it seemed his hair would come undone and fall about his face.

Thorkell said slowly and loudly, as one who speaks to a stupid child, 'What sword do you carry?'

The Laplander made the motion of carrying a heavy load. When the men had quietened again, Thorkell said, 'Have you a weapon?' He pointed to his own sword on the table. The Laplander went forward to take it up, thinking Thorkell had given it to him. Thorkell snatched it away only just in time.

'Speak to him, Wolf,' he said. 'I do not know how to make him understand.'

Wolf came forward and took the little man by the arm and went through the dumb show of fighting with a knife, then an axe, then a sword, even of wrestling.

It was at the last that he made the mistake of gripping the Laplander's arm too tightly. It seemed that the man thought he was actually being attacked. What happened then was too fast for most of the men to see properly. First they saw Wolf smiling, and grappling in play with the Lapp. Then they saw Wolf's legs disappearing over the little man's shoulder, and Wolf stretched out on the pebbles, the breath knocked quite out of him.

The little Lapp went forward and helped him up again. Wolf rubbed his shoulder painfully and said, 'Do your own talking now, Thorkell. I had almost as soon fight Aun Doorback.'

Then Gnorre came forward and whispered in the Lapp's ear. The man grinned and went to the table, 'Horic Laplander,' he said, 'no axe, no sword, no knife. This.'

He pulled from his pouch a thin length of tarred twine. There were four knots tied in it along its length. Thorkell put out his hand, in wonder, to touch it, but the man jumped back and shook his head. Gnorre said, 'You must not touch it, Master. It is a magic thing.'

'What does he call it?' asked Wolf, bewildered.

Gnorre spoke to him again, and the man said, 'Windmaker. Horic bring whatever wind ship wants. Untie knot, wind blow; tie knot, wind go.' Then he laughed aloud and stared from one face to another, in wonder, for no one believed him.

Thorkell said, 'No good. We have too many lunatics in the ship's company already. He must go back to Lapland with his winds.'

Aun stepped forward and said, 'If you send this man away, I shall go too. He will take the good winds with him.'

And three or four other men spoke up then and said that they would follow Aun and give back the knucklebones.

Thorkell was about to tell them to go when Wolf whispered and a smile came over Thorkell's face.

'Aun,' he said, 'you seem to spend your life fighting other men's battles, but I think none the less of you for that – unless you become too great a nuisance. You must remember that I am the shipmaster. Now, I will tell you what we will do – if this Horic is as good a wizard as everybody seems to think, let him do something we can all see, something useful to our enterprise, and then I will let him sail with us, for he seems to have strength enough to row the boat himself, without any help from us!'

Gnorre spoke to Horic, telling him to make a magic that would help the ship. Horic nodded and then bent down low over the ground, seeming to search among the coarse grass for something he had lost. Everyone watched him carefully now. Even the children were still.

Horic picked up something from the ground. It was a small black beetle. He stooped then and found a twig. All men watched him as he pulled out one of the black hairs of his head and carefully tied one end round the beetle's body and the other end to the twig. Then he pushed the twig a little way into the sandy ground and sat down near to it, watching.

The beetle began to walk round the twig, trying to get away, but he was tethered by the long black hair. All he could do was to go round and round. As he walked about the twig, the hair wrapped itself shorter and shorter until the beetle was only an inch from the twig.

By now men were beginning to think that this was only a jest that the Lapp was playing on Thorkell, and they began to laugh. But the little man looked up sternly and waved them to silence. Then, as the beetle approached the twig on the end of the hair, he looked up towards the wooded hilltop, his yellow face anxious, his narrow eyes keen and watchful.

'What in Odin's name is he doing?' asked Wolf.

'He is bringing you shipmen,' said Gnorre, in a hoarse whisper.

Now Thorkell watched with great concern for he was anxious to make up a full crew before he sailed. Yet every day's delay was a serious one, for these wandering men were impatient and would hand back the bones if they did not sail quickly.

Now the Lapp was trembling with an inner excitement and Thorkell saw that the beetle had almost touched the twig.

Suddenly it moved its hard-shelled back against the slip of wood, and Horic, gazing up the hill gave a little cry of pleasure and pointed towards the woods with his yellow hand.

They all turned and followed his gaze.

From between the hanging pine-boughs two men came, a young one and an older man, staggering as though they had come far across the mountains and through the woods.

The older man's head was covered by his long cloak, but all men saw that the young one had hair the colour of corn. The two waved joyously, as though with relief, and began to descend the hill towards the village. Thorkell shook his head in wonder then held out the bones to the Lapp. For a moment his eyes were fixed beyond the world's edge and he did not see them. Then he awoke and took the bones and stood by Gnorre to watch the two come down.

Aun said, 'The young one will make a proper Viking in time.'

So Harald and his father Sigurd came to the village at last.

4. The Ship-Naming

IN THE feast hall men were merry. Spruce boughs lined the walls, turning the long log shed into a forest glade. Resinous pine-boughs burned in iron wall-sockets, throwing their flickering light over the many laughing faces of the shipmen and the villagers who served them with mead and corn-wine, or carried in the great wooden platters laden with barley bread and fish, or tender sucking pigs.

The smoke of the fire in the middle of the hall blew back in gusts from the high chimney hole, for the wind was in a bad quarter. It was blowing out to the mouth of the fjord, and when that happened the smoke always seemed to come back, thick and choking, into the feast hall. But this night no one minded that, for all men spoke with great enthusiasm of the voyage they were about to make, no man knew where, in a great new ship as yet without a name.

Harald said to his father, 'It was a journey worth making, that through the forests, to reach such a place as this, and to be accepted among such men as these.' The boy's bright eyes lingered on the gay figure of Thorkell, who had dressed his beautiful hair with gold braids for the feast and wore a sky-blue cloak that seemed to be woven of the very texture of summer.

Harald's father, Sigurd, curled his lip a little disdainfully. 'It is always thus, my son,' he said, 'before a voyage. Men seem heroes in the torchlight at a feasting. But we must wait till the harsh salt cakes on their hands and the bitter wind tears their fine cloaks from them before we can judge whether they be true men or no.'

The boy gave a quick glance towards his father, an angry comment already forming on his lips. Then he thought the better of it and said nothing after all. Yet in that moment Harald hated his father a little for those slighting remarks about Thorkell Fairhair.

Seated next to Thorkell at the head of the long trestle table was the village headman, an old peasant with a fine leathern face, whose white hair hung down in snaketails on either side of his head. He wore a thick frieze wrapper about his shoulders, for he was a sick man and the wind that blew down the valley at night-time brought on his rheumatism. Although a horn of corn-wine was set before him, he did not taste it, for he was an abstemious man who had never drunk anything but water from the springs, or at the best, goat's milk, when there was too much to be made into cheese. But this he did only infrequently, for he looked on such drinking as waste. A man might drink in five minutes enough milk to make a cheese that would last a family a week, he said to himself. This headman's name was Thorn. He was as sharp as his name. Although his hands were now too crippled to hold a stick, all the boys went in fear of him, and stopped whatever they were doing when he hobbled along the village street. It was this Thorn who had conceived the idea of building the longship and of sending it out to bring back treasure to the village. It was Thorn who had said, 'I choose Thorkell Fairhair for her master, if he should travel this way before we have finished her.' And all the villagers had agreed in their council, for every man liked Thorkell, and would trust their venture in his hands.

So it was that Thorn sat at Thorkell's side. And at last Thorn said, 'Master Thorkell, all goes well. The ship is ready and the crew chosen. If this wind holds, it will carry you out to sea tomorrow to begin your viking. But one thing is lacking. The ship has not been named, nor has she an emblem carved on her prow as most of our longships have. A raven or a dragon or a wolfhead.'

Thorkell smiled down at the old man lazily in the torchlight. 'Master Thorn,' he said, smiling, 'how call you this wine before the corn has been put into the mashtub and wetted?'

All men listened as he spoke, some puzzled, some laughing. The old man blinked up at Thorkell, 'How call you it?' he said, wondering. 'How can we give it a name, for it is not yet made. It is nothing until the water is put on it and the corn has fermented. Nothing. It has no name.'

Thorkell said, 'What right has a man to call his sword "Brainbiter" until it has bitten a brain!'

The old man smiled tolerantly and said, 'We are talking of our ship – not of wine, or of swords, Thorkell.'

Thorkell said, 'Should a man name his ship "Land Ravager" if she is destined to sink before ever she sights land to ravage?'

When he said these words, many men crossed their fingers or spat upon the floor, to keep away the evil omens. 'He should not have said that,' whispered Aun Doorback, looking first over his right shoulder and then over his left, to see if the wicked ones were listening.

Thorkell sensed the unrest about the table at his words and he laughed loud. 'My friends,' he said, 'we are fighting men, not shivering old women, to be frightened with a strange word! I tell you that nothing ever happens unless it is fated to happen, long ago, before today or yesterday. Before last sowing or ten sowings before that. What happens was written down by Odin when the world was first made. It is there, in his writings, and nothing a man says can change it. Now, be still.'

'What then will you call the longship, Fairhair?' asked the old man, Thorn, impatiently. 'We built her and gave our money for her. We must know what her master will name her.'

At that moment Thorkell paused in his drinking and with a shrug of his broad shoulders stood up, so that all men watched him, wondering. Thorkell Fairhair pointed down the long table towards the Finn, Gnorre, who was at that moment hacking away with great concentration at his piece of salted beef. All men's eyes turned on the Finn, who looked back wide-eyed and surprised.

'Tell me your name, friend,' said Thorkell. 'I have forgotten it in the excitements of the day.'

The Finn said, 'Gnorre, Master. I am from Finland. I told you so earlier.'

Thorkell smiled again. 'By what other name are you known, Gnorre?'

Aun Doorback's face flushed and his great red hand began to fumble for his axe. But Gnorre patted him gently on the arm and whispered, 'Have patience, Aun. Perhaps he means well. You shall kill no more men for my sake. I can fend for myself, come the worst.'

Gnorre stood up, a strange bent figure in the torchlight, which played about his thin lined face. Then he spoke so proudly that all the hall was still and men listened.

'I am Gnorre Nithing, shipmaster,' he said. 'I took the knucklebones from you today as a Viking, not as a prisoner to be handed back to those who would slay me for my past misdeeds. Now stand I here a warrior with a warrior's weapon and who takes me shall need to be a good swordsman.'

With that Gnorre leapt backwards with a speed that startled every man. And they saw that his sword, Grunter, was out and shining in the torchlight.

Then Aun Doorback had moved and the bench fell over, scattering the men who had been sitting at it among the rushes.

A woman screamed and one of the villagers dropped an earthen pitcher of wine. But Thorkell never moved a muscle. His gay face still smiled fixedly and his golden hair wafted softly in the breeze that stole in through the hide covering of the door.

Then he stretched out his hands towards Gnorre and Aun, almost in an attitude of pleading. 'I have picked two real men, my friends. I know a man when I see one, never fear. But when I asked your name it was so that everyone should see what I mean. Nothing more. All Finland must come to take you back, Gnorre, if they want you. But they must find their way beyond my sword guard to do it.'

Now Aun and Gnorre looked at each other like fools, a smile of embarrassment on their faces. The men who had fallen to the floor got up and scratched their heads, puzzled. The headman, Thorn, shook his grey head a little more, petulantly.

'Gnorre Nithing,' said Thorkell, 'you have given our ship her name. She shall be the *Nameless*. She shall wander as you have done, Gnorre, an outlaw of the seas. Perhaps all men's hands will be against her, as they are against you. But though she may be nothing at her launching, she may prove to be something at her beaching when she returns. Then we will give her another name, you and I.'

At first there was a hush in the long room, then everyone began to talk at once, and though the villagers did not seem to like the name, the shipmen were pleased with the way in which Thorkell had chosen it. For it seemed to free them of all responsibility. Now they would become outlaws, their own masters, to do as they pleased, obeying only their shipmaster, Thorkell.

Now men began to call to the villagers to fill up their wine-pannikins again, and here and there they began to slap each other on the back, sometimes a little too hard. And just when it seemed that the feast might become an excuse for rough horseplay among the Vikings, Horic Laplander leapt on to the table, a weird misshapen figure in his bundled clothes, with his thick pigtail flying out behind him.

Now he whirled about in a strange winter dance of his people, striking grotesque attitudes, of bear or wolf and even of a pine tree. His padding feet now grew as noiseless as those of a mouse and he danced hither and thither among the drinking horns and dishes without disturbing a thing. The men of the village, whose own dance was a heavy-footed stamping affair, gazed open-mouthed at his skill.

Then even Horic appeared to tire. He sank down in the middle of the table and seemed to roll himself into a great ball. In this position he stayed still for such a space as a man might need to count twenty. Then without warning he sprang into life again, his hands held upwards and outwards, his feet wide apart and his thick body swaying. No man understood the language he spoke, for it was of the farthest northern forests and not spoken along the fjords for many hundreds of years. But they knew that Horic was telling them a story – a grim tale of the great forests and the wolves and the bears, and, worse still, of the old gods who demanded sacrifices in return for a good harvest, or a good reindeer foaling, or a good catch of fish. And they shuddered as they heard the gods speak through Horic's mouth, heard the forests sigh in his deep breathing, heard the wolves howl about the winter stockades, or the bears grunting outside the doors when all else was still and the children were asleep.

Now no one drank any more, or bothered to eat, though they still held their bread in their hands. Many even lost all knowledge of where they were, for the man's spell was so strong.

And then, when all stared at the Laplander, and even the torches set along the walls had stopped flickering, there came a great laugh from the darkness outside, and a moment later the hide covering at the doorway was flung aside with a single rough movement. The men in the hall turned slowly round, bemused, to see who had come, and then the spell was broken and Horic was no more than a little Laplander squatting on the table. The one who stood in the doorway had broken the magic, like an earthenware pot, it seemed.

Immensely tall and swarthy-faced, his raven hair hanging below his dark and burnished helmet, the newcomer stood, his long black cloak reaching down to the straw on the floor. Men saw that his strong arms were bound about with ring after ring of gold. They saw the deep tattoo marks across his forehead and cheekbones, the oiled beard and the curling moustaches. This was a fine man, thought those who did not know him. This is an evil omen, thought those who did.

Thorkell gave a little gasp, 'Ragnar,' he said. 'Ragnar Raven! I thought not to see you ever again!'

Ragnar smiled, a soft, dangerous smile, showing his white teeth. 'Do you mean "thought not" or "wished not," Thorkell Fairhair?'

Thorkell's face stiffened slightly and a cold air blew in through the open doorway from the fjord. He stepped forward.

'Enter and sit at the tabletop, Ragnar,' he said. 'We are blood brothers and come what may you shall share my fortune.'

Men moved away to let the proud stranger sit beside their leader.

5. The Blood-Launching

THE *NAMELESS* still stood on her stocks, above the runway of planks that led down to the waters of the fjord. With the arrival of Ragnar Raven the wind had changed and blew across the sea inlet towards the village, so that it would have been madness to push the longship out only to have her dashed on the rocks that lay below the launching-place.

Men began to whisper, their heads together, saying that Ragnar had brought the venture ill-luck. Some men even said that, were it not that they loved Thorkell, they would have handed back the knucklebones and have gone on free up the fjord to find another ship.

Harald and his father kept together, for they were from inland and knew none of the others, the seafarers. Harald said to his father, 'I am afraid that this delay will spoil the crew.' Sigurd laughed and said, 'Sailors always grumble. Once they feel the planks bucking under their feet and get the sound of the sea-mews in their ears, they will forget all this. A Viking is born, my son, and never escapes his destiny.

As some men love horses, and others love hunting wolves, so a Viking loves ships, every plank and rope of them, and he is never happy unless he is riding the track of the whale, treading the path of the gannet.'

Harald said, 'All the same, this Ragnar makes me wonder whether the venture will turn out well.'

Sigurd said, 'You are a young fool to bother your head with such thoughts. Ragnar is but a man, though a strong one. He can only do what Odin will let him. And we can only do what Odin will let us. So what can you change with all your worrying? You are but an ant crawling on a hunter's boot. That boot may carry you a long distance and you will think that life is good to you. Or it may crush you, then you will know no more. If you are a sensible ant you will not worry your head to discover what makes the boot move, for it will not alter your condition.'

The boy scratched his head and looked puzzled. Then he walked away and watched the villagers loading the *Nameless* with its tackle and threading the stay ropes through the pulleys that should hoist the mainsail.

On his way back to join his father he came upon Horic Laplander, sitting under the lee of a rock and holding a short length of tarred twine. The man was smiling, his eyes half-closed, and rocking back and forth. Harald saw that there were four knots in the twine that the man fingered so lovingly.

He tapped the Laplander on the thick shoulder. 'What are you doing, friend?' he said curiously.

Horic came out of his trance and whispered hoarsely, 'This is a bad wind for it keeps us ashore, quarrelling. I have just asked for a good wind to blow, now I must untie it so that it may come down the fjord and carry us out to sea.'

With a deft movement of his yellow hands he slacked the knot and gave it a tug. Then he shut his eyes and rocked back and forth again. Harald stood amazed and wondering. The wind which had been blowing into his face, slapping it roughly as he stood, ceased suddenly, and for a moment there was a complete stillness. Harald looked round and saw that the smoke from the chimney holes was going up straight. Then, as though a great door had been opened somewhere up the valley, a low roaring noise came, growing louder and louder. At first the smoke still eddied, then it flicked like a whiplash and began to flurry. The pine trees high on the hilltop gave a faint sigh, then they too bent under the blast and began their own roar.

Now the wind struck Harald at the side of the head, and the smoke swept into his eyes. From the huts a man shouted, 'Praise Odin, the Viking's wind has come!' And everywhere the cry went up, 'The Viking's wind has come!'

Now all was bustle in the village. The headman hobbled out and said, 'Odin is pleased with our venture and wishes you to begin without delay. He has sent you a good wind.'

Only Horic still smiled, inscrutably, his length of twine now twisting in his yellow fingers, his eyes half-shut and his face contemptuous.

Sigurd said, 'This is beyond my knowledge. All men know that there are land breezes and sea breezes and that they come at different times of the day. But this is no ordinary land breeze to come at midday, after three days of the other. I cannot understand it.'

Harald said, 'I am happier than I was, Father. If Horic sails there is one whose magic will put a check on Ragnar.'

Sigurd looked at his son, wondering, then said, 'Go into the feast hall, son, and eat well. You seem a little light-headed with hunger. Anyway, it is no bad thing to sail on a full stomach. Perhaps you will not want to eat for a day or two after we get started.'

Harald ate with the others while the villagers piled the provisions for the voyage near the shore – oatcake, barley bread, salt beef, pork and herring. Three large casks of fresh spring water stood among the other things, the most important of them all.

An hour later, Thorkell and Ragnar came out of the headman's hut, followed by Wolf, who now seemed crestfallen at having been replaced in his leader's affection. The headman was arguing loudly with them. He was saying, 'But Thorkell, you have a full crew. Your friend Ragnar has

no place in the ship and you know it. He is an extra man and we all know that the gods do not like an extra man.'

Ragnar spat towards the fjord and said, 'Old wives' tales!'

This angered the headman. His hands began to shake violently and his daughter had to support him or he would have fallen on to the pebbles in his rage.

Thorkell patted him on the shoulder gently. 'Do not frighten yourself, Thorn,' he said. 'Ragnar once saved my life and I owe him that. Now he goes where I go, if he chooses; and this time he does choose. We can say no more.'

Suddenly Ragnar turned on the headman and said, 'If that is all you are worrying about, an extra man, we can arrange that, old man. Under the old law a launching demands a blood sacrifice. Surely there is one among the crew who would lay his head upon the slipway to fulfil the ancient command?'

The headman glared up at him, speechless for a moment. Then he said, 'This village is a peaceful place. We do not sacrifice in the forest temples as they do in some parts. We are a free folk here and have been so since we formed our village settlement. Let who will pray to the gods of blood, we will not. Sooner than our ship went down the slipway through blood, I would burn her. She is ours, to do with as we please, and no one, not even Thorkell, shall tell us what we must do.'

Ragnar shrugged his shoulders and began to walk away whistling. Thorkell stared after him in anger for a moment, then helped the old man to his seat on the shore, near the slipway.

By the early afternoon all was ready for the launching. The crew stood on either side of the longship, resting their hands against the strakes, waiting to take the strain when Björn and his men had knocked away the supports with their great mallets. Then the Vikings would push their ship down the runway into the water. Only Rolf Wryneck was aboard, holding his steerboard loosely, waiting to act when the ship was afloat, his thin neck twisted round and his sea-blue eyes misty as he gazed towards the bluer waters of the fjord.

Harald stood just beside his father, who was the first man at the bow of the ship, on the steerboard side. 'May she float well,' he prayed, his eyes half-closed. His father smiled and said, 'Never fear, son, she will. The men who made her might make one worthy of Odin!'

Hasting heard this and sucked in his breath loudly. 'That was a foolish thing to say, Sigurd,' he said. 'That is tempting Odin to make her sink.'

'On my own head be it,' said Sigurd, who was not a superstitious man. Then the last prop was knocked away, and Thorkell shouted, 'Vikings, take the strain – steady her – now heave!'

As he called out the last word, every shoulder was bunched, every arm tensed, all muscles strained. And when men thought that the longship would never move, she began to slide forward like a living thing.

But Sigurd let her go a little too late, and as she thrust forward, he lost his balance and toppled sideways in her tracks. Harald saw it happen and opened his mouth to shout, but he could not save his father. Then the Vikings on the steerboard side saw Sigurd twist sideways and roll from the slipway, and many thought that he had come away unhurt. But those who dared to look saw that his rolling had been a little too late. All heard the bone of his leg breaking, and the man's stifled gasp. Then the *Nameless* slid smoothy down the slipway to the water.

Harald bent over his father, holding back the tears that burned his eyes. Yet even in his anguish he heard Ragnar's voice, 'I said that the old laws demanded a blood-launching, old man. Well, we have one now – and no extra man in the crew!' There was sardonic laughter in his voice. Harald shook the spurting tears from his eyes and tried to lift his father's body.

Sigurd opened his eyes and smiled grimly. 'I am not ready for Valhalla yet, lad,' he said. 'A broken leg mends easily with care, and if it doesn't, why, I have another leg!'

When he had said this, Sigurd fainted with pain. Thorkell patted Harald on the back and said, 'You have a brave father, boy. Let us hope his son is as much a Viking.'

The headman had Sigurd carried into his own hut, to be tended by his daughter. Then all the crew clustered on the shore, as though nothing had happened worth noticing, for the *Nameless* was riding the rough fjord waters like a swan, graceful and strong. The Vikings sent up a great cheer and some of the villagers began their uncouth dance on the shore, relieved that their vessel had not let them down.

At last Harald made his way to the headman's hut. His father was sleeping, but the headman's daughter said, 'He will be well again, one day, never fear. We shall care for him. He commands that you go on your voyage as though he were with you.'

'But I cannot leave him,' said Harald.

'Is the son less of a Viking than the father?' asked the girl.

Harald stood ashamed. The girl smiled at him then and said, 'This is his home now, as it is yours when you are not voyaging. Come and say goodbye to your father before you sail, that is all. Now go and get your things together, for Thorkell will not be pleased with you if you lag behind at the sailing.'

Harald went out of the hut. Men were loading the provisions aboard, and the Vikings were already choosing their places in the ship, and packing their few belongings into the sea chests on which they sat to row. Here and there along the side of the *Nameless*, men were hanging their shields, one overlapping the other, to keep the water out in a high sea.

Harald stood irresolute for a moment, then suddenly he felt that he must ask Odin to look after his father while he was away from him. An idea struck him and without looking back at the ship, he turned and ran as hard as he could up the hillside towards the great forest.

At last, tired and panting, he stood on the outskirts of the wooded heights. Choosing the greatest pine he could see, he slipped off his gold arm-ring and flung it up into the boughs, saying, 'An offering, Father Odin. It is all I have to give you. May my father prosper and be made whole again.'

Then he turned to go down to the ship again. But as he went he began to recall how he had rejoiced when his father had come striding towards Gudröd's Hall, laughing, and bearing that same gold ring.

'Wear this, my son,' he had said. 'And may fortune smile upon us all the days it clasps your arm.'

Now he had thrown away his father's precious gift. Suddenly it did not seem the right thing to do. Moreover, his father had prayed for success to fall upon *them*, not him alone. As he stood under the great pine tree, Harald, his dark northern superstitions stifling his reason, feared that by giving away the ring, even to Odin, he was somehow working against, and not for, his father's chances of survival.

With a low cry, he began to climb the pine tree. It was not easy. Nor was the ring at first visible. But at last he saw it, dangling precariously, between two small shoots. Ignoring the difficulties, and the pain of the ascent, he clambered up towards it. And, as he reached out to take it, he begged Odin to forgive him.

'One day, I will make you a finer offering, Father,' he said. He put the ring back upon his arm. And then he froze in a sudden fear. He heard voices below the tree. And one voice that he already knew. He looked down cautiously. Three men stood at the edge of the wood, only a few yards beneath him, talking earnestly and smiling wickedly. One of them was Ragnar. The others were not of the venture and Harald did not recognize them. Yet he saw by their ornaments and their black hair that they must be of Ragnar's own folk, Danes.

Ragnar was saying, 'So, my friends, this is your chance. Ride fast and tell them up the fjord that we sail today. Yours is a bigger ship and should find us before we are far from shore. Have no fear, Thorkell will do as I wish.'

One of the others said, 'Then perhaps we can take the *Nameless* without having to fight?'

Ragnar turned on him with a black scowl. 'Not even I can make Thorkell lay down his arms. No, he will fight, whatever happens. I meant that I can cause him to furl sail if it seems that we have too great a start on you, so that you may catch up. And don't forget, I shall have to make a pretence at fighting by his side. See that your men know that. I do not want them to come at me like boars, or they will take an arm from me by mistake!'

Harald said grimly to himself, 'An arm for a leg, Ragnar! You deserve it!' Then the tears flooded his eyes again and blinded him. When he looked again they had gone, and Ragnar was striding down the hill towards the longship, waving to Thorkell.

Harald followed after him at a distance, wondering what he could do to prevent Ragnar's treachery. One thing he dared not do and that was tell Thorkell about it yet, for there was no proof. Whatever he did must be done when they were well afloat.

Harald stopped at the headman's hut. His father greeted him warmly and kissed him on both cheeks. 'Go, my young Viking,' he said. 'And may Odin heal my leg well enough for me to follow you on the next ship that sails from this fjord. Now go, and all fortune with you. If you stay longer I shall forget that I am a warrior.'

But Harald was not yet a warrior. The tears ran down his cheeks unchecked as he clambered into the *Nameless*.

6. Strange Happening

THE *NAMELESS* moved slowly away from the shore, heading towards the open sea which lay not much more than ten miles away. Harald stood beneath the mast, looking up at those of the villagers who ran alongside, on the rocks above the fjord, keeping up with the ship for as long as they might, and shouting down messages of goodwill to the crew. Then his eyes filled with tears and he lowered his head.

When he looked up again, the village on the shore was out of sight. The great adventure had started. Now Harald's heart lifted and he began to think more calmly about his father's misfortunes. He consoled himself by thinking that Odin had wished it to happen as it did. And Sigurd would be the first to agree with that, Harald felt sure, after what he had said earlier.

Now Harald looked about him in the longship. The oarsmen seated on their sea chests had stopped rowing, for the wind had freshened enough to carry them well away from the rocky shore and out in the middle of the fjord. The great coloured sail was unfurled, and bellied out strongly, proudly displaying its bright coloured stripes. The white pennant stuck out almost rigid, towards the bow of the boat, in the following breeze.

Harald sat down, over the loose planks in the middle of the ship, below which the provisions and weapons were stored, the latter oiled with pig's fat and wrapped in sheepskin to keep them dry. Beside him sat four others, playing dice and telling tales already. There were sixteen oar-ports on each side of the *Nameless*, which meant that she needed thirty-two oarsmen to keep her going well. Thorkell as the leader, and Rolf as the steersman, stood in the stern. Ragnar, self-appointed as second-in-command, stood in the bow, acting as a look-out. So were the forty shipmen disposed in the *Nameless*. The five who rested replaced oarsmen as they became tired, and were themselves later replaced by others who had enjoyed a spell away from the oars. Though, once out in the open sea, it was not the custom to use oar-power – and then the men rested, waiting for the first sight of land.

Overhead the afternoon sky was clear and blue in the sun's light. The white gulls swept here and there about the ship, sometimes just skimming the mast-top, as though they were curious about this new creature that had come to ride the waves with them. One gull even alighted on the high golden prow, just above Ragnar's head, and seemed to regard him for a while, critically, before flying away to its fellows with a harsh squawk. At this, many of the Vikings smiled, and one or two of them even laughed aloud.

'A gull can judge a man,' whispered Björn to Hasting, for neither of them had any love for this arrogant newcomer to the crew.

Hasting said, 'He holds the place that you should have by rights, my friend. You built this ship and none knows her better than you.'

'That's as may be,' said Björn, who was a reasonable man. 'If Thorkell says that Ragnar is to be second master of her, who am I to deny it?' And he went on whittling at a piece of oak which he had brought with him on to the ship. The oak-chips lay about his feet, gold in the sunlight, until the wind whipped them away and over the side of the *Nameless*.

At length Rolf Wryneck called out to Harald, telling him to come and try his hand at steering. The boy forgot his lingering sadness, in face of this high honour, and moved over the gently swaying deck. As he passed along the shipside, the men he knew called out to him, smiling and patting him on the back, to keep his courage up. Aun Doorback pulled him aside and said, 'Your father is a fine man, lad. And with strong arms like these of yours, you will do him justice on this voyage.'

Harald went on along the deck feeling pleased at the big man's words. Rolf Wryneck said, 'Watch me for a few minutes, lad, and then see how you can hold her.'

Harald did as he was told, and then took the long horn-shaped haft. The ship was now his, his to command and steer. He felt the steerboard shudder, then pull away from him, and, when he had used all his strength on the haft, felt it strike a course and hold it. He had the illusion that the ship was a living thing, like a horse, and that for a moment he had mastered it. Rolf was watching him, a bright light in his eyes. He smiled to see Harald's new confidence and said, 'Ships be like any other creature. Show them who is master and they will obey; but once let them have the upper hand and they will run wild and break their backs in rebellion.'

Thorkell had watched all this, and laughed to hear Rolf's words.

'Does she ride well, you old gossip?' he asked Rolf.

Rolf shook his head, in his strange twisted way, and grinned, 'Aye, Master,' he said. 'She rides smoother than any ship I have ever held except the *Gullchaser* that I made my first voyage in.'

Thorkell saw the reminiscent gleam in the man's eye. 'What became of her?' he asked.

Harald saw that Rolf's eyes were wet now. 'She tried to leap a rock off the Northumbrian coast, Master,' he said. 'I was the only one to come away from her, and sometimes I wish I had stayed with my fellows. I have this twisted neck to remember that rock by. Some say I broke it that day, and that it never set right.'

'Odin is keeping you for greater things,' said Thorkell. Suddenly Harald felt his tongue unlocked and he dared to speak. 'Shipmaster,' he said, 'there is something which weighs on my mind. I would tell you of it.'

Thorkell smiled down at him. 'If you wish to ask for Rolf's job, save yourself the trouble. Rolf steers very well for my purposes.' Harald would not be put off now by such jesting. 'Shipmaster,' he said, 'I fear there is treachery aboard, to rob us of the *Nameless*. I heard men talking in the woods. Ragnar's men.'

Thorkell's eyes narrowed and his lean jaws twitched. He glanced over his shoulder and then said, almost in a whisper. 'Tell me no more, boy. A little bird has already whispered to me about something.'

He saw the boy's wide-eyed incredulity, and patted him on the arm, saying, 'When you become a shipmaster, you develop eyes in the back of your head. And even the gulls bring messages to the man who can understand them.'

Then he went amidships, without another word, leaving Harald staring after him, dumbfounded, and knelt down by Horic, who was sitting away from the other Vikings, looping and unlooping his length of twine and mumbling to himself.

Harald wondered at this. It seemed that Thorkell wished to speak secretly with the Laplander, for no man could hear the words he spoke. But then Harald saw Horic rise and point back the way they had come, and then nod his head violently at something which Thorkell had said. After that, Thorkell came back and stood near the steerboard, but now with a distant, abstracted air, as though there were weighty things on his mind. He was a man who had more to work out than his years would let him do easily, it seemed. Rolf, who was wise in the ways of men, put his strong sinewy hand on Harald's arm, and nodded in the direction of their shipmaster, as though to say, 'Keep out of his way for the moment. Something troubles him, and a man who is troubled in his mind might bite and do hurt without intending it.' So the boy watched carefully, but did not think to speak with his leader as he had done but a little earlier.

In fact, none of the men spoke to Thorkell. He stood, chin in hand, his back against the ladder that led up to the platform at the stern of the longship, his eyes dark and foreboding. Even Ragnar, the arrogant Ragnar of but a few hours before, glanced back a time or two, and then decided not to disturb the young warrior's thoughts.

At length the afternoon gave place to early evening, and as it was springtime, the dusk came on quite soon afterwards. Now the air became sharper and a salt tang came to the nostrils of the Vikings. The sea was not far away. Now the birds that circled the masthead were not gulls alone, but also those feathered inhabitants of the deep-sea rocks, the cormorant and the shag, flying who knows whither? Carrying the spirits of drowned seamen who knows where? The Vikings looked upwards and shook their heads with foreboding.

Once a goshawk, from the woods high on the hills that overlooked the widening fjord, poised high above them and seemed to set the pennant of the *Nameless* in its cruel eye, as though to swoop down. Then it decided that this was not its true prey, and swept away from the scene in a broad swoop of wings, away, away, towards the dusky forests.

Then Harald noticed something unusual about Thorkell. The young man was listening, listening, not seeing, for sight over any distance was impossible now. It was as though he was listening to the wake that his ship made; listening even beyond that wake; beyond the village from which they had started that day . . .

And suddenly he made a sign to Horic, who crouched beside him looking up.

Harald looked towards Ragnar, almost instinctively. The tall Dane was listening too. His white hands were clenched hard on the gunwale nearest to him, his body was tense. Every muscle in his dark body seemed to be waiting for something.

The men playing dice or yarning together did not notice these things. They only smelt the salt in the air and heard the different cries of the deep-sea birds. They only heard Thorkell's voice, a new and urgent voice that they did not know, shout out, 'Steersman, set course to shore. There we shall spend our first night's voyaging.'

Some of the men sighed with relief as the *Nameless* pulled into the shore and they knew that they would not spend their first night fighting the rolling waves that swung down from Iceland towards the Pillars of Hercules.

So the longship beached in the dusk, less than five miles from where it was launched. Those who wished slept aboard, for a long tarred cloth was stretched over the centre-posts that stood one on each side of the mast. Those who wished went ashore and slept in their sheepskin bags, under rock or bush. Though they were not allowed to make a fire, by Thorkell's strict orders; no man knew why.

That night Thorkell said to Harald, 'Boy, your father broke a limb serving me. Under our law I am now your father, being your accepted leader. That is my obligation. Until you can fend for yourself, you are my son. You will sleep near me and do as I say.'

Harald secretly laughed at the idea of having a father so young as Thorkell; yet in his innermost heart he was proud that this warrior should take him as son. He bowed his head in acknowledgement and got into his sleeping bag at Thorkell's feet.

Then Harald fell fast asleep, without another thought of the ship, or the voyage, or Thorkell, or Ragnar, or Horic – or even of his dear father, five miles along that same shore, lying in the hut of the kindly headman, Thorn.

When he woke, a chill air blew about him. Even the woods above him were still, as though the birds were not yet sure of themselves. He looked across at Thorkell, who was awake and staring out towards the fjord. Harald followed his gaze and saw that the waters were now leaden, and still ruffled, as though a great storm had swept them in the night and had not yet died down

Thorkell said, 'Make ready, boy, for I shall not wait long here.'

Then Harald went aboard again, but noticed that Thorkell was walking with Horic, and that Ragnar was behind them, pulling at his beard with anger.

The longship sailed again before the Vikings had fed. They ate what they could aboard as the dawn came slowly across the sky behind them. Some ate of oatmeal, soaked in fresh water, others of barley bread, and yet others, the hardiest of the voyagers, of dried fish. This was a meal to turn the squeamish stomach, for the herring were strong in smell and taste, and might not be enjoyed by any but the toughened traveller.

Soon the *Nameless* began to rock. Harald looked ahead and saw great foam-headed breakers. They were approaching the sea – that vast world which the poets had called 'the gulls' way,' 'the whales' way,' 'the track of the dolphin,' and other fanciful titles. To Harald it was something new and different and frightening. A young Viking among Vikings, he was, in his heart, afraid. Though he would have lost an ear rather than admit it. The sea was before him. The deep, salt sea!

Now the sailors put out their oars and helped the sail to do its work, and Harald heard many words spoken that he had not heard before, for these men knew what it was to fight an incoming tide. They knew how a tide will first warm, then blister, then crack the skin of their hands; will bend the back and then bring it nigh unto breaking. These were old Vikings, who knew the sea as a friend, and enemy, a grave.

Then at last, when the ship was moving smoothly again and the breakers were less noticeable, Harald looked back and saw the rocky headlands and the high forests only distantly. He knew that they were now truly a-voyaging!

Some of the men had gone back to sleep, even the oarsmen, their blades pulled up and safe against the rollers. Even Ragnar, at the bow, resting his great dark head down on the gunwale . . .

Then Harald woke with a start. Thorkell's voice said, 'Care, take care to steerboard, watch for the wreck!'

All men looked where he pointed. On the surging waves rested the remains of a longship. She rolled carelessly with the tide, a neglected thing, her bright planks ignored by all but the seabirds that already sat upon her, gossiping. What had been her sail, a white sail marked with a black raven, floated in bellying ripples about her. Her oars jostled each other about her sides, for she lay turtle-wise, her loose keel uppermost.

A great gasp ran along the *Nameless*. This was the end all sailormen feared – dreamed of, and feared. Now men clustered along the gunwales to see what there was to see.

A covey of gulls swung about and about the wrecked longship.

'Something must be living here,' said Björn, who knew every mood of the sea and of its birds.

Thorkell said, 'Head towards the wreck, Rolf.'

The *Nameless* shuddered like a shot goose as she turned her golden prow to where the seabirds were quarrelling.

Aun said, 'Odin save us from such an end, Gnorre.'

Gnorre hung on his oar and did not speak.

Harald, curious, thought he saw a hand raised, and dark hair floating with the tide. For some nights after, he even thought he heard a hoarse voice screaming for help. But he was not sure. All he knew was that Thorkell shouted, 'Ease away, Rolf. A Viking clings to the spars. Alongside and get him aboard.'

Then Harald saw Ragnar unhook the long seal-spike that hung beside him at the forward end, and lean over the bows, looking intently into the sea.

Gnorre, who stood as he rowed, said, 'He means to save the man.'

Aun, standing beside him, said, 'Who knows?'

Then the *Nameless* swept past the wreckage and Ragnar turned back with a shrug of the shoulders, and a grim smile towards Thorkell.

Harald ran to the steerboard side but could see no man. 'Hold course,' called Thorkell, with a sigh.

Horic whispered to himself, but every man near him heard, 'Look, there is blood upon the point of Ragnar's seal-spike.'

When the Vikings turned to look, Ragnar took the long harpoon and held it in the sea, so that the running waves covered it.

'I have known men take a fish or two this way,' he said with a smile, to the oarsman who sat nearest him.

Wolf Waterhater, his red hair wet with sweat, did not smile back at him.

7. The Gulls' Way

FROM THE day when the *Nameless* had run upon the wreckage, many of the Vikings hated Ragnar. For, like all true seamen, the voyagers both loved and hated the sea, but above all regarded her as a constant danger; and they felt bound in a strange way to give aid to all who suffered by the sea, even though the sufferers were men whose ships they had themselves wrecked in a sea-fight. Against the merciless waves, all Vikings were brothers, save in the most extreme cases when, by giving help to the wrecked, they might endanger the safety of their own longship.

Yet, among all voyagers there were those with the hearts of wolves, who gave no quarter to any man. These were the fierce brutes who sailed down upon holy places and burned and pillaged without compassion. Ragnar was such a man.

But as the *Nameless* pushed on across the northern sea, the Vikings had other things to occupy their minds. When they had muttered to each other for a while, they forgot the wreck and turned to their task of bracing the sail, or rowing when the winds lagged. Once they had to take buckets and bail feverishly when they struck a patch of water that rose above them like the foothills above the village they had left. Harald, seeing the great waters rising high above him, wanted to cry out in fear, for it seemed that they would topple down upon the frail shell in which he sailed, to crush everything into oblivion. He could not see how any craft might survive such a smashing blow. But though he was terrified, there was nowhere he might run, to escape the fury of the salt waters. He stood rooted and would undoubtedly have been swept overboard had not Gnorre pushed a rope into his hands and yelled in his ear, 'Grasp this for your life! The sea does not play bower-games!' Harald saw that all the others were clutching tight to anything that might be at hand. Even proud Ragnar held the ladder near the forward platform, his head bent as though he wished to evade the full force of the blow.

Then the green mountain of water crashed down upon them and for a while Harald only knew that a rushing, roaring nightmare had enveloped him. He heard nothing but the sound of great waters; he tasted nothing but bitter brine; and he was drenched through and through, as though the sea had penetrated to his innermost heart.

At last he shook the water from his eyes and ears and was able to look about him. The oarsmen were lying sprawled in the lee of their sea chests. Only Thorkell and Rolf stood erect, and both were smiling. It was that strange smile which put new heart into Harald, and he tried to smile too. Thorkell saw the boy's grin and beckoned him to come aft. 'That was but the pat of a bear-cub,' he said to the boy. 'When we face the big seas beyond the islands, you will feel the weight of the grown bear's paw!'

Now the sun came out and the *Nameless* ran into clearer waters. The men took off their leather tunics and rubbed each others' backs with rough cloths, to get warmth into their bodies again. It was then that Harald saw Aun's back for the first time without its rough covering of bear-hide. It seemed to the boy that the breadth of his back was almost as great as the span of a child's arms, held outstretched. But what most interested Harald was the great blue dragon that was tattooed there, its head between his shoulder blades, its tail disappearing somewhere into the rough leathern breeches that he wore.

It was with something of a shock that Harald saw Gnorre's back, for it was so thin and bunched, and worse still, it was covered with white weals, criss-crossed in many directions, the marks of a vicious whip. It seemed that Gnorre Nithing had not escaped unhurt from the land where he had killed a man. Harald felt very sorry for him, but wondered how such a man could possibly be the warrior men thought. For Harald had little experience of men and expected all fighting men to be cast in the same mould, that of a godlike hero, a Thorkell, or even a Ragnar.

Later, when the shipmaster had sanctioned an issue of the warming corn-wine that was kept in stone bottles under the planking amidships, the Vikings let the mainsail do all the work, while they sat round in the sun, talking and singing. Rolf sang a song which they all seemed to know, for they joined in the chorus, thumping out the rhythm with their fists on the planks beside them. To

Harald it was all new and he listened, wide-eyed, his mouth half-open, to the tale it told.

It was the story of a hunter who slept in a cave one winter's night, warm and contented, only to find in the morning that the heap of skins on which he had rested was a sleeping bear, drowsy with hibernation. When the song came to the point where the hunter put out his hand and felt the animal's wet muzzle, Harald gave a little gasp, and Wolf Waterhater slapped him on the back and said that he had once done the same, only the creature turned out to be a whale. Harald told him not to be so stupid, for whales didn't live in caves. Wolf said quite solemnly, 'Oh, this was a cave under the sea. As a matter of fact, it upset me so much that I have avoided water ever since.'

The rough men about Harald laughed at the lad's expression, for although he had been taken in by Wolf's serious expression at first, he knew that he was being teased and felt angry that Wolf should imagine he would believe such nonsense.

Then Wolf pretended that Harald meant to strike him, so still sitting, he clasped the lad round the waist and began to wrestle with him. Then, when he had tired of this, Wolf slung the lad over to Aun, who ruffled his hair and poked him in the ribs playfully – though hard enough to make Harald gasp – and so passed him round to Gnorre, who let him get up after giving him a slap. Yet it was all done with good humour, and Harald's expression of annoyance at Wolf's yarn had soon passed away.

Horic, who had watched the horseplay, said solemnly, 'That is good advice, Harald. When you are angry, go and wrestle with your friends. It will bring smiles back to your heart and you will forget your anger.'

Aun said, 'What do you know of wrestling, little monkey?' He looked so fierce as he spoke that Harald thought a quarrel was about to begin, but the others laughed. Then Horic, still smiling, leaned over and grasped Aun's thick wrist and slowly twisted it until the great man lay face downwards on the boards. And when Aun had beaten with his other hand three times, to signify that he would give in, Horic let him rise again, rubbing his wrist as though it hurt, but smiling now.

'You see,' said Horic, 'Aun was angry. Now he is glad.'

'Yes, glad you let me get up again,' said Aun. 'But never fear, monkey, I will get the better of you one day.'

'Perhaps when I am asleep,' said Horic. 'Or better still, when you are asleep, and dreaming!'

It was during these early days of the voyage that Harald learned of the many proverbs with which Norsemen sprinkled their talk. One of them that stuck in his mind went: 'Praise no day till evening, no sword until tested, no ice until crossed, and no ale until it has been drunk.' This was a saying which reflected the Viking's cautious approach to many things in life. Yet there was another side to the Norse character that was also shown in the tales they told each other. It was a love of exaggeration that made them roar with laughter when it figured in a tale they were listening to.

For instance, there was the story of the brothers, to whom bad news was brought; one of them grasped his spear-shaft so tightly that the imprint of his fingers bit deep into the hard wood; another was playing chess, and crumbled the ivory chessman to pieces as he gripped it; the third was cutting his fingernails and sliced his finger down to the bone without noticing it, such was his rage.

As these tales were told, the men of the *Nameless* howled with glee at each succeeding exaggeration, and even vied with each other to make up still more impossible incidents.

Yet, despite this fanciful yarning, when it came to their own experiences, they were tight-lipped and dour, for to be called a boaster was considered worse than being called a thief. To be called a murderer, of course, meant hardly anything at all, since it depended on whether the man one had murdered had a weapon in his hand. If he had, then no man thought more of the incident.

Harald learned much about his fellow Northmen in the three days they spent in crossing the northern sea. But he learned little more of Ragnar, or even of Thorkell, for now they kept themselves away from the others and spent much time under the platform aft, talking quietly.

Björn said to Hasting, 'Yon Thorkell must make the best of a bad bargain, I fear.'

Hasting replied with a wry smile, 'I think he has bitten off more than he can chew, bringing Ragnar aboard.'

But Kragge, who was passing at the time, stopped and looked down on them sourly. 'Let not your tongues wag too fast, my friends,' he said. 'This Ragnar may well be a better man to follow than Thorkell. I have watched him closely these two days and he seems to be a man's man, even if a maid may not like his face so well as the golden-haired lad's.'

Björn, who respected Thorkell and hated Ragnar, said, 'You are a fool, Kragge. Are there any more fools aboard this ship like you?'

Kragge made a gesture of the thumb behind him. 'Gryffi and Ivar, and a dozen others, think the same,' he said. 'We are not voyaging for our health, my friend. We come for treasure, and we count that leader a good one who takes us to where treasure may be found.'

Björn looked back at him with dislike, but said, 'How do you know that this Ragnar will lead you to treasure?'

Kragge said, 'I know the sort of man he is. I was farthest forward when he took the seal-spike and rode beside the wreck. There was a man there, clinging to a spar. And that man knew Ragnar, for I heard him call on him by name. You others could not hear that for the pounding of the waters on the ship's sides. But I heard it. And I saw what Ragnar did with the harpoon he held.'

Hasting said, 'Go back to your friends, Kragge, for you are a fool to follow such a man.'

But Kragge said, 'And you are a child, Hasting, not to see that this Ragnar, being so ruthless, is such a leader as would stop at nothing once his mind was set towards a thing. He is the man to bring us to our hearts' desire. He is a man to be followed.'

'Aye, and feared,' said Björn, turning his head in disgust.

'Who thinks worse of a man for that?' said Kragge. 'That is what a leader should be, for if we fear him it means that our enemies must surely fear him more!'

He went back to his fellows at Ragnar's part of the ship and soon seemed to be telling them what had passed.

Hasting said, 'I have seen this happen before, and often it means that a ship does not return, for when the crew divide, the ship becomes her own master, and then breaks her sides on the teeth of the rocks.'

Björn said, 'Perhaps it is not as bad as we think. Perhaps we shall become a crew again when we sight land. It is this sea-crossing that upsets a man's mind. It comes hard, even to a Viking, after a winter spent on the sheepskins by a hall fire.'

Harald was lying close to them when this happened, his head pillowed on a coil of rope. He heard it all without meaning to. When the men had finished speaking he went to Björn and told him that he had heard. 'Well, then, boy, you have heard, that is all,' said Björn. 'Which captain would you follow?'

Harald said, 'I gave my word to Thorkell, and him will I follow through thick and thin, wet and dry, sun and shower.'

Hasting said, 'You are a true Norseman, lad, like your father, Sigurd. One day, if sea and rock will let you, you will grow to be a Viking.'

Then Aun, who had been sent to act as look-out, called through his cupped hands, 'Land ahoy! Land on the starboard!'

Harald ran towards Aun and stared in the direction of his pointing finger. A thin blue-grey haze seemed to rest on the surface of the waters, far away. Then it would disappear and Harald would wonder whether his eyes had played him tricks; whether indeed that haze existed at all. Then, when he had rubbed his eyes and had come to the conclusion that he had imagined it all, the haze would appear again, a fine ribbon, as distant and as flimsy as a dream.

Now all the Vikings ran to the starboard side and peered under their hands. They knew what to look for and there was no doubt in their exclamations of surprise and joy.

Thorkell gave the order for all men to eat and drink their fill, for soon they would be able to replenish their stores, and in any case, if there was fighting to be done, it was best that it should be done on a full stomach, provided there was time enough for the meal to be digested, and, from the look of the land, he said, they would not beach for another two hours.

8. The First Prize

IT WAS at this point, when the seamen were sitting on the deck, knife and drinking horn in hand, that Aun shouted out once more.

'A ship, a ship, lying in our course!'

This time Harald had no difficulty in seeing what had excited the great look-out man. Rising and falling with the surging tides was a small boat that carried a square sail. It was too far distant for him to see more, for the vessel looked no larger than a small seed rocking on the waters.

Now the men of the *Nameless* flung down their bread and their meat, and drank off their fresh water at a gulp. The deck-boards amidships were raised, the weapons distributed to their owners without delay. Once more Hasting caressed his axe, Dream-maker, and Rolf Wryneck his dagger, Battlefang. Only Horic was without a weapon, and, though he protested, Thorkell made him take a sword out of store, an unnamed rough-cast blade, meant for such an emergency.

'See that it does such work as to deserve a name tonight,' joked Wolf Waterhater. But Horic looked utterly lost, holding such a blade.

Now Thorkell became their leader again, wearing such an expression of severity on his youthful face that all men obeyed him without question.

He gathered the men about the platform at the stern, and standing above them told them what they were to do. First, the sail was to be furled and taken down, and they were to row to within a distance such that the other vessel would not see their oars. Then they would pull in the oars and drift, each man hidden under the platforms, or lying close to the ship's sides, covered by skins or old clothes. On no account was any sound to be made. The *Nameless* was to appear deserted, as though the crew had abandoned her and she was left derelict.

All save Ragnar warmed to this stratagem. He only spoke up, saying, 'Why do we not sail right in and take her direct, without such mockery of battle?'

Thorkell smiled down on him and said, 'If this ship comes from the far coast, as I think she does, her shipmaster would see us coming and would turn for his own shore, to reach haven long before we could hope to catch him. Then what sort of welcome would we receive, think you? A hornet's nest about the ears, and the end of a short voyage for us all!'

Some of the men, including Aun and Hasting, laughed and jeered a little at Ragnar, when this answer was made. But Kragge and Gryffi mumbled and muttered that Ragnar's was the right way of tackling the problem. At last this whispering faded, however, and all men did as they were bidden.

To Harald, lying half-stifled under a pile of sacking, the waiting was never-ending. He thought that surely night must have fallen before he heard voices, speaking in a language which he did not know. Then he heard Gnorre whisper to Aun, 'If this should be my day, I will take your greetings to your brother, though we were enemies in life.' Then he heard Aun say, 'I send him no greetings, brother. See that you stand back to back with me and we shall live to take a hundred more ships.'

There was a silence then, and Harald found that his teeth were chattering violently. Under the pile of sacking, he clutched tightly at the long spear that Thorkell had given him.

So tightly, in fact, that for a moment he wondered whether his fingers would leave their imprint in its shaft, like the one in the saga he had heard. This made him laugh at himself, and he began to understand how men went 'berserk'. He had never seen a Berserk, but he had heard many tales of them, for of all the Vikings they were the most respected. They were men who tore off their shirts and ran half-naked into the fray, careless of life, trying to take as many men to Valhalla with them as they could. Strangely enough, they lived to see many battles, most of them, whereas the saner fighters lasted a much shorter time.

As he lay under his sacking, Harald recalled that his father had once said that a good average for any man was a round dozen of battles. After that the chance of survival became gradually smaller and smaller. His father had gone on to say that this didn't apply to a Berserk, for they were usually so drunk, one way or another, that they fell lightly and seemed to survive where a normal man would have broken his neck. He instanced one case where one Thor Baldhead, a notorious Berserk along the fjords, had fought with great distinction in eighty-five affrays, both great and small, in all places from Orkney to Miklagard. This Thor had once run amok in Frankland and had cut his way thirty yards into a solid phalanx of guards, until he reached the horse on which the King of the Franks sat, petrified. With a last sweep of his axe he had struck off the horse's head and was then borne down by the spear-points of a dozen guards and left for dead. At dawn the next day, when the old women were searching the field for treasures, one of them had trodden on his finger and wakened him. He jumped up, wounded all over his chest and arms, and they had thought he was a spirit and had run away.

Then Thor found a mail shirt belonging to one of the Frankish king's guards, and a helmet that one of the Vikings had left lying about, and had walked all the way back to the coast, a distance of twenty miles, unmolested. A month later he was back in Norway, and ready to go a-viking once more. This Thor, said Harald's father, died at the age of forty-two, a great age for a Viking, from an adder's bite when he happened to be trespassing in the garden of a Moorish Caliph in Spain. It was a sad end, thought his comrades, for the physician who treated him did not know of the Viking hatred of dying in bed, and so poor Thor died a cow's death, with two Arab slaves holding him down as he tried to struggle to his feet.

All these things came to young Harald's mind as he lay under the sacking, listening to the voices of the strangers in their square-sailed boat.

Then he heard the grating of wood on wood, and knew that the ships lay alongside each other. Suddenly a whisper ran through the *Nameless* . . . and all men lay tense and sweating, grasping sword or mace or heavy axe.

Then the tumult broke loose; light came upon them all, either because they had flung off their covering, or because the boarding party had dragged the sacking and skins aside.

Now the deck of the *Nameless* was a swarming mass of men, thrusting and stabbing and slashing at each other.

Harald saw Gryffi go down, a spear through his breast. Then he saw Kragge standing over Ivar, his knife Homegetter darting here and there, and at each thrust drawing a howl or a curse.

Aun and Gnorre were by his side, back to back, scything great swathes of men before them. And now Harald saw that Gnorre was smiling and even singing, a long low rhythmic tune, which Aun caught up in the chorus, so that they both were singing aloud at the end. And at the end of each verse, a man fell, and another verse started.

Once a man fell at Harald's feet. His face was daubed with a blue paint, and his red hair was tied with bone pins. His eyes rolled horribly up at the boy and he seemed to be trying to get up and thrust with a long sword. Harald gripped his spear-shaft so hard that his hands became quite numb, and for the life of him he could not have stabbed down at his enemy. Then, as a thick haze seemed to drift across his eyes, a sword came out from behind him and the blue-painted man lay still. Harald turned, bewildered, to see Horic's bland smile. Then the boy realized that each of the Vikings of the *Nameless* had paired up, and were standing back to back. Horic had silently chosen to be Harald's war-friend. The boy smiled back, feeling rather sick, and Horic grinned as he kissed the blade of his new sword. 'This Pict-pricker,' he said, solemnly.

It was at this stage of the fight that many men heard a curious and monotonous chanting from above. They looked up to see Thorkell, his golden mail-shirt discarded, his wild hair flying about his shoulders, his pale blue eyes full of an empty ecstasy. In his hand the sword whirled so rapidly that the sun seemed to create a new globe of light about him. Harald understood the man's secret then; he was a Berserk. That was why the others followed him.

Then Harald had his second shock. Ragnar was by Thorkell's side, stripped to the waist, his black head beside Thorkell's fair one, his great axe whirling in time with his friend's sword. And together they sang a song which must have been rehearsed in many such a fray as this, for no syllable fell out of place.

For a while, the fighting below seemed to eddy and still itself. Then, with a frightening scream, the two men leapt down.

Harald closed his eyes, feeling weak at the knees. He was angry with himself at feeling so, and at the same time half ready to call out for his father, as he used to do when a small boy. Then something else came into his heart; a man was but flesh and blood, after all, his brain said. What one can do, another may attempt! And now he stepped forward, his spear-shaft held loosely, his eye on the alert for an enemy.

But he was too late. The fight was over, and the *Nameless* looked very different from what it had been but four days before. The other vessel had put grappling hooks into the gunwales of the longship and so could not get away easily. What remained of her crew were huddled in the other boat. The Vikings swarmed aboard her, led by Thorkell and Ragnar. Harald and Horic followed close, but Aun and Gnorre stayed aboard their own sea-home, binding each other's wounds.

In the excitement, Harald had scarcely noticed what manner of men they were fighting. Now it was obvious that they were coastwise Picts of Caledonia, men much like Wolf Waterhater. Harald turned to see that Wolf was still aboard the *Nameless*, cleaning the points of his mace and affecting not to notice what went on. Then Harald recalled that Wolf too was a Caledonian, and that these were his own people. He could understand why this terrible fighting man did not wish to board the enemy.*

* History tells only of the most important happenings, the most forceful people. Sometimes it has to neglect the life of ordinary people so as to stress the victories of a king. So, always there is a part of any community that lags behind recorded history. There is always a part of any country that will not keep abreast of the beliefs of the times. There are people even today who believe that it is unlucky to sit thirteen at a table.

So, in many parts of what we now call Scotland, there were villages and even whole areas, in the eighth century, which had not become Christianized. This especially applied to the mountainous places, where communication was difficult.

And some of these folks, 'Picts' (or 'Painted ones,' as their Romanized name implies, because of their use of woad), still believed in the old gods, to whom sacrifices were made before the coming of Christ – such as

Now all was still. Thorkell, his wet hair swept back, and a shirt flung across his shoulders, was standing to face a group of Caledonians, who clustered about an old man dressed in black robes, and wearing a round hat of catskin.

No one spoke for a while, each trying to break down the pride of the other. Then, at last, the old man whispered to a blood-stained warrior who stood beside him, and the man, wiping the drops of sweat from his tired eyes, translated to Thorkell. 'My master says that he intended no battle to you. He came to take what he thought was an abandoned ship. That is the law of the sea, in all Christendom.'

Thorkell said, 'We are not Christians, my friend. We are Vikings. But say on. Perhaps you will tell us a story that will make us laugh.'

The man looked put out, but he turned again to his chief, the old man wearing the catskin cap, and listened to his instructions. Then he spoke again, 'My master says that he has nothing to offer you for the ransom of the crew and the ship, but that he will pray for the success of your enterprise farther north.'

Lugh, Mabon, and Belatucader . . . Time moved slowly in those distant days.

Yet these people were not deficient in other respects. They were good fishers, good herdsmen, good craftsmen in iron and in the precious metals. It is not wise for us to belittle the intelligence, or the civilization, of any people simply because they do not hold the same religious beliefs as ourselves.

Thorkell said, 'Thank your master for his prayers, and tell him that we pray to different gods. Tell him that we will be satisfied with his ship and with whatever cargo he carries.'

At this Ragnar smiled in his black beard, and Harald wondered what would come next. Then, to his great surprise, the old man in the catskin cap stepped slightly forward and said, without the aid of an interpreter, in good Norse, 'Young man, you are a knowing one. I will not try to deceive you further. We are not of the new religion, as you will know. I am a druid.'

He waited, expecting that the Vikings might be impressed. But they were hard men who were not concerned with a man's religion, but only with their own gain, with fighting, with their own gods, with the nature of sea and herring-shoal. Thorkell said at last. 'We do not care what you call your gods. We fought you fairly for profit. Now we are entitled to your ship and to whatever she carries. We are also entitled to you – though Odin forbid that any of you scarecrows would interest us. If we were on our way back, well, we might take you with us as a midsummer sacrifice in the forests – but as slaves you would not be worth your carriage and victuals.'

Now the old man frowned, but Thorkell's smile and his glance at the sword he carried made him talk on.

'Young Berserk,' he said, 'we are not a rich folk, for we must often pay two dues, one to the Christian church and one to our own secret college. What we have here is dedicated to the sun god, Lugh. We came out to sink it in the waters for him, where he sets. To touch it would bring disaster upon yourselves and on us.'

Ragnar said, 'We will fend for ourselves. Show us the treasure.'

The Vikings laughed, until they felt their longship jolt against the captured vessel, and sensed the deck-boards shuddering beneath them. Then they looked back in surprise. Wolf Waterhater was standing at the side of the *Nameless*, a long knife in his hand, the knife that had severed the grappling-ropes. His face was stern, so that even Thorkell knew that it would be of no avail to command him.

'What must we do, Wolf?' he said, seeing the widening space of sea between the ships.

Wolf Waterhater shrugged his shoulders and said, 'I say, leave the Pictish ship, Thorkell, and let them sink their treasure where they will. That is what I say.'

Thorkell turned to the old man and said, 'Go your ways, father. My men and I will go back to our ship. May your old god help you in your need.'

The man in the black robes and the catskin cap smiled slowly and said, 'It is a pity that you do not give us back the man who cut the ropes. He is a Pict. I can see it in his face.'

Ragnar said bitterly, 'You can have him. He is a nuisance to our venture.'

Thorkell looked stern. He loved Wolf. Then from the *Nameless* Wolf's voice came back, 'No, black master, if you want me you must swim for me – as must all the others!'

With that he hoisted the sail again, and since he had a following wind, swept past the captured boat for a distance of three lengths. Then he threw down the staying-stone and waited.

The Vikings laughed again and leapt overboard, to swim to the *Nameless*. Harald found himself in the salt water alongside Horic, who swam like a fish and ducked him many times before they boarded their own ship again.

When they were all aboard, Thorkell said, 'We have lost five men. Where are they?'

Aun and Gnorre got up from their seats and said, 'We did not wish to waste any time, Thorkell. We put them over, on the far side, while you were gossiping.'

Then they all laughed, all except Wolf, who seemed more interested in the strange signs that the old man in the black robes was making than in anything else.

'Come away, Wolf,' said Björn. 'He is not your master.'

Wolf shook his head sadly. 'One never knows, friend,' he said. 'Their arm is still a long one.'

Then Thorkell ordered the sail to be hoisted, and Harald noticed that the thin haze had become a clearly defined coastline.

9. The Visitor

DARKNESS HAD settled on the rocky inlet where the *Nameless* lay. The Vikings had lit a fire on the shore and clustered round it, wrapped in their sheepskins, eating pieces of salt pork, which they grilled on the ends of sticks.

Now, when the fight was long over, Harald found himself shivering from crown to toe with the delayed shock of the battle. He began to remember things he had seen at the time but had half-forgotten since, in the excitement of pulling in to shore. He remembered some of the horrors of the fight and Harald shuddered and turned away from the fire.

Behind him lay a dozen of the Vikings, on heaps of sacking, all of them wounded, in leg or shoulder or chest. Kragge sat with Ivar, whose right arm hung limply from a great sword gash. Ivar was gripping his underlip with his teeth, trying not to show that he was in pain. Kragge was telling him some long story, meant to take his mind off his wound. But Ivar was not listening, Harald could see that.

Hasting had taken an axe blow across the thigh, and lay asleep near Björn, who washed the wide wound in fresh spring water to keep the inflammation away. As Harald came up, Björn smiled a little sadly and whispered, 'Hasting will not fight again, lad. The best he can hope for is a thatched hut and a herd of cows. He will go on a crutch for the rest of his days.'

Harald said, 'He would rather die, I think, Björn.'

Björn said, 'He may yet do that, Harald, for these are cold nights to be sleeping out in.'

Harald tried to make signs then that Hasting was awake, so that Björn should not say anything more. But Hasting had heard what was said. He made no reply, but only turned himself over and hid his face in the sacking.

Aun, Gnorre and Horic sat together, unscathed. They ate warm oatcakes and drank corn-wine, which they had heated in their cups at the fire. They offered some to Harald, but he refused it, not liking its sour taste. He sat down beside them and said, 'We did not come out of that very well, did we?'

Aun said, 'It was a foolish venture, for we gained nothing and though we slew the greater part of their crew, we have lost some good men. Five I threw overboard myself, with Gnorre's aid, and here are two more who may not last the night out.' He nodded back to where Hasting and Ivar lay.

Gnorre said, 'Yet a start had to be made. A crew is not a crew until it has fought together, whatever the gain. That is the price one pays.'

Horic sat smiling, twisting his length of twine, saying nothing. Harald had the feeling that the Laplander did not care for battles, though he fought fiercely while in them.

'Now there will be nothing but rowing for us all,' said Aun. 'We have lost the relief men, and unless we pick up two others when this night is over, you may still live to see Thorkell and Ragnar at the oars.'

Harald turned to look towards the leaders at this. They sat apart from the Vikings, talking heatedly. Thorkell was waving his right hand about, and thumping it into the palm of his other, as though to emphasize the points he was making. Ragnar was shaking his head gravely. Harald wanted to creep nearer to them, to find out what they were saying, when there was a sudden blast on the horn from the Viking who was acting as scout on the hilltop above. All men who could left the fire, for its glow would make them an easy target to anyone above who could use a bow. They ran into the shadows, drawing knives and swords, unhooking the axes from their girdles.

There was a silence; then at last the sound of one man coming down the pebbled slope above them. Harald shivered as he heard the small stones falling on to the beach. He was not a coward, but he felt the spear he held shaking violently. He hoped that if there was to be an attack, he would not have to strike at anyone. He had not yet recovered from the shock of the earlier encounter; another on the same day would be too much.

Then a man came into the glow of the fires, and the flickering light glinted on the copper armbands and neck-ring which he wore. Upon his head he had a broad-brimmed iron helmet, which flung his face into shadow. A long parti-coloured cloak of red and green worsted hung from his shoulders, secured with a bronze brooch.

He was a small dark-haired man, though his shadow made him look bigger. He carried an iron-shod staff in his right hand, but no other weapon that could be seen.

Beside the fire he halted and looked round inquiringly, a smile on his dark face. Aun muttered, 'That is a brave man, to walk into our camp smiling and without a sword.'

'He claims a herald's privilege,' said Gnorre. 'He must come from the king of these parts, whoever he is.'

Now Thorkell stepped forward, his own sword sheathed, and said to the stranger, 'Do you come in peace?'

The dark man laughed and said, speaking Norse easily, 'I might ask the same question of you, Viking, but I do not wish to insult you.'

Ragnar joined Thorkell. 'If I were to lay this blade once across your neck, you would join your fathers,' he said. 'How would you like that?'

The small dark man stared back at him and said, 'If I blew once upon this whistle, a hundred arrows would turn you into a hedgehog. How would you like that?'

Thorkell laughed and said, 'We are tired from a voyage and have lost some good men. If you wish to fight, let us wait till the morning, and when we have had a night's rest, we will come up the hill to you.'

The dark man said, 'I know of your fight this afternoon. It was my folk you killed. I am pleased to see that they gave a good account of themselves too. I am pleased, too, that you let my father sink his treasure where he wished. Had you taken it from him, we should have shot you through with arrows an hour ago when you were all round the fire. We are a lawless people in many ways, but we insist on serving our gods as we wish and without any hindrance.'

Ragnar said, 'You speak up bravely for a little man.' There was an insulting smile on his face as he spoke.

The other said, 'Better a small warrior than a tall coward.'

Ragnar said, 'There is light enough here for us to try each other's skill with any weapon you name.'

Thorkell was silent, for it was against the law for any man to prevent another from fighting, if he thought fit. Though they all saw that he was displeased with Ragnar. Even Hasting said, 'That Ragnar will be the end of us all, unless a check be put on him.'

Aun fingered his axe. 'I wish I might let Peacegiver talk a word to Ragnar,' he said.

'There may come a chance,' said Gnorre.

The small dark man by the fire glanced up the hill as though wondering whether he should blow his whistle.

Then he shrugged his shoulders and said, 'If you will come to my steading as guests, so be it, and none shall harm you. If you still wish for death, so be it, and none shall hinder you from having it. I do not care. I only speak the words of my father who sent me to you.'

Thorkell held out both his hands and said, 'We come as guests, chieftain. I will speak for my crew. Is that good?'

The other said, 'That is good,' and took Thorkell's hands in his own.

It was at that moment that Aun saw Ragnar make a slight movement, as though to draw a knife. Such an act of treachery would bring death on them all, he knew. He sprang forward, dropping his axe on to the beach and flung both arms about Ragnar. In the shock of the impact, both men stumbled and fell. Even as they did so an arrow stuck quivering in the spot where Ragnar had been standing.

The Vikings gasped. 'There are sharp eyes above us,' whispered Horic, smiling secretly. 'They see all.'

Thorkell still held the other's hands. They smiled at each other. 'Your friend is hot-tempered,' said the dark man. 'But then, it appears, so are my own watchers, so that makes all even.'

Now Aun let Ragnar rise again. For a while the two men glared at each other like wolves about to fight. 'I shall not forget you, Doorback,' said Ragnar darkly.

'I shall be ready for you, Raven,' said Aun. 'Come for me when you please.'

Then the Vikings followed their leader up the hill, carrying their wounded, but leaving six men to keep a guard on the *Nameless* as she lay beached.

10. After the Feast

AFTER THE feasting, Harald lay in the dark of the long pine hall, wide awake. He could not get off to sleep partly because of the excitements of the day, partly because of the groaning wounded who lay near the fire in the centre of the hall; but perhaps most of all because of the memories of the feast that had only just ended, memories which flooded in a great noisy tumult through his head.

Once again he heard the wild music of harp and flute that had filled the hall; he saw the dancers, skipping like elves above the crossed swords, their fierce faces lit with an ecstasy he had never observed on a man's face before. He saw in his mind's eye the long trestle table, with its torches set along it and the meat and drink scattered here and there in profusion. And at the head of the table, the old chief, Dubghal and his son, Feinn, with bright Thorkell between them, all of them laughing and singing as though they had known each other always. The boy recalled how, at a certain point in the feasting, Feinn had taken out his razor-keen hunting knife and had nicked Thorkell's wrist and his own and had placed them together so that their blood mingled.

Then the Vikings and the Picts had roared with approval and had slapped each other so hard on the back that at least three fights started – and finished just as quickly when the old chieftain glared down the hall.

And he recalled poor Hasting and Ivar, propped up against the wall, their faces ashen pale, the food beside them untouched, their weak hands letting drop the wine horns that their comrades offered to them. Ivar had stared blindly towards the table, now without power of speech; Hasting had tried once or twice to speak to Aun, but could not make his voice heard above the general flurry of sound in the hall.

These things had impressed Harald deeply; but perhaps even more disturbing was his memory of Ragnar, seated down the table from his friend, brooding darkly and never saying a word to anyone, hacking savagely at the meat which was placed before him and drinking constantly of the strong heather-honey ale of which only the Picts held the secret. At first, they had all watched Ragnar anxiously, since they were afraid that he might start a quarrel out of jealousy. Yet as the evening wore on, and nothing untoward had happened, they had forgotten him.

Once Thorkell had looked round the table and had asked for Wolf, but no man had seen Wolf that night. Someone said that he had volunteered to stay with the *Nameless*, and that had satisfied Thorkell. The old chief, Dubghal had said wryly, 'That Wolf is one of our folk, I think. I should like to speak with him.'

The young chief had said quickly, 'He has lived with the Northmen almost all his life, father. You cannot call on him.'

Harald had wondered what this meant and Horic had said in a whisper, 'They of the old faith choose a red-haired one to lie on the stone at Midsummer. I think Wolf was wise to stay with the *Nameless*. It is every man's right to choose the manner of his own death!'*

Then, when the Picts had sung and told their stories, the old man Dubghal had asked if any of the Vikings had a skill in entertaining, and Horic had been pushed forward to do his winter dance on the long table. This time he improved on his earlier performance, for he brought the creatures of air and forest into the very hall. Standing in the flickering torchlight, he had extended his long arm towards the rooftree, and everyone had not only heard, but seen the wild geese coming down from Iceland and flying south through the firesmoke, to disappear before they reached the far wall. Then a bear had walked in at one door and out of another. At last a wolf had howled outside the hall and Horic had made the motion of inviting it in; but by this time the Picts had had enough of the illusion and the old chief, afraid that one of them might hurt the Laplander in his excitement, had bidden the entertainment to stop. Later he had called Horic to him and had offered him much gold to stay with them, for he knew that the

* Horic was referring to the druidic sacrifices, performed on Midsummer Day, at dawn-time, when a red-haired youth was chosen to represent the Sun-god. By dying on the sacrificial stone, this youth was thought to bring sunshine and hence growth to the crops. He died for the people.

Laplander was of the same old faith which he himself followed. But Horic had shaken his head and had said that he only did these things for amusement's sake, and that if he were forced to do them, his power would leave him. So Dubghal had reluctantly let the little man take his place at the foot of the table once more.

And Harald recalled all these things as he lay in the darkened hall, the feast now ended. Here and there through the gloom, dark figures moved, though whether they were Vikings or Picts the boy did not know. And at times a strange whispering started up and seemed to pass through the hall before it faded and died. There was an air of general unrest about. But at last Harald fell into a light, troubled sleep, in which green-eyed wolves looked round the trunks of pine trees at him and called to him in Ragnar's voice . . .

Then suddenly Harald was awake again. The fire had gone out completely now, but the hall was full of movement. Then there was the flash of flint on iron and a torch flamed out. Harald saw that the Vikings were on their feet, their weapons drawn. There was a great shout in his ear. Aun yelled, 'Out steel, we are betrayed.' Then the hall was full of leaping shapes and swords rose and fell, vicious in the dim light.

Harald found himself between Aun and Gnorre. Horic was somewhere behind them, grunting as he struck out. A Pict, wearing feathers in his helmet, came at them. Harald saw the mad light in his eyes as the man thrust out with a long leaf-bladed sword. The weapon seemed to flash before the boy's very eyes, then the man screamed and tumbled forward with the impetus of his rush, almost knocking

Harald's feet from under him. Aun bent and swung up his axe again. Gnorre said, 'Don't fall, lad, or it will be your end. Keep your feet and we may win to the door.'

They began a slow rhythmic movement across the hall. They passed Björn, who stood over the bodies of Hasting and Ivar. He was beset on every side, but spared a word as he swung his axe. 'Do not stay, Aun Doorback,' he said. 'If Odin wills it, I shall come down to the ship again. If not, then he means me to travel with these two Vikings home.'

Harald saw that Hasting and Ivar had not survived their wounds, gained earlier in the sea-fight. Then he saw Thorkell at the far end of the hall, surrounded by their dark-skinned enemies. Feinn, with whom he had taken the blood-oath that night, pressed close at him, taunting him. 'So this is what men mean when they say: "Trust a viper before a Viking!" I had not thought you would so soon forget your friend's promise.'

Thorkell swept his long blade about the circle that tried to close on him. 'It is you, Feinn, who are the breaker of vows. I have done nothing worse than trying to get a night's sleep since I last saw you.'

Feinn and his followers laughed in derision, and lunged in at the golden-haired leader.

Gnorre looked round and said, 'I do not see Ragnar, or any of those who follow him rather than Thorkell. Come, Aun, we must spare a blow for Thorkell before we go!'

The four of them pressed forward to where their leader fought. He was a fine sight, even though outnumbered. His hair was disarranged and his shirt of mail pulled on

carelessly. Even the strappings of his hide breeches dangled behind him as he shuffled now in this direction, now in that, to meet and slash at a foeman. Yet, for all that, he looked a hero, even the son of Thor himself, thought Harald.

Aun yelled, 'Up Thorkell! Up the *Nameless*!' Gnorre joined him in the cry, but Horic and Harald were silent. Yet all pushed on, and now, with the men beside him, even Harald felt a strange desire for battle. It seemed to him that now they were fighting with good cause, and not merely to win treasure. They were fighting a treacherous enemy, for their very lives, and to save their leader, to whom they had pledged themselves.

They took the Picts by surprise. Some of them turned at Aun's first shout and put up sword or small buckler as defence. But two at least of them were too late. Peacegiver rose and fell, rose and fell. Horic's rough sword thrust to left and to right. Then a bundled dark shape launched itself at Harald. He heard Gnorre's shout of warning, but it came too late. The man was on him, stabbing furiously with a short dagger. Harald felt the blade sear his shoulder, and then, in a great anger, he shortened his spear, and using it like a sword, struck with all his force at the man who attacked him. He felt the jar of the blow along his arm and then the man seemed to run on past him, sideways, dragging the spear from his grasp.

Gnorre said, 'Your first blood! Hail, Viking! Thorkell shall give you another weapon now.'

Harald's heart swelled, for he saw Thorkell's eyes glance at him and a grim smile come across his leader's face.

Thorkell had seen him fight his first battle. Then a great wave of nausea swept over the boy, and he wished that the Pict had never run at him.

The next thing he knew, he was standing next to Thorkell, and they were all pushing their terrible way to the open door, through which Harald saw the stars shining out of a deep blue-black sky.

Behind them, still clustered in the hall, were their enemy. Feinn was leaning against the wall, his hand over his chest, the dark blood ebbing between his white fingers, a vicious grin on his swarthy face.

Harald heard him gasp, 'Thorkell Traitor, though you leave me so, my gods will follow you. Their arm is long.'

Thorkell's face twisted in a smile of sadness. It was as though he wished to go to Feinn. Then with a shrug he remembered where he was and they turned to go through the door into the night.

Yet, even as they turned, a dark shape lying in the doorway moved. A man raised himself on his elbow and flung the short axe he had clenched in his hand. The blow was meant for Thorkell, but Gnorre saw the axe as it flew through the air and stepped towards it, keeping it from the leader. Harald heard the haft thud on Gnorre's temples, and stepped across to catch him as he fell. Aun gave a great roar of anger and struck down towards the floor. The man lay still.

Gnorre was unconscious and the blood flowed down his face. Aun took him on to his broad back and carried him. Horic and Thorkell paused for a moment in the doorway. They called to Björn, but he would not come. He still stood over the bodies of his comrades, singing quietly to himself, a terrible rhythm of death, like the song that oarsmen sing when they battle against a contrary tide.

'Up – ay – aa! Up – ay – aa!'

His sword struck again and again. His eyes were glazed. He did not know where he was, it seemed.

Thorkell whispered, 'Odin holds out his hands for Björn. He will never come away now.'

Then he called out softly, 'Farewell, Viking. We must go down to the ship your hands built. May they build even better ships where you are going.'

Harald felt the hot tears running down his cheeks. He saw that Thorkell was crying too. As they turned, Björn snatched up a pine torch and was swinging it round him as he shambled towards the ring of men who waited, like hungry wolves, for his great strength to fail.

When they were halfway down the hill that gave on to the beach, they looked back at the sudden glow in the sky behind them.

'Björn has made himself a funeral pyre,' said Aun. 'Now if Feinn lives, he must build himself another hall!'

Then they saw the *Nameless*. She was already afloat and ready to move away. Thorkell shouted, and down below them Ragnar answered, 'Hurry, Thorkell,' he said. 'We had given you up for lost. The tide pulls us away. Hurry!'

They struggled over the rough shingle and on into the water, breast-high before they reached the longship. Rough hands dragged them aboard. Harald saw Gnorre's eyes flicker, and he heard him whisper something to Aun, who bent over him like a mother over her child.

Horic whispered, 'Gnorre's wound is not deep, lad. Sleep happily.'

Then Harald fell his length on the hard wet boards, exhausted in body and in mind. He did not hear the gulls crying or the wind slapping against the great mainsail. He did not hear Thorkell's harsh words to Ragnar, or Ragnar's ironical laughter. Nor did he hear Ragnar say, 'You are a fool, Thorkell. I and my band raided their treasure house while you slept. We have brought enough away to make us all rich men. And that is the thanks I get!'

Thorkell said, 'You traitorous dolt! I had taken a blood-oath with Feinn.'

Ragnar pulled at his black beard and said, 'The oath bound you, not me, my friend!'

Harald did not see Thorkell strike the Dane full across the face then, for all men to watch. The boy was deep in sleep.

11. Harald's Dream

THE *NAMELESS* rode wearily in the northern sea. It was now the best part of a week since she had put out from the rocky inlet under Feinn's steading. It was such a week as made Harald think lovingly of the days when he lived ashore in Gudröd's hall, with solid ground beneath his feet, a good meal three times a day and a warm bed to go to at night, out of the winds. The northern sea held no such comforts. Often the Vikings were wet and hungry, and often they must watch or row all night so that they might sleep in the sunshine on deck the next day. Harald thought many times of his father, almost tearfully now, wondering if his leg had mended well . . .

During the week since the fight in the hall, the *Nameless* had put into shore twice, when Thorkell had sighted smoke rising above a village. They had been lucky enough to attack without warning and had carried away enough provisions to keep them fed, but without any luxuries. The first village had been an easy one to surprise, since most of the men were away on a hunting trip into the mountains.

They had stormed the low stockade and had carried off meal and meat. Kragge had fired a hut or two before anyone could stop him. In this affray Wolf had stolen a little pig, but a small black-haired girl ran after him towards the longship, crying so bitterly that he had stopped and given it back. He gave the child a bracelet from his arm, after which she wanted to come with him on to the *Nameless*. But Thorkell made him take the child back, almost to the gates of the village. As he waved goodbye to her, an enthusiastic shepherd put an arrow through Wolf's ear, which caused him great discomfort and made his comrades laugh, to see him jumping with rage, shaking his fist at the marksman, and waving to the little girl – all at the same time.

The second foraging expedition was not so fortunate, generally. It was a much larger settlement, some of its houses being made of stone. The Vikings got into it easily enough, for it was night-time and the place was poorly guarded. But once inside, they found it more difficult to make their escape. Both women and men attacked the Vikings with whatever weapons lay at hand. One buxom woman laid open Kragge's head with an iron ladle. Three others caught Rolf and flung him into a deep midden pit, almost dislocating his steering arm. It was only with great difficulty that Aun and Gnorre pulled the steersman up again, after which all men walked at some distance from him.

While this foray went on, men from a neighbouring settlement made a detour and got down to the *Nameless* in the shallow bay. They were still striking at the ship's sides with heavy wood-axes when Thorkell's band returned.

Luckily Björn had built a ship to last and they had done little damage when the Vikings trapped them, between the cliff and the sea. At first Thorkell would have struck off their heads, on the sand, for his anger was so great that a plank of the *Nameless* should have been touched by an enemy. Then he listened to Ragnar's counsel, and took the protesting men aboard to act as oarsmen, and later to be sold as slaves. They all felt that they deserved this fate, since they had interfered in a quarrel that did not concern them and had tried to damage a fine ship which had done them no harm.

The captured half-dozen were young red-faced foresters, well used to hard work. They were chained at the ankles, but their arms were left free, so that they might row without hindrance.

At first they were wrathful and silent. They even dared to sneer in Thorkell's face when he spoke to them, telling them that if they behaved themselves he would try to find a good master to sell them to. But their bravado soon left them as the *Nameless* pulled out farther and farther into the northern sea. Then first one, then another broke down and wept. They began to implore Thorkell to set them ashore again and promised that they would pay a handsome price for their freedom. This made the Vikings laugh, for they knew that the men were lying, and had no more money than would buy a truss of hay for a horse. So it was that the twelve men of the *Nameless* who had been lost in the earlier fighting were replaced by the six Pictish slaves. It was a poor exchange, but better than none, for by now the ship had need of every hand she could find.

The quarrel between Ragnar and Thorkell had healed itself, up to a point, and now even Thorkell liked to lift the deckboards and gaze down on the great bundles of gold torques and gorgets and drinking-cups that they had amassed in that treacherous raid.

So, one way and another, the voyage went fairly well until a storm blew up late one afternoon and carried them eastwards, far from any land. One man of the *Nameless* was swept away when a great wave struck the ship on the beam. He was a Viking named Smörke, who had lost three brothers in the northern sea already. He had often said that this voyage would be his last, but all had laughed at him. As he was swept overboard, Gnorre swore that he heard the man yell out, 'There, I told you so!'

They all ran to the side, but there was nothing to be done. Smörke was borne away in a swirl of water, and the last men saw of him were the bull's horns of his helmet.

'That will confuse Odin,' said Horic. 'He will think that Smörke died in battle. A man should have the sense to take off his helmet if he is going to die in the sea.'

But for all that, the Vikings were sorry to lose a good sailor. Yet the storm was so violent that they did not mourn for long. Their attention was needed for other things.

Harald suddenly felt older, much older. Now the sea was an enemy, he thought, a ravenous salt beast that for ever gnawed at the timbers of a boat, and no friend. The boy smiled bitterly as he recalled his joy on setting out over the fjord, so long ago it seemed now. He remembered the smooth glassy sea, so harmless and so mirror-like, a deep blue-bronze, with the rich amber sun shining across it.

Harald stood upright, clutching the swinging gunwales, the bitter salt spray smashing hard at his face and over his drenched body. He remembered Gryffi with the spear in him, Björn swinging the torch in the great hall, the faces of Ivar and Hasting as they sat dumbly against the wall, the man he had killed . . .

He did not feel the spray then. He was lost in a dream, his wet golden hair stuck across his wind-reddened face; his cloak heavy with seawater, yet flung out in fitful gusts behind him as the gale tore at it, making its edges ragged. Harald's pale-blue eyes stared blindly through the thick spume. He did not see it, did not feel the storm, even for a moment. Now he was back in memory on the fjord, with the amber sun staring at him from the west, casting a broad track towards him, magnificent and grim as blood. And over this ghastly sea of his memory, a deep and echoing voice seemed to say, 'Come, young Viking. Come, come, come, come. Walk on the Whale's Way, pace the Path of the Dolphin towards me. Come to the sun, warrior-lad, come, come, come . . .'

He began to sway on his feet, and it was then that Aun caught him and carried him into shelter under one of the platforms. 'The lad is suffering from a fever,' he said to Thorkell. 'He has seen too much and suffered too much since we started out.'

'Yet he shapes well,' said Thorkell. 'He will make a good Viking yet.'

Aun said, 'He won't unless we treat that wound in his shoulder. The young fool has said nothing to anyone about it, and now it is inflamed and swollen. If you won't care for the lad, as you ought, since his father is maimed for you, then let me take him over. I am prepared to do my duty if you are not.'

At first Thorkell was angry that Aun Doorback should speak like that to him. Then he made himself smile as he said, 'I am sorry, Aun Doorback. I have had little experience at being a father to anyone. But I shall improve with time. Have patience with me, and in the meantime, let us both be father to the lad.'

So it was that Harald found himself a second father, in the middle of the northern sea in a storm. He almost found death too, that night, for the ship's mast snapped and crashed through the roof where he lay, missing him by the breadth of a child's hand. Yet such was the lad's fever that he knew nothing of these things for many days, until he was told.

12. A Ship and a Sword

IN THE days that followed, the Vikings were beset by sore trials. Now though the storm wore itself out, they had to row from dawn to dusk to make headway. Their hands were raw and their backs breaking. One of the slaves fell into a stupor and at last lay still. Thorkell had him put overboard for there was no one to tend him. Then the fresh water ran out and now men dared not row for thirst. They tried drinking corn-wine instead, but that left them stupefied and witless and they lolled about the decks, disinterested in life. Nothing that Thorkell or Ragnar could do would rouse them.

It was while they were in this condition that a cargo vessel passed them, at a distance of not much more than a hundred feet. It was a high round-bellied tub, carrying two sails, a Frankish trader, a privateer, laden with amber and bear pelts and reindeer hides; a ship of the south, anxious to spoil the icy north, crewed with hard men who felt themselves to be man for man as good as any Viking of the fjords. This ship had sailed in upon a quiet village, too busy with its own affairs to think of guards, and had come away laden to the gunwales with enough barbaric finery to keep the Frankish Court in high glee for long enough. Thorkell had quickly judged it to be a Frankish ship, and wished that they could have boarded it. But the merchants on board the vessel could see the sorry plight of the Vikings, as they rolled on the decks of their mastless ship, and they came to the side of their boat and looked down on them, jeering. When Ragnar shouted back at them, they challenged him to come aboard and fight their champion on the foredeck. Such was Ragnar's rage that he would have gone, not seeing that it was a trick. But Thorkell held him back, and the Franks passed on unharmed and laughing.

'One day you will laugh on the other side of your face,' yelled Ragnar, who hated to be bested.

'Good riddance!' shouted the Franks, and Black Ragnar beat his forehead on the gunwales with rage.

The following morning, shortly after dawn, another Viking longship rode confidently up alongside them and flung grappling irons over the side of the *Nameless*. Her seamen could see well enough the plight of Thorkell's ship and looked for an easy prize, but when their leader saw who was captain of the *Nameless* he climbed aboard and flung his arms round Thorkell and kissed him on the cheeks. It turned out to be his cousin, Knud, whom he had not seen for three years. Knud gave the Vikings two kegs of water and a sack of meal. He told them that if they steered due west they would strike an easy coast where the forests came down to the sea. There they might make another mast from some tall tree.

In return, Thorkell told Knud that a big Frankish trader had passed them but a few hours before. Knud slapped him on the back and said, 'Tit for tat! If I take anything worth having, I will keep a share for you!'

Then his longship, which he called *Hungry Hawk*, set course and bore down after the ship which had so insulted Ragnar. 'Strike off the captain's head for me,' yelled Ragnar. Knud laughed back. He was more interested in plunder than in killing.

During the days that followed Harald slowly recovered from the effects of his exhaustion and of the poisoned shoulder which had laid him low. Aun and Gnorre took it in turns to sit with him and to put cold water pads on his arm and chest to keep down the fever. Horic and Rolf came when they could and told him tales when he was able to understand them again.

Horic had a lovely yarn about two brothers who went hunting bear in the great forest of Lapland. Their names were Festi and Vlasta, and they were great hunters but a little simple in all other respects. One night as they sat by their fire, Festi saw a big bear looking at them. He told his brother to make ready the pot and took his bear-knife and went after the animal. The bear ran away, but Festi soon caught up with it and, after a short struggle, was able to kill it. Then he thought that he would play a joke on his brother, so he skinned the bear and got into the skin, intending to frighten him. He made his way silently back through the woods until he came to a rock, near the fire where he had left his brother and, after making a great growling, leapt out into the firelight. But instead of his brother, a great bear sat by the fire, just finishing off the last of Vlasta. The real bear and the imitation bear stared at each other for a while, then each gave a yell and ran away, the bear back into the forest, and Festi to his village. But when the villagers saw Festi coming, they thought that he was the great bear that had terrified them for so long. Three strong men ran to meet him, and put three arrows into him as he ran towards them, because he was so wrapped about with bearskin that they did not recognize his shouts for help.

Most of Horic's stories were about bears. And they usually ended with someone getting eaten. He would roar with laughter when he came to that part and would rock backwards and forwards until he made Harald feel quite giddy. Then Rolf would come in and tell Horic not to be a barbarian. He would push him out and try to teach Harald the art of navigation. Rolf was a very kind person in spite of his forbidding appearance, and Harald came to like him as much as any of the Vikings.

One day Thorkell came into the hut below the platform. He smiled down at Harald wearily. The boy saw that the warrior's hands were callused and raw, as though from much rowing. He moved with a bent back, stiffly. His fine golden hair was tangled and matted now, and was tied in a rough knot. His blue eyes were red-rimmed and tired.

'It has been a hard row, Viking,' he said to Harald. 'You must hasten and get well, then you can give us a hand.'

When the tears of weakness gathered in the boy's eyes, Thorkell bit his lips and looked sheepishly down at the floor.

'I was teasing, lad,' he said. 'There will be time enough another day, mayhap. Look, Aun tells me it is time to bring you these gifts.'

He put two packages on to Harald's lap, one as small as his hand, the other as long as his arm, both wrapped in oiled cloth. Harald tried to unwrap the small one, but his sick fingers only fumbled at the knot which held the package together. Thorkell took the gift and slashed the string with his knife. Then carefully he unwound the cloth. A perfectly carved model of a Viking longship lay in his hand, gleaming white, fragile and beautiful. Harald gave a gasp of excitement. His hands lay on the sheepskin coverlet. Thorkell put the ship on the boy's lap, where he could touch it.

'Björn made it,' said Thorkell. 'It is of ivory that someone brought from Miklagard long ago. Björn carved it when he made his first voyage, when they were becalmed in the White Sea. He told me that he wanted to give it to you after your first battle. He is not here to give it. It is yours, Harald Sigurdson.'

Harald remembered poor Björn, fighting alone in the long hall, a torch in his hand. The tears filled his eyes again.

Thorkell said, 'Do not weep for Björn. That is the death he wanted. He is a lucky man. Not all of us will die so well.'

He unwrapped the long package. Harald watched him and saw, slowly revealed, a sword. At the sight of it he felt exhausted again with wonderment and could only sigh. The polished hilt was of ebony, inlaid with rings of silver; the pommel was a globe of rock crystal, carved into the shape of an acorn; the guard was a curved cross-piece of bronze, chiselled to form ivy tendrils curling round a bough; the blade was long and leaf-shaped, with thin runnels going its length, from hilt to point. It shone blue-black in the dim light of the cabin. He did not dare to touch it.

Thorkell smiled happily. 'Take this,' he said. 'It was made for me when I was but a little older than you are now. It was my warrior-gift after I had been lucky in my first foray. Now I give it to you, and may it bring such luck to you as it has done to me.'

When he had said that, he laid the sword across the boy's knees and went from the cabin, turning back only once, to smile down at Harald. The boy gazed stupidly at the two precious gifts and wished that his father were there to see them. Then he fell into a contented sleep, and dreamed that he was running down the path back to Gudröd's hall with the gifts in his hand to show his father. And when the door opened at his shouts, he saw that not only his father but his mother also stood on the threshold, waiting to welcome him. And Harald wept in his sleep, for his mother had died when he was very small, and he could not recall her face.

It was while he was weeping thus, in his sleep, that Aun came in and shook him gently and woke him.

'Good fortune!' he said. 'We have run upon a fleet of Orkney fishermen, eight smacks in all. They will tow us back with them.'

Harald said, 'Are they our own people?'

Aun answered, 'Yes, all Northmen, though they sailed out to Orkney a generation ago. We are in luck's way, Harald. Now you will get well again, and we shall have no more rowing for a while at least!'

As he finished, a strange man wearing a woollen cap over his grey hair looked into the cabin. 'Is this the young warrior?' he said, and Aun nodded. The man came forward and gently examined his shoulder. 'My wife, Asa, will know what to do with that,' he said. 'She is a great woman for herbs.'

'That is Olaf,' said Aun. 'He is a fisherman and a farmer, and has a family of his own; a prosperous man, who will look after us now.'

And truly the Vikings of the *Nameless* needed someone to look after them, for the breaking of their mast came near to costing them their lives. No man had tasted water for two days, and they were too weak to battle any longer against the sea which seemed determined to keep them from the shore. Yet, even though they suffered agonies of thirst, they had agreed to let the sick boy have what water there was. Harald never knew this. No Viking would tell him a thing like that.

13. Olaf's Steading

OLAF'S HALL was a comfortable place, built solidly of wood and set in the shelter of a large rocky hill. A great fire of driftwood always burned, and Asa saw that the rushes on the floor were changed regularly, although her sons grumbled at having to do this. There was enough work cleaning out the byre and gutting the fish, they said. But they always obeyed their mother.

Asa was a plump woman with a red, smiling face. Her fair hair was bound in a scarf of blue linen. Her sleeves were always rolled back over her strong arms, for there was ever a job to do, either milking or baking or washing, and she had no daughters to help her – only three huge sons, lazy louts, she called them, though she loved them dearly.

Asa's great sons were all red-headed, as their father had been before he became grey. They were Sven, Rollo and Ottar. Each day they could, they went down to help in the task of getting the *Nameless* ready for her next voyage.

The battered longship lay, a hawk among gulls, in the midst of the fishing-smacks, in the little grey stone harbour under the shadow of Olaf's hill. Seabirds screamed over her as the men worked hard, stepping the new mast, renewing the tackle and recaulking the seams. Thorkell was hard at work every day, whatever the weather. He gave himself no rest. His once-beautiful eyes were now always red-rimmed and bloodshot. The winds were cruel to the eyes.

Under Asa's care, Harald grew well again, though at first she had almost despaired of him. Once she came to his bedside when he lay in a troubled sleep, crying out to his father, telling him of the man he had killed. Asa saw the boy's pale hands and his sunken face. She saw the sword and the ivory longship that he always had at the side of his bed, and for a moment she had an impulse to destroy them in her anger.

'A fine lot of warriors you are, to bring a lad to this, with your swords and silly boats,' she said to Aun, who only scratched his head and looked away. 'Butchers, I call you! I pray that Odin never puts such tomfoolery into my lads' heads!'

But her prayer was made a little too late. Asa's three huge sons grew to love the *Nameless* as they worked on her in the harbour, and one day when they were shown the treasure that was placed for safety in their father's strongroom, their eyes glistened with envy. That night they told their father that they wished to sail with the *Nameless* when she left again. Olaf shrugged his shoulders. He did not tell them that it would be hard for him to make a living without them, farming and fishing. He only said, 'You are of age. You will do as you please.'

That night he said to his wife, 'We must pull in our belts a little when the boys have gone.'

Asa flew into a great rage, but she saw that it was no use arguing. Olaf had left his people in Norway, and she hers. Their sons were only doing the same. 'Very well,' she said at last, when her eyes were dry, 'then I shall keep Harald to make up for them. He shall be our son.'

Olaf smiled sadly and patted her gently on the shoulder. 'He is worse than our lads,' he said. 'He is already a Viking. They are only fisherfolk, though they have big arms and bigger ideas!'

And Asa knew that he was right. The next day she asked Harald if he would stay, but he shook his head and said, 'I have a father already, Asa, and I promised him to make the voyage. He lies sick and I must go back to him one day. Besides, I am pledged to Thorkell and must follow him until he sets me free.'

Not all men were so loyal to the young leader, however. While the Vikings were resting on the island, Kragge went round to many of them, spreading tales of Thorkell's lack of leadership. Many now began to look to Ragnar, who had after all got them the treasure they carried. Indeed, before a month was out, only a handful still thought of Thorkell as their true shipmaster. These included Rolf, Aun, Gnorre, Horic and, of course, Wolf. Harald did not know of this treachery, but even if he had, Thorkell's place in his affection was too high for him to be replaced by any living man but Harald's own father.

At last the *Nameless* was ready again, and looking as bright and fresh as when she had been launched. Provisions were laid aboard, and there was some feasting in Olaf's great hall, though it had an air of sadness about it now. Olaf's sons were there, and three of their cousins, big men like themselves, who wished to leave the island and sail away on their adventures.

They were all waiting to take the oath, but Thorkell was still down at the harbour, with the longship. At last he came up the path to the hall. All men heard his slow, shuffling step. They watched him stand by the doorway for a while, fingering the rough wood of the doorposts. When he looked up, his half-closed eyes seemed to look beyond them. Olaf said, 'Drink a cup of wine in celebration of your sailing, Thorkell.' And he stepped forward and handed a cup to the young shipmaster. But Thorkell put out his hand to the side of the cup and grasped the empty air. Men drew in their breath. Olaf led Thorkell towards a chair, but he could not see it and fell down beside it. Gnorre whispered, 'He is blind. Great Thor, we have a blind captain!' Then all men except his friends shrank from Thorkell. They helped him to his feet and led him weeping to his bed.

That night, Olaf's sons and their cousins took the oath to Ragnar, and the others, who sided with Ragnar, took the oath again, now no longer Thorkell's men.

When Wolf went to comfort Thorkell, the young leader struck out at him, but Wolf only smiled and put his arms about him.

'I will be your eyes, Thorkell Fairhair,' he said, 'You have lost nothing.'

'I will be your right arm, Thorkell Fairhair,' said Aun. 'You have gained something.'

'I will be your spell-master, Thorkell Fairhair,' said Horic, crying a little as he said it. 'You will gain everything.'

'Where is Harald,' said Thorkell, pushing them away. 'Where is my young Viking?'

Harald stepped forward and stood by Thorkell. The leader put his hand on the boy's shoulder and said, 'Are you with me, lad?'

Harald said, 'I would try to kill anyone who asked me that but you, Master.'

Thorkell smiled then and said, 'So be it. Now I know that I have lost little.' And with that he fell into an exhausted slumber while his friends watched over him.

14. The *Nameless* Sails Again

ASA TURNED Thorkell's eyelids up as he slept. She said to Aun, 'I have seen such blindness before among those who come here. It is the bitter wind which scours our island and blows dust into the eyes.'

Aun said, 'Will he see again?'

Asa said, 'Only Odin can say that. I have known such eyes to see again. He should stay here indoors and not go on to the sea.'

Aun answered, 'He would rather be blind than leave the sea.'

Asa said, 'He is a fool then, like you, and like my own sons. One would think their mothers were seals. Look, I will give you herbs with which you must make a poultice, then bandage them to his eyes. He must be kept quiet, in the dark and away from the wind. Then perhaps Odin might take pity on him and let him see. Who knows? We can only do our best.'

Aun turned to Harald and said, 'Thorkell is a difficult man to treat. He will knock my teeth out if I try to make him sit still. You are the one to do it, boy. He will listen to you.'

The next day a great crowd of islanders gathered above the stone harbour, and a pathway was cleared for the longship between the clustered fishing-boats. The Vikings went aboard, led by Ragnar, who took Kragge as his second-in-command. Wolf and Thorkell came last. Harald led Thorkell by the hand and many women wept as they watched this. As Thorkell went up the plank, he stumbled and almost fell into the water. One of Olaf's sons said, 'Thank goodness we have a leader who can see.'

Ragnar heard these words and strode down the longship to where the man sat. He said in a loud voice for all to hear, 'Though the Vikings have elected me their leader, Thorkell is still my blood-brother, young sniffling. Were we in open sea, I would have you whipped for what you have said. But since we have not started, then get up and go back to your cow-byre where you belong.'

The young man's face flushed with embarrassment. He said, 'I am sorry, Ragnar. I will beg Thorkell's pardon.'

He went to Thorkell and knelt before him but Thorkell pushed him aside and paid no heed to him. Ragnar felt that the young man had been punished enough and sent him back to his seat.

Olaf, at the dockside, was furious with his son and wanted to go aboard and thrash him. But Asa said grimly, 'Leave him be, husband. Between the two of them, that Ragnar and that Thorkell will bring the young lout to his senses!'

When the *Nameless* sailed, Thorkell sat in the darkness of the rear cabin, with Harald by his side. Now he obeyed the boy for he trusted him in a way that he trusted no other man on board, not even faithful Wolf, who would have leapt overboard at the merest whisper from his master.

While they were still rowing and before their sail had caught a good wind, Ragnar stood on the forward platform and spoke to all the Vikings. He said, 'Sea-warriors, we sail southwards now for Ireland where there is great treasure in the holy places. The Christ-men lay up great stores of gold. It does no good lying there in the dark. We Northmen can use it to good advantage. Let it be ours to take back to the fjord. How say you?' And they all roared and cheered these words, save only Thorkell's friends.

In the darkness, Thorkell said, 'These same Christ-men can bear pain, they tell me. Is it so?'

Gnorre said, 'They are men, like anyone else. Any man will bear pain if he has to.'

Wolf said, 'I think they are more than ordinary men. I have heard that their holy men go out of their way to find pain, so that they may master it.'

'I have heard that, too,' said Aun. 'Their leader did just that, in the time of the Romans. He seemed to seek death, so at last the Romans gave it to him, when they nailed him on to a cross.'

'I like the sound of these Christ-men,' said Thorkell. 'They would make good Vikings.'

'Many of them were Vikings, long ago,' said Wolf. 'They went to Britain in their own sort of longship when the Romans were there.'

'I beg your pardon,' said Gnorre, 'but the Romans had gone.'

'I tell you the Romans were there,' said Wolf.

'It all depends on what you mean by Romans,' said Thorkell, his mind taken off his pain for a while. 'So they were Vikings, were they?'

'In a way,' said Wolf, 'though they went to stay, not to plunder like us and then to go back home.'

Aun scratched his head. 'What difference does it make where you live?' he said. 'There is only eating and drinking and sleeping, call it home, call it what you will.'

Thorkell, who loved an argument, as did most Northmen, especially if it were on a point of life or death, said, 'Some ways of living are better than others. A man's life is better than a pig's, for instance. Do you deny that?'

Aun said, 'No, but a god's life is better than a man's.'

'Yes,' said Gnorre, 'the gods feast and fight all the time and never have to row longships through contrary tides.'

Thorkell said, 'How do you know what the gods do? Have you ever seen them? Do you know anyone who has seen them?'

Gnorre said, 'No, but every man *knows* that the gods do this or that. It is in the stories.'

Horic said, 'In my stories bears can talk, but have you ever heard bears talk?'

Aun said, 'Be quiet, Horic, you are simple and do not understand arguments about these things.'

Thorkell said, 'Horic is right though. We know nothing for sure. We do not even know whether we shall eat our dinner today. I did not know I would be blind, but I am blind.'

Aun said, 'Do you deny that we shall go to Odin when we die, then?'

Thorkell said, 'I cannot answer that, but I will tell you a story. Two Vikings sat in a longship, chained to a log, for they had been taken prisoners in a sea-fight. They had such an argument as we are having now. Then one of them said, "Look, the headsman is coming with his axe. We shall soon know the answer, friend." The other one said, "I am first so I shall know first." His friend said, "That is a pity, for you will not be able to tell me. Let me go first." But the other said, "No, it is my turn. But look, I will take this cloak pin, and if I know anything after my head is off, I will stick the pin into the log I am sitting on. Then you will know." And that was what they agreed to do.'

'What happened?' said Harald, who had been listening excitedly, though not daring to speak before.

Thorkell grinned. 'When the axe fell, the pin dropped out of the Viking's fingers.'

'So nobody knew,' said Gnorre.

'Oh yes they did,' said Wolf. 'It is obvious, even to a fool like you, that there was nothing after death.'

'No,' shouted Aun, 'only obvious that there was no control of one's fingers after death, and any fool should know that, even you, redhead!'

By which time Thorkell was in a fine good humour, in spite of the glowing pain that never lessened, and the *Nameless* was well out in the open sea and setting a course south-westwards.

15. Leire's Dun

LEIRE'S DUN was built on a promontory, backed by a gaunt purple mountain. Though to say built is not an accurate description; it had been added to as occasion demanded, its houses of widely differing types flung together helter-skelter in haste. At first there had been only a rough stone hut, to which Leire had come from Ireland, foraging. He had killed the shepherd who built the hut and had lived there himself, his small boat having been wrecked on the treacherous rocks that lined the narrow channel below the neck of land. Soon he was joined by others, each of whom had made a house for himself, of wood or wattle or rough stone mortared with mud. That was many years ago, though Leire's descendants still ruled as chieftains in the place. Now there was a street and a square of sorts in Leire's Dun, and in the square a strongroom, sometimes used for storing wood or even fish, sometimes for keeping prisoners for whom a ransom was expected. For Leire's Dun was nothing more nor less than a pirate stronghold. The custom of the place was to lure passing ships on to the dog-toothed rocks

that lined the narrow channel by lighting beacons on either side of the channel, as though there were a clear way between. Then when the ships had struck, the curraghs from Leire's Dun would put out and salvage what they could, in kind or humankind, if the humankind were still living and saleable in any slave market. It was the dear hope of the village that one day a ship might run aground without breaking her back, then they would have a vessel that would let them forage out beyond the islands, where there would be good pickings from the ships that passed back and forth with holy relics and church treasures. But alas, no ship had ever survived the dog-toothed rocks, and so the pirates of Leire's Dun still relied on their curraghs, long clumsy shells of tarred cloth or hide, stretched over wooden frames, able to hold a dozen men, the biggest of them.

These men were of many kinds, of all races that lived along the western seaboard of Britain, but most of them Celtic. They were rough-living, hard-dying scoundrels to a man, who feared nothing, and loved nothing but gain, come at it how they might. Their chief, Leire, who bore his great-grandfather's name as a point of primitive honour, ruled them like beasts of burden, nothing more. He was a massive one-eyed brute himself, almost bald, and with a hunched back as broad as a table top. His men whispered that he was hunched up like that from peering into treasure chests, for it was rumoured that he was extremely rich, though no man dared ask him outright. It was enough to ask him for one's rightful share after a wrecking, let alone pry into his private affairs. But where Leire hid his treasure, no man knew. His house was large and rambling, for he had added to the small original hut that his ancestor had stolen; yet its rooms were empty, but for the haphazard rubbish that a sea-dweller might be expected to accumulate, fishing-nets, oars, benches, and even two comfortable beds, taken from a wrecked ship. Though Leire never slept in a bed himself; he preferred to lie hard on a pile of sacking. Inquisitive men had even searched these beds in his absence, hoping to find his treasure. But the beds held no such secret.

Not that any man would have dared even go into his house, except on piratic business, had he been there. If he had discovered anyone in his house, he would either have killed him outright or have thrown him into the strongroom in the square to howl away his days, without food or water, as a warning to the rest of the village.

But, however strong Leire was, he could not have kept his power in the Dun had he not had a body of cut-throats who were sworn to serve him to the death. These numbered twenty, a pack of blood-thirsty hounds rather than men, the most terrible of whom was Aurog, a monstrous creature, dumb from birth, who thought in his half-witted way that Leire was a god. Aurog never left his master, and tasted all food before Leire dared to eat. It was said that Leire found Aurog on the mountainside when the monster was a tiny baby and had brought him up as his own. Those who knew of such learned things said that Aurog was more like the Minotaur of Crete than any man should be, except that he didn't have horns on his forehead.

The short curly black wool of his head reached down to his shoulders, and over his chest. His nose was flat and his mouth unnaturally broad, with thick pendulous lips and great jowls that shook when he moved. Once a drunken Pict had removed Aurog's shoes when he was asleep, to see if his feet were of humankind, or cloven hooves. Aurog had awakened and crushed the man to him, breaking his neck So no one ever knew the truth.

Everyone of Leire's Dun prayed that Aurog would one day meet his match. Many men prayed that Leire himself would find death soon. Yet in spite of this dissension, most of the ruffians who inhabited the hovels on the promontory had to admit in their hearts that Leire had more luck than any other man when it came to luring a ship on to the rocks. He could find a treasure-boat in a barrel of apple cider, they said, and left it at that.

Leire sat in his house, with his bodyguard about him. Aurog gnawed at a beef-bone by his side. Leire, who suffered from an interminable itch, scratched constantly. Now no one noticed it any more, they were so used to it.

Leire had just had great news from the north. A messenger had run in that afternoon, one of a team of relays which Leire kept along the coast, to say that he had heard of a great Viking ship that was coming down south between the islands. The man said that it sailed slowly and appeared to carry much weight, and when Leire had asked what emblems the ship bore, the man had said, 'Nothing. It flies a white pennant, but there is nothing carved either at bow or stern.'

'Nothing,' said Leire, scratching. 'Well, out of nothing may come something!' Everyone had forced a laugh at this, except Aurog, who never laughed. He had munched on at his bone.

16. Thorkell's Peace

A STRANGE peace now came upon Thorkell. He understood well enough that Ragnar had taken over control of the *Nameless*, yet he made no mention of it. He seemed to accept it – as he did his blindness – as being inevitable. He did as Harald told him and often the two would sit in the semi-darkness of the aft-cabin, talking for an hour at a stretch, while sometimes Aun, sometimes Horic, sometimes Gnorre would come in for a few moments, when they were not needed in the ship.

Once Thorkell had stood on the aft-platform, sniffing like a blind greyhound, his head held high. Harald was by his side, ready to prevent him from falling if the ship rolled too wildly. Kragge, yarning below with a group of his fellows, looked up and said, 'Look at blind Balder; he has the young spirit of sunlight with him.'

Someone said, 'They might be brothers, from the colour of their hair.'

The name 'Balder' stuck to Thorkell, though it was never said either in his presence or that of Ragnar, who, for all his masterful ways, his cruelty and his treachery, still admitted his blood-brotherhood with Thorkell, and would have thrashed any man who openly insulted Thorkell.

No man could fully understand Ragnar, but once Aun said quietly to Gnorre, 'Yon man is a villain, yet he has certain good qualities that I cannot understand. He will work or starve with us, claiming no privileges. He stole the treasure, yet is ready to share it even with those of us who hate him for his deceit in getting it.'

Gnorre said, 'I hate him, Aun Doorback, yet I too can see some sort of good in him. I think that once he was truly a worthy friend for Thorkell, but that somehow he fell on evil times and became bitter. Now I think that he is a thing of ambition, from his head to his toes. He is all greed – all but a faint shadow of what he was before, that lurks behind his ambition and his greed; and that shadow is his love for Thorkell which has never died fully.'

Aun said, 'I have seen such a thing between brothers. They may quarrel and even do each other a great hurt. Yet underneath there is a strange kind of love for each other. I think I loved my own brother – I certainly wept for him in the dark when no one was there to see – but I believed you did right to kill him, for I knew that he was evil.'

Gnorre said, 'Sometimes we kill the thing we love. Sometimes we see in our brother or even our close friend a part of ourselves. If we kill our friend for evil, we still weep because we have killed a part of ourselves in doing so.'

Wolf Waterhater, who had come up while the two were talking, said, 'You Northmen are like old gossips by the chimney fire. You are for ever either killing something or explaining to each other why it should be killed. Can you never leave life and death alone?'

Aun said, 'We are a people not yet born. We are struggling to explain life and death to ourselves. When we all understand what life and death are, then we shall become a united people, like the Romans of old, or the Greeks.'

Wolf said, 'Many folk in Frankland and England and Spain, think you are nothing but savage axemen. They would not believe you if you said such things to them.'

Gnorre said, 'No one will ever give us time to explain. If we put ashore anywhere, immediately men run to meet us and shoot us with arrows. In England, the fierce islanders have even nailed the skins of flayed Vikings on their church doors.'

Aun said, 'Yes, such treatment gives a man no heart to land bearing gifts and sweet words. If you know that they will try to kill you, it is only natural to take an axe and kill them first.'

Wolf began to laugh. 'You are a pair of old hypocrites,' he said, slapping Aun on the back and then rubbing his hand as though he had struck a lump of hard wood. 'I do declare, you had never given a thought to it all till this moment. You have always sailed where you wished and plundered as much as the enemy would allow you!'

When he had gone, Gnorre said, 'Doorback, he doesn't believe a word we have said.'

Aun said, with a twisted smile, 'No. Do you?'

Then they went back to their oars and forgot their talk.

Later Ragnar stood on the forward platform and shouted out, 'Soon we shall pass across the route of the

Christ-men. Their ships pass back and forth to Ireland and we may have the good fortune to meet one of them. They are not fighting men and no doubt we should overcome them easily. Therefore, I say to you now, that if any man in this company has no heart to fight with these long-robed prayer-makers, then him I will excuse. He may take his share of what treasure we find if he will. He need not if his manhood will not let him!'

In the cabin Thorkell said to Harald, 'Ragnar speaks to them fairly, boy. Yet there is no honour in taking a few goblets from old men whose minds are set on their cloisters and their prayers.'

Harald said, 'I have not given much thought to riches. If I had, then I might not worry how they were obtained. At the moment, I wish only to prove myself a warrior so that I can go back proudly to my father. I would not wish to fight a holy man who carried no weapon but his holy book.'

Thorkell placed his white hand on the boy's shoulder. 'I think as you do, Harald, yet it has taken this blindness to make me see more clearly. For a blind man there is no day, no night; it is all one interminable darkness in which he sees only when he is asleep, and they are dreams. And last night I dreamed that a man came to me. I saw him so clearly that at first I thought that it was day and that I had my sight again. This man was dressed in a long gown of rough linen and he wore the top of his head shaven close. He carried a paper in his hand and smiled and then read it, looking up at me from time to time. Then he spoke to me, in Norse, saying, "Thorkell Fairhair, sometimes called 'Skullsplitter', I have been sent to greet you and to tell you that all will be well with you. There will inevitably be trials, as there must be for all men, but if you are honest with yourself, all will be well." Then he made a mark on the paper he carried, as though he had my name recorded there.'

Harald said, 'What manner of man was he, master? Would you know him again?'

Thorkell smiled and said, 'If I could see him I should. He was of middle height and his face was thin and pale, but patient-looking. I saw that he had a mole by his right nostril. Yes, I would know him again.'

Then he sank so deeply into his own thoughts that Harald left him, going out quietly on to the deck to take his turn at the ship's work.

Just before middle day, as the *Nameless* skirted a long island that lay low in the sea, they all heard a sound of singing borne to them across the waters from beyond the island. Ragnar's nostrils twitched like those of a hunting dog and he nodded to his men to hold ready.

The long ship nosed round a rocky tongue of land and then Ragnar ordered the oarbeats to quicken, for immediately ahead of them lay a heavy slow-moving ship. Peering between the shields that were slung round the gunwales, the Vikings saw that though this ship bore a square hide sail, she was propelled also by many oarsmen, who sang at their work, for the currents about the island were at variance with the wind, because of the shallow channels wherein the tides turned back upon themselves.

Harald told Thorkell, 'By their long robes and shaven heads, I think these are the men we spoke of earlier.'

Thorkell did not speak, but lay down on the thonged bed and buried his face in the coverings.

The *Nameless* ran swiftly athwart the other ship and then Ragnar ordered that his oarsmen should stay their vessel. The *Nameless* stopped so abruptly that the other ran on and bumped against the longship's side, knocking the oars out of the hands of three Vikings, who rubbed their wrists ruefully and swore to have vengeance.

Ragnar stood in the prow and called to a long-robed man who stood on the platform by the mast of the holy ship. 'What treasure have you aboard?'

The holy man called back in a voice almost as strong, 'Nothing that we have is our own, neither our immortal souls nor anything else, sea wolf. Delay us no longer for we go about our Master's business.'

Ragnar scoffed and said, 'If what you have is not your own, then you will not mind if we take it from you! As for going about your business, that depends on us; we wish to go about our business, and that involves keeping you a little longer.'

The cowled man under the mast said, 'You speak too well to be a fool, so I will ask you again to go your ways and let us do the same. Good journey to you and may God guard you.'

He spoke to his own oarsmen then as though the interview were at an end. This angered Ragnar who leapt aboard the other vessel, to be followed immediately by a score of Vikings. Harald saw the grey-robed oarsmen rise from their benches and go to meet the warriors, their sleeves rolled up and their fists clenched. Many of them were great raw-boned men who must have spent more time at the oar than at the altar. One red-faced man with the shoulders of a blacksmith met Kragge and punched the Viking so hard beneath the ear that he fell over, carrying Sven and Ottar with him. The Norsemen still in the *Nameless* laughed loud at this and cheered on the big monk, who then looked sorry for what he had done and tried to help them up again. But Kragge, furious at this assault, drew a short knife and ran in on the big oarsman. He flung up his arms and fell to the deck. Aun Doorback clutched his own axe and swore that if he were within reach of Kragge, the man would go headless to Valhalla.

The fight, such as it was, was soon over, for the monks did not pursue their first advantage, and the Vikings were not there to play games of courtesy. Soon men were coming back to the *Nameless* with heavy sacks and barrels, calling out to those who still sat aboard that the treasure was worth a better battle than that. Gnorre turned his head away. 'They can take it who will. I want no share of it.' Many others agreed with him, but did not say so openly, as he had done.

At last Ragnar was left alone on the holy vessel. He told the oarsmen that they might go on to wherever they were bound. Their leader said sadly, 'Now that you have taken away our reason for travelling, we have little reason for breaking our backs against the tides. If our entreaties will not touch your hearts to return the property of the Church, we shall return whence we came, sea-thief.'

The last word seemed to nettle Ragnar who turned on the man and said, 'You should be thankful that we have taken only your chalices and salvers, and not your heads and hearts.'

The cowled man said, 'Perhaps you have taken our hearts.'

Ragnar said, 'Then your hearts are trumpery things of gold and silver. I thought that you were of rarer metal than that!'

The man in the cowl said, 'You are not only a common water rogue, you are a blasphemer. If one of your men will give me an axe, I will break a vow and take your head from you. Who offers me an axe?'

No one stirred in the *Nameless*, though Sven said, 'This is a real man, despite his robes.'

Aun turned on him and said, 'What do you know of real men, farmer's boy?' Thereafter Sven and his brothers were silent.

Ragnar, beside himself with rage, shouted, 'Will no one lend this Christ-man an axe, if he wishes to commit suicide?'

The Vikings sat mute. Ragnar turned to the *Nameless*. 'Two of you,' he shouted, 'bring this praying beggar aboard. He shall come with us and taste Viking mercy at my leisure.'

The cowled monk waved aside the two men who came to fetch him. Their names were Thurgeis and Hageling. They were quiet-natured men, who had no wish to harm the holy man. They allowed him to step aboard the *Nameless* without hindrance. When he stood aboard the longship he turned to his crestfallen followers and said gently to them, 'Return home, brothers, and pray that these heathens come to God in good time. Do not pray for me, I command you. Goodbye.'

He did not look at them again. He went where he was told and sat on the bench by the mast. The holy ship pulled away and sailed south-westwards then. This time the oarsmen were silent.

Harald noted the cowled monk's bearing and his quiet devotions as the longship set course once more. He turned to Thorkell and said, 'I can understand why they followed this man. He has a strong bearing.'

Thorkell said, 'Is his face thin and pale?'

Harald said, 'Yes, Master.'

Thorkell shuddered a little and then said, 'Can you see his nose? Is there a small mole beside his left nostril?'

Harald watched the man closely, as he raised his head towards the heavens and his cowl fell back on to his shoulders.

'No, Master,' said the boy. 'The mole is beside the right nostril.'

Thorkell lowered his blind head. 'That is the man I was shown in my dream,' he said. 'Now my fate comes upon me.'

17. The Meeting of the Dreams

WHEN HE had thought the matter over for a while, Thorkell asked Harald to lead him to the holy man. Harald did as he was bid. The man looked up and saw that Thorkell was blind. He rose and took his hands.

'How did your blindness come, my son?' he said gently.

'It came with the wind and the rock-dust on a northern island, Christ-man,' said Thorkell, at first a little angry that the man should call him 'son'.

'Then take care of yourself,' said the monk, 'and God may let you see again, for it is only the outer casing of the eye that is troubled. The precious sight of the eye is still there, but cloaked with pain. It is sometimes the same with a man's spirit; the spirit is good enough, but he has let it become surrounded by disease. The disease of the spirit, and that is more deadly than the disease of the flesh.'

Thorkell made a movement of irritation. 'I did not come to hear a sermon,' he said. 'I hold to other gods than you. I came to say that you shall come to no harm on this ship, if I have the power to prevent it. If you should be sold into slavery, then I promise to buy you from Ragnar, and will turn you free straightaway. You will not be kept against your will once we strike shore.'

The holy man smiled and said, 'Thank you, Viking. But it is something which you must decide. I am content, whatever God asks me to tolerate. I will only tell you that this is, in its way, a joyful meeting for me.'

Thorkell broke in scornfully, 'Joyful? To be held captive by men you do not know or love?'

The monk said softly, 'But I do know you. I saw you in a dream I had but last night. I saw the very bandage about your eyes, and in my dream you told me that the cruel winds of Orkney had blinded you. That is why I asked but now – and you gave me the self-same answer. Then I knew that I was sent to you with a purpose.'

Thorkell clapped his hands to his bandages, as though he would tear them off. But the fit passed and his hands fell again. He turned from the monk and said, half to himself, 'So we met in our dreams, the two of us. It was meant to be, all this. Now I know the answer to one thing at least, that there is another world, another life, beyond that which we know waking.'

He walked back slowly to the cabin, no longer leaning on Harald's shoulder. It was as though he had found direction, blind as he was. To Harald it seemed that Thorkell had grown older, much older, in that last hour.

When night fell, the *Nameless* was still ploughing a southerly course. She was among the narrows between the smaller islands before Rolf realized it, for he had never navigated this stretch before. Then they all were concerned

to hear not only the dull booming of surf on both sides of them, but the vicious rushing of water about some rocky outcrops before them.

Sven said, 'We should have made landfall earlier, while there was still light to see by. This is a shallow, treacherous sea, I have heard.'

Even as he spoke a beacon flared up to their left. Then, almost within a breath of the first, another to their right. Gnorre said, 'Praise Odin, now we may steer through the channel between the rocks.'

Within the pull of five oars later, the *Nameless* shuddered in every timber, then groaned, and then gave a great heave like a stag when the spear probes deep, and turned half-about, her deck tilting so high and violently that men fell hither and thither, sliding down towards the frothing breakers that now ringed the longship.

Thorkell gave a great cry, as though of agony, and stumbled out from the cabin, tearing off his bandages in a vain effort to see. Aun ran and grasped him, then clutched hard to the mast so as to save him from being swept overboard by the great waves that washed the doomed vessel. But for her loose keel, the *Nameless* would have broken her back there and then. As it was, she took the violence of the first shock, then pitched sideways and filled almost straightway and began to settle. At the least a dozen Vikings were thrown into the darkness and went swirling away to their deaths, silently, as though they had never been.

Then the longship settled, heeled half-over, and men the Vikings did not know were scrambling over her like flies about a meat-bone. They were laughing and shouting to each other joyously. Some carried torches, and by their light the Vikings saw that these men had come out in long tarred curraghs.

Harald tried to draw his sword, but a great skin-clad man clubbed him viciously at the side of the head. As the boy fell, he saw Aun shielding Thorkell from the assault and trying in vain to reach out for the axe which Gnorre offered him. Then as Harald lost consciousness, he saw Gnorre fall face downwards, and the axe flying from his hand and over the side of the longship.

18. Leire's Strongroom

THE SCORE of Vikings who had survived the wreck lay on the damp earthen floor of Leire's strongroom. Leire looked down at them from the stone steps that led to the street above. Aurog was behind him, slavering like an animal. Leire said harshly, 'Which is your leader?'

At first no one stirred, for the Vikings had been cruelly treated on their march up the stony pathway from the sea. Then Ragnar raised himself on his elbow and pointed to Thorkell. 'That is our shipmaster, man. But as you see he is too sick to be meddled with. I am his second and will take on my shoulders what you may ask.'

Aun said to Horic, 'He has some good in him, after all.' But Horic's head only swayed weakly, as though he were too far gone to understand the words spoken to him. Gnorre lay between the two, his eyes closed and his face twisted with pain from the great club wound at the back of his head.

Leire smiled down at blind Thorkell, who sat with his hands clasped about his knees, his head sunk. 'I shall regard the blind one as your leader,' he said. 'He will be responsible in my eyes for whatever you shall do.'

Then he went out and a short while later two men came armed with spears and flung pieces of smoked meat into the dungeon. The Vikings ignored it, though the monk, who was still with them took up a piece and ate a little of it. 'Forgive me, friends,' he said, 'but I have been fasting for three days and now I must eat or I shall lack strength should I need it.'

No one heeded his words, so he munched on silently. At last he went to Harald, who lay beside Thorkell, staring up at the little square of window that stood at street level.

'Try to eat something, my son,' he said. 'You must keep strength in your body. God would wish you to make the best of this adventure.'

He smiled as he offered the lad a piece of the meat. Harald overcame his repugnance at the sight of it and tried to do as he was told.

The day passed slowly. Men spoke little except to ask how their friends had died. Rolf Wryneck was among the dead. By some fatal irony, his neck had been broken with the first shock of the wreck, for he stayed at his steerboard till the last, trying to steer away from that awful rushing water. The fate he had escaped five years before had now come on him again, when no man thought it would.

Ottar, the son of Olaf and Asa, was dead too. He had died bravely, trying to fight with the wreckers, barehanded. His two brothers, Sven and Rollo, still lived, but their cousins were among those swept overboard in the first rush of the sea over the gunwales.

Harald gazed up at Thorkell's hopeless face and wished that he had the words to comfort him. But Thorkell was beyond consolation for the time being. He had spoken but once, and that was to ask if the *Nameless* was a wreck. When he had heard that her ribs were stove in on one side, he had laughed and said, 'Thank Odin that he has prevented this rabble from sailing her.'

Then he fell silent and brooding and had not spoken again.

As darkness came on, men came with small clay lamps, filled with oil and burning twisted hemp for a wick. Others brought in two pannikins of water. They all waited until Thorkell had wet his lips before they drank. The monk was given his share like the rest and the pannikin handed to him with a certain respect. His bearing throughout the day had impressed them all, though they would not have admitted to this weakness.

When he had drunk, Ragnar came to Thorkell and took him by the hand, kneeling before him. 'I ask forgiveness, brother,' he said. 'It was my evil-doing that brought this disaster upon us all.'

Thorkell's lips twisted for a while, trying to speak. Then he said softly, 'Get up from your knees, Raven. Kneel to no man, brother. If you have been a fool, then you have been a fool – but that is no reason to kneel! In any case, I know now that this would have come upon us whatever we had done.'

He took Ragnar's hand and pressed it. Ragnar turned from him then for the tears were beginning to run down his gaunt and swarthy cheeks. 'I shall repay your kindness, Thorkell,' he said.

'Whatever you say, you will never become Ragnar Dove,' said Thorkell; 'it will always be Ragnar Raven.'

'They understand each other,' said the monk to Aun. Aun nodded. 'They are not saints, Christ-man,' he said, 'yet there is a strange good in them both, if a man will only try to look for it.' The monk said, 'Yes, so is it with all men, my son.'

Aun said, 'If you call me son, must I then call you father?' He was already laughing, in his old jesting way. The monk laughed too. 'No,' he said. 'Your father was a bear from the forests! No, you can call me John, if you choose, for that is my name.'

'John! John! John!' said Aun, trying the name over on his tongue. Then he nodded, 'Very well, John,' he said. 'That is what I shall call you.'

Towards night, Ragnar made a man hold a blanket over the window-hole so that none of the folk outside should see them. Then he called the others into a circle and said, 'Vikings, if we stay here we shall grow weak and lose heart. If we are to escape from this dungeon, it must be soon. When shall it be?'

There was some argument, then Rollo said, 'I say that we should go at dawn-time. That would give us time to sleep and refresh ourselves.'

Ragnar slapped him on the shoulder and said, 'That was in my own mind too, young Viking. Now, say on, Rollo, and how shall we go from here?'

Rollo said, 'I have tried the window bars and they are too strong for a man to move them. There is an archway of stone in the wall behind you, but that is shored up with stout planks of wood and will lead nowhere. The only way is through the door at the top of the steps and into the street.'

Ragnar said, with a slight sneer, 'Have you set your back against that door, Rollo?'

Rollo nodded his head. 'It is a good three inches thick, Master,' he said. 'I felt it with my finger and thumb as they dragged me in.'

Ragnar said, 'Then how shall we go through that door, friend?'

And Rollo scratched his head, defeated. Ragnar said then with a smile, 'Well, what muscle cannot do, guile must. I will open the door at dawn, and be you all still as mice in the thatch at wintertime.'

He stood up then and said, 'How many will come with me?'

Most of the Vikings put up their hands to show their willingness. Those who did not were Thorkell, Wolf Waterhater, Harald, Horic, Aun Doorback and Gnorre Nithing. The monk stood with his arms folded. He did not join in the discussion at all.

When they had decided that they would escape at dawn, the Vikings became more jovial, for it was as though a weight had been lifted from their minds by the decision to take action.

Now men began to hammer on the door and call for meat and wine. Ragnar pushed a gold coin that had not been stolen from him under the door and soon one of the guard brought in a wooden platter of bread and smoked fish and a great stone jar of a rough-tasting mead.

'You robber,' shouted Ragnar, in pretended rage. 'You have cheated me, bringing only the orts from another's table, in return for a true gold piece.'

The man shrugged and grinned, presenting his keen spearpoint at Ragnar when he moved towards him. Ragnar saw three more men standing behind the guard, in the narrow doorway, their axes ready. He made no further demur and the door was shut once more.

'We shall need much good luck at dawn,' he said with a grim smile. 'It is a narrow place and one man could hold it against twenty, if he were armed and they barehanded. Well, we shall see.'

Those who were planning to escape sat about the meat and wine and made themselves a feast. Though the others were invited to join them, they did not do so for there was little enough food and drink, and those who were going at dawn would need as much sustenance as they could get.

Only Thorkell sat with them for a moment or two and drank from Ragnar's clay cup to wish him luck. There were fourteen of them, all strong men, most of them scarred in many battles. Yet now they seemed innocent and young in Harald's eyes, as though they were untried boys about to perform an act of dedication. In the flickering light of the little lamps, their eyes were bright and anxious, and looked up at Ragnar when he spoke, as though he knew the secret of eternal life.

Aun turned away, his head down. He wished that he were making the attempt with them, but he could not leave Thorkell. A blind man could not make such a hazardous attempt, for he would endanger the safety of the others. That had been understood by them all from the start.

Now the feasters became merry and called on Horic to amuse them before they lay down to rest. He stood in the torchlight with a little pebble in his hand, on his flat palm for all to see. 'Watch the mouse,' he said, and swiftly waved his other hand over the pebble.

The Vikings saw the long tail and the grey fur and the bright beads of eyes as the tiny creature held up its head and wrinkled its nose.

Aun said to the monk, 'What think you of that, John?'

The monk smiled and said, 'That is wonderful.' But to him the stone had never changed, though he knew that the Vikings had seen a mouse.

Horic passed his hand over the mouse again and it had gone. The Vikings cheered him and shouted, 'Another trick, Horic! Another one before we go!'

Horic took out his length of twine. It dangled from his fingers. 'This twig will flower,' he said. All men but the monk saw the twine stiffen and then climb upwards in his fingers until it stuck up as straight as a twig.

Yet at that moment a man outside the window coughed and a woman in the street laughed out raucously. Horic shuddered and the twig fell, to become a length of twine once more. He turned to the Vikings and said, 'The magic has gone out of me. It will not come again tonight.'

Then the Vikings shook hands with each other and many of them kissed Thorkell as though they were going on a long journey and would wish an older brother farewell. He did not speak to them, but the tears ran down his face unhindered.

Then Ragnar blew out the lamps and the Vikings made themselves as comfortable as they could, those who were going with Ragnar in one group, those who were to stay behind in another.

In the darkness Ragnar went to Thorkell and put his arms round his neck lovingly. 'Goodbye, brother,' he said. 'When I hated you most, I loved you most.'

Thorkell said, 'In Valhalla there will be no more hate, only love. There you shall tell me of this escape.'

Then they parted and were silent, though no man slept much that night.

When the dawn came and the chill winds blew into the dungeon, Harald raised himself on his elbow and waited. Ragnar rose silently and went to the door. He peered a while through the great keyhole and then whispered, 'Guard! Hey, guard!'

At length, Harald heard the shuffling of feet outside and the sound of a smothered yawn. Ragnar turned to those in the room and put his finger over his lips.

'Guard,' he said again, through the keyhole. 'Are you listening to me? Harken then, there is one in this place who wears a necklace of gold that would buy a man twenty horses. He lies asleep now near my feet.'

The guard mumbled sleepily for a moment and then made a slight exclamation of surprise. Ragnar sensed his growing interest and said, 'He lies ready for the plucking, warrior. He is an old enemy of mine and I tell you because I would pay back old scores. If you wish for a fortune, then it is yours, but you must take it with your own hands for I dare not touch him. I am afraid of him.'

Ragnar waited long then and it seemed to them all that the trick would not work. The man outside moved away from the door as though he were listening for something. All in the room lay still, scarcely breathing. Then Ragnar said, 'If you tell others, they will share it. If you take it, it will be yours alone – and you will bring vengeance on my enemy for me.'

Ragnar lay on the top step, a smile on his face that was not good to see. Harald shivered to see the thin lips almost bitten through by the strong white teeth.

Then the door began to creak slightly and, in the uncertain light of the early dawn, began to move. Ragnar moved back with it, so as not to be seen. When it was open a foot wide, the man peered forward, a rough sword in his hand. Still Ragnar did not move. The guard leaned, so as to see the man who lay near the foot of the steps, as Ragnar had said. As he did so, Ragnar suddenly sprang into life, and with a cruel lunge, slammed the thick oaken door hard on the man and his weapon. The head and sword-arm were trapped as in a vice. The man had only time to give a sharp gasp when Ragnar had struck him with clenched fist hard on the temples, and the sword fell into the dungeon from the unclenched hand. Then Ragnar swung open the door and the man dropped down the steps, limp as a pennant drenched in a heavy sea.

Ragnar stooped to pick up the sword. He spared a glance at the man and smiled grimly. Rollo went over and lifted the man's head by the hair then let it fall. With that one blow Ragnar had broken his neck. The Vikings smiled and rubbed their hands together in admiration. They would have cheered had they been able.

Harald did not dare watch them go through the door. When he looked up again they had gone. Aun was staring at the closed door, his fists clenching and unclenching.

At length he rose and opened the door cautiously. Then he bundled the dead guard outside and shut the door again. Thorkell, his red eyes still closed, whispered, 'That was well done, friend.'

19. The Awakening

IT SEEMED that day would never come. The dawn lingered over Leire's Dun as though wishing to torment the waiting Vikings in the dungeon. They lay with closed eyes, listening, but for a while all that they heard were the cries of swooping gulls above the village roofs, and the distant thudding of the sea on the rocky shore.

At length they heard footsteps outside their door and an exclamation of surprise; then the feet running away, and others coming. A head looked in at the window-hole for an instant, then the great key turned in the lock again.

'They have discovered the dead guard and have found that our comrades have escaped,' said Horic. Aun only nodded. He sat holding Gnorre's cold hand, speechless with grief.

No one came to bring them food that morning. Footsteps and quiet whispering voices sounded in the street. There was a strange tension everywhere. It seemed as though folk wanted to laugh uproariously, or cry out loudly, yet held back those sounds.

Thorkell stopped rocking backwards and forwards and said, 'I do not like it. I thought they would have come to us here, to find out what they could about the escapers. They are leaving us alone, deliberately.'

The monk John kneeled in a corner and prayed quietly.

Harald, his nerves on edge with waiting, walked round the low dungeon, examining the walls, to give his mind something to bite on. He stopped by the archway at the back of the room; it was blocked in by thick planks of oak. Yet there were interstices between the boards. Harald felt a cold air sweep through them to his face. He peered through the cracks, but could see nothing. Yet it seemed to him that a distant low booming came up from behind that door. He told Horic, who said, after he too had listened, 'That is the sea.'

The others came and listened and Thorkell said, 'Doubtless there is a long tunnelway behind these planks, which comes out above the shore somewhere. It would need a giant's strength to move these great pieces of wood, though, for they are sunk into the ground and wedged hard at the top of the archway. Could you move them, Aun?'

Aun Doorback let go Gnorre's hand and moved slowly to the door. He tested it with all his strength, and said at last, 'If I were rested and had good food inside me, I might move a plank or two. But my strength has gone from me since the wreck, Thorkell.'

He went back to his dead friend and sat silent. John knelt in the corner and prayed again. Harald began to bite at his fingernails. The time must have been midday.

'They have great faith in their planks,' said Thorkell.

'Either that or the mouth of the tunnel is guarded,' said Horic. 'Or perhaps it comes out high above the sea.'

'Are you hoping to escape, Thorkell?' said Aun, moving his eyes slowly towards the leader.

Thorkell passed his hand across his eyes and said, 'Perhaps. Perhaps I might not be a drag on you if we could get out from this place.' He said no more, but sank his head again in his hands and brooded for a while.

Suddenly wild horns skirled in the village and skin drums began to throb in a strange savage rhythm. All in the cell looked up. Then Harald went to the high window and jumped up so as to see outside. He shrank back with a sudden cry for he had seen a hand, a white hand, resting at street level, just outside the window. He did not see the arm or the body – just the hand, and it was still.

He gave a gasp and turned to tell someone of this, when the door burst open and without warning the dungeon seemed to be full of wild-eyed villagers, who jostled with each other to get at the captive Vikings. In less time than it would take for a man to count twenty, the tribesmen had bound their prisoners by the wrists and were dragging them up the steps towards the street.

Outside, the Vikings blinked in the bright light. They saw the mud hovels, the thatched roofs, the small square teeming with shouting folk. Above them the seabirds shrieked as though to be in company with the savage inhabitants of Leire's Dun.

Harald, who walked next to John, turned his head as soon as he got into the street towards the window of the cell. Sven was lying there, an arrow in his chest, his arm flung out so that his hand lay by the side of the window. The Vikings saw this and gasped. Then they looked towards the centre of the square where the greatest shouting was to be heard. A heap of bodies lay tumbled on each other – Kragge, Thurgeis, Rollo, and all the rest, man for man, each one pierced by an arrow. Ragnar lay on the top of the heap of dead. His eyes were rolled back and his teeth bared in a savage grin. In his right hand he still clutched a long thick tress of black hair. Three arrows pierced his breast, their broken shafts hanging down as though he had tried to tear them out.

Thorkell said, 'Why are you so stricken, Vikings? What can you see?'

No one would tell him, but at last John whispered to him, 'Thorkell, my son, your comrades who went from the dungeon have met disaster. They lie dead before us.'

Thorkell said, 'Is Ragnar with them?'

John said, 'Yes, Viking. He died a brave death. All his wounds are at the front.'

Thorkell said, 'You speak well, John, for a priest. You would have made a good warrior with a little teaching.'

John said, 'I am a warrior in my way, I thank God. I will say a prayer for our dead.'

Thorkell noticed that now he said 'our' as though he was one of the Viking band. Thorkell smiled and said, 'I cannot think that your God would approve of your new alliance, John, but no doubt it will do no harm. At least *they* all know the answer now . . .'

He said no more, but allowed Leire's tribesmen to lead him to the whipping-posts that were set where the crowd was thickest. Each Viking was bound to a stout pine stump, his hands above his head. Those who still wore shirts had them torn away. Even the monk's vestment was ripped down. Harald saw that his back was hard and muscular. The crowd jeered and hooted them. Aun's back was laid bare and the tattooed dragon was exposed to view.

'I will make that beast writhe for mercy,' said a great savage, whose matted hair almost hid his face. He twirled a heavy whip with many weighted thongs. It hissed in the air like a family of vipers, suddenly awakened from their sleep.

Aun said, 'It would need a better man than you, ape-man.'

The whipman spat at Aun in his rage. Aun merely smiled and shrugged his broad shoulders.

John, bound next to Harald, whispered with a smile, 'Have courage, boy. The pain of the body soon passes. It is the pain of the spirit that hurts. If your spirit is strong, then slave body will obey it and will bear the pain. I shall pray for you.'

Harald thanked him. Then Leire stood on the roof of a low hovel and taunted them. He told them that they must pay for the disobedience of their fellows. Especially must they pay for the death of Aurog, his dear friend, whom Ragnar had throttled while the arrows were still in him.

Thorkell spoke up then and said, 'We are willing to pay Ragnar's debt, then, pig-face, for he would have paid ours. Only I ask you to spare the boy and the priest. They are not to blame for anything.'

Leire said, 'You must all taste the mercy of Leire, my friends.' He was angry that Thorkell should have insulted him, for he could see that many among the crowd enjoyed the Viking's taunt.

Thorkell said, 'Stay, snout! I am the leader of this band. I will take the whipping for them all. Is that a good bargain?'

Aun said, 'That you shall not, Fairhair. I am as good a man as you.'

Leire said, 'Hark at them, these seacocks, they even quarrel about who shall die first! Nay, nay, blind one, all will be beaten.'

Thorkell said, 'As well ask a mangy wolf for the bone he gnaws. Well, trough-grubber, I make you a last offer – do not let the bargain pass, it will not be offered again. Look, I am a blind man, but I will fight you, or any warrior you have that dares meet me, but let these others go back untouched to their prison.'

Aun shouted, 'Why should you have the pleasure, Thorkell? Look, midden-grunter, I will fight any two men you have, yourself included, if you count yourself as a man!'

At this the crowd yelled with joy at the Viking's bravado. Leire's sullen face flushed. He shouted to the whippers, who rushed in and began to wield their vicious flails.

Aun was still yelling taunts at Leire when the man who whipped him staggered with exhaustion. Now the crowd was silent and breathless. The dragon that had once circled the great Viking's back had disappeared.

At last Leire said, 'Enough! There is always another day.'

The whippers wiped the sweat from their faces and bodies, thankful to rest.

The square was empty now. Only the seabirds still wheeled above it as the afternoon sun began to sink in the west.

20. Aun Doorback

THE DUNGEON was twilit when Harald came to his senses again. At first he wondered where he was. Then he saw Horic bending over him and he remembered. Horic said, 'Your back – does it hurt, boy?' Harald sat up and shrugged his shoulders. Then he gave a wry grimace but did not answer. Horic said, 'You were lucky. They were merciful to you because of your youth. They dealt quite kindly with the priest too, though he begged them not to.'

Harald looked round the cell. Aun was lying in the corner, muttering terribly to himself. His face was drawn and horrible to see. He looked more like a vengeful fury than a man. The others did not go near him at that time. John came across to the boy when he saw that he had awakened. He smiled down and put his hand on Harald's shoulder gently. 'God be praised,' he said, 'for He has given Thorkell back his sight. When the first lash fell, so great was Thorkell's rage that he went berserk, and the scales fell from his eyes with wrath, and he sees again now! Look at him!'

Thorkell was standing, his back all bloody, but his head erect, by the high window. Wolf was by his side. They were talking in an undertone together. Now they seemed as they were when Harald first met them on the shores of the fjord, two close friends, with no Ragnar to come between them. Wolf seemed happy, as though even his tortured back was worth having if it brought Thorkell's friendship with it.

Horic said, 'Sometimes suffering brings a reward with it.'

Aun looked at him, then at poor Gnorre's body which still lay in the corner, and growled menacingly. John said, 'Aun is taking it all very hard. But he will recover. He is as resilient as a tough old oak tree.'

Thorkell turned then, and though Harald saw that his young face was lined and begrimed, he was smiling. He came across to the boy and said, 'Well borne, Viking! I will give you another sword one day, if we ever reach our fjord again.'

Then he went across the cell and spoke to Aun, at first gently, then almost harshly. Aun recognized the voice of his master and stopped growling like a wild beast. Wolf joined them. Harald sensed that they were planning to escape, and now the heart of each of them was bitter against his captivity. Better to die, thought Harald, than live such a life. The face of the monk, John, had lost some of its gentleness and was set in firmer, more warrior-like lines. But for his cropped hair, it would have been hard to recognize him as a religious man, for his habit was now torn and hanging about him, only held to his body by its stout rope girdle.

That night no food was put into their cell. They had therefore been almost twenty-four hours without breaking their fast. Nor were they given lamps that night.

Thorkell said grimly, 'Well, we can work as well in the dark, can we not, Aun?'

Aun said, 'We must find a flint or two from the floor of the cell, if we are to dig, then it matters not whether we have light or not. We can feel to dig, like the mole.'

Thorkell said, 'I have become so used to the dark that I am not troubled.'

So, while they could still see in the twilight, they grubbed up a few long flints from the earthen floor of the dungeon, and having chosen the sharpest, sat down to wait for night to come. There was much to do and they knew they must waste no time.

When it became so dusk that none could see into the dungeon from the street, they began to scrape away the hard-trodden earth at the base of the arched doorway. It was a mighty task for men whose strength had been sapped by privation and punishment, yet they worked on and on, for they knew that their lives hung on this effort.

As one tired, so another took his place, Harald working as hard as the rest of them, until after two hours of scraping and digging, they had got down almost to the base of the deep-sunk planks that blocked the archway. Once, as they dug, footsteps had sounded outside their door, and for a while they had lain silent, until the steps had gone away again. Then they worked more feverishly than before to make up for the time they had lost.

At length, when the first of the grey flickers of dawn began to creep over the eastern seas, they had moved the earth away so that the planks might be swung outwards into the dungeon to let them pass into the far tunnel. Then they stopped and each shook hands with the other solemnly.

'We must keep together while we can,' said Thorkell, 'yet if one of us lags, the others must leave him, or we shall all die. Leire would not tolerate another escape.'

John kneeled down in his corner and said a prayer for them all. He stayed a while by Gnorre's body, though Aun pushed him away a little too roughly. 'This is not your concern, Christ-man,' he said, 'let Gnorre go to his own gods. Do not meddle.' John forgave Aun, for he knew how much the great Viking had loved the dead outlaw. He smiled up at Aun's wrathful face and went to join Thorkell.

Then they began to move the planks, each man straining with all his might, for it seemed that they had been sunk in the earth for many years. When they moved the first, a small trickle of earth and stones began to fall into the dungeon. When they had moved the second, that trickle became a stream, and now the very archway began to tremble.

Thorkell said, 'Stand back, or we shall be buried. That archway is ready to fall. Those planks have held up the whole side of this dungeon.'

But as yet the space was only big enough to let Harald pass through into the tunnel. Suddenly Aun pushed forward and stood in the archway, holding up his hands and taking the weight of the structure on his broad and mutilated shoulders. Harald saw the pain it caused him to touch the rough stonework, but the Viking's face was set. His voice was now hoarse and commanding. 'Move the third plank, you fools,' he said. 'I cannot wait here for ever. Move it and pass through. I will follow.'

Thorkell said, 'It is madness, Aun, for once the third support has gone, you will be left with the whole weight of the rock wall on your back.'

Aun stared into his master's eyes sternly. 'Do as I say, young man,' he commanded. 'Do you not recall my eke-name?'

'Aun Doorback,' said Horic; 'but you are truly named.' Then they swung the third plank away and passed through into the tunnel as fast as they might. As Thorkell went through last, a shower of big stones fell about his head, and above them there was the awful sound of rock, straining against rock, an immense subterranean tension, like the creaking of a gigantic door of stone.

Thorkell heard this. He heard Aun's deep and laboured breathing as his great thews and sinews stretched and almost broke beneath the titanic strain.

'Come with us now, Aun, or it will be too late,' he said.

Aun only cursed at him, telling him to go away. Harald saw that the man's eyes were closed and that his face worked with a dreadful spasm. The priest, John, went to Aun and prayed beside him. Aun's eyes opened wide and rolled horribly. The foam was now flecking his lips. He used his last breath to shout, 'Go, all of you, or may Odin's ravens peck out your eyes! I can hold it no longer.'

Thorkell said, weeping, 'Aun, beloved warrior, come with us. We will all hold up the roof while you get from under it.'

Aun spat at him and whispered, 'I stay with Gnorre.'

Then there was a fearful grinding of rock above them and the very floor beneath their feet seemed to shake in sympathy. Thorkell led them away from the doorway and into the passageway. As they stepped back the rock fell, massive, stirring up clouds of dry dust. Aun's great scarred hand stuck out from between the immense boulders that fell. Nothing more of him could be seen. The great hand clenched and then unclenched. It lay still. Thorkell bent and kissed the gnarled fingers. Then as other rocks began to fall about them, they turned and made off, bent double, along the passage, towards the sound of the booming surf.

21. The *Nameless*

AS THEY ran on that nightmare journey along the twisting tunnel, the light filtered through to them gradually and the sound of the sea became clearer and clearer. Once they passed through a great cavern, where the tunnel widened out suddenly, to give on to this broad space, from the roof of which hung strange growths of weed, and the floor of which was deep in ancient shells, the fossilized remains of a much earlier world. Then they had passed through the green gloom of the cave to the tunnel again, though now it became much wider and higher, and they were able to run without bending low.

Harald gasped, 'That would be a fine place to hide one's treasure.'

They all laughed, in spite of themselves, that the boy should be thinking of treasure at such a time.

'Perhaps Leire does,' said Wolf Waterhater, stumbling on, his hand clapped to his side, for he suffered from a painful stitch.

Then, suddenly the light came full into their faces as they turned a sharp corner, and they stood out on a platform of rock above the sea.

As Thorkell came to the entrance of the passageway, he stopped short and gave a great gasp, his finger pointing below them and to their right. They all followed his gaze.

On a rocky shoal, between two long, dog-toothed ridges on which the sea broke in a foamy spray, lay the *Nameless*. Her mast was shattered and her mainsail dragged with the tides. She lay on her side, the waves breaking over her, the currents flowing through her broken sides. The Vikings drew in their breath, in compassion for their ruined longship.

Thorkell wiped his hand across his face. 'Well, at least we know the end of her,' he said sadly. 'None of those land rats will ever sail in her now!'

Then he turned his head and they all looked below them. The rock fell steeply from the cavern, but not too steeply for men who had already braved so much. Far beneath them lay a strip of sand, and pulled up on to it, three or four curraghs of different sizes.

'That is our goal,' said Thorkell, as he leapt down the rocky slope. The others followed, now careless of life or limb. The cold dawn air chilled them but set their blood tingling. They were filled with a strange excitement. The smell of the sea, strong and heady, made them drunk. They shouted a war-cry as they leapt.

Then from above and behind them they heard another shout. Horic, who was last in the line, turned and stopped for an instant. He saw a tall dark shape on the rocky hilltop above the passage-way. It was one of Leire's guards. Horic saw him thrust out one arm and draw back the other. He ducked, expecting to hear the arrow whizz over his head. It struck him between the shoulder blades. He flung up his arms and with a high cry, pitched forward, to fall before the others. He rolled quickly down the slope, taking with him a runnel of pebbles. Thorkell stopped for a moment as Horic's body struck the sharp rocks below. 'He was dead before he reached the beach,' he said. 'Crouch low and run for your lives. We must not stop now.'

Once an arrow whirred above them. Once a shaft glanced on the very rock where Harald had leaned a second or two before and shattered itself to pieces, flying on through the brightening air with the vicious sound of a hornet.

Then, sobbing and gasping, they reached the beach, and staggered over its soft surface towards the tarred curraghs.

They lay unguarded, their paddle-oars stacked beside them. Thorkell and Wolf rocked one of them, the smallest, until it was clear of the clogging sand, and then all pushed the flimsy shell to where the breakers ran in on to the pebbles. John and Harald carried four oars. They clambered into the curragh while the others pushed on until they were waist deep. Wolf groaned with pain as the salt water bit into his raw back, but still he pushed.

Then Thorkell yelled, 'Aboard, Wolf, the tide will take her now.' First one, then the other, scrambled into the curragh. The light shell seemed to shudder with their weight. A flurry of waters struck her and for a moment she hung, turning back towards the shore. The four rowers worked like souls damned to bring her out to the current again.

At last she swung free of the shore and began to move out of the shallow channel where the *Nameless* lay, and so beyond the far ridge of rocks, into the open sea. Now their spirits lifted, despite the great sadness of their lost comrades. For a while they sang wordless songs, out of the bursting fullness of their tormented hearts.

And so singing and weeping and rowing they passed out of sight of the rocky coast on which lay Leire's Dun. It was only when they met the great untamed rollers of the ocean that they came to their senses and realized that they had no water, no food, little clothing. Then they remembered their wounds, their weakness, their madness at leaving the land behind them with so little preparation for a voyage.

Wolf said, 'We had little luck with the ship we named *Nameless*. What shall we name this one, shipmaster?'

Thorkell smiled grimly and said, 'I have learned that a ship lives up to its name. Nothing comes of nothing. Very well, then; let this be *Landfinder*. And I pray to Odin that she finds us a good shore to land on before long.'

Wolf said nothing, but from his look as he lowered his head, Harald saw that he had little faith in that prayer. Harald turned to John. The monk's eyes were closed, but his lips were moving in syllables which the boy did not understand. Yet the monk rowed as steadily and as strongly as did Thorkell himself.

Perhaps there is some hope, thought the boy, when he saw this.

A gannet flying low seemed to say, 'Perhaps . . . Perhaps.'

22. The End of the Voyage

THE THREE days since they had taken to the sea again had been days of steadily growing despair. Now the battered curragh lay, almost waterlogged, at the mercy of the sea. Three of the paddles had been swept from nerveless hands and had floated away beyond all chance of recovery. As Wolf's had gone, he had said, ironical with exhaustion, 'Goodbye, dear friend, and may we never meet again!'

Then he had burst into loud laughter which had weakened him so much that Thorkell had been forced to turn and strike him across the face to save his reason.

John still had an oar and he pushed this way and pulled that way, more to give himself something to do than with any hope that his puny efforts would change the course of the curragh.

Harald sat, over the knees in water, his hands on his thighs, staring at the bottom of the tarred craft. The sky was dark above them now, and the great grey-green waves rose mercilessly higher and higher about them. Sometimes they lay deep in a twilit trough; sometimes, with a sudden

frightening swing, they climbed effortlessly to the summit, and the waters rushed past them as they rose, sickeningly powerful.

Harald tried to remember what his father looked like. But found that the image would not come to his mind now. He tried to recall the name of the old headman in the village on the fjord, but that eluded him too. There was nothing to think about. Even the man he had killed no longer seemed frightening. The boy tried to make up a song and was actually singing its first harsh note when between his feet, the floor of the curragh split, and a spar of splintered wood appeared as though from nowhere, ripping its way through the flimsy shell, and striking violently on the lad's legs, numbing them with the great force of the blow.

Almost immediately the crazy vessel sank beneath them. They were sitting down upon the waves at one moment, then they were standing in the great waters without any warning.

No one spoke, but each grasped the wooden rim of the waterlogged craft. They stared through each other, seeing nothing but the surging mountains of water, their teeth already chattering with the shock of the sudden immersion.

Then Thorkell came out of his trance and said, 'Ragnar.' It was merely that one word, spoken so softly that Harald only just heard it. He did not look at Thorkell's face. He only saw the red hands slowly unclench on the rocking shell and then disappear. It was some time before Harald understood that Thorkell had gone. He did not feel sorry. He did not feel anything. It was as though only his own hands existed now. There was no sensation in the rest of his body. He began to wonder with what part of him he could see, or think, or hear. He knew only his own hands, chafed raw and cramped. As he looked at them he saw that the ends of his fingers had gone white, very white, down to the first knuckle joint. He wondered why that was. Then he heard Wolf shout out, 'Where has Thorkell gone?' As though Thorkell had walked out of the feast hall without saying where he was going.

John looked towards the swaying breakers. Wolf understood what he meant. He gave a hoarse cry and loosed his grip on the curragh. He had disappeared as soon as his hands let go.

Harald looked at his fingers again. They were white now to the second joint. Then to the hand itself. He watched his fingers loosing the rim of the curragh. The waters swept in at his mouth and he gave up trying to breathe. He began to slip away from the curragh.

Then John clasped him and brought him back again, holding him between his own two weakening arms. A curious gull swept above them, almost alighting on the curragh to see what they were. But at that moment John raised his head and the timid bird swept on up again, into the salt-laden air.

The bird wakened Harald once more. He saw the white flash of its wings, that almost touched his face as it rose, screaming away from them. The bird's cry stirred the boy's memory to life again. He now saw Gudröd's hall clearly again with the flames licking round it, reflected in the dark tarn; he saw the deep forests through which he had trudged with his father; he saw the village nestling by the fjord. Then he saw his father's face. He remembered it now. It came closer and closer to him, bigger and bigger. Now it was very near his own. At first it towered over him, then it came down and down, until it almost touched him. He saw the hair, the eyes, the mouth, all separately, then all blurred.

He heard his father's voice. It said, 'Steady with him. He had almost gone. Lift him aboard. Gently, gently, Rurik! The lad isn't made of iron.'

Then Harald saw that it was not his father after all. Suddenly he felt unsafe. 'John! John! Where is John?' he shouted.

The Danes looked over the side of their longship. They saw only the swirling wastes of water. Their fat, dark-haired shipmaster rubbed his chin. Then he went to where the boy lay, wrapped round with woollen blankets. 'Sleep now, lad,' he said, 'John is with you, John is well.'

Harald smiled and tried to put out his hand. 'Good John,' he said. 'Where is he?'

His hand had moved but a few inches when the boy sank into an unconsciousness as deep as the sea he had been saved from.

The shipmaster said, 'There will be time enough when he is well again to tell him that there was no John there when we found him.'

Indeed, of all the longship's crew, Harald was now the only one left. John had held him afloat just long enough for the Danish ship to sight him and then, his work finished, had slipped beneath the waves.

23. The Village by the Fjord

IT WAS high summer and the forests above the fjord were a full, deep green again. The sun glittered across the broad water as though there had never been winter in the world, and would never be winter again. The blue-grey woodsmoke rose straight up from the cottages that lay along the shore, and children ran after each other, brandishing sticks for swords.

Behind the huts, tethered cattle grazed on what they could find. The pigs, as ever, rooted cheekily wherever they wished and only lost their smug air of self-confidence when the headman's dog, Brann, ran out from his master's hut and chased them grunting away.

Outside the headman's hut sat three men, on a bench in the morning sun. Old Thorn cupped his horny hand about his ear to hear what was being said. He paid great attention, like an aged but earnest scholar. Sigurd sat attentive too. One of his legs was still bound thickly with a flannel wrapping and he carried a stout blackthorn staff. These men listened to the one who sat between them. He was a raw-boned young man, his light hair cropped short, his lithe body dressed in a simple rough tunic of linen. He was talking gravely and with a quiet confidence. The old men nodded as he spoke. Sometimes he would make a wide gesture with his hand, as though explaining something, when the others would follow his every movement with their pale-blue eyes, as though they were hungry for information. Then they would nod and smile at each other, having understood his words.

At length a young girl came out of the hut, bearing a big clay pannikin of milk. She offered it to Thorn first, but he waved her aside. She stood irresolute for a moment, about to offer it to Sigurd. Then her father spoke, almost in reproof, 'Give it to the Viking, girl,' he said testily. 'Give it to Harald Sigurdson. He has been where none of us will ever go. He has come back to us from the belly of the sea.'

The young man looked down. 'We lost your longship, headman,' he said.

Thorn looked across the fjord to where the woodsmoke rose from another settlement.

'A ship can be built again,' he said. 'But a true man once lost is lost for ever.'

After a while Sigurd said, 'They are building a longship over there. Will you go and take the knucklebones from her master?'

Harald looked down at his deeply scarred hands. He felt the itch of the wounds across his back as he leaned against the wall of the hut. His mind suddenly flung him the picture of his white fingers slipping from the curragh's rim.

'Maybe, maybe, father,' he said. 'Who knows? There is time. But come what may, one day I would wish to talk with John's brothers again, to tell them about him.'

Thorn said, 'You have sailed with men, Viking. The world will never see their like again.'

Harald smiled sadly, 'Who can tell, headman?' he said. 'Perhaps there will be others as good. Perhaps one day their longships will sail the seas as thick as seeds on a lake.'

'Hm, perhaps,' said Thorn, taking the milk-bowl, 'but I doubt it.'

Harald's father said, 'I have a hankering to go where you have been, son. Perhaps to make a home alongside Olaf on Orkney.'

The old headman said, 'I have often told you, Sigurd, that there is always a home for you here, by the fjord. Will that not do for you?'

Just then a fresh breeze blew in from seawards, carrying on it the sharp tang of salt. Two white gulls swooped up from the blue waters and on over the pine woods above the village, and out of sight. Sigurd sniffed the air and followed the flight of the birds.

'Ah, they are free creatures,' he said, still looking up. 'My leg is much better than it was, since seeing you, Harald. Perhaps if we waste no time we shall be there before they launch her.'

He put his hand on his son's strong shoulder and stretched his leg, trying it.

Thorn looked bewildered. 'Where are you going?' he said. 'Are you not happy here?'

Sigurd and Harald smiled back at him gently and then gazed over the fjord to where the longship was a-building.

Old Thorn shook his head sorrowfully, 'Ah, Vikings! Vikings!' he mumbled. 'There's no understanding them. They are tied to salt water as a prisoner is tied with chains! No, there's no understanding them! They're either madmen – or heroes!'

He called his daughter to lead him back into the warmth of the hut. He was still shaking his head.

The Road to Miklagard

Contents

About this Book

In *Viking's Dawn*, I described how a young Northman, Harald Sigurdson, sailed on a voyage with Thorkell Fairhair about the year AD 780, and how, after many adventures in Scotland and the Hebrides, he returned home to the village by the fjord, the sole survivor of the ship's company.

The Road to Miklagard is set about five years later, when Harald has grown to be a warrior, respected in his village, and describes how once more he has the urge to 'go a-viking'; but this time his travels take him farther afield – to Ireland, where many kings still reigned; to Spain, where the victorious Moors had set up their Muslim kingdom; to distant Miklagard, or Constantinople, where the wicked Irene fought to gain power over her weak son, Constantine, so as to rule the Eastern Roman Empire herself; and finally, across the great plains of what is now Russia, and so home again.

On such occasions, many men set out, but few returned. Yet such was the Viking wanderlust that the hazards of their journeys in no way deterred them; indeed, one can imagine that the possible dangers lent attraction to their voyages!

They were a grimly humorous people, who loved nothing better after the voyaging and the fighting were done than to sit at the feast-board and spin their long and sometimes impossible yarns about the places they had been to and the wonders they had seen.

Besides, they were insatiable treasure-hunters; and who would *not* sail halfway round the world if, at the journey's end, there was waiting such wealth as might stagger the imagination to dream of it, even!

To the Northmen, Miklagard was the storehouse of such riches; the magnetic City of Gold. So, it is inevitable that at last Harald Sigurdson must find his face set towards Miklagard.

HENRY TREECE

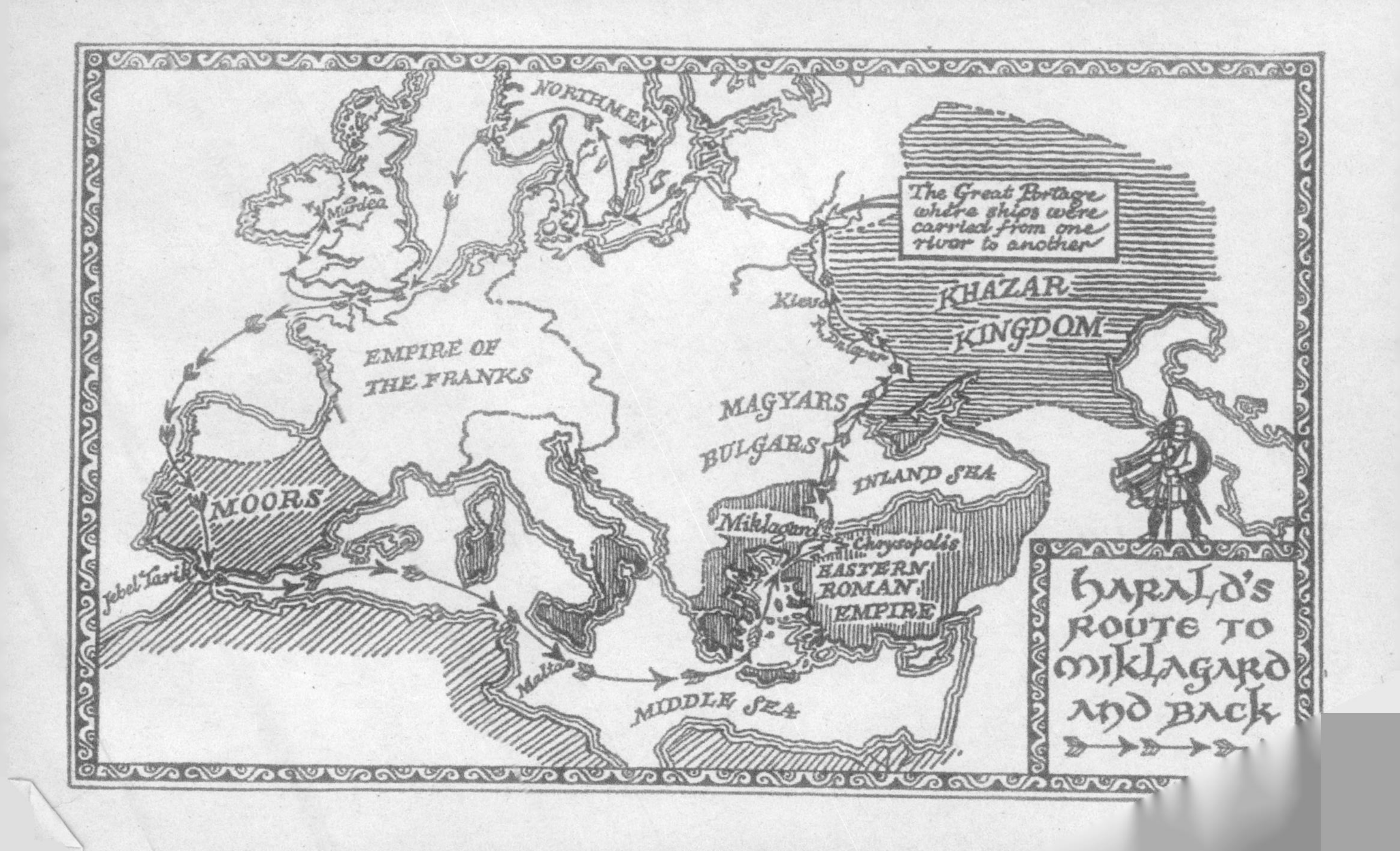
Harald's Route to Miklagard and Back
NORTHMEN
Mirdea
EMPIRE OF THE FRANKS
MOORS
Jebel Tarik
Maltao
MIDDLE SEA
The Great Portage where ships were carried from one river to another
KHAZAR KINGDOM
Kiev
R. Dnieper
MAGYARS
BULGARS
INLAND SEA
Miklagard
Chrysopolis
EASTERN ROMAN EMPIRE

PART ONE

1. The Dark Stranger

THE LATE afternoon sun burned a deep copper-red behind the gaunt hills of the west, slowly sinking to its salty bed among the great grey breakers beyond Ultima Thule, the Last Island, whose silvery beaches of a myriad shells were strewn with the countless wrecks of all the fine longships that had never come back to the fjords. And now they were no longer fine; only grim spars of blackening, salt-encrusted wood, home for the barnacle, playground for the merry barking seals who danced in the secret silver light of the moon, calling to each other in their age-old language, the tongue of those who were familiar with all the rocks in all the seas of all the world – long before man had dared leave his caves to paddle his frightened little shell of a coracle across the width of a meadow stream.

A tall, golden-haired boy sat thinking things as he watched over a herd of swine on a little plateau of green grass, at the edge of a thick beechwood, high up above the dark green waters of the fjord.

'I am Harald Sigurdson,' he said to himself sadly; 'the son of a great sea-rover. Yet I have made only two voyages, and now my dear father is dead and gone to Odin. We shall never sail together again; and all I am fit for is to watch that old Thorn's pigs do not get carried away by a wolf, or eat something which disagrees with them!'

He gave a wry smile of resignation and looked down at his hands and arms. They were burnt almost black by the sun, and scarred from finger-tip to elbow. And as he looked at each scar, he recalled the occasion which had created it . . .

'This one came when I fought in the torchlight beside Bjorn, in the long-house in Pictland, when they betrayed us while we slept. Poor Bjorn, rest in Valhalla . . . And this one came when I tried to drag the rocks off great Aun Doorback, as we escaped from Leire's dungeon. May Aun be happy in Valhalla with his comrade, Gnorre Nithing . . . I almost wish I were with them, to hear the tales they will tell . . . And this scar came when I struggled with the sinking curragh, far off the coast of Caledonia, with John the Priest supporting me until the Danish longship found me . . .'

Harald Sigurdson passed his hand over his eyes and said, 'Dear John, we shall never see your like again. The priests who have come here are not of your mettle, good friend. They think more of words than deeds. Alas, that I shall never see you again. Your heaven is not my own.'

He glanced over his shoulder, down the steep hill, to where the village lay, snuggling along the shore of the great fjord. The blue woodsmoke was twisting now as the sun set. They would be laying the tables with barley bread and a roast pig, filling the drinking horns with honey mead and heather ale; all for the feast.

Harald must be there, he knew, for he was the shipmaster of the village by the fjord, after his experiences a-viking, adventures which no other man in the place could equal. Yet his heart was heavy.

'My father should be the shipmaster,' he said to himself. 'I am not worthy to step into his shoes. But he is gone, gone after only one voyage with me . . .'

Bitterly he recalled the one foray they had made on a sleepy little coastal village in Northumbria. The Northmen had been confident that all would be well, that they would return to their ship with bags of barley meal and baskets of eggs. Then Sigurd had been struck down by an arrow that flew out of the darkness, and the others had turned to find their longship ablaze . . . They had sailed, empty-handed, carrying their dead leader, in a ship that more resembled a funeral pyre than a vessel. Harald remembered how they had wallowed offshore, trying to put out the blaze with their cloaks, with salt water from their helmets, even by rolling on the flames, stifling them with their own bodies.

It had been a sad homecoming for them, for that ship had cost the villagers three years of harvest to buy. Old Thorn, the headman, had been furious, waving his stick and spluttering all manner of curses on the weary Vikings who dragged the charred hulk ashore.

Yet even Thorn had let fall a tear when they carried the body of Sigurd up the runway, back to his lonely hut, for of all men, old Thorn most loved and respected Sigurd, the noble warrior who had chosen to make his home in the sprawling wattle-and-daub village by the fjord.

And now Sigurd's only son, Harald, sat mourning for his father at sunset, among the grubbing swine at the edge of the high beechwoods.

But at last he rose and fastened the hide strapping round his breeches, getting ready to go down to the feast.

'Only the bear's widow mourns for more than one day,' he said, recalling an old Norse saying. 'And she soon gets caught!'

He was about to lay his stick on the back of an old pig that would not herd with the others and come down the hill, when he heard a sudden quick movement among the bushes just within the wood. He waited for a moment, expecting to see a fox or a badger, but when nothing appeared, he forgot the noise and turned once more towards the little path that spidered its way downwards to the thatched roofs of the village.

And at that moment, a man ran out from the beechwoods, swift as an attacking wolf, and kicking Harald's feet from under him, sat astride the boy, his knees pinning Harald's arms. The pigs grunted and stopped once more, searching for something else to eat among the heather-covered rocks. The man above Harald snarled, 'If you shout I shall kill you. Believe me, I am a hungry man. I set no store by the laws of this place.'

Harald did his best to smile up at him and said, 'By your black hair and the sort of brooch you wear, I judge you to be a Dane. We have a saying in my village: "Trust a snake before a Frank, a Frank before an Englishman – but do not trust a Dane at all!"'

The man grinned down with fury and said, 'It is true. I am a Dane, and I am proud to be such. But that is neither here nor there. I am a hungry man at this moment, and I swear by my gods and yours that I will let nothing stand between me and my hunger. I want only one of your pigs, a small one will do. But I cannot carry it whole into the forest. I shall kill it and carve it here. So lie still, for I intend only to give you such a knock on the head as will keep you quiet until I have done what needs to be done.'

He leaned over and took up a round stone that lay by them. Harald tried to move, but was powerless under the great weight on his chest. So he smiled again, as the man raised his hand, and said, 'My friend, why should you knock me on the head, when I can help you? I thought you Danes were better bargainers than that.'

The Dane said, 'Why should you help me to steal your swine? That does not sound likely, coming from a Norseman! No, I must knock you on the head, my friend. You are too strongly built for me to take any chances.'

He raised the stone once more, taking aim. But Harald looked up into his dark eyes with his own sky-blue ones and smiling still, said, 'Very well, what must be, must be; but let me tell you before you go to all this trouble that I would willingly give you a fat pig, and help you to skin and carve it. They are not my pigs, and the man to whom they belong is no special friend of mine.'

Slowly the Dane let fall the stone and got up from Harald's chest. He looked very tired, and Harald observed that a trickle of blood had run from a wound in his shoulder and had dried on his arm. In spite of his rich clothes and his gold-studded belt, he looked like a man who was near the end of his tether.

He stood watching the boy suspiciously. 'You must go before me,' he said 'Choose me a good pig and do what needs to be done. If you try to trick me, I shall . . .'

But even as he said that, Harald's leg shot out, striking the Dane at the side of the knee. He staggered, with a hoarse cry, but before he could regain his balance, the boy had slipped sideways and had flung him face-downwards on to the springy turf.

'Now,' said Harald, drawing the man's arms behind him as he sat astride the Dane, 'who shall be knocked on the head, my friend?'

The Dane said, 'I am a fool, and I deserve to die for trusting the word of a Norseman. Kill me and I shall be satisfied.'

But Harald said suddenly, 'Why should I kill you? You look like a warrior to me, and it would ill-become a swineherd to kill a warrior with a stone. No, instead, I will offer you friendship. You shall come down to the village with me and eat your pig there. What do you say to that?'

For a while the man did not speak. Then at last he said, 'No, I would rather be killed by a swineherd than let any gap-toothed villagers jeer at me for being caught so easily.'

In reply, Harald got off the man's back and stood away from him, his hands open, palms upward, to show that he carried no weapon, not even a stone.

'I am no boaster,' he said. 'I would not say that I had caught you by a trick. But later, when you have fed, if you still wish to die, I will borrow a sword from someone and will do what you ask, decently, in the proper manner.'

Then he took up his stick, and ignoring the Dane, gathered his pigs together into a neat herd, and started off with them down the hill.

When he had gone twenty paces, he heard a cry behind him.

'Wait,' shouted the Dane. 'I will come with you. We can talk about swords when I have a meal inside me.'

Harald nodded and said, 'That is just what I told you, my friend.' He handed the staff to the Dane.

'I see you are limping, my friend. Lean on this. I can drive the pigs on with a smack of the hand.'

The Dane took the staff, wondering. Then he smiled and said, 'Judging by the size of your hands, my friend, I wager the pigs would rather be struck with your staff!'

So, laughing, they reached the village.

2. The Feast and What Befell There

OLD THORN was beside himself with rage when he saw the guest he was to entertain. Though half-crippled with rheumatism, he bobbed up and down in his anger on the hide-thong bed where he usually lay, and threatened Harald with his stick, saying that the village had little enough for itself, without giving entertainment to good-for-nothing Danes, who ate up all they could, then brought their families in longships the next year to pillage their hosts.

As he raved in the smoke-filled hut, the Dane shuffled his feet with irritation; but Harald still smiled as he laid his hand on the man's shoulder.

'Send him away, and send me, Thorn,' he said softly. 'My father would have counselled you as I do. My father, Sigurd, would not have forgotten the laws of hospitality.'

Thorn's eyes goggled and a vein stood out in his thin neck. But at last he was quiet again and said, 'Be it as you say. He shall stay as long as he wishes. But mark me, he has the look of a pursued man about him, and that bodes no good to anyone. What if he is a nithing, then? What if his king sends for him, and takes our heads too?'

The Dane said, 'I am no nithing, old man. As for my king, he is dead and will never send here for me. He was my brother, and I should have ruled in his place, but for my taste for sailing the seas in longships.'

When Thorn heard that their visitor was of royal blood, he put a rein on his temper and even tried to smile.

'Well, well,' he said, 'then you still may be useful to us. Though you have indeed a look about you which I have seen on the faces of men who are pursued.'

The Dane said, 'We are all pursued, old man; and the one who pursues us will get us, each one of us, in the end.'

Old Thorn, who was very superstitious, crossed his fingers at those words, to keep away Loki, the evil spirit, who listened at the chimney hole to what men said.

Harald laughed and said, 'So, you have been a-viking, Dane! What sights did you see?'

The Dane snorted and replied, 'Such sights as may not be told, young fellow, for fear of keeping sleep from a boy's eyes for a year or more!'

Harald answered, 'I could match them, Dane.'

But the Dane had turned and was looking across the village compound, up towards the hills again, listening, as though he expected someone to come leaping down the heather-covered rocks towards the houses.

Then the horn sounded to summon the villagers to the feast in the long-hall.

Soon the oaken table was thronged about with men and women, for this was not a warrior-meeting, where only the men gathered; and soon the long pinewood hall was thick with smoke from the wood fire in the centre, so that one could hardly see from one side to the other. The village folk ate their pork and barley bread ravenously, each trying to outdo his neighbour and to get good value from the occasion, for each had contributed his share. Then, when the mead-horn had passed round the board a time or two, and the heather ale had been poured into the great helmet and sampled by all, men began to cry out for a song.

The village sagaman, old Nessi, so old that he had to be carried in his chair by two boys wherever he went, began to strike on a little drum with the flat of his dry old hand, giving himself a rhythm to work to. His drum was an earthen gourd, covered by a tight and thinly-scraped sheepskin, bound about with deer sinews. It gave off a sharp little note that cut through the talk about the table and caused all the villagers, even the most quick-tongued woman, to fall silent, while the bard declaimed his words.

> *'There are three things a man should fear,*
> *A wolf, a sword, and a woman.'*

He sang, smiling wickedly.

The men began to laugh and the women to make angry faces at the old poet. But when the uproar had died again, he started again more seriously and sang,

> *'It came from no man knows where;*
> *It hides beneath the deepest rocks;*

It will not be wooed with promises;
Yet most men love it better than life itself.
What say you, wise ones, that it is?'

The hall was filled with the voices of men and women, who tried to guess the answer to the riddle. But at each attempt, the sagaman shook his head and smiled.

Then he looked towards the Dane who sat between Thorn and Harald, at the head of the table.

'You seem to be a quick-witted fellow,' said the bard. 'Will you not try to guess?'

The Dane shrugged his broad shoulders and smiled. 'I shall not need to guess,' he said. 'For I know what the answer is. I made up that song myself, at my brother's house in Hedeby, many years ago. The answer is: *Gold*, nothing more!'

At first there was silence, then there was an excited shouting among the people. The sagaman smiled and said, 'I recognized you, Arkil the Prince, as soon as you came in. That is why I tried your own song on you. Here, take the drum; I hand it to a better bard than myself.'

The people clapped Arkil on the back and made him go forward, against his will, to stand beside the fire and sing them a song. He struck the drum a time or two, but then flung it back to the sagaman, saying, 'I can get along better in my own way, Nessi the Bard'.

And he began to clap his hands against each other, making many different sounds, and many complicated rhythms. The folk in the hall would have been well contented to hear him clapping like that for long enough, but the Dane suddenly began to sing in a deep musical voice:

'Away where the seal plays,
In the light of the dying sun,
Where the wave rocks forever
The white bones of the great sailors,
And the ghosts of all longships
Swing on the tides,
There have I been.
I have been where
The halls of the sunset
Echo with song, echo with voices
Of all the great army
Of those who have left us,
Left us to roam.'

As he stood there, in the flickering firelight, a strange look came over his face. He seemed to be asleep, or voyaging in a dream among the islands of his song. And the folk in the hall gazed at him raptly, sharing his vision.

Then suddenly the door was flung open and a great gust of cold air scattered the ashes of the fire, and brought everyone back to the world they knew, with its harsh chill.

'Who has opened the door?' shouted old Thorn angrily, grabbing his stick to lay it about the shoulders of the man who had been so careless.

But then men gasped. Standing in the doorway were two strange and frightening figures. They were bigger men than anyone at that feast had seen before, bigger even than Aun

Doorback himself had been. Their long black hair was knotted up with bone pins, and about their bodies they wore thick corselets of horsehide. Each carried a long, leaf-bladed sword of bronze and the firelight glistened on the broad streaks of blue which stretched across their dark cheeks. They smiled grimly to see the fear they had roused among the villagers.

Then one of them spoke. 'I opened the door, old man,' he said. 'Will you beat me with your little stick, then?'

Old Thorn was a brave man, despite his age and his rheumatism. He began to rise, saying, 'Aye, that I will, whoever you may be!'

But Harald pulled him back on to his seat. 'Take care, Thorn,' he said. 'These are lawless Irishmen; I see that from their coloured breeches, which are such as their inland tribes still wear. Do not anger them.'

When their first shock was over, many men cursed themselves for obeying the old feast laws, which decreed that they must leave their weapons at home; while the women wished they had their ladles or rolling pins.

One woman, Thora, the niece of Thorn, a strong-armed creature with a great reputation for keeping her husband in order, rose and called out, 'If only I had my skinning-knife, you rascals, I'd make you skip back to Ireland, and glad to go! That I would!'

Then the other Irishman spoke, coldly and viciously, 'If we had the time, woman, we would teach you the lesson your husband should have taught you by now. But we are not concerned with you folk. Our man stands there. We have followed him half over the world and shall not let

him go for the threats of a roomful of midden-churls and their women.'

He pointed with his sword at Arkil the Dane, who still stood by the fire, the sagaman's drum by his side on the table.

Arkil shrugged his shoulders, 'You have come a long way to find me. Now let us go outside and settle this quarrel properly, as men should, without disturbing the feast.'

The Irishmen smiled grimly and shook their heads.

'What we have to do shall be done here, without delay,' said the first one. 'We cannot risk losing you in the darkness again.'

They saw that Arkil was trapped, with his back against the table, and they saw also that he carried no sword or axe. They moved across the space towards him, their blades raised to strike. The horrified men and women about the tables saw that the Dane still smiled, and made no attempt to run from the threatened blows.

Yet as the first great Irishman struck downwards with his sword, the Dane flung the sagaman's drum at him with all his force. The earthen jar shattered to pieces with the impact, and the Irishman staggered backwards, with a cry of pain, his hands to his face.

Then there was a great shout from the head of the table and Harald leapt forward, scattering dishes before him in his haste. He could not reach the second Irishman in time to grapple with him, but did something even more terrible. As he passed the fireplace, he snatched up a flaming log and flung it at the barbaric figure. The Irishman swung round, trying to ward off the brand with his sword, and in that moment, Arkil leapt upon his back, bearing him down.

Men rushed from the nearest end of the table now, anxious to attack the first Irishman, who had recovered from the blow he had received from the drum; but they were too late. Harald had kicked the half-blinded man's feet from under him and was sitting astride his back, his fingers deep in the man's black hair, banging his head rhythmically on the hard earthen floor.

Soon Arkil rose, smiling strangely, the sword of his opponent in his hand. He said simply, 'That one will not spoil a feast again. Now let me take his brother outside, Harald, my friend. He shall have better treatment than he would have allowed me. He shall take his sword with him into the darkness.'

No man, not even Thorn, could deny Arkil his right in this matter. And shortly the Dane came back into the hall, carrying two swords this time, and smiling as one who could now get on with his supper without fear of interruption.

But first he flung the two swords on to the sheepskins beside the walls, saying, 'The village boys will play happily with these. They are of no worth. I doubt whether a man could cut himself with them if he tried!'

And to the sagaman he said, 'One day, my friend, I will repay you a golden harp for that drum, for it saved my life this night'.

Then he stood near Harald and took him by both hands. 'May the seas have me and the crows eat my heart if I am ever false to you, my friend,' he said, in the time-honoured oath.

And when he sat down again, he put his hand inside his tunic and drew out two things; a long package and a round one. When he had unwrapped the deerskin from the long package, the villagers saw that it was a knife of gold, its hilt carved and moulded so beautifully that all the women gasped with envy; its blade chased from end to end with fine runes, which glistened in the torchlight.

The round package, he opened more carefully, and then let fall a glittering cascade of coloured stones on to the table, where they lay, glinting beautifully as the light from the wall-torches touched them. Now all men rose to their feet in astonishment, and Arkil smiled and gathered his treasure once more into the bag.

To Thorn he said, 'You were right, headman, I was pursued; but I am pursued no longer. Those who came after me to regain their giant's treasure are no more.'

Thorn said, 'You have stolen a giant's treasure, have you! And an Irish giant at that! Well, and what do you mean to do now, Arkil the Prince?'

The Dane smiled and said, 'I propose to gather a shipful of fighting-cocks about me and to go back and steal the rest of his treasure, for this is but a tiny drop in the ocean.'

Thorn's eyes gleamed as red and green as the jewels themselves with greed. He said, 'My stepbrother, Alaf, who farms higher up the fjord, has a good ship, which he is a little too old to sail in now. I have no doubt that I could persuade him to sell it to you for that bag of pretty stones.'

The Dane smiled slowly and then said, 'This bag of pretty stones, as you call them, would buy a ship made of gold with sails of silk, old man. Nay, nay, I will buy your stepbrother's ship with three of my pretty stones at the most – not a grain of dust more!'

Thorn's face showed his annoyance and for a moment it looked as though he might quarrel with Arkil the Prince; but he saw the reason in what the Dane said, for after all, this man had risked his life to gain those precious stones, and the boat was worth no more than Arkil said.

But Thorn was not a man to be beaten in a bargain.

'Look you, Prince,' he said at last, 'buy my stepbrother's ship, and I will provide her with a stout crew from the men of my village.'

The Dane screwed up his eyes, amused now. Then he nodded.

'That seems a good plan, headman,' he said, 'for I have seen that your village breeds good men. But what price must I pay for their service? I cannot imagine that you offer them for the love of it.'

Thorn's long forefinger drew a little pattern on the oaken tabletop as he spoke. 'I shall ask two-thirds of whatever treasure you shall bring back, to be given to the village. For after all, it has not done badly by you in your need.'

Arkil clapped the old man on the shoulder.

'By Odin,' he said, 'when I next go to market to buy a cow, I shall take you with me, old man. There is not a better bargainer in the northern lands than you. Well, I agree to what you ask, for if we find the treasure I have mentioned, one third of it will satisfy me – and will keep me in comfort for the rest of my days.'

So they shook hands on the bargain, and the next day Arkil and Harald went with Thorn to Alaf's steading, higher up the fjord. Alaf accepted the price the Dane offered without any argument, for he was not a shrewd haggler as Thorn was.

Alaf's longship lay in the cow-byre, where it had been dragged when he gave up voyaging five years before. It was a well-built boat, but a bit heavy, the Dane said, for the rivers it would sail up in Ireland. He would have preferred a ship broader in the belly and sitting lower in the water.

'But beggars cannot be choosers,' said Thorn, 'and I am setting you up with a crew straightaway; you will have no seeking to do.'

The Dane looked at him through narrowed lids.

'My friend,' he said, 'with my knowledge of the treasure, and my reputation in my own land, I could fit out fifty little ships like this, at one whistle.'

Then, seeing Thorn's crestfallen expression, he touched him on the arm and went on, 'But I should find no better men than those of yours if I went whistling along every fjord in the northland.'

So they paid for the longship, which Arkil named *Seeker*, and the next day twenty men dragged her on rollers down to the village.

3. The Sailing

ARKIL FOUND no difficulty in getting together his crew. The real difficulty lay in picking twenty out of the hundred men who jostled round the table, anxious to sail with him. Harald sat with Arkil at the table, for the boy was named shipmaster without any argument, while Arkil held himself merely to be the leader once they were ashore in Ireland.

So, just as Thorkell Fairhair had done, five years before on that very spot, Harald gave the new crew the knucklebones, as symbols that they were signed on as crew members in the *Seeker*. And each man, as he took the bones, gave his solemn promise to obey orders and to fight for his comrades, whatever the odds.

Many good men came up to the table that day, laying their weapons before their new masters and naming them as they took the oath. There was Haro Once-only, with his sword, Alas; Sven Hawknose, with his axe, Sweetheart; Elf Elfson, with his axe, Trouble-me-no-more; Kran the Lark, a great singer, with his dagger, Forget-me-not; Jago

Longarm, with his axe, Wife's Lament; Skirr Barrel, a great drinker, with his mace, Thunderstone; and many more. Harald had his long sword, which had belonged to his father once. It was called Sigurd's Darling, and had a curiously carved hilt of walrus ivory which was the envy of all who saw it. As for Arkil, his only weapon was the golden knife, which he called Heart's Desire. He refused to accept any offer of a weapon, for, as he said, when he needed a weapon, one always seemed to come to hand, whether it was a drum or a log out of the fire. And such weapons did not need cleaning and oiling as swords did!

There was only one mishap before they sailed. It happened when they were stepping the mast. A sudden gust of wind swung the loose pole sideways, pinning Skirr Barrel against the gunwales and breaking his arm. But he took the event with all good humour, and said that in any case he had three casks of heather ale to finish up before it went off, so he did not mind, provided that they took his cousin, Radbard Crookleg, with them in his place.

Arkil the Prince did not care for the look of this Radbard, whose red beard gave him a shifty expression, and whose badly set leg caused him to walk with a slight limp.

But Harald accepted Radbard gladly, for he knew the man to be a true sailor and a brave warrior. As it happened, this Radbard was a lucky choice, and when he looked back on the affair, Harald was compelled to think that the gods who had sent the sudden puff of wind to pin Skirr Barrel down had acted well.

So, when she was laden with dried meats, barley flour, five kegs of water and three of heather ale, all stowed beneath the deck, *Seeker* pulled away from the village, and at last came into the open sea.

The men soon settled down to their new life and the voyage was an uneventful one, save for the occasion when they tried to board a tall ship, which wallowed clumsily off the Anglian coast.

Then, to their cost, the Vikings found that the vessel was full of archers on their way to Frankland. Elf Elfson and three others were lost in that affair, though they took more than their own number with them to Valhalla.

After that, both Harald and Arkil took a turn at the oars. And on the fifth day out, just when their water was finished, they sighted the port of Murdea, which Arkil told them was the nearest point to the kingdom they were making for.

It was a squalid-looking harbour, with wooden houses seeming to hang above the water, supported on piles which were gradually rotting, to let their loads heel slowly over into the dark and rubbish-littered tide. Over the township, which was set on a low hill, a heavy cloud of smoke hung perpetually, as the grey seabirds flew in and out of it, crying discordantly.

Kran the Lark blew his nose lustily and said aloud, 'Even a blind man would know when he had reached Murdea!'

Sven Hawknose tugged at his long yellow moustaches and said quietly, 'Could a blind man find his way back home *from* Murdea, think you, Kran?'

Then there was silence on board *Seeker*, for they had all heard of the cruelties practised on Vikings who were unfortunate enough to get themselves captured in the townships they sacked.

But Arkil cheered them up by saying, 'You need have no fear here, my seacocks! I know the headman of Murdea as well as I know most of you – better, if the truth be told!'

'That isn't saying much,' said Haro Once-only, grinning, 'for we are a simple lot. We must be, or we shouldn't be here now!'

When they had furled the sail and rowed to their anchorage, they climbed ashore, up the dangling rope ladder, leaving Jago Longarm and another Viking to guard *Seeker* till they returned.

'Have no dealings with the townsfolk,' warned Arkil as they left. 'Give them no offence and they will not harm you.'

Jago grinned up at him and touched his sword-hilt lightly.

'Have no fear, chieftain,' he said. 'The ship will be here when you want it again.'

The Vikings walked in a body up the winding street, followed by a group of hangers-on and children, who admired their helmets and their various weapons, noisily and with many gestures.

Sven Hawknose flung a coin to one of the raggedest of their followers. He picked it up and then spat on it, before flinging it back at Sven's feet.

'Now you know,' said Harald, laughing, 'Keep your money in your pouch, Sven; it is a bad bargain to throw it into the gutter without even getting thanks for it.'

Sven muttered angrily and said that if he could lay his hands on that ragged rogue, he would cut his hair for him – with an axe.

The headman of Murdea greeted them at his tumbledown door, but the look on his face was one of annoyance rather than pleasure. And when they were all inside, he said hurriedly, 'My friends, things are not now as they once were here. The Vikings have made a bad name for themselves, and the folk of the town say they will stand it no longer. I who am half a Viking, my father having been a Dane, think that it is stupidity, but my wife, who is Irish, sides with them and says that the Northmen are a curse from God for our misdeeds in the past. Whatever is the truth, I do not know; but all I can tell you is to go away from Murdea with the next tide.'

Arkil thanked him for his advice and then bought wine from him. They all sat together on the floor and drank from the few cups that the headman possessed, passing the vessels from one to the other.

Harald noticed that the headman himself refused the wine, saying that he was suffering from a chill on the stomach and could not appreciate it. Harald spoke about this to Arkil, saying, 'It is a bad sign when a man will not drink his own wine. I have heard of travellers being poisoned by that trick before now The headman must drink his own wine, then we shall be sure that he has dealt with us in good faith.'

So Radbard held the man still while Harald poured a cup of the tart wine down his throat. The man protested and spluttered a great deal, but did not fall dead; and so the Vikings were satisfied.

Then suddenly the guard they had put on the street door, Goff Goffling, ran in and shouted out, 'Come quickly, my masters, there is such a light shining down at the harbour as can mean only one thing!'

The Vikings raced down the rough street, Harald and Arkil in the lead, full of foreboding. Their fears were realized, when they turned a corner and saw the *Seeker* a mass of fire, down to the water-line, and already foundering.

They found Jago Longarm lying with his head dangling over the edge of the harbour jetty, a great wound in his back. He smiled up at them as they lifted him up and said, 'Four of them will greet their gods tonight, master. But I am sorry about the ship.'

Then he died without speaking again. As the *Seeker* slowly settled down in the water, the body of the other

Viking guard floated up to the surface for a moment. All men saw the colour of his tunic and recognized it. Then he went down in the suction of the sinking ship.

Haro Once-only turned towards the town, pulling at his moustaches and cursing horribly. He was a notorious berserk and had to be kept under control when any trouble started, or he was inclined to rip off his shirt and run screaming at the enemy, dealing dreadful slaughter. It was a madness that ran in his family, for his six brothers had also been berserks, though they had not lasted as long as Haro, who had never received a wound in more than fifty affrays and five voyages.

Arkil went up to him and said softly, 'Patience, friend Haro. I too am of the same turn of mind. My own shirt will seldom stay on my body once I feel the little hairs prickling at the top of my neck. But patience, we must wait. One day we will burn this rat's nest out, and then our two will be avenged.'

Now they had no ship and no food, and a hostile township before them. Arkil turned away from the harbour suddenly and strode towards the biggest house he could see. The others followed him. It was the house of a rich merchant, it turned out, and soon the Vikings had broken open two sacks of meal and had filled their flasks with clear grape wine.

'At least we shall not starve for two days,' said Arkil, 'and that is all we need if I can find my way through the bogs again.'

As they left the silent house, a shower of arrows came at them from the other side of the street. No one was hurt, but Harald felt one shaft pass between his arm and his body, and afterwards saw it still quivering in the door he had just passed through.

'That is a good omen,' said Arkil, 'and, it seems to me, we shall need all the luck we can get.'

Then, led by Kran, whose voice sounded out over the town like a great bell, the Vikings sang their war-song as they marched up the narrow winding street to the top of the town. No further harm came to them, though they often saw men run round corners, or draw back from windows as they passed, and not one of the crew but expected to feel an arrow shaft in his back a moment later.

At the top of the hill stood a little white church, with a small square tower. Haro was all for going inside and sacking it, but Harald took him by the arm and said, 'But for one of those men who follow the Christ, I should not be here today. If you lay a hand on the Christ-man's belongings, you will have me for an enemy, my friend. And I should not like that, Haro.'

Haro grinned and punched Harald in the chest. 'No, nor should I,' he said. And so they passed over the hill without burning that church.

As for the Vikings, they were not so happy after an hour's walking, for the memory of their lost comrades had come back to them, and made them wonder whether the treasure they had come to seek was not guarded by ill-fortune. Besides, they had now begun to strike the marshy land, where habitations were few and far between and the roads had almost ceased to exist.

But Arkil strode on purposefully, giving no hint of the doubt that had already come into his own mind.

4. Dun-An-Oir

ON THE third day after their retreat from Murdea, the Vikings lay down, exhausted, in a little green gully that gave them some slight shelter from the night wind. Their clothes hung in shreds and each man was filthy with mud from the waist down.

Now their minds were filled with nothing but the thought of that everlastingly green countryside, where the ground gave suddenly beneath one's feet, to leave one floundering in the choking slime.

'We cannot go on much farther, Arkil,' said Harald himself. 'I have known many hardships, but this is the worst; yes, even worse than the flogging-post at Leire's Dun.'

Arkil licked his dry lips. 'Have courage, Harald boy,' he said. 'We have not much farther to go, if my reckoning is right. There is a great blue hill, shaped like a cow's back, with hawthorns growing the length of it. And on the other side of that lies Dun-an-oir, the Fort of Gold. That is our journey's end.'

Haro Once-only said sharply, 'You should not use such words, Arkil the Prince. Odin might make it your journey's end in all faith.'

Arkil said, 'I am weary, Haro my friend. Do not tease me or I might hit you with my fist, and then you would fall into such a dreamland that even you would not care what Odin thought!'

Haro shrugged his shoulders and said, 'I wish you would, for I am dying slowly of hunger and thirst. Two cupfuls of porridge is no food for a grown man like me to live on for three days.'

Arkil said, 'Tomorrow you will feast on sweet sheep-meat and the crispest of rye bread. Have patience.'

Then, to keep the men's minds from hunger and thirst and cold, Arkil said, 'There is not a poet among you all, save myself. Listen, I will tell you a verse I have just made:

'The white shears cut the green,
But the shears are not of iron
Nor the green of grass.'

Sven Hawknose said, 'That is an easy one. I have known children make better riddles. That is a seagull skimming over the sea.'

Arkil said, 'You are right, Sven. But can you make one which I could not guess?'

Sven said, 'Yes, I give you this one:

'This shining snake has no home
And so must make one in the white rock;

But it is chased away by the red river
And can rest nowhere.'

Arkil said, 'You are clever, but not clever enough, old friend. That is a sword making a wound.'

Then Harald said, 'You both rhyme like young girls in the bower. Let me tell you one, and if you guess this, I will let each one of you give me a kick:

'When we have you not
We want you;
But when we have you
We do not know.'

The Vikings sat and scratched their heads, making many guesses, but not one of them right. Then, when they had given up, Harald said, 'It is sleep; and that is what I am going to have now.'

So without another word he wrapped his tattered cloak about him and, snuggling close against the side of the gully, he fell into a doze, which at least kept his mind from thoughts of food and drink. The others followed suit, tired by their long march, and when the sun rose again, they set off towards the west and, after much floundering in the marshland, rested once more on the peak of a little hill.

It was then that Goff Goffling ran back to Arkil, saying that he had seen two wonderful things; to the west he had suddenly glimpsed the hill shaped like a cow's back; and below the hill they were on, he had seen a herd of horses, with only one man to guard them.

This news cheered the wanderers immensely, and Arkil and Harald crept quietly to their hill's edge to test Goff's words. True enough, in the morning haze they saw the great hill shaped like a cow's back, beyond which lay the Fort of Gold, their destination; and below them, a great herd of horses grazed, guarded by a tired-looking horseman, his black hair held up by pins, his legs encased in coloured breeches. Arkil noted that the man carried a long bronze sword and a cruel-looking lance.

'The important thing is not to give him time to use them,' said Harald, 'for he looks like a warrior who would sell his life dearly to protect such fine beasts.'

Arkil nodded and whispered, 'Is there anyone among us who can throw a stone, young friend?'

Harald nodded and said, 'Radbard Crookleg can hit a sparrow with an acorn at twenty paces.'

So they signalled back to Radbard, who found himself three good-sized stones and then began to creep down the hillside towards the horseman. The Vikings watched him go, holding their breath with anxiety.

The horseman's back was towards them, and men soon began to chuckle as Radbard drew nearer and nearer. Then something happened which put their hearts in their mouths, for suddenly the great black stallion on which the man sat raised his fierce head and gave a high warning neigh. Immediately the herd swung round, stopping their grazing, snorting and whinnying. Radbard stood up then and threw with all his might. But the stallion had seen him and reared in anger. The stone missed the rudely awakened rider, but struck the horse on the neck.

With a high bound, the startled animal swung round, flinging its rider down, and for an instant all was panic among the great herd.

Then Arkil was on his feet. 'Run, run,' he shouted, 'before the man is up again!'

And like a ragged army, the sixteen wanderers streamed down the hill towards the swirling horses, each man grasping the mane of the creature nearest to him.

The guard had been kicked on the shoulder and sat ruefully rubbing his arm as Harald came up with him. He glared ferociously at the boy, but brightened up when he saw Arkil, who knelt down beside him and shook him by the hand. 'Why, Saidhe, old friend,' he said, 'and to think that I did not recognize you!'

The Irishman grinned painfully and said, 'Arkil the Prince, and to think that you dare come back here after what giant Grummoch vowed to do to you! But it is good to see you again, and I can tell you that King MacMiorog will not turn you away this time, especially as you bring such fine men to fight for him.'

Arkil said, 'That is as may be, Saidhe! But our quest is for our own good, not King MacMiorog's. Where is giant Grummoch at the moment, my friend?'

Saidhe rose from the ground and whistled his black horse back to him; the half-savage creature snorted violently at the nearness of the Vikings, but his master whispered something to him, and he became calm once more.

Then Saidhe replied, 'You are in luck. Giant Grummoch is away in the north, at the court of the High King, asking the hand of his beautiful daughter. So you will be able to talk to King MacMiorog without interruption for a while.'

And so it was that the Vikings rode over the hill shaped like a cow's back and saw for the first time Dun-an-oir, the Fort of Gold.

To many of them, this was the most splendid place they had ever seen, and they began to say that neither Kiev nor Miklagard itself could be as wonderful, though of course they had not seen either.

Dun-an-oir lay golden in the morning sunshine, surrounded by a high stockade, a place of many fine houses, with the woodsmoke curling up blue above the thatched roofs.

Goff Goffling groaned and pointed to the many heads which nodded on tall pikes the length of the stockade wall.

'You treat your visitors badly,' he said to Saidhe.

Saidhe grinned and said, 'There is not a Viking head among them all, my friend. King MacMiorog is a good Christian and would not decorate his city with the heads of heathens.'

Harald was less concerned with the heads than with the vast herds of black cattle which grazed quietly here and there across the broad plain.

'Indeed, King MacMiorog must be the richest king in Ireland,' he said enviously.

But Saidhe once more shook his black head until the bone pins in his hair began to jingle.

'Nay, nay, young friend,' he said. 'He might be if Giant Grummoch were not here. MacMiorog owns only that which Grummoch will let him own; for he is like a carrion crow who feeds on the best meat himself and leaves little enough behind for the lesser birds to pick.'

Harald said, 'Why does your king allow this giant to go on living off him? Could he not arrange for the giant to join his fathers in whatever heaven giants go to?'

Saidhe shrugged his shoulders, though it seemed to hurt him to do so after his fall, and said, 'MacMiorog was born a coward. He is a strong fighter when his opponent is afraid; but his courage fails him when he meets opposition. The warriors of Dun-an-oir hold him in some contempt and will not attack Grummoch for such a king. So Grummoch rules the roost and makes a good thing out of it, while MacMiorog sits biting his fingernails in his palace, dreaming of the day when the gods will snatch Grummoch away.' He paused a while and then added, 'But so far the gods seem to prefer Grummoch to remain down here on earth with MacMiorog. His reputation seems to have gone before him to heaven!'

At last they came to the stockade gates, which opened to them after Saidhe had blown three blasts on the horn which hung beside the lintel.

The herd of horses galloped first through the stockade and turned off into a protected paddock within the city, led by the black stallion. Haro Once-only turned longing eyes after them.

'Alas,' he said, 'we might have done well to keep a firm hold on those beasts, for we may need them sooner than we think.'

Saidhe said grimly, 'If things go well with you, the King will give you horses to ride on. But if they go badly, you will not need horses again.'

While the men were wondering about this, Saidhe led them to a long house of timber and thatch, the broad door of which was adorned with seven white skulls, nailed to the timbers with iron spikes. He pointed at the skull in the centre and said, 'This one came from Orkney to put an end to Grummoch, but the crows had him within five days.'

Then they passed by the guard, who lolled against the doorpost, leaning on his spear, and so into the great hall itself, where the King sat on a painted throne, made more comfortable by coverings of sheepskin.

MacMiorog stared at them through the smoke of his hall and spoke to a little man, dressed in black, who sat on the floor beside him.

The Vikings heard him say, 'Here, Cormac, are the men you promised me in your dream, the Lochlannoch, men of the waters. Mayhap they will put a swift end to our troubles, then we shall sleep soft o' nights once more.'

The King was a bent and wizened creature, a young man grown old before his time. His thin black beard and

moustaches gave an air of weakness to his pale face, and even his narrow crown of beaten Irish gold sat crookedly and comically upon his head. He flung back his shawl of red and green wool and beckoned to Arkil, who had stepped up before the throne.

'I am glad to see you again, Prince Arkil,' he said, in a soft and womanish voice. 'We thought your head might have come back sooner than your body, for Grummoch sent the two fierce brothers after you. Did you not meet them on your way?'

Arkil bowed a little and said equally softly, 'Yes, King MacMiorog, I met them, and drew their teeth for them. Their bodies have long since fed the fishes of the fjord.'

The King pulled at his beard and forced a smile. 'That is good,' he said. 'For if they had brought your head, it would have been no use to me. There is no space on my door for another one, you see. But coming with your whole body, and with such a goodly company of sea-rovers, you may well be of use to me.'

Arkil said, 'You wish us to put an end to giant Grummoch, is that not it?'

The King nodded, his thin lips smiling cruelly.

'You are still as keen-sighted as ever, Arkil,' he said. 'Let us pray that Grummoch does not draw the shades of night over those eyes.'

Haro Once-only was becoming tired of this talk, for he was a direct man, and he said suddenly, 'The giant who can do that has yet to be born.'

The King turned his gaze on Haro, as though he had never seen such a creature before, but Haro was not a man to be frightened by a look and he stared back, until King MacMiorog had to give him best and look away.

'Every cock can crow loudly enough in the daylight on his own dunghill,' said the little man in black who sat by the throne, 'but how many cocks dare crow at night, when the fox sniffs under the perch?'

Haro stepped forward then and flung his sword, Alas!, at the feet of MacMiorog.

'Before Odin, I will take that giant's head if it is the last thing I do, just to show you that this cock has spurs as well as a singing voice!'

The King pushed the sword away with his foot as though it were a distasteful thing to him, and said, 'Prince Arkil, a true captain keeps his hounds on the leash. See that this dog is muzzled before you bring him before me again.

At this the Vikings in the hall began to shout out, and some of them even drew their swords and daggers, so that the guards at the door prepared for battle there and then, and were not at all happy about their prospects.

But Arkil held up his hand for silence and then he said, 'King MacMiorog, we have an old saying in the north. It is this: the wolf whose foot is caught in a trap cannot afford to snarl at the hunter. Think on that saying, King, and we will come before you tomorrow and listen to you then.'

He turned to go, but King MacMiorog called him back, smiling now, and said, 'I was only trying to test your mettle, my friend. Now I know that you are men of good heart and so I give you my trust.'

Then he clapped his hands and slave women came forward with horns of mead and platters of sheep-meat and good barley bread. The Vikings sat on the rush-covered floor and ate their fill, and when they had finished, the King spoke once more, saying, 'My friends, you shall live to call me a generous master.'

Sven Hawknose called out, his mouth full of meat, 'We have no masters but Arkil and Harald!'

MacMiorog smiled bitterly at him and went on, 'That is so, I used the word merely as a term of friendship towards you. But I will proceed. This land is ravaged by a giant, as you know. I cannot turn my own men against him, for they fear him; and besides that, I must confess that they do not love me enough to risk their lives for me. So it will fall on you to rid the land of this plague. And in return, you shall take away with you as much of the giant's treasure as you can carry, each man a sackful.'

Arkil stood up before the king and said, 'If we kill Grummoch, we shall take all his treasure, my friend, have no fear.'

King MacMiorog bit his lip and then said, 'Very well, that is as may be; you have a name for being harsh bargainers, you men of the far north. Let it be at that.'

But Harald was not satisfied, for he did not trust this black-haired king with the crooked crown. He rose and went forward, saying, 'Take my hands, King, and swear by your God that you will give us leave to take all the giant's treasure.'

King MacMiorog glowered at Harald, who was only a boy in his eyes, and said, 'I will swear to Prince Arkil, but not to you.'

But Arkil said stoutly, 'Swear to Harald or not at all, for he and I are as two brothers in this matter.'

So King MacMiorog took the oath, holding Harald's hands, and then he promised that he would show them where the treasure lay, so that there might be no error when the time of trial came.

5. The Island Treasure House

THREE DAYS after their arrival at Dun-an-oir, the Vikings lolled before the cave entrance on the little island in the lake, below the hill shaped like a cow's back. They had made their home there since the night King MacMiorog had shown where the giant's treasure lay, and each day some of them rowed back to Dun-an-oir to fetch food and drink for the company.

They sat in the sunshine, wondering when giant Grummoch would return to Dun-an-oir, speculating on the nature of the treasure, and working out ways of transporting it back to the coast when they had won it.

Haro and Goff Goffling were in the middle of a tremendous argument on the matter when Sven, who had climbed the one tree on the little island, shouted out that he could see a wagon train approaching Dun-an-oir across the green plain. He said that there were at least ten wagons and that they were drawn by white oxen. It seemed to his eyes that the giant was riding at the head of the column on a black creature, but he could not tell what the creature was. Arkil, whose eyes were keener than those of a hawk, climbed up the tree beside him and said that the creature was a bull. He also said that the giant seemed even bigger than when last he, Arkil, had been in Dun-an-oir, and that was saying much.

Then there was much excitement among the Vikings, for each man wanted to climb the tree and see this giant; but the tree was not strong enough to hold them all, and there was no time for them to take turns in climbing it. They were all sent to their various hiding-places, and Arkil himself rowed the little boat round to the far side of the island so that Grummoch should have no suspicion of their presence.

The waiting was terrible for them all, and the only thing they could do was to lie quietly, chewing on the strips of dried meat which MacMiorog had sent them that day. It was almost sunset before they heard the sound of voices on the far shore, and saw the flare of torches start up as men began to load boats and rafts on the other side.

Arkil passed the message round that they were all to lie still and not to attack until he called out like a sparrowhawk; then they were to fall on the giant in a body and put an end to him as swiftly as could be managed.

It was then that they heard Grummoch's voice for the first time, and so strangely high-pitched was it that Haro laughed aloud. Goff punched him in the mouth for that and a fight would have started there and then, but for Arkil's warning that the two would lose their share of the treasure if they did not quieten down immediately.

Then the Vikings heard the sound of oars splashing in the waters of the lake, and saw the flare of torchlight growing nearer and nearer.

And suddenly a big boat drew alongside the small landing-beach and they saw for the first time the giant, Grummoch, as he waded ashore, carrying two great sacks on his shoulders.

Harald, who had once known the massive Aun Doorback, gasped in mute astonishment, for this was a bigger man than he had ever dreamed of. Grummoch was the height of a man and a half, and was as broad across the shoulders as three men standing together. The slaves who came after him, carrying their loads, had almost to run in order to keep up with his monstrous strides.

From the corner of his eye, Harald saw Arkil wipe the sweat from his forehead, in anticipation of the fight that must surely follow the arrival of such an opponent.

Then Harald had a closer view of Grummoch, in the light of the many torches. His red hair hung in two great plaits, down each side of his head, and was braided with strands of gold wire. His thick red ears carried rings in the shape of half-moons. His massive arms were laden with bracelets of gold, twisted in spirals; and his fingers glimmered in the light from the many rings which encircled them. From head to foot, this giant was a treasure-house in himself. His rich red tunic was embroidered with silver and gold; rubies and emeralds gleamed on his embossed belt; his sword scabbard flashed with the fire of many amethysts; even the strappings about his gigantic thighs were thickly garnished with studs of coral.

As Harald saw the ease with which Grummoch rolled away the great boulder at the mouth of the treasure cave, his heart fell, for he and many others had tried for days to roll away that stone, without success.

Their plan had been that they were to attack when Grummoch had entered the cave, and before his slaves could reach him, for it was thought that in the restricted space of the entrance the giant would have less chance of using his great strength on the Vikings.

And then Arkil gave the cry of the sparrowhawk, and all men saw him break cover and run shouting towards the cave, Harald close on his heels. As the Vikings rose, baying like hounds, the slaves dropped their burdens and their torches and ran screaming back to their boats. Some of them dived into the lake and began to swim for the other side, made afraid by the terrible appearance of the attackers.

Harald entered the cave five paces after Arkil, but even so was too late to save his friend. Grummoch was holding Arkil's body as though it had been a child's doll made from rags, swinging it like a bundle of straw, as he turned to face the onrush of Vikings. And all saw, in the torchlight, that Arkil's brave head was loose on his neck. They had no further need to speculate on his fate.

As Harald ran whooping at the giant, Grummoch flung Arkil's body at him, sweeping the boy aside. But as Harald fell, he saw Haro Once-only, his sword between his teeth as he tore off his shirt, racing at the giant. There was a great roar, and then Harald got to his feet once more to see the Vikings swarming round their gigantic opponent like hounds about a stag.

How long that grim battle went on, no one will ever know, but to all men who survived the affair, it seemed like a year rather than an hour.

Men flew hither and thither, once Grummoch could get a grip on them, and then lay gasping and coughing out their life on the floor of that terrible cavern. But at last sheer weight of numbers bore the giant down, and Harald came suddenly behind him and struck him with all his force at the base of the neck with the flat of his sword.

Grummoch gave a loud groan and sank down, dragging six men with him. Goff Goffling, who fell beneath the giant in that tumble, gave a high shout and then lay still for ever.

In his berserker fury that Grummoch should have killed Arkil, Haro Once-only, whose right arm dangled limply by his side, would have run his sword through the giant with his left hand; but Harald stopped him, saying that they might use him as a beast of burden, if he was not wounded too badly.

The irony of this pleased the Vikings, and they set to, to bind the giant with all the leg-strappings and ropes they could find.

And when the count of the dead was made, they found that they had bought their victory dearly, for of the sixteen Northmen who had waited outside the cavern that night, only nine would live to share the treasure. Among the dead were Arkil, Goff Goffling, Sven Hawknose and Kran the Lark. Their comrades wept that such fine warriors should be sent packing to Valhalla so hurriedly, and without their treasure.

But when they carried the torches to the far end of the cavern and saw what they had gained by their battle, even

those Vikings who had loved the dead men best were forced to agree that such a price was not excessive for the riches that were now theirs.

Piled high against the far wall were sacks of Frankish and English gold; goblets and trenchers of rich Miklagard ware; coronets and sceptres such as would have rejoiced the heart of a score of Caesars; and swords and scabbards of such richness that the Vikings almost wept to see their flashing beauty.

Harald stood gazing, amazed, at the show before his eyes, when suddenly Grummoch began to groan and tried to sit up. Four of the Vikings flung him back and sat on him to keep him down. He glared up at them and rolled his eyes horribly.

But at last he felt able to speak and then he said, 'It comes to every man that one day his dearest treasures shall be taken from him. I have worked hard for mine, but the will of the gods is stronger than my own arms. I do not complain. He who is strongest shall deserve the most. I am glad that I was beaten by real warriors, and not by the minions of that lapdog MacMiorog; moreover, if the truth be told, I am glad that I put an end to so many before you others got me down. I can say no more.'

Then Harald replied, 'Grummoch, you speak like a true man and a great warrior. Will you come with us as a slave, or shall we put a sword into you now and have done with you? It is your right to choose.'

And then giant Grummoch said, 'It was foretold in my runes when I was a little lad that I should one day become a slave to men of three colours – golden, black, and red. You, I see, my boy, have golden hair, so that is the first part of my rune come to pass. I do not complain. Now let me rise.'

But the wily Vikings would have none of that. Radbard Crookleg, who was skilled in blacksmithery, got out a pair of gyves which he had forged the day before in Dun-an-oir, and with the help of three others beat them on to the ankles of Grummoch, who groaned loudly all the while, saying that he would do them no harm if they let him get up freely.

And when at last the job was done, they cut his bonds and he rubbed his great arm muscles and grinned like anyone else. He was in a way sorry, he said, to have killed Arkil, for he had always had a soft spot for the Danish prince, although he had known all along that he must one day kill him.

The Vikings were sitting about in the cave, sharing their dried meat with Grummoch, when suddenly the entrance was lit up with the flames from many torches. King MacMiorog stood there, surrounded by his guards, smiling evilly as he gazed at Grummoch.

Harald said, 'Well, King, we have captured your giant, and now we shall go on our way with his treasure as we arranged in your hall.'

But MacMiorog said, 'Yes, you will go on your way, but without his treasure. For that I regard as being mine, after all the suffering I have endured from this giant these many years.'

Then he nodded to his guards and two of them stepped forward, their swords drawn, to put an end to Grummoch. But Harald and his men rose and stood before the giant, to protect him.

'Step closer at your peril,' shouted Radbard, his smith's hammer still in his hand. 'This giant is ours, to do with as we please now, for he is our slave, and his treasure is ours likewise.'

Then MacMiorog gave a shout of anger and called on his men to rush in and finish the Vikings; but such was their fierce appearance in the torchlight, with the blood still on them, and their faces twisted in anger at the betrayal, that the King's men thought twice about it, and would not do as MacMiorog said.

So, followed by the taunts of the Vikings, and the highpitched laughter of the captive giant, the King and his men made their way back across the lake.

And when they had gone, Grummoch said, 'From now on he is your bitter enemy. He will poison you if you eat the food he offers. He will do all he can to kill you while you are in his land. Take my advice, and let us all go round to the back of the city without delay, for there are my own ox-wagons and oxen. We might well use them to get to wherever we are going, and for my own part, I should be glad of a change of scenery for this flat green plain is bad for my temper and my rheumatism.'

And so it was that the Vikings loaded the treasure on to the rafts and at last on to the ox-wagons and set out towards the coast once more, even before the sun rose.

Their dead comrades they left in the cavern, lying side by side, each man holding his weapon so that he should be able to protect himself and his dead comrades in the long journey that must be made through the darkness to the land of everlasting light.

Grummoch agreed to roll the boulder back across the mouth of the cave, so that no man should ever disturb them again.

6. The Bargainers

ON THE journey back to Murdea, it was agreed that Grummoch should be allowed to travel on one of the wagons, since his heavy leg-gyves made walking extremely painful to him. In return for this kindness, the giant went out of his way to make himself as friendly as possible to the Vikings, sometimes playing to them on a little bone flute which he always carried, and on which he was a marvellously clever performer, and sometimes by telling them stories to while away the time. Usually, these tales were told in a high voice, punctuated by many interruptions when Grummoch stopped to laugh at one of his own jokes for he was an inveterate leg-puller, and for a giant had an amusing sense of humour.

Harald came to like him in the three days during which the wagon train wound its way towards the coast, and he would often sit alongside the giant, listening to his yarns.

He learned that Grummoch came from a poor farming family in Caledonia, one of many children, all the rest of them being of a normal size. When Grummoch was still small – only twice as big as he should have been – he had beaten many boys three times his age in fair fighting, but had always been thrashed when he got home for bullying his fellows. Also, he was in constant trouble for being greedy, when in fact he had eaten only half as much as he needed for that big body of his. He told Harald that from the start his mother hated him, for even as a baby he exhausted her, so that she could not carry him about or nurse him. Later, as he grew older, the other young lads of the steading refused to let him share their sports of wrestling or javelin-throwing because he always won; while the girls ran screaming from him if he asked them to dance in the harvest festivities.

The only thing his village would let him do was to work; and every farmer vied for his services when there was any manure to load, trees to cut down, grain to draw, ditches to dig. Yet though he did three times as much as a normal man, he was always cheated when it came to being paid, for it was commonly held in Grummoch's steading that the gods had given him a big body but a small brain.

Grummoch stood this treatment for some years, he told Harald, and then one day he decided he would not tolerate it any longer; so he began by filling the village pond with boulders which no men could ever drag out from the mud again; then he rolled two great hay-wains down a hill, breaking down twenty yards of dry stone walling in the process; after which he went into the church and pulled on the bell-ropes so hard that the top of the tower came down through the roof and shattered the font.

After that, he had to go on his travels, for all men's hands were turned against him. Even his mother shouted out down the road after him that she hoped never to see his evil face again.

'But,' said Grummoch almost tearfully as he told Harald of this, 'it comes on me more and more often that the one thing I would most love would be to see my dear mother again, before it is too late.'

Bit by bit, the Vikings got the rest of his story; how he walked to the coast, stole a curragh and sailed it single-handed to Ireland; how he begged his bread there, playing on his flute and performing deeds of strength; how one day he overcame a great champion at a fair in the Blue Mountains; and how at last he took service with King MacMiorog, and seeing that monarch's great luxury, decided that he too would amass such a fortune as would one day buy him a royal bride.

He ended his story by saying, 'And that was just what I had managed. It was her dowry that I was bringing home the night you attacked me. But for you, I might now be the son-in-law of the High King himself. Alas, alas!'

But Grummoch was by nature a light-hearted creature, and soon he was fluting again, as merrily as ever. Indeed, his company was so diverting that before the Vikings reached Murdea again, their sorrow for the loss of Arkil and their comrades had much abated. For that was the way of life, they agreed; one met a man, and then lost him – all as Odin wished. It was best to accept what the gods decided, without complaining, for whether one wept or not, it made no difference. As for Grummoch, he had soon accepted the fact that his treasure was lost to him, but Harald told him that if he would come back with them to the village by the fjord, he would arrange it that old Thorn should accept him as a villager and should pay him a share equal to that which every other man would get; at which Grummoch seemed genuinely pleased.

Two miles out of Murdea, the wagon train came upon a party of Danes, who were riding on stolen horses inland. They were greatly interested in the giant and in the contents of the wagons, and when Harald told them the story, their greedy dark eyes lit up so brightly that had they not been put off by the looks of the wagon-party they would have attacked there and then.

Their leader, a gaunt-faced man called Riggall, said that he was anxious to profit even if only a little by the meeting, and suggested that since they would need a ship to carry their treasure home, he would sell them his ship, which lay in the harbour at Murdea, for one sack of treasure.

But Harald said, 'We too have a ship lying in the harbour at Murdea. It is a blackened hulk and lies at the bottom, among the eels. No doubt your ship lies alongside it, if we know anything of the people of that town!'

From the look on the Dane's face, the others could see that Harald's words had hit their target.

But the Dane was not to be beaten, 'Look you, bargainer,' he said, 'in three days, my own son-in-law, Borg, will pull into Murdea with a small ship, just such as could be managed by a small crew, as you yourselves are. Give him my ring, and tell him to sell you his boat fairly. Say that if he does not, I will give him a taste of my belt when I see him again.'

Harald took the ring and thanked him. The Dane held his hand for a moment and said, 'Is this not worth something, dear friend?' And he kept holding Harald's own hand so tightly that at last the boy signed to Grummoch, who flung the man a hunting-knife set with amber, and with a hilt carved in the shape of a prancing horse. This pleased the Dane so much that he shouted after them, 'And tell my son-in-law, Borg, that he must deal kindly with you or I will find my daughter another husband.'

So it was that they came to Murdea once more, to be met by a shower of arrows fired from the very church tower which they had spared on their way inland.

This time Radbard Crookleg was hurt in the neck. The shaft entered at one side and came out at the other. This angered his comrades so much that before Harald could stop them, they had barricaded the doors of the place, and, setting faggots of wood before it, had set light to it.

Grummoch consoled Harald on the way down to the harbour by saying that he had seen with his own eyes the priest and five men climb out of a little window at the back; so they at least would be safe.

'Why did you not tell the men, so that they could have driven them back into the flames?' asked Harald, wondering.

Grummoch shrugged his shoulders and took out his little flute. 'I am a Christian myself, Harald,' he said. 'Though I have always been rather a poor one, I fear.'

Then he began to play a restless little tune, and Harald could get no more out of him.

They camped at the harbour side, and suffered no more hurt from the men of Murdea, who were impressed by their fierce faces and fine weapons. On the third day, the Danish ship sailed in, and after Harald had given the Dane's message to Borg, the bargain was made, and the newcomers went on inland with half a sack of treasure and a full team of oxen and wagons.

Then, by common accord, Harald Sigurdson was named the master of their new ship, which they joined in calling *Arkil the Prince*, after their dead leader.

Harald said, 'By Odin, I swear to deal fairly with you all, and as you deal fairly with me, so may we all prosper. Has any man a word to say to that?'

As he waited for their answer, the gulls swirled over the heads of the men in the bobbing longship, and the smoke from the hovels at the waterside swept across the oily swell.

All men were silent, save only Grummoch, who stretched and scratched himself noisily. 'Yes, shipmaster,' he said, with a little smile 'I have a word to say.'

They looked at him in surprise.

'Say on, Grummoch, then,' said Harald.

And giant Grummoch yawned and said, 'My word is this: let us set sail without any more talk! For I am anxious to see this village of yours!'

Haro Once-only raised himself from his pallet of straw on the deck and said grimly, 'That is well said, little giant; for if you had spoken a word against Harald, Radbard and I would have fed you to the seagulls.'

'Yes, in little pieces,' said Radbard in the high whistling voice that was his since his arrow-wound.

Then they all laughed and Grummoch said, 'Dear little ones, you had better think about yourselves, for if you do not get better soon, it is you who will go overboard to feed the white chickens!'

Yet, in spite of the laughter and taunting, Radbard and Haro were well cared for by the sea-rovers, for they were brave comrades, and the first lesson a Viking learned was to stand by his shipmates through thick and thin.

Haro's arm had been broken in the cavern-fight, but was now set in splints and gave him little discomfort provided that he did not roll on to it in the night. When that happened, the other Vikings would clap their hands over their ears, in pretended horror at the things he would find to say.

As for Radbard, his wound had been less dangerous than had at first appeared, for the arrow had passed through the muscle of the neck and not through his gullet. All the same, the wound gave him so much pain while it was healing that he could only speak softly and on a high note, like a little girl – which went comically with his great hairy beard and his fierce face.

So it was, when they had stored their food and water under the afterdeck of the ship, and had packed the treasure down snugly below the maindeck, wrapping it round with sacking and sheepskins, that they prepared to set forth. The great weight of the gold they carried caused them to ride low in the water, and they needed no further ballast.

'May Odin send us a safe crossing, without a storm,' said Olaf Redeye, cousin to Haro, 'for this is ballast which I would die for rather than fling overboard!'

Giant Grummoch said pleasantly, 'You are very concerned about my treasure, little Northman! What about me, the founder of the hoard, how do you think I feel about losing it to you?'

Olaf said, 'We have an old saying: "A clean shirt to a pig; gold to a Pict." Neither of them understands the worth of such things, you see, Grummoch.'

Grummoch said, 'I cannot reach you, little Olaf, for these gyves stop my free movement; but if you will come here to me, I will take you by the hand and show you what a friend I can be to you.'

He held out his massive hand, invitingly, but Olaf shook his head with a sly smile.

'Nay, Grummoch,' he said, 'but I need this hand for rowing, I thank you! Perhaps we will shake hands when we land in my country, for then my six brothers will be there to see that you let go when I yell!'

Grummoch nodded, reflectively, and said sadly, 'That is the trouble, no one will ever be my hand-friend. I once shook hands with a German bear, but he howled so loudly, I could not make myself heard when I asked him what was the matter.'

By this time Harald Sigurdson was at the steerboard, and called to them to take their places at the benches with the oars, for, he said, if they did not get started soon, they would have the good men of Murdea aboard to burn them off the face of the seas.

And certainly there was a nasty-looking crowd already assembled at the dockside, muttering and pointing angrily at the Vikings. But Grummoch merely yawned again and called out to them, 'Would any of you brave souls like a little trip round the harbour before we start on our voyage?

We will not charge you anything, and will set you safely ashore again when you have had enough!'

The men at the harbour's edge began to shout abuse at the Vikings, so Grummoch called again, this time to the one who seemed to be their leader, 'You, good sir, with the bald head and the big nose, what about you? You look to be a rare sea-rover, will you not come with us?'

But he got no polite reply, and so, with stones and refuse whistling round their ears, the Vikings set forth from Murdea, ten men in a little ship full of treasure, to make the long and tedious passage round the south coast of England, and up past the land of the Franks.

They put in for food once more at the Isle of Wight, and were not dissatisfied with the treatment they received there, for some of the islanders spoke a dialect similar to their own, having themselves come from Jutland many generations before.

So all went well for the first three days, but, early on the fourth, something happened which was to change the whole course of their lives.

7. The Small Dark Men

IT WAS a grey grim dawning, with bursts of rain scudding down from the north and the whipped ocean rolling strongly against the prow of the *Arkil*. The high sail was useless since the change of wind, and Harald and Grummoch pulled it down together, being buffeted mercilessly as they clung to the writhing canvas with frozen hands.

The other sea-rovers lay wrapped in their sheepskin cloaks, under the gunwales, sleeping as best they could, for their hands were already blistered with the rowing they had done the day before.

But Grummoch said, 'We shall have to waken them, shipmaster, for this is a wind that must be fought with more than snores!'

Harald woke Olaf only and asked him if he thought they might put ashore in the land of the Franks, at some quiet village, for example; but he shook his head and said grimly, 'Frank and Northman, fire and water! I had as soon jump overboard now – they killed my father and three of my cousins last summer, trying to teach them to be Christians!'

So there was nothing for it but to wake the sleepers and set them rowing against the tide. Both Harald and Grummoch took turns at the oars, for with Radbard and Haro sick, they were short-handed.

But by midday, the weather grew worse, and soon a great gale began to sweep out of the north, rendering the oarsmen as weak as kittens, drenching them through and filling their hearts with fear.

Haro called Harald over to him and said gloomily, 'It comes over me that we shall never get this treasure back to the fjord, shipmaster. It weighs the ship down, and soon we shall be foundering if these waves do not slacken. Besides, the boat is so heavy now that we need a crew of giants to move her through such a swell.'

Harald nodded, thoughtfully, and said, 'Let us have courage for a little while longer, Haro, and then, if we can do nothing better, we will lighten the load a little.'

He went back to his oar, but did not say anything about this conversation to the others, for they were all anxious, to a man, to get this great hoard back to their village and live lives of comfort evermore.

By early evening time, their next misfortune happened. Radbard went aft to broach a keg of water and came running back to say that it was all brackish and undrinkable. The men of the Isle of Wight had tricked them, it seemed, selling bad water for good gold, despite the similarity of the language they spoke.

Harald and Grummoch went aft to taste the water, and agreed that it would poison a man.

It was then that the gale caught them and drove them southwards like a leaf falling from a high oak tree, powerless, swirling hither and thither, out of control. Harald shrieked for the men to draw in their oars, but his words came too late; three oars were swept away, out of the weakened hands of the rowers.

So, as night came on, the *Arkil* went her own way, far off the course Harald had set, until at last Radbard cried out that if the storm did not die away soon, they would eat their next meal in Africa.

He was not far wrong. The storm grew from fury to fury, throughout the night, and all through the next day, lashing the little longship as though it was a hated thing, almost turning it turtle a hundred times, snapping off the mast, breaking in the gunwales on one side, and straining the stout oak strakes to the utmost of their strength.

Now the battered Vikings had no heart left for anything but to huddle close to each other, in whatever shelter they could find, which was little enough. Even the stoutest stomached of them had been sick, and not a man but was frozen until he could hardly speak.

Then, as the utterly chill dawn of the third day struck across their ravaged deck, the wind fell and the seas rolled back to their accustomed places. And far on the steerboard bow, Harald at last sighted a thin grey shape low on the horizon.

'Yes, that is land,' said Grummoch, 'though who should know which land it is, we have been so buffeted! And I for one do not care which land it is, for if we can only reach it, I will never set foot on a ship's deck again.'

And others, even the hardiest of the Vikings, said the same thing.

Then the problem was taken out of their hands, for on the larboard beam and bow suddenly appeared three ships, long and low in the water, gliding towards them like sea snakes, catching the morning wind in their triangular red sails.

Harald rubbed his eyes and said, 'I have never seen such ships before; they are built for speed and even if we had our sail and our oars, we could not escape them.'

Radbard, who stood with him at the gunwales said in his high voice, 'It is not the ships which worry me, it is their crews. Look, they are little dark men, not sea-rovers at all.'

Grummoch shaded his eyes and there was fear in his voice as he spoke. 'We can expect no mercy from them, my friends,' he said. 'I know their like. For the love of god, strike off these gyves so that I can at least defend myself when they draw alongside.'

Then, to the horror of all the Vikings, Harald said, 'We have no hammer, Grummoch. It went overboard in the night and I could not save it.'

At this, Grummoch gave a great cry and jumped overboard. Radbard tried to stop him, putting out his hand, but it would have been as easy to hold back an oak, falling in a high wind.

'He will drown, with those leg-gyves on,' groaned Radbard. 'His ghost will never let me rest for what I did to him.'

But Haro said, 'You should be worrying about your own ghost, my friend, not Grummoch's, for the men who are coming to board us do not carry bunches of flowers in their hands!'

Now Grummoch had disappeared among the breakers, and the Vikings turned, to sell their lives as dearly as their failing strength would let them, each armed with a weapon from the store they had taken from the cave.

And as the sharp-prowed ships cut in at them from all directions, their gunwales lined with dark-faced men, Radbard shouted suddenly, 'They may take our heads, but they shall not take our gold!'

Then, before anyone could stop him, he had torn back the plank that led beneath the deck, and all men saw him give a great heave at the oak bung in the ship's bottom.

The green sea rushed in, ice-cold and hungry, about the waists of the Vikings in a flash.

'Radbard, you fool!' shouted Harald, as he saw the man flung down beneath the deck planks by the onrush of water.

Then they were in the sea, with the *Arkil* sucking at them as she sank, and the three cruel-looking ships above them, treading them down into the waters it seemed, and the little dark men grinning above them, their white teeth gleaming in the early morning sunlight.

8. Slave Market

FOR YEARS afterwards, the events which followed came to Harald like a strange dream; first someone leaning down and trying to pull him up into the boat, then the sensation of falling again, clutching out and missing his hold, and then the green swirl of waters above him while the harsh keel of the boat rolled over him, forcing him down and down, until he thought that his lungs would burst. Then, at last, coming back from a dark and rushing nightmare to find himself lying on a white-scrubbed deck in the sunshine, between two rows of black-legged rowers and the taut red sail above him, bellying in a following wind . . . And, best of all, Radbard and Haro lying beside him.

It was some time before Harald discovered that his legs were bound – and that none of the rest of his crew besides Radbard and Haro had been picked up. When he knew that, his sunlit mood turned to one of black despair.

Radbard, who had miraculously shot up to the surface when the *Arkil* sank, was grim and tongue-tied; Haro sat nursing his aching arm, too deep in despair to speak, even to his dear friends.

Shortly after Harald's senses had returned to him, a tall man dressed in a long white robe and wearing a red turban came down between the sweating oarsmen and kneeled beside him. Harald noted that his long brown fingers were covered with gold rings and that his curved sword had an exquisite hilt of chiselled steel, set with amethysts.

The man smiled at him, showing his perfectly white teeth, and began to speak to him in a soft and musical voice. But his words were strange and Harald could not understand him. The man made several attempts to make his meaning clear, but Harald shook his head.

At last the man shrugged his shoulders and began to make signs. He pointed to the hide bonds which fastened Harald's ankles, then he made the motion of counting out money from one hand to the other. Harald understood. 'You want us to pay you to let us free?' he asked.

But the other did not understand and smiled, nodding his head.

Then, with a cold shudder, Harald said, 'Are we slaves?'

The man heard the one word, and nodded happily, 'Slaves,' he said, recognizing that single word, 'Slaves, you slaves!'

Radbard heard this and turned away with a groan. Haro put up his good hand to his eyes for they had filled with tears.

Harald clenched his teeth and said to the man, 'If I had a sword I would give you the payment you deserve.'

But the man still smiled and shook his head, not understanding. Then, seeing that he would get no further with these three rough bears of the north, he shrugged his shoulders as though he had done all he could and went back to the helm, swinging the long narrow ship towards the shore, which rapidly grew nearer and nearer, until Harald could actually distinguish the shapes of gaily clothed men and women moving in the sunshine before the white houses.

Soon after that they were running in alongside a low jetty, and then that same man with the red turban came to them and indicated with his long white staff that they were to disembark. But this time he did not smile, and when Radbard rose slowly, he felt the weight of that white stick, suddenly and viciously. Harald stopped, aghast, and then, with a slow cold anger, turned and struck the man a blow with his clenched fist between the eyes.

'No man shall treat my crew like that while I am here to prevent it,' said Harald, glaring round him. But Radbard shook his head gravely. 'That was a daring thing to do, Harald,' he said. 'Now look what the results may be.'

The tall man sprawled on the sun-dried planking of the jetty, holding his head and speaking to his followers in a vicious tone of voice. These followers ran immediately to do his bidding, and soon came back from a shed with a smouldering brazier.

Haro said listlessly, 'It would seem to be their custom to brand rebellious slaves. I had not thought to be branded when I set out from Murdea with my share of the treasure glittering in my dreams. Alas, but a man's life is quite unpredictable!'

Radbard said, 'I have a dragon tattooed in the middle of my chest. I hope these fellows do not mar the design with their clumsy botching. What do you say if we offer to brand each other, to see that the job is done properly?'

Then they were dragged forward, towards the brazier. A thick-armed man bent over it, blowing the coals to white heat with a little sheepskin bellows. They saw that an iron lay in the fire, getting hotter and hotter. A small crowd of men and women had gathered now, anxious not to miss any entertainment that might be offered by the slaves, and the man in the red turban, who had now regained his former air of authority after his blow on the head, was talking excitedly to the crowd, explaining some point or other, which necessitated his waving his hands violently up and down.

Harald said, 'I think he is telling them that we deserve the punishment. He wishes them to think him a just man, doubtless.'

Radbard said, 'It comes to me, from the look of these folk and the shape of their houses, that we must be in that part of Spain where the Moors have come to live. And if that is so, then we must expect to find them a very just people, for their Caliphs make strict laws, causing them to be respected in this part of the world. We can look for justice, no doubt.'

Haro grinned and pushed away a man who had gripped him too strongly by the shoulder of his injured arm. 'Yes, but what if we do not care for their justice, friend?'

Harald said, 'We are Northmen, not Moors, Radbard. Our justice is what I would go by, not theirs. Besides, he deserved the blow I gave him, according to any man's justice, for he struck you when you were unable to move any faster.'

Radbard smiled and said, 'Very well, you are the shipmaster and I obey your orders. What shall we do?'

Harald said, 'We must make it unpleasant for them if they try to harm us. That is as far as I can think, with these three ruffians hanging on to my arms.'

Suddenly a great hush fell on the chattering crowd, and then the man in the red turban gave a signal to the guards who held Harald. They dragged him towards the brazier and then waited. The man in the red turban spoke harshly to the one who bent over the flames, and as he straightened, the hot iron in his hand, Harald gave a great cry, 'Up the North!'

He heard his cry echoed by Haro and Radbard, behind him, and then he lunged forward with all his strength, snapping the hide thong which held his ankles. He felt the thing go, and with his new freedom he kicked out, catching the brazier with the side of his foot and scattering the coals among the crowd. He heard men and women cry in sudden alarm, and then he had shaken himself free, and was punching out to left and right. He had time to see that Haro and Radbard were doing the same, and then, overpowered by sheer weight of numbers, Harald sank down to the ground, half-suffocated by the Moorish sailors who clutched him wherever they could get a hold.

For a moment, he saw nothing but legs and feet, and was momentarily afraid that they might trample him to death. Then he heard a strong voice cutting through all the hubbub, and suddenly he found himself free again, and looking up at a short, squat man who wore a round helmet and an iron breastplate, and whose skin was very much lighter than that of the pirates who had captured him. This man's high boots were of the old Roman pattern, as was his short purple cloak and the broad sword which swung in a moroccan leather scabbard at his right side. He seemed to be a man of power, from the way in which he addressed the pirate captain in the red turban.

Harald could not understand his speech, for he spoke the Arabic of the Moors; yet even Harald could recognize that his manner of saying the words was not that of the sea-rovers who had bound him and brought him to this place.

Suddenly, when all was still again, the man touched Harald in the side with the toe of his fine riding-boot and said, 'Well, and is this the sort of behaviour one would expect from a slave?'

Harald stared at him in wonder for he spoke the tongue of the north – though not like a Northman, but like one who had learned the words in his travels there.

Harald stared him in the eye and said, 'I am Harald Sigurdson, a shipmaster. These men have attacked my ship, *Arkil*, and have caused us to scuttle her off this coast. Now they treat us like beasts.'

The man nodded and said, 'You are their rightful prize, my good fellow; they are slave-runners and do not go out to sea for the fun of it. They plan to sell you in the slave market, at a good price, for you are all young men and have plenty of work left in you, if a man only knows how to fetch it out of you!'

The man in the red turban now came forward and began to argue with the other, who answered him in Arabic. At length the newcomer turned and said to Harald, 'This captain says he wishes to punish you all for your rebellious behaviour, to leave such a mark on you as will warn other good men that you are savage beasts and must be watched.'

Harald answered, 'Then he is a fool, for we only did what any warrior would do, no more. We are not savage beasts, but good Northmen, whose only wish is to go about our own business without interference from any man.'

The man in the helmet tugged at his dark beard and smiled a little grimly. 'I am a Frank,' he said, 'and so I have some knowledge of you good Northmen, and of the business you like to go about!'

Radbard broke in, saying, 'What, you a Frank, and you side with these heathen?'

The man said, 'I was captured in battle, my friend, and so became a slave, as you are. But my master, Abu Mazur, is an enlightened man; he used me sensibly, making me his emissary up and down the land, for this and that. I am contented. I have known worse masters, and Christian ones at that.' He paused for a moment and then smiled and said, 'You should have no cares about my fate, for after all you too are heathen, my friends!'

Harald said, 'Look you, master Frank, we are in a sad plight. Let us have done with talk of heathen and such like. Will you help us?'

The other smiled and nodded. 'I shall, my friend,' he said. 'For I shall buy the three of you now, if I can get you at a reasonable price, and if you will promise me that you will not get up to your berserk tricks as soon as you leave this place.'

Harald answered, 'I do not like being a slave, but you seem a fair-minded man for a Frank, and I will promise that we will not try to break your neck, or even to run away for the time being. Is that enough?'

The man nodded and added, 'If you break your word, it will go uncomfortably with you, one way and another. I say no more; Abu Mazur is a good master but a cruel enemy. That is his rule of life.'

Then he left the Vikings and began to bargain with the man in the red turban.

And so it was that soon they were dragged to their feet and had their wrists tied tightly with thin hide thongs. Then they were pushed towards the man in the helmet, who mounted his black mule and turning said, 'Follow me without causing any disturbance. My wagon train waits at the outskirts of this town. We have a long journey to make.'

They did as they were told. On reaching the busier part of the town, they came upon a broad square, set round with many-coloured awnings.

'Is this a market?' asked Radbard, who thought they might buy food.

'Yes,' answered the Frank, smiling down on them from his saddle. 'Look at the merchandise they sell here and be thankful.'

The wondering Vikings did as they were told and stared at the bright stalls. Under every awning sat a slave-master, with his wares: men and women and children of all races, it seemed, and all tongues. There were bright-haired children from England, standing sullenly and glowering at these foreigners who inspected them as though they had

been pigs at a fair; red-haired Caledonians, who pulled away and bared their teeth whenever a prospective buyer went towards them; great laughing Africans, who went out of their way to attract a kind-faced purchaser; small slant-eyed Tartars, who squatted nonchalantly, as though they were at home, and did not seem to care what happened to them as long as they were alive; restless lithe Armenians, who held out their delicate hands to passers-by, asking to be bought and fed.

Radbard said that he thought he saw three Northmen, who had once sailed with him beyond Orkney, but the Frank said that he did not mean to buy any more Northmen that day. Three were enough, he said, and if they protested, he would sell them back into this market and have done with it.

They did not protest, but walked on with him to the outskirts of the town. And there, drawn up beside a wayside inn, were the four wagons, with their patient oxen already in the harness, waiting to go. Harald noted grimly that a dozen riders, with lances, accompanied the wagon-train, so that all thoughts of an escape while on the journey faded from his mind.

Then they were told to get into the first wagon, which they did without further protest. In it were three Bulgar boys, who wept incessantly. The Vikings tried to console them, but found that it was impossible to do so; the Bulgars seemed to enjoy their grief more than their consolation. So, since the wagon was thickly laid with straw, and since they were still fatigued from their long sea journey, the Vikings gave up trying to help their fellow-slaves, and curled up, like dogs, and fell asleep.

When they awakened, it was almost evening time and the red sun struck sadly over the harsh countryside, showing them the nature of the land they had come to – a great, undulating plain, with sharply serrated hills on the skyline; a place of small, dried-up bushes and great fissures in the reddish earth. A place where the sun shone down unmercifully in the day, and the frosts broke up the soil cruelly in the night.

The Frank brought them a dish of broken meat and a pannikin of harsh red wine each. Then they went back to sleep, lulled by the rocking of the wagon.

It was to be a long journey, down to the truly Muslim south, where the Moors had settled in their many thousands, bringing their language and their customs from the east, setting up their bulwark of Islam in the western world.

And it was to this strange world that the three exhausted Viking sea-rovers were now travelling, slowly, inevitably and sadly; three free men who were now slaves; three men who had recently been as rich as Caesars and were now poorer than the poorest goosegirl along the far northern fjords.

Harald once said this to Haro, on the journey; but Haro only turned over in the straw to find a more comfortable spot and muttered thickly, 'The black beetle climbs up the table leg, but there is a hand waiting to crush him when he reaches the top.'

PART TWO

9. The House at Jebel Tarik

AUTUMN passed, and then slow-footed winter. Now, with the coming of spring and the reopening of trade in the Mediterranean, the great white house of Abu Mazur was a hive of activity, for the Master himself was coming down from his winter residence to be near his galleys and his ledgers, at Jebel Tarik.

The three Vikings stood on the high terrace that looked down on to the busy harbour. They saw the red flowers in their gilded urns, hanging heavily over the marble balustrade, teased by the light spring breezes; they saw the many broad white steps that led down and down and down, until they were as small as steps in a dream, to the broad and crowded wharf, where Abu Mazur's heavily-laden galleys bobbed lazily on the blue tide, waiting the signal that would send them to far Cyprus, or Crete, or even to Byzantium.

Harald stood gazing at the ships, tugging impatiently at his long golden plaits; in his mind's eye he saw himself, with his companions, in the prow of such a ship, cleaving through the blue waters to freedom, to adventure, to far Miklagard itself . . .

Haro came up to him and touched his arm. 'Do not brood, shipmaster,' he said gently. 'The captive wolf wears out his heart walking round his cage; you are a man, not a wolf; do not wear out your heart, Harald.'

Harald turned away from his friend with a great sigh. Haro shrugged his shoulders and began to flick pebbles over the edge of the balustrade, on to the broad white steps. They bounded down and down, until they were impossible to see for their smallness in the distance. Sometimes the cluster of guards who always stood halfway up the steps glared back as the stones passed by them, looking up at the Vikings with annoyance showing on their dark fierce faces. Once a pebble struck one of these men, a great fellow wearing a gilded helmet with a tall yellow plume. He swung round and shouted at Haro, shaking his long curved sword at him. But Haro only smiled sadly and then flicked another pebble. He knew that the soldiers were not permitted to come through the upper gateway and on to the terrace. He knew also that house slaves were considered as men of some importance and must not be beaten by mere soldiers. The Frankish Captain, Clothair, had told him as much.

Clothair had been very helpful, in his rough way; he had seen that the three Vikings were given easy tasks, indoors, and had even sent a teacher to them, to give them at least a little insight into the Arabic tongue. This had helped to keep their minds occupied during the long winter days and nights.

Now at last they were to see Abu Mazur, the Great One, the richest merchant of Jebel Tarik, their master.

Radbard said, 'I have been dreaming of my house by the fjord these last few nights, Harald. My mother will be missing me now that the sowing-time has come again. Since my father died, I alone have put the barley seeds in the ground, and my mother will expect me to do it this year too. She will not let my cousins do it; she says the seed would never grow if such young ruffians laid their hands on it.'

Harald said sadly, 'You will not be there to do it this year, Radbard.'

Radbard thought for a moment and then said, 'I have been thinking, Harald, that if we could get past the guards, we might hide in one of those great ships and at last sail away from here.'

Haro shook his head and said grimly, 'Radbard, my friend, no men, not even men like us, could pass those guards down there; and even if they could, there are more guards at the bottom step, and yet more guards on the wharf. There must always be at least a score of guards between us and the wharf; a man would need the hammer of Thor to make his way to the ships.'

Radbard said, 'Perhaps, perhaps, Haro; then might we not go out the other way, through the house?'

Harald smiled ruefully and said, 'That is worse; we do not know our way. There are many courtyards, and passages, and high walls. One room leads into another and then another, and that into a courtyard, and that into more rooms, until a man might go mad, trying to find his way outside. I was lost there once, myself, when the slave-master sent me with a message to one of the cooks. Luckily, Clothair found me, and brought me back to my sleeping-place, or I would have beaten my head on the wall with hopelessness.'

Haro nodded his agreement. 'Yes,' he said, 'I have seen the places you speak of, and there are guards everywhere, in niches, in towers, on the walls, in the courtyards; everywhere. It is not possible.'

Radbard turned away from them without saying any more.

Haro came up to Harald and whispered, 'I do not like the way friend Radbard is looking, shipmaster. He means to run away, of that I am sure. And if he does that, then he is as good as a dead man.'

Harald nodded. 'Yes,' he replied. 'That thought was in my own mind about him. But what can we do?'

Haro answered with a grim little smile, 'Once, I would not have thought twice about the problem; I should have gone with him, against all the odds in Islam, against all the Moors in creation. But now, with an arm that will not always do what I bid it do, and a heart that has been softened by the good food and drink of this place, I hesitate. Yes, I too wish to see the north again, but not from above, as a spirit in the air! When I go to the fjord once more, I wish to greet my friends as a man, like them!'

They would have gone on discussing this for a long while, for the Northmen loved argument, but just then the silver trumpet blew within the house, and then there was a great shouting and a scurrying of feet. The slave-masters were runing out on to the platform where the three friends were, urging the many slaves of the house to hurry and assemble there in neat rows, for the Master, Abu Mazur himself, was already at the main gate, and coming to inspect his new stock as the first thing he did on his arrival from his winter residence.

The Vikings kept together, standing with the others in the second row – Romans, Turks, Franks, Africans – all whispering in their excitement, in their many tongues, for this was a great occasion.

Harald saw that Clothair was waiting by the inner door, his helmet carrying a new red plume, his breastplate burnished until it sent off blinding rays in the morning sunlight. Then the trumpet blew again, but more softly this time, and Clothair suddenly fell to his knees beside the door, bowing his head until the red plume almost touched the white marble flagstones of the terrace. Abu Mazur appeared.

He was an old man, but still very upright and dignified in his bearing. His high turban, surmounted by a silver cross set within a crescent moon, made him look even taller than he was; as did his long, sky-blue robe, which reached down in straight folds to his feet. His thin, bejewelled hand rested on the silver pommel of his curved scimitar. His long, noble face, its narrow chin fringed with a wisp of grey beard, was set in gently quizzical lines, which were etched deeply in the sallow skin, giving him a curiously humorous look. He was most obviously a man of great wealth and power, yet a man of simple but refined tastes, and a man of good humour.

He paused for an instant and spoke to Clothair, bidding him get up from his knees and explain which were the new slaves who must be inspected.

Clothair rose but did not move when his master moved. Then the Vikings saw that he was waiting for someone else to pass through the pointed doorway before he followed Abu Mazur. It was a young girl of not more than sixteen years, who walked with the lazy grace of a panther, secure in the knowledge of her father's wealth and power. A tall Nubian who stood next to Harald whispered, 'That is Marriba, the Master's only child. She will be a princess one day, perhaps a queen, who knows? He would lay down his life for her, my fellows.'

Haro sucked in his breath and said dreamily, 'I think that I would lay down mine for that lady. She is the most beautiful one it has been my fortune to set eyes on.'

Harald smiled at him and whispered, 'Wait till I tell the girls of our village by the fjord, Haro the Heartless! They will pull your plaits off in their jealousy!'

But Haro went on gazing at Marriba, sighing all the time, as though he were not a warrior but a silly little boy outside a sweetmeat booth on a fair day.

Yet Harald had to agree that Marriba was a most impressive creature; though she was young, yet her almond-shaped face had an air of dignity beyond her years. Her skin was of a light golden colour, her hair as black as the raven's wing, her eyes great and round, fringed with dark lashes, soft as the doe's eyes, yet capable of flashing with anger it seemed.

Harald said softly to Radbard, 'It comes into my mind that I would like to see a girl of the north now, my friend;

someone with long flaxen hair and sky-blue eyes; someone whose skin was like cream, not dark ivory.'

Radbard shrugged and said, 'I am only interested in the seas and the forests and the fjords; I do not worry my head over skin like dark ivory, my friend.'

Then the two great ones were almost beside them, and Clothair gave Harald a warning glance, to show him that he must keep silent until Abu Mazur had passed.

But Abu Mazur did not pass so easily. Instead, when he stood opposite Harald, he stopped and looked the young Viking up and down.

'Are these the seacocks from the north?' he asked the Frank.

Clothair bowed and nodded. Abu Mazur stood still, fingering his grey beard with long fingers, his surprisingly dark eyes fixed on Harald's. Harald stared back at him, wondering why this old man should concern himself to look so long into a slave's face.

Then Abu Mazur said, 'You are a bold young man, I can see that. Who is your father? He must be a great warrior.'

Harald stood up as straight as he could and looked above the Moor's head.

'My father was Sigurd of the three swords. He was the greatest warrior of his lord's host. He was the bravest seafarer along the fjords. Now he is gone and his only son is a slave among folk who hold to other gods.'

Abu Mazur considered him for a whole minute, never taking his dark eyes from the young man's face. Then, his voice very quiet, he said, 'And does his only son consider that he is a warrior, too?'

Harald thought that there was the slightest taunt in the words and he replied with heat, 'Give me a sword and I will meet any two of your guard here, on the steps, in return for the freedom of my two companions.'

Abu Mazur smiled and nodded his head. 'I had heard that you Northfolk were great bargainers, and it seems to be true. Well, I will take your word for it that you are what you say, for I cannot allow my slaves to fight with my guards, who are all valuable and highly-trained soldiers and needed for other things. But I will do one thing for you; I will allow you to do that work in my house which best suits you. Now what task would you prefer, son of Sigurd?'

Harald's mouth became a thin hard line. He said abruptly, 'I am no slave to work in other men's houses. I am a warrior and a sea-captain. I know nothing of maids' work.'

Abu Mazur's grave face still kept its deep lines of humour, but his dark eyes seemed to shroud at these words, and something harder seemed to come into them. He passed by Harald without saying another word. But he stopped once again before Radbard and said gently, 'What is in your mind, Northman?'

Radbard said simply, 'In my mind there is nothing but the sea and the planting of the barley seed, master.'

Abu Mazur answered just as simply, 'I cannot give you the sea, but you shall plant what seed we have.'

Then he passed on along the line and they lost sight of him as he turned to the other slaves.

But Marriba stayed behind a moment longer, looking Harald straight in the eye with her own great eyes. She smiled, ever so little, and said softly, 'You crow loudly, seacock; I wonder if you can peck as well?'

This made the other slaves laugh, and Harald was angry for an instant. Then he shrugged and looked away from her, afraid that he might say something which he would regret later.

Later that morning, as the three Vikings sat on the steps, trying to scratch runes on the marble with sharp pebbles, a little hunched man came to them, his head shrouded in a massive turban, his body clothed in a much-patched shirt. He spoke harshly, as one who addresses his inferiors. 'Come with me,' he said, 'the Master has given me command over you. I am the gardener and you are to serve me in the garden of the great courtyard.'

The vikings halted in their scribbling and then, ignoring him, went on with their scratching. The little man jumped with rage.

'Come, when I command,' he said, 'or I will see to it that you are well punished. You will get to know soon enough that I am a person of some power in this house.'

Haro was nearest to him, sprawling on the white steps and trying to draw a ship with the wind full in the sail. It was the only thing he could draw, and he always took great pains over getting every strake drawn correctly, though without much imagination. So the gardener's words passed over Haro's head; he did not even bother to look up.

But suddenly the little man's foot came down on Haro's hand as he drew, harshly and cruelly.

'Let me show you what manner of man I am,' shouted the gardener.

Haro stared at his bruised knuckles for a moment, then, rising slowly, reached out and took the man by the neck and the leg. He held him for a moment, then calmly leaned over the balustrade with him. The guards below looked very small and far away. Their words did not reach the top of the stairs though they talked loudly.

The gardener began to cry hoarsely.

Haro said, 'And now let this show you what manner of man I am!'

He made to swing the gardener out into space, above the dark blue sea. Harald and Radbard sat looking at this, smiling all the time, the pebbles still in their hands.

Then suddenly Haro swung the little man back on to the steps and let him fall roughly on the marble. He lay there for a while, his hand clasped to his heart, as though he expected it to fail at any moment, his brown eyes wide with terror still at the memory of that long sheer drop.

Then Haro knelt gently beside him and said, 'If a Northman had trodden on my sword hand as you did a moment ago, he would now lie dead, with such wounds on his body as would frighten a dragon to dream of! Are you not lucky, O little gardener-man?'

The man tried to speak, but could not get his breath.

Haro went on, 'Know then, little gardener-man, that from now on you are graced by the company of great warriors, who will deal harshly with you if you so much as raise your voice to them again!'

He waited for a moment, until the man had regained his breath.

'Now, good little gardener-man, lead on and we will follow; but see that you set us gentle work to do, or by Odin, I will drag you from your bed one night and finish the journey I was about to send you on today. Come on, get up and we will follow you!'

The man needed no second bidding, but did as Haro had said. So the Vikings became gardeners in the house at Jebel Tarik, all because Radbard had had a desire to plant the barley along the fjord, as he had always done since his father, Radbard the Horse's Face, had passed away to Valhalla.

10. What Happened in the Great Courtyard

THE GREAT courtyard was a most magnificent place. It stood in the utmost centre of the vast house of Abu Mazur and was the joy of his heart, next to his beautiful daughter, Marriba.

Its broad floor was paved with porcelain tiles of many colours, laid out in the coiling arabesques of a Persian rug. In the centre of the tiled space was a fountain, made of alabaster and edged with beaten silver, in the shape of a snake coiling round a pomegranate, the sparkling water issuing from the snake's upturned mouth.

On all four sides of the tiled space were arcades, formed by arches of terra cotta, supported by veined marble pillars of such slenderness that one stood amazed that these delicate stalks should carry such weight.

Within each arch was a garden box of black marble, its sides overflowing with the luxuriantly flowering plants –

red, yellow, blue, purple, orange and violet, so that the cool air was always filled with the scent of blossom.

This courtyard was not open to the sky, but had a double canopy, the upper sheet of which was of thick samite, striped with red and gold; and the lower sheet of which was of a delicate thin-spun silk, almost transparently woven. This allowed the light to come down from above, while keeping off the strongest blows of the sun at midday. It also had this purpose, that it allowed one to observe the colours and the flights of the many captive birds which were kept there, within the two sheets – whose voices, mingling with the voice of the fountain and of the small aeolian harps set on the roof, gave to this courtyard an air of Paradise.

When Radbard first entered the place, he shrank back almost in fear and gasped, 'No, not yet! I have not died yet – or have I?'

After Harald had assured him that he was still flesh and blood, Radbard said, 'But it is impossible. When I said I wanted to plant seeds, I meant on a wind-swept upland, with the salt in my face, strong hairy barley seed that doesn't mind if a bullock tramples on it; not this sort of garden, where the flowers are like delicate princesses who would shrink from the touch of such rough hands as mine!'

Haro said, 'We shall get used to it, friend! It is like fighting in a battle; the first time one sweats and can hardly hold one's sword still. But after that, one talks to one's side-fellow as one advances, discussing the weather, the crops, the next feast, and so on.'

Harald said, 'You both talk like old women; I am all for doing something useful. Come, the water is cool and our feet are hot; let us wash them, that makes good sense.'

So the three Vikings took off their heavy goatskin shoes and bathed their tired feet in the rich fountain, while the little hunched man who was their master wrung his hands in fear lest Abu Mazur should pass through the courtyard while they were about their ablutions. But the Vikings ignored him, and Abu Mazur did not pass through the courtyard so all went well.

Nevertheless, Marriba, who was watching them through the grille of an upper window saw it all, and told her father, who smiled and said, 'They are three devils, my daughter, and I do not know what I shall do with them. Perhaps I shall come to like them one day – and perhaps I shall have to turn them over to the executioner. Who knows?'

Marriba pouted and said, 'But father, do not let us dispose of them until they have entertained us a little more. They are droll, these bears of the north! We have never had such funny ones before.'

Her father had given her a wry look and then turned back to his accounts, which were long and tedious, since he was so wealthy and involved in business. He was not the sort of man who leaves all his affairs to a secretary; for, as Abu Mazur knew well enough, in such matters no secretary is ever as trustworthy as one is oneself.

So life went on quite smoothly for the three sea-rovers, at their work or their rough play in the great courtyard. Their work was very light and consisted mainly in watering the many plants and in sweeping and keeping clean the bright tiles of the place. Sometimes this became tiresome to the Vikings and then the master gardener was teased without mercy and more than once was held, head downwards, over the fountain, when he had spoken too irritably to one or other of his slaves.

Once Haro said, 'I pity that little gardener-man. If I were such a man, I think I would swallow that prickly cactus and so put an end to my worries!'

'I cannot understand why he does not report us to Clothair and get us whipped or put on to a heavier task,' said Harald. 'There is something strange in our being allowed to stay here after the things we do.'

Radbard said, 'There is nothing strange in it. If he were to tell Clothair, then he would be punished or his position taken from him, for not keeping better order. That is all.'

Nevertheless, the antics of the Vikings had been observed by one pair of sharp eyes, and Abu Mazur's mind had been troubled to think that there was any sort of disobedience among his slaves. The result was that one day the three Vikings came to work in their courtyard to find three well-armed guards lolling against the pillars, seemingly resting from more arduous duties outside.

Haro went up to their leader and said insolently, 'Good day, General. You appear to be fatigued, my friend. Would you care for a dip in the fountain? It is most refreshing, I do assure you.'

The guard, who was a massive man, stared down at Haro from beneath his heavily-lidded eyes, then, showing his white teeth as he spoke, said, 'I am not Rajik, the little gardener, my friend. I am a warrior and I do not make a habit of letting rug-headed barbarians up-end me over fountains. Go back to your tasks, or you may feel the butt end of my lance in a place where you would not find it welcome!'

Haro stepped back a pace and said gently, with a slow smile on his face, 'Now I am nearer to you, I notice that you smell, dear Captain. Let me repeat that a wash would do you no harm.'

Harald ran forward now and tried to drag Haro away, but he set his feet resolutely and would not budge, not even for his friend.

The guard still lolled against his pillar, but with a slight movement of his hip swung his heavy dagger round to a position where he could reach it easily.

'Go back to your tasks, slave, and do not meddle with affairs which might bring your stay here to an abrupt conclusion,' he said. Now Harald was greatly worried for he saw that Haro's face had begun to twitch and that he was tugging at the short plaits which hung beside his ears, things which always happened when the man was about to run berserk.

He stepped forward to grasp Haro, but even as he did so, the Viking launched himself at the great soldier, taking him off his balance and tumbling him on to the gay tiles of the courtyard.

Haro was about to leap on to him, but Harald saw that, if he did, he would be jumping to his death for the soldier had drawn his dagger and was holding it upwards so that the Viking would fall upon it.

Then behind them there was a scuffling of feet and Harald turned to see the other guards running across the courtyard.

At the same time, Radbard thrust a sweeping broom into Harald's hand, and offered another to Haro, who stood breathing fiercely, willing to grasp any weapon which might aid him against the guard.

And at that point, Marriba, opening her window to find out what the noise meant, saw the three great Vikings, standing in a triangle, and warding off the blows rained on them by the guards, whose weapons were long narrow-bladed axes, set with sharp spikes.

'Quickly, quickly, father,' she called. 'Here is a sight one does not see every day!'

She jumped with excitement, like a little girl, when Harald suddenly bent his head to let an axe sweep over him, and then, with a lightning movement, brought up the end of his broom into his opponent's body. The man staggered back and fell into the fountain, winded.

At this Haro gave a great laugh and brought down his broom-handle fair and square on the right shoulder of his guard, causing the man to drop his weapon, and fall back, groaning with pain.

Radbard had seen these things and, anxious not to be outdone by his companions, was driving his opponent before him, as a dog might drive a rabbit.

Haro and Harald were laughing and shouting now, forgetful of their situation, when suddenly the voice of Abu Mazur came down to them, commanding and hard.

'Stop, this instant, all of you,' he said. 'The next man to strike a blow will row out the rest of his life in my prison galley!'

The men all looked up at the window where their master stood, his lean face working with anger. The guards picked up their weapons and stood sheepishly beside the Vikings, their heads bowed in shame.

Harald stared back at Abu Mazur, defiantly, but now even Harald felt the great strength of the other's eyes and looked down, to see Marriba smile suddenly, a small and impertinent smile, as though she was saying that her father held no terrors for her, and that she would see that all went well.

Later, standing before Abu Mazur in his small room, the Vikings heard him say, 'My house is a place of peace and industry. You men of the north have spoiled that peace, and seem to have no industry in you. I could pass such a sentence on you, my friends, that you would never raise a finger against authority again – but I shall not do that, for I understand a little of what passes through your minds, having been a soldier myself once in my long lifetime, and having known what it is to suffer imprisonment. This time I shall not punish you; but be assured that should you ever give me cause to raise my voice against you again, you will find me to be such a man as will bring terror to your minds whenever you think of me again.'

As the Vikings went from the room of Abu Mazur, they saw Marriba playing with her pet leopard in a little alcove. She smiled at them and said softly, 'You are fortunate that I did not tell my father I hated you. If I had done that, who knows what would have happened to you?'

Then she went on playing with the leopard, pulling his tail and tickling his furry ears. The Vikings passed by, prodded on by the spear-butts of the guard who escorted them.

When they were again in their quarters, eating rye bread and drinking barley broth, Haro said, 'For that young woman, I would lay down my life. She is the most beautiful creature I have seen.'

Harald said, 'Yes, she is beautiful, but I think she is perhaps cruel too. Did you see how she teased the leopard cub?'

Haro said, 'I would gladly become a leopard cub and be teased by such a princess.'

But Harald only struck him on the back, making him splutter, for his mouth was full of rye bread, and said, 'Take care that Loki is not listening behind the curtains, or you may wake to find yourself a leopard cub in all truth one day!'

11. The Empty Bed

FOR THREE weeks after the fight in the courtyard, the Vikings went on quietly and obediently with their work. And then something happened which led to even stranger things.

They were being marched to their work in the garden one day, by their master, Rajik, when they passed by the prison room in which new slaves were sometimes put until they grew more accustomed to the idea of servitude. From the high barred window floated a man's voice, young and strong and full of an infinite yearning. The vikings stopped dead and listened, for it was a voice which spoke their own tongue. And the song it sang was this:

'I have sailed in the northern seas,
Taking the Whale's Way,
Over the Gannet's Bath,
Among the ice-capped breakers;
Song-drunk and drifting,

Over the lift and the drop of green waters,
Into the sun's eye, into the West.'

Radbard's eyes filled with tears and his lips trembled when he spoke. 'That is a Northman,' he said. 'A sea-rover – a seabird whose long wings are clipped.'

Haro bit his lip thoughtfully and said, 'He is young and will feel the pain of imprisonment. But perhaps in a day or two he will see sense. He will see that a man could be in worse places than this.'

Radbard Crookleg clenched his fists and shut his eyes. 'For some of us,' he said, 'death itself would be better than slavery.' Harald said slowly, 'I am as true a sea-rover as any man, but what good does it do a man to pour out his soul like that, into the foreign air where there is no one to help him?'

They had forgotten Rajik, who had stood aside while they spoke, smiling softly to himself. Suddenly he came forward and whispered, 'Who says there is no one to help a sea-rover who wishes to break from his cage? Who says that a man might not get away from this house, if only he had the right friend to help him?'

Radbard turned and stared at Rajik, who shrugged his shoulders and then continued to walk towards the courtyard. They followed him, for now the song had finished and all was silent in the high prison.

Rajik said nothing more that morning, but often seemed to fix his eyes on Radbard especially, as though he expected the man to open the conversation again. Harald and Haro watched their companion closely, for he appeared to be moody now, and when they met again in the eating hall, they saw that Radbard had taken a bench near to Rajik and was talking excitedly and in a low tone to him. Rajik was replying quietly, glancing over his shoulder many times as he spoke.

Haro said to Harald, 'There is a bird that will fly before long, unless I am mistaken.'

That evening, Harald put his hand on Radbard's shoulder and said, 'Friend, we have been together for a long while. Let us stay together now, for the time may come when we shall find a way towards the north again.'

Radbard stared at him like a man in a dream and said, 'Let us stay together, yes. Let us all go north together now.'

Harald turned away from him and said to Haro, 'He speaks like a man who has drunk some drug and does not understand.'

Haro shook his head and said, 'I fear that Radbard's mind is clouded, Harald. I have seen Northmen grow like this before when they have been locked up too long. Their senses leave them and they beat their brains out on stone walls, like a bird trying to fight its way out of a cage.'

They decided that they must keep a watchful eye on their companion from that time onwards, and if possible prevent him from talking too much with Rajik, whose conversation seemed to trouble him.

Two nights later Harald woke from a frightening dream in which he was chained down in a cave on the seashore. As the green tides flowed higher and higher into the cave, Harald saw a large basking shark which tried to get to him. He shouted at the creature in his dream, telling it to beware for he had his father's sword by his side – though even as he dreamed these words, he knew that his hands were tied and that he could not defend himself if the tide rose so high that the shark could get to him. It was at this moment, when the breakers were already rolling over his body, that he woke up with a great start and sat up, mopping his forehead with his hand.

He looked about him, to make sure that he was not in the cave, and then he saw that Radbard was not lying beside him as he usually did. The coverlet was flung back from his pallet of straw and Radbard was not to be seen in the long dormitory room.

Harald touched Haro lightly on the face and woke him. 'Our seabird has flown, it seems,' he said. 'Come, we must find him before he runs himself into mortal danger.'

Swiftly the two men rose, passing between the beds of the other slaves and through the open door, where their guard snored at his post, his helmet on the floor beside him, and so out into the long corridor.

The moonlight glimmered on to them as they passed between the pillars of the cloistered passageway, and at length they ran through the nearest courtyard and so into another passageway, this time shut off from the light.

Once more they moved silently past a sleeping sentry and as they rounded the next corner, saw a white figure disappearing under an archway.

'That may be Radbard,' whispered Harald, as they ran.

'It looks more like a woman than a man, for it is dressed in long white robes,' said Haro. 'Yet we must make sure.'

Once as they ran a sentry stretched his arms and yawned, and the two men were compelled to draw aside into a little alcove until the soldier had grunted and settled himself to sleep again. Then they passed on, through the great courtyard where they worked each day, and into a square, high-ceilinged chamber.

It was there that they almost ran into the figure in white, for it had stopped and was bending over someone who lay on the floor.

Harald saw immediately that it was Radbard whom they had pursued, though he was dressed Moorish fashion, his face half enshrouded by a hood, his waist encircled by a broad black sash.

They came beside him and touched him on the shoulder. He turned to them a face contorted with horror, and pointed to the body on the floor. They bent over the man, and saw that it was Clothair. He was dead. A dagger had been driven into his back, between the joints of his body armour. Harald bent and looked at the weapon; it had a long, red-leather hilt.

Then he looked at the empty scabbard that swung from the black sash at Radbard's waist. 'Did you kill Clothair?' asked Harald, striving to keep the horrified disgust from his voice.

But Radbard only shook his head, helplessly. 'He was dead when I stumbled over his body a moment ago. I had no dagger. This robe and scabbard were left for me by Rajik, who showed me how I could escape this night when all the guards were drugged.'

Haro said grimly, 'Then friend Rajik has tricked you, Radbard. For now suspicion will fall on you and if they catch you, your end is certain.'

Radbard said simply, 'Rajik always hated Clothair, he even told me so. Well, what shall be, shall be; there is nothing more to say.'

He stood in the glimmer of moonlight like a man in a drugged sleep, hardly able to care for himself.

It was then that Harald's sharp ears caught the sound of shuffling footsteps along a far passageway. He signed to the others to be still and said, 'There are men at the end of that passageway. Where does it lead?'

Radbard said, 'That is the way to the treasure chamber. Rajik showed it to me only yesterday.'

'Then that is where we shall find him, and take our vengeance on him,' said Harald, suddenly angry with a cold and fearsome anger.

12. The Vengeance of Abu Mazur

AT THE corner of the passageway, the three Vikings halted. Before them, in the semi-darkness, a group of figures moved slowly and quietly, as though they were engaged in some arduous task. Harald's keen eyes picked out five figures, dressed after the manner of the house-guards, and led, it seemed by a small crooked man – Rajik the gardener.

'They are armed,' he whispered to Haro, 'for I see the glint of sword blades.'

'One of us carries a weapon, too,' said Haro ironically, holding out his hand. Harald saw that he had taken the red-hilted dagger which had killed their friend, Clothair.

It was then that they heard Rajik's unmistakable voice.

'Go quietly, my comrades,' he said, 'for soon we shall come out into the great chamber, and then we may need to have our wits about us!'

Almost as by instinct, Harald leapt forward, crying, 'Your wits will not save you now, Rajik the serpent! You have murdered Clothair and tricked our brother, Radbard! Now you would rob your master!'

There was a frightened cry in the gloom of the passageway, then muffled oaths and words of anger, as the robbers realized that they were assailed not by the guards of the house, but by three slaves.

There was the sound of boxes being flung to the ground hurriedly, then the Vikings were among the robbers, grappling with them before they could bring their swords into action.

In the half-darkness, it was impossible for the Vikings to fight with the skill which was theirs by day, but they gave a good account of themselves. Radbard was the first to speak, after the battle had started. His comrades heard him say, 'And that is for you, Snake Rajik, and for Clothair who was a good friend to us in his way!'

They heard Rajik's high voice call out for mercy, and then a groan took the place of his crying and he fell.

Haro was fighting like a berserk now, holding two men at bay with his long-bladed dagger, and driving them back down the passageway, towards the treasure chamber.

Harald had grappled his opponent round the waist and was slowly bending him back, when he felt a sharp pain in his side and then knew that he had been wounded and could exert his great strength no longer. 'To me, Radbard,' he called hoarsely. 'I am hurt and cannot hold this one much longer!'

A great blackness, blacker than the night itself, swept over Harald's eyes, and as he heard Radbard's feet shuffling towards him, he fell, unable to hold the enemy at bay any further.

Radbard reached forward and took Harald's opponent by the hair of his head and dragged him forward, and even as Radbard struck the man at the nape of the neck with his hard clenched fist, a great light shone on them from the high chamber, and Abu Mazur stood there, surrounded by a dozen guards, the torchlight glinting on their helmets and poised javelins.

The fight in the passageway ceased, suddenly, as a thunderstorm when the sun breaks out again and the air is still.

Then, in the great hall, Abu Mazur sat in judgement, the fighters standing or lying before his gilded chair, the guards standing in a circle about them, fierce in the flaring torchlight.

'What has any man to say before I speak?' the master asked, turning his eagle's eyes upon them all in turn.

Rajik, still shaken by the great blow which Radbard had dealt him, flung himself before the gilded chair and held out his hands in supplication.

'Listen to me, master,' he said. 'I am your good servant and have always served you faithfully. Tonight I heard strange sounds and came here to find these three Vikings dragging your treasure from its resting-place.'

Abu Mazur nodded and said, 'Who are these men who were fighting with the Vikings? I have not seen them before.'

Rajik said, 'They are good true men of the town, of Jebel Tarik, old friends of mine. They were drinking with me, as friends do, in my little room that you let me have, in your graciousness of heart.'

'And who killed Clothair?' asked Abu Mazur, gently, for he had always trusted the Frank and was sad to see him lying dead before him.

Rajik pointed an accusing finger at Radbard. 'That one did it. He struck him down with the dagger which lies before you now.'

Abu regarded him steadily for a moment and then said, 'The thing which lies before me is called Rajik – for Rajik killed Clothair, and Rajik brought in these murderers to steal his master's treasure.'

The gardener began to protest, but Abu Mazur waved him to silence.

'Have no doubts, Rajik, I was well aware that you were plotting against me. After all, I must keep my spies like any other rich merchant in these troubled times. And I know these friends of yours. That one is Rajam the sheep stealer – his father was hanged last year in Africa; that is Bela Tok, who killed a shepherd outside Granada three weeks ago; and the others, who are dead or unconscious, I do not care which, are also known to me.'

Rajik gazed at him in bewilderment. 'But, master, you said you had never seen them before.'

Abu Mazur passed a weary hand over his forehead and said, 'No, I have not seen them, but my spies bring me accurate descriptions, you dullard. I have eyes in my mind, too, friend Rajik, which is something you have not – nor will you live to have now.'

At this, Haro, although wounded deeply in the neck, gave a great shout of laughter and clapped the wretched Rajik on the back, almost knocking him flying. 'There,' he said, 'but it takes a big wolf to catch a little wolf! Friend Rajik, you are nicely in the trap now. Let us see you wriggle clear this time!'

At this the guards would have silenced Haro, but Abu held up his hand, ordering them to let the Viking be.

Then he addressed them, saying, 'My rough northern friends, for now I believe you are my friends, I am grateful to you. You shall not find me a forgetful master, and from this time your lives may perhaps be sweeter. Your chieftain, who lies wounded before me, shall have Clothair's place in my household and you shall help him in his task. Who knows, perhaps one day you may become my guards.'

Then he gave orders that Harald should be carried carefully to the physician, Malabar el Arrash, who lived in the house, to be treated for the sword-cut which had pierced deeply into his right side.

As the Vikings rose and followed the guards who carried their friend, they heard the voice of Abu Mazur once more speaking to Rajik and the robbers who had tried to steal the treasure.

'As for you,' it said, 'your traitorous eyes shall not see another dawn. You shall die where you stand now, and your fate shall be a lasting warning to any others who think to gain easily by night what I have spent many hard days in getting.'

Radbard said, 'He deserves his fate, for he would have brought it upon me, but for your friendship, my brother.'

After that, they did not mention Rajik, the little gardener-man, again. Nor did they ever walk through that echoing hall where the sentence had been passed.

13. To Sea Again

HARO'S neck soon healed, but spring had turned to summer before Harald was well, nor would he have walked again had not the great skill of Malabar el Arrash been devoted to its full on his behalf.

But now, as the first heavy heat of the summer sun began to beat down, already almost unbearably, on the city of Jebel Tarik, the three Vikings sat once more on the white terrace overlooking the steaming harbour.

The two others were teasing Harald, for he was wearing his helmet and armour for the first time since he had been appointed to fill Clothair's position.

'Why did you not let them cut your hair, King Harald?' asked Radbard, mischievously, for he had now regained something of his old spirits. 'Your helmet does not fit properly. It was made for a man with short hair.'

Harald said, 'No man shall cut my hair, friend Bald-head! I would rather have my own hair than any helmet!'

This annoyed Radbard, who was going very thin on top, and he immediately began to grapple with Harald, trying to roll him on the ground.

Then suddenly Haro began to whistle, warning them that someone was coming, but it was too late. Marriba stood behind them, smiling, her leopard cub on a golden chain at her side.

'What a pretty picture, Captain Harald,' she said, 'to see a great warrior rolling on the floor like a little boy.'

Harald looked up sheepishly and then, unable to say anything, took an apple from his leather pouch and flung it into the air. The girl watched it go, wondering, and then saw Harald rise to his feet, pull out his sword with one swift motion, and, as the apple came down at arm's height, cut it through downwards and then, almost with the same movement, across, so that the fruit fell in four even parts at her feet.

The look of amazement on the girl's face was such that the three Vikings burst into a roar of laughter.

Haro said, 'He is a show-off, is this Harald, Princess. Look, if he will give me his sword, I will show you one even better than that.'

Marriba said slyly, 'You are still a slave, Haro Roughneck. You are not allowed to have a sword, like Harald.'

Harald said, 'I am the Captain here, my lady, not you. If I give him a sword, that is my affair.'

But although he spoke abruptly, it was not through anger, but to cover his embarrassment that a girl should have seen him wrestling like a little boy on the ground. Then he handed his sword to Haro, who took three figs from his pocket and, having disposed them evenly in his left hand, flung them all into the air at once. As they came down in the sunlight, he struck at each one, neatly and quickly, with blows like those which a cat gives to a rolling ball of wool. The three figs lay on the white marble pavement, equally divided. Haro tossed the sword back to Harald, who caught it.

'Not a bad sword,' said Haro, carelessly, 'though I like one a little heavier in the blade. That is a lady's toy.'

Laughing, the girl turned to Radbard and said, 'After that is there anything you dare do, Crookleg?'

Radbard scratched his nose for a while and then said slyly, 'Yes, but it has nothing to do with swords, my lady.'

'So much the better,' said the girl, 'for this cutting and carving becomes tedious after a time. Well, what can you show me?'

Radbard simply said, 'This, and no more!'

He turned suddenly and snatched up a handful of pebbles from the edge of the steps. A large black carrion crow was sitting on the red roof, at the edge of the platform. Swiftly Radbard threw at the bird, which seemed to expect something of the sort and was ready to fly away. The first pebble struck the bird on the body and toppled it down the roof, but it rose again and was almost away when the Viking threw again. This stone brought the bird back to the eaves, fluttering. Radbard raised his hand to throw the third pebble, but Marriba held his arm.

'That is enough, barbarian,' she said. 'I do not love those birds, but I will not have you kill one just to show me your skill at throwing pebbles.'

Radbard shrugged his shoulders, and the bird, glad of the respite, gathered itself and flew away over the house, crying hoarsely.

'All the same,' said Marriba, when it had gone, 'I have never seen such marksmanship before in my life. A man like you does not need a sword, Radbard Crookleg, when there are stones about to throw!'

With that she went away, and Haro watched her go, sighing and holding his hand to his heart. The other two then rolled him on the ground, telling him that he was a dolt and a love-sick clown.

That afternoon a messenger came to fetch them into the presence of Abu Mazur, who met them with a grave face.

Radbard whispered, 'I know what it is, she has reported me for throwing at that bird, and now we are all to be punished.'

But it was not that at all.

Abu Mazur allowed them to sit down, a privilege which amazed them, and then said to them slowly, 'My friends, my dear daughter, Marriba, is not well. Her delicate constitution was not intended by nature for the heavy heat of this city and I am afraid that if she stays with me in the house here through the summer, she may come to harm. My good doctor, Malabar el Arrash, of whose skill you already know a little, tells me that my daughter must go to a more northerly climate, away from this heat, if she is to retain her health and happiness.'

Radbard said absently, 'Along the fjords now they will be sailing in their boats with the red and white sails, and already men will have returned to the villages with stores of treasure . . .'

Abu Mazur's sharp eyes silenced him in his dreaming. 'I do not speak of the far north, my friend,' he said sternly. 'That is a place where only bears and wolves live. It is not a place for such a frail flower as Marriba. Remember that.'

There was a silence then, and Abu Mazur rubbed his chin thoughtfully. At last he spoke to Harald alone, ignoring the others.

'I trust you, Northman, and so does my daughter. In recent weeks I have come to believe that I trust you more than I do any of my servants, of whatever race or quality. If I gave you charge of the fast ship which is to take my daughter to the northern islands, what would you say?'

Harald fell to his knees on the floor and said earnestly, 'I should thank you most deeply, Abu Mazur. I can say no more.'

Abu Mazur said quickly, 'I should not ask for any more, Northman, except that I should require you all to kneel before me, and putting your hands within mine, swear on your honour that you would obey my daughter in all things and would never question her judgement.'

The three men kneeled before Abu Mazur and took that oath.

With a wry smile he said gently, 'It is my right and my duty to convert men such as you to the true faith, to Allah, but I am not always strict in these matters for even good men vary so much in their beliefs. If you were of my faith, I would ask you to swear on the Beard of the Prophet, perhaps, and that would be binding; but I ask you to swear on your honour as fighting men of the north, and I know that you will not betray me.'

Haro said swiftly, 'May Odin's ravens peck out my heart if I disobey your daughter in anything she commands, be it great or small, for I would willingly die for her.'

Abu Mazur touched him gently on the shoulder and said, 'You are a good man, though a fool in many ways, Northman. Take my daughter to her relatives in the islands, where the air is fresh and sea-borne, and the sun strikes less shrewdly, and when you return with her at the fall of leaf, you shall all be made freedmen, to go or to stay here as you wish.'

Then he clapped his hands as a sign that the audience was ended and the three Vikings walked down the long arcades, unable to speak for the joy that was in their hearts to be going in a ship once again.

Marriba watched them from her window grille and smiled, though when her father came into her room to tell her the result of the meeting, she lay back in her bed again and put her hand over her eyes.

'Oh, father,' she said, 'the heat is so oppressive. I can hardly stand it. I shall die, I know I shall die.'

Abu Mazur bent and stroked her head lightly. 'Patience, my lamb, patience my chicken,' he said soothingly. 'In two days from now you will be on the seas with our brave Vikings to look after you. Then your spirits will rise again and you will be my lovely daughter once more.'

Marriba shrugged petulantly and said, 'No, I shall not! I shall die, I tell you, father, and then you will be sorry for bringing me here to Jebel Tarik where the wind is as hot as a furnace and the stones burn one to touch them.'

Her father tiptoed sorrowfully from the room to fetch the physician, but as soon as the door curtain had swung to, Marriba jumped from her bed and ran to the window grille, to see if the Vikings were still in sight.

But they were not; now they stood looking over the harbour wall at a low and rakish vessel with a triangular sail of red and gold.

'Ten oar ports and a steerboard like one of our own longships,' said Harald, pointing.

Haro gazed in silence at the high sharp prow and the bright steel grappling hooks. A great lump had risen in his throat and he was afraid of crying if he tried to answer.

Suddenly Radbard began to shout and dance and cry, all at the same time. 'By Odin,' he said, 'a ship! A ship! A ship!'

Then, with the tears streaming down their cheeks, they began to hug each other like clumsy bears.

PART THREE

14. Marriba's Command

ONE DAY out from Jebel Tarik, Harald stood at the helm, holding a north-easterly course through the torpid blue waters of the Middle Sea. Once more he felt the salt upon his face and his heart rejoiced. Radbard and Haro stood in the prow, pointing excitedly at this and that – a white gull swooping low over the water, a brightly-coloured sail on a distant ship, anything.

Marriba sat under an awning aft, stroking her leopard cub and sometimes deigning to speak to the old woman, her personal slave, who accompanied her. This old woman, Lalla, was a devout creature, for ever at her prayers, and hating the whole idea of a voyage, even though Marriba told her again and again that they could come to no harm, with the Vikings to guard them, and ten fierce Syrian oarsmen, who were as able with a sword as with an oar or a sail. But still the old woman shook her head mournfully and wept that she had ever come to this . . .

Sometimes Marriba strummed on a golden lute that her father had given her as a parting present, and then the sweet music seemed to echo in time to the beat of the oars and the cry of the seabirds, and all seemed gay in the sunshine.

Often they passed other ships belonging to Marriba's father, which always gave a loud call on their trumpets to show that they recognized their master's fast ship and were paying their respects to it.

Harald was thinking how beautiful Jebel Tarik had looked, as they sailed away a day ago, set in terraces on the high rock, white and red and yellow in the morning sunshine. It had quite gone from his mind that he had ever been a slave there, and now when he looked back, it seemed a place of good fortune – in spite of the fact that to get there, he had lost many friends, a ship, and a load of treasure.

His thoughts swung back to his comrades – Haro, Goff, Sven and the others ... yes, even the giant Grummoch, who had looked like becoming a true sea-rover and then had jumped into the water and put an end to himself rather than be taken by the Arab pirates ... What a shame it was, thought Harald, that one lost one's shipmates! And how glorious it would be to sail with all the good men one had ever known, in the biggest longship of all time, to the west, to the west, to the west ...

But now he was sailing to the north-east, he reflected, half-sadly for the moment, and he knew only two men in this fast little ship.

He was roused from his daydream by a blast on the silver whistle, which Marriba used to call her shipmaster to her, on her father's orders.

Harald beckoned to Radbard, who ran aft and took the helm. Then he made his way to the girl as she sat under the striped awning.

Marriba smiled at him and indicated a cushion at her feet with a motion of her hand.

'Sit down, shipmaster,' she said, gently. 'There is something I wish to say to you, now that we are over a day at sea.'

Harald still stood, feeling that he should not show any familiarity with his master's daughter; but Marriba pointed to the cushion again, this time imperiously. 'Remember, you swore to obey me in all things – yes, in all things, Captain,' she said, smiling.

Harald frowned and said, 'What shall be, shall be. What is it that troubles you, Lady Marriba, then?'

Marriba smiled sweetly at him and said, 'Nothing troubles me, Captain; and nothing is going to trouble me, either. You will obey all my commands, and then nothing will trouble me. Is that clear?'

Harald nodded, puzzled. 'Yes,' he said, 'I shall obey you in all reasonable things.'

Marriba said sternly, 'You will obey me in all things – reasonable or otherwise, Captain. For that is the oath you took to my father, and that is the oath he will expect you to keep.'

Harald said, 'Yes, but if you ordered me to run this fine ship on to a rock, not even my oath would make me –'

Marriba stopped him with a wave of her hand.

'I should not do anything so stupid,' she said quietly, 'for we need this ship to take us to Byzantium, don't we, Captain?'

Harald jumped to his feet. 'What do you mean, Byzantium?' he said, in amazement.

'Just that, Captain,' said Marriba, fingering the silky ears of her leopard cub. 'I am ordering you to change course, and to set this ship's nose towards Byzantium, or Miklagard as you barbarians call it, towards the Empire itself. Is that clear?'

Harald said thickly, 'No, it is not clear. I am to take you to the northern islands, a day and a half away, to pass the summer there with relatives who expect you.'

Marriba sighed and said, 'How dull you Northmen are. A man of the south would have seen my point immediately. Well, if you must know, my dear relatives in the northern islands will wait for me in vain. They are old and dull and would be no fun for a young girl like me to pass the summer with. I am going to pass the summer, and longer than the summer, with someone more to my liking, dear Captain.'

Harald gazed at her with wide-open eyes.

'You know someone in Byzantium?' he said slowly.

Marriba mimicked his slow speech. 'Yes, dear Captain,' she said. 'I know a prince there, a Roman, who wishes to marry me. Is that clear?'

Harald stood back a pace and rubbed his forehead.

'But does your father know about this?' he said.

Marriba smiled wickedly and answered, 'No, dear Captain, he does not; and who is there to bother him with such news? You will take me to my prince in Byzantium, it is an old arrangement with us, and then everyone will be happy.'

Harald said, 'But what if I refuse?'

Someone had stepped behind him. It was Haro. He put his hand firmly on Harald's shoulder and said, 'You will not refuse what this lady asks you. You have sworn an oath, as I have, and you will obey her.'

Harald looked into Haro's eyes and saw that he was deadly serious.

'You are bemused with this young woman, Haro,' said the shipmaster. 'Abu Mazur didn't mean us to obey her in things like this.'

Haro answered calmly, 'Who are you to decide what Abu Mazur meant? Do your duty as a Captain, Harald. And if I am bemused with her, well and good, that is no crime. I shall see her delivered safely to her prince if it is the last thing I do.'

Radbard met Harald outside the awning and said, 'I have heard what has been said.'

Harald said, 'You must be the final judge, Radbard. What do you say?'

Radbard Crookleg scratched his long nose and then smiled at Marriba over Harald's shoulder.

'I have always wanted to see Miklagard,' he said.

And before Harald could reply, Radbard had walked back to the helm, to swing the ship round so her prow faced towards the east.

Marriba said nothing, but picked up her golden lute and began to strum lightly.

Harald stumped away to the prow of the ship and stood staring into the white foam that lashed about the bow. But at last even he relented and by evening time sat with the others under the awning, eating and drinking and telling those immensely long tales which all Northmen rejoice in.

15. The Ship of War

EXCITED as they all were, the trials of the many weeks which followed caused Harald to doubt his wisdom in agreeing to the long voyage to Miklagard.

When they drew too close inshore off Tunis, a dhow came out after them, and though they easily outstripped it, yet they lost three Syrian oarsmen in the flight of arrows which followed them.

Marriba said bitterly, 'If my father knew of that, he would have the crew of that dhow strangled with bowstrings.'

Harald retorted, 'If your father knew, he would probably reward them all for trying to recapture his wicked daughter.'

But this only made Marriba laugh and Harald said no more.

Again, they almost ran aground on the coast of Sicily, and were chased by a long warship which got close enough to fling out its grappling hooks. Harald swung the helm hard over, almost capsizing the shallow craft, and unseating the oarsmen, who by this time were ready to surrender to anyone who looked fiercely enough at them; but they got free again, and put in at Malta to replenish their food and water, which had only been sufficient to take them to the Balearic Islands in the first place.

At Malta, yet another misfortune befell them, which made Harald feel that the hand of Odin was turned against them on this voyage. Wandering in the woods above the shore, while the water-skins were being filled, Radbard trod upon a viper and was bitten deeply in the ankle. He struck off the creature's head and then tried to let out the poison from the wound with his sword. Harald and Haro found him, hours later, staggering about in the woods, his eyes wild, and babbling that he must get back to the fjord to plant the barley seeds for his old mother.

Harald examined their comrade's leg. It was very swollen and had red streaks running up it towards his body.

'There is nothing we can do, friend,' said Haro, when he saw this. 'Radbard has run his course. It is the will of Odin.'

Later they fetched the old woman, Lalla, who was skilled in herbal medicines. She clucked her tongue against the roof of her mouth and said that if they had been back home, she would have known just where to find the right herb to cure this snake sting – but here, ah no, it was impossible. Allah wanted this man, she said, and it would be wicked to keep Allah and Radbard apart.

As she said this, Radbard's mind seemed to clear for a moment or two and he even smiled grimly at the old woman.

'Be assured, old one,' he said, 'it is Odin who requests the pleasure of my company at his feast, not Allah! And I am ready to go.'

Harald was holding him at the time, and felt Radbard's head suddenly go slack on his shoulders. He laid the man down gently and then they covered him with boughs and turf, for the wood there was too green and damp to make a funeral pyre.

On the way to the ship, Harald dried the tears on his cheeks and said, 'Haro, my only friend, this is a bad voyage. But I swear to you that I shall make Miklagard pay for this. I shall leave that city as rich as a prince, or shall die there!'

Haro did not answer and they went back to the ship in silence.

When they got aboard, Harald solemnly handed Radbard's sword to Marriba. 'Here, lady,' he said with a quiet bitterness, 'this is a present from the man you have killed by your wilfulness.'

He was sorry he had said this when Marriba suddenly burst into tears. But after that, she regarded Harald very oddly, at times, as though she wished to punish him for his words to her that day.

Then their luck seemed to change without warning. A week later they ran in north of Crete, to be met by a large Roman man-of-war that stood high out of the water. There was no escaping this time, and indeed Harald had little heart to try that trick again. He merely ordered the rowers to leave their oars and get out their swords. Then he walked to the prow and stood waiting for the first men to come at him.

The Roman ship flung out a grappling hook and drew the other ship alongside. Three officers, splendid in golden armour, jumped lightly down beside Harald, their swords rattling in their scabbards.

'What cargo do you carry?' the first man asked in Arabic.

Harald said, 'A woman, nothing more.' He was weary of the whole voyage and would almost have surrendered Marriba at that moment, so annoyed was he at the loss of Radbard.

The officers strode down between the Syrian rowers to the awning where Marriba sat, putting on a brave face, twitching the strings of her lute, as though she were accustomed to such situations every day.

When they reached her, they bowed and smiled courteously.

'On what errand do you travel, lady?' said their leader.

Marriba smiled up at him and whispered something which he had to bend to hear, her voice had suddenly gone so weak.

To Harald's great surprise, the officer bowed again and said for all to hear, 'A thousand pardons, lady. If I had known, I would not have put you to the indignity of answering my questions.'

As he spoke, the other two officers knelt before Marriba, their heads bowed low.

Haro nudged Harald and whispered, 'If they do not take care, they will break their long noses on the deck boards!'

Then the officer spoke again and said, 'The times are dangerous ones, Your Highness, and our Emperor Constantine, your beloved, would think ill of us if we allowed you to travel further without our escort. Indeed, great lady, if I confess the truth, we have been watching for you these three months, up and down the islands, for your message that you would find some occasion to travel east before the summer was out pleased the Emperor Constantine greatly.'

Harald hissed, 'To think that all the time she was planning this trick! I will never trust womankind again!'

Even Haro looked a trifle put out as he heard the officer's words.

When these men had gone, with many bows and a great swirl of their purple cloaks, Marriba beckoned to Harald and said slyly to him, 'So now you know, great Captain! I am to be betrothed to the Emperor in Constantinople. Are you not glad that you did not disobey me now, when I ordered you to sail here?'

Harald said angrily, 'What would your good father say to such a match? You are a Muslim and this emperor is no doubt a Christian, of some sort.'

Marriba said quietly, 'Be assured, friend Northman, he is a very great Christian; one of the greatest! And so shall I become, in due course, for there are some trifling obstacles to be cleared away, I understand. First this lover of mine is already betrothed to one Rotrud, no doubt an ugly creature, the daughter of that Frankish king Charles, who lets himself be called "The Great".'

Even Harald gasped at her insolence, for he and his folk had good reason to fear the name of Charlemagne.

'And what is the other obstacle, O Powerful Queen?' he asked, in as bitter a tone as he dared.

Marriba examined the nails of her right hand negligently and at last said, 'My Constantine's mother, Irene, a woman of Athens and no true Roman, seems bent on making trouble. I gather that she hopes to rule here herself, and so did not take the oath of fealty to her son. But we shall attend to that matter when I am installed in Byzantium, friend Harald, that we shall! Then there will be no obstacle.'

Harald said slowly, 'No, no obstacle then, my lady. And how old is this Emperor of yours?'

Marriba struck three light chords on her lute before she answered, and then she did so with a defiant expression on her ivory face.

'He is fifteen, great Captain,' she said. 'But fifteen in a brave warrior is the match of twenty in, say, a mere seaman, shipmaster!'

Harald stared at her aghast; then he controlled himself and strode to the prow of his ship to supervise the loading of certain delicacies which the officers on the warship had decided it was wise to offer to the beautiful young lady who had come so far to marry their Emperor. Not that they were afraid of her or of him, but it was as well to keep in favour – with both sides if possible – and in any case they would report all they knew, as soon as they landed, to the Lady Irene, the Emperor's rather overbearing mother, from whom they drew a second salary, after the little Emperor had paid them off with his miserable pittance.

On their high deck they looked down on to the fast ship of Abu Mazur. Their Captain, the one with the hooked nose and the curly black hair, who had spoken to Marriba so respectfully, said to his two lieutenants, 'Well, gentlemen, the situation grows more and more amusing! He sends us to meet her and guard her to the port; she sends us to capture her and, if possible, to drown her quietly, off whichever of the islands is the most convenient! Which shall we do, gentlemen?'

The two lieutenants grinned at each other, admiring their reflections in each other's armour. Then the elder of them turned, twirled his long black moustaches and said silkily, 'Let us take her back safely, my Captain. It would be more amusing – I should love to see what old Irene says when this young Arab lass begins to queen it over her in the Court!'

'Done!' said the Captain, slapping the other quite gently on the back. 'So that is settled! She lives, for the time being! And now we will go below decks and drink some of that sweet white wine I had brought on board this morning. It looks superb, gentlemen, quite superb! Far too good for the likes of poor soldiers like us!'

They went below laughing gaily. Harald watched them from his ship and wondered what had pleased them so hugely. It was perhaps just as well that he did not know.

16. Miklagard

THREE days later the two ships had passed between the many islands and had reached the Sea of Marmara, had skirted the Golden Gate and were running into an anchorage but a stone's throw from the great golden-roofed Palace of Justinian.

Though the heat beat down unmercifully, to be reflected from the oily water, Marriba had decked herself out in a robe and cloak of heavy silk, and had braided her raven-black hair with thick pieces of corded ribbon, shot through and through with strands of gold and silver thread.

She stood upon the deck, among the rowers, gazing in wonder at the many glories of this Miklagard to which they had come, the Jewel of the World.

Beyond the battlemented walls, set round with dark cypress trees, rose tier after tier of roofs, some red, some green, some golden, surmounted again by immense domes, that glistened gloriously in the sunshine, and great arches supported by twisted columns of marble; and over these yet again, high towers and minarets, that seemed to reach up through the deep blue sky to heaven itself. The Vikings saw the immense aqueducts which spanned the vast city like many-legged monsters of white stone and pointed in awe.

'Aiee!' gasped Haro, 'but they are impossible! No man could put stone on stone to grow so high up towards the clouds! I shall never believe it! And when I leave this place, I shall know that it was all a dream!'

Harald laughed at him and said, 'If ever you leave it, friend!'

And everywhere they looked, there was such magnificence; northward, across the Golden Horn, was the suburb, Pera, two miles away, its layers of white houses rising up from the blue waters towards the bluer sky, like some fantastic betrothal cake, set with olive trees; and eastward, a mile across the Bosporus, lay Chrysopolis, purple-roofed and splendid above the water, its harbour gay with the many-coloured sails that bobbed lazily on the swell.

Harald grinned and said, 'And do you recall, Haro, that when we first looked down on King MacMiorog's cattle ranch, we said that it must surely rival Miklagard!'

Haro nodded and said, 'It was to this place what a ladybird is to a stallion!'

Then the many trumpets blew and at the signal the two ships pulled into the white-stoned harbour.

'Look, look!' said Marriba, excitedly, 'in that litter with the purple canopy decorated with silver! That is the Emperor, he has come to meet me! Oh, look!'

Harald and Haro nudged each other and stood aside to let the girl go forward on to the plank. The three officers from the war vessel waited on the harbour to lead her to the Emperor Constantine.

Harald and Haro followed at a respectful distance, staring about them at the many soldiers, all in their golden armour and red cloaks, or draped in long purple vestments as they sat on their motionless white horses, their black helmet plumes nodding in the morning breeze that blew down, soft and odorous, from the high city.

Marriba stood before the litter, which was carried by four great Negro slaves. She seemed irresolute and nervous, as though now that she had reached Byzantium, she wished she could be back in the safety of her father's house at Jebel Tarik, where she was the most important person . . .

Then the curtains of the litter were drawn aside and the Emperor slowly got down on to the red carpet which had been spread on the harbour stones.

Haro's eyes grew wide and his mouth fell open.

'What!' he gasped. 'Can that be the Great One we have come so far to meet!'

Constantine was a weak and sickly child, there was no gainsaying it. His thin fair hair hung lankly down his pale face, his light-blue eyes seemed faded and almost colourless; his small red mouth was as petulant as a baby's. And not all the bright, tall diadems, the robes and cloaks, stiff with fine metals and jewels, could make him look other than what he was.

'Poor little puppet!' said Harald, under his breath.

'I would rather be a shepherd lad along the fjords than this pretty doll,' said Haro, in contempt.

The many officers bowed low before the Emperor, and even Marriba knelt on the stones, for the red carpet did not reach as far as the spot where she was made to stand.

The Emperor Constantine looked down at her haughtily, his heavy-lidded eyes half-closed. Then he extended his thin pale hand, heavy with pretty rings, and speaking in a high voice, bade her stand by him.

When she had done this, he looked past her and said slowly, 'Where are the brave men who brought you to Byzantium? Where are the men who stole you away from your father to bring you to me?'

Marriba was about to speak when the senior officer said, 'Most High, there are the Syrian rowers, still sitting in the ship.'

The Emperor waved his white hand languidly and said, 'I do not mean the rowers. Their work is finished now. I give them the ship they sit in for their pains. They may go when they will and row away, wherever they please. That is all one to me. I ask who was the captain of that ship, the one to whom thanks must be given for this lady's safe passage here.'

The officer turned and beckoned to Harald and Haro to step nearer the Emperor.

'These are the men, both Northmen, Most High,' he said.

The Emperor Constantine gazed at them for a moment or two, his petty mouth half-smiling. Then he said abruptly, 'Those who know how to steal such a lady from her father might one day know the way to steal her away from me. That must not be. Take these men to a place where they will steal nothing else. What is done to them there, to prevent them from harming any other man, I care not.'

While the Vikings were still numb with the shock of this command, many soldiers closed in on them from every side, and they felt their arms being dragged behind them and pinioned.

Harald shouted out, 'Lady Marriba, help us! We served you well!'

But a soldier clapped his hand over Harald's mouth, and he could say no more.

Marriba did not look at him. Her head was bowed and she did not seem to see what was happening. Then, struggling as violently as they could, the Vikings were dragged away from the harbour.

17. The Challenge

THE ADMIRATION with which the two Vikings had first greeted Miklagard had now turned to disgust and even hatred. The narrow cell in which they had spent their last three days was dank and stinking; its earthen floor was covered with a mess of rotting rushes; the only light came down to them from a window set high in the wall, and level with the pavement of the street outside, for this cell was partly an underground structure.

Twice a day, a sour-faced gaoler thrust two flat pannikins into the cell; the one containing a mixture of broken rye bread, pieces of cold meat, and grease-scummed gravy; the other filled to the brim with water, which, more often than not, was cloudy and of a rusty-brown colour. Always it was brackish and next to undrinkable.

The Vikings complained loudly, but the gaoler ignored them and went away after he had pushed the repulsive food at them.

There was one other occupant of this cell, a bent and wizened old man, dressed in a single garment of rough sacking. His hair was quite white and his eyes sightless. When he heard them complaining, he said haltingly, in a dialect which was a mixture of Arabic and Greek, 'This food is not so bad; it has kept me alive for twenty years! Be thankful that they left you your eyes to find the food when the gaoler brings it in. They were not so kind to me, my friends.'

The Vikings wondered about the terrible nature of the crime for which the old man had been so punished, but one day he told them that he had once been a Chancellor in the court, and had been thrown into prison, blinded, in the time of the Emperor Constantine Copronymus, because he would not confess that he had received bribes from certain of the bishops.

Haro said directly, 'And did you receive bribes?'

The old man shook his head and replied, 'No, but that made no difference. They did not believe me. They blinded me in their usual manner, by making me look at a white hot iron held close to my eyes. It has happened to countless people in Byzantium, and will no doubt happen a countless number of times again. You are lucky to have escaped it. It is a distressing thing to happen, especially to a young man, and I was only thirty at the time.'

Harald said bitterly, 'It seems to me that Miklagard is most like a beautiful but cruel woman, nothing better.'

The old man smiled and said, 'I could give it a harsher name, but there, I am old now and must not shorten my days by hatred.'

Haro said, 'But things are changed now, surely; that happened many years ago. Now that there are new monarchs, why do they not let you go free?'

The old man answered, 'They have forgotten me, my friend. One expects no justice in Byzantium, in any case. It is a hard city. And anyway, if they set me free, I should starve, for my family has gone away, and I have nothing. I am content here, that is all. So you see why I do not complain about the food, bad as it is; it keeps life in one's body.'

Another day Harald said to the old man, 'Why do you want to live? This life is a living death, no more.'

The old man shrugged his white head and said, 'No, one lives after a fashion. You see, every other day a little street beggar comes to this window and tells me what is going on in the city, what is happening at the Court, and so on. In that way I live, for I can picture the scenes in my head, as though I had my eyes again; and at night I dream that I am amongst the courtiers again, listening to gossip, meeting the new arrivals at the Court, and such like. Yes, it is a sort of life and I would rather have that than have no life at all.'

Then he went on to tell them many things; that Byzantium was not a happy city; that the taxes were always high, and no justice to be had; that the Court, the Church, and the Judges were all corrupt; that Irene the mother of the Emperor-to-be, hated her son and wished to rule herself over the Eastern Roman Empire.

'She refused to take the oath of fealty to him,' said the old man, 'although all the others did – the provincial governors, the ministers, the senators – even the artisan guilds, the common workers, you know. But not Irene! No, she has already tried to break off the young man's betrothal to the daughter of Charlemagne, in case her son might become too powerful if the marriage took place. And' –

here his old voice fell to a whisper – 'they tell me that in a great quarrel with him, in the full Court, some days ago, she even threatened to have him blinded, if he did not mend his ways and obey her in all things.'

Haro blew out his cheeks and said, 'I thought my old mother was strict when she used to thrash me with a broom-handle, but that was the gentlest of love compared with this. No, friends, I would not be a little emperor for all the wealth of Miklagard.'

The old man smiled and said, 'And Miklagard, as you call it, is very wealthy, very rich. I know that from my own experience here. There are treasure houses of the Court situated in many unlikely places throughout the town, and even beyond the town walls. Look, just to show you . . .'

He took up a straw and began to sketch out a plan of Miklagard in the soft earth of the floor. Harald and Haro watched, amazed at the old man's detailed knowledge, though he was blind.

'There,' he said, when he had finished. 'I have shown you ten treasure houses. What think you of that? And I know only a little of what must be the final truth.'

The two Vikings surveyed the sketch earnestly, letting it bite into their memories like acid on a plate of metal.

'Wonderful,' they said. 'And are you sure that this will not have changed since you have been in this prison?'

The old man shook his head. 'They have never changed, those treasure cells, since Byzantium was founded. They will not change now.'

That night, as they lay trying to get to sleep on the hard floor, Haro whispered to Harald, 'If ever we do get free, I know one way of getting our revenge on that little puppet of an Emperor!'

'So do I, my friend,' said Harald. 'But how should we carry it away with us?'

Haro whispered, 'Let us cross that bridge when we come to it, shipmaster! First catch the pig before you eat him!'

The next day they evolved a plan of escape, though when they told the old man, he only laughed and said that it would never work. All the same, they determined to see what would happen.

So Harald climbed on to Haro's shoulders and when the passers-by became most numerous, began to call out in his rough Arabic, 'There is not a man in Byzantium I would not fight! Not one I would not meet, with my right hand tied behind me! No, not one!'

For a time, no one answered Harald's hoarse cries. Then a passing beggar-man, trundling a solid-wheeled cart, flung an armful of refuse – old rags, bones, and pieces of broken metal, into the cell.

This time Haro took a turn on his friend's shoulders and cried, 'The men of Miklagard are cowards! They are rats, ruled over by a puppy and a cat! Nothing more – just rats!'

The blind man in the corner cried out in fear at this, saying that the secret police of the city would surely hear and then they would all regret those words.

'For they will leave you no tongue with which to make your apologies,' he shouted.

But Haro shouted back, 'I am not the man to make apologies! I say that the men of this dunghill are cowards; such cowards as would be laughed to scorn along the fjords, where men take a pride in answering any challenge, whencesoever it comes!'

Suddenly, Haro noticed that the bustle outside the cell window was still. A shadow fell upon his head and at eye level he saw a pair of feet, wearing heavy red and gilt sandals which reached so high that he lost them above the small window.

Once more he called out, 'I challenge any man, yes, any man, to combat; and I will bet my tongue that I will beat him in fair combat, though he has a sword and I a stick.'

And when Haro had finished, a deep voice from the street said loudly, 'Do you then, hairy one? Let us see what you have to say when I come down to you!'

The gilded feet passed from before the little opening, and then the sun shone down faintly into the cell again.

The old man clucked miserably to himself in the corner, while the two Vikings stood back against the wall and waited for what should happen – each one already feeling the searing iron on his tongue, before his eyes, in imagination.

Then at last the grumbling gaoler flung open the door, and a man stood beside him on the upper steps – a man so immense that he had to bend to come under the doorway and down into the cell.

Harald stared at him in admiration, for he was a soldier and was dressed in all the golden glory of an officer of the Byzantine Guard. His purple cloak swung heavily behind him; his gilded scabbard slapped against his great thigh. This was a man above ordinary men, thought the Vikings.

As he walked down among the rotting straw, he pinched his aquiline nose delicately and blew out his curled moustaches in disgust. Then he came on towards the two men, who stood to face him, trying to put on the bravest face that hunger and exhaustion would allow them.

'Which of you two challenged me a moment ago?' he said, his thin lips curled into a strange smile.

Both men spoke, 'I did!'

He smiled and then called to the old man who was praying in the corner, stiff with fear, 'Which of these two challenged me, old fellow?'

The old man said, 'I heard no one challenge anyone, lord.' The splendid soldier stood back for a moment, his hand on the hilt of his great sword.

Then he said lightly, 'Two heroes and a wise man in one small cell. I did not think Byzantium could boast such a gathering.'

His quick eyes surveyed the Vikings from head to foot; it seemed to them that he noticed everything. And then, after a long silence, he said, 'To fight with you would be to waste good men, for I should assuredly kill you.'

The Vikings burst out at this, suddenly angry, but he waved them to silence with a commanding gesture and went on, 'You are real men, I can see that; and warriors, I can see that also, from the scars you bear. I observe, moreover, that you come from the north – by your accent and by your fondness for bears' claw necklaces!'

Harald broke out, 'What is wrong with that? We killed the bears ourselves to get the necklaces! We did not buy our trinkets from any goldsmith's booth, my friend!'

For a moment the officer regarded Harald sternly, as he twisted his own gold chain between his strong brown fingers. But at last he smiled again and said, 'Have it your own way, Northman. But let me speak; I say that I would not fight you and kill you – if such were my fortune; I would rather buy you and use your courage and your strength.'

Then for a moment his gaze rested on the old man in the corner. 'You are not of the north, I know, old one. You are one whom we all know, we of the Palace. Yet I will buy you too, and though I have no use for you, I think you could find a better home than this for yourself. What say you?'

But the old man shook his head. 'Thank you, Kristion,' he said. 'For it is Kristion, I know; no other man has such a voice and such a heavy footfall! No, thank you, Captain of the Guard, but I am too old and too weak to beg my bread in the streets where I once rode in glory.'

The Captain, Kristion, strode to him and took him by the shoulder. 'Don't be an old fool,' he said, smiling. 'You can go to my sister's house, in the country. Her children need a tutor. That would be easy for you, and the children are gentle little ones.'

He turned to the Vikings. 'I offer you a place as soldiers in the Palace Guard – in Irene's Company. You will get food and clothes, and enough pay to enjoy yourselves on without being pampered. Will you come?'

Harald and Haro stepped forward, smiling, their hands held out. 'We will come,' they said. 'That is, if the old man will agree to leave this place too.'

And when the old man was turned round, so that the question could be put to him again, they saw that he was crying like a child.

The Captain, Kristion, turned away suddenly, flicking his cloak hem over his own eyes. He went up the steps in silence, and at the top turned and said, 'There will be some trifling matter of signing the papers of purchase. I will return tomorrow, Guardsmen, have no fear. And when I do, see that you spring to attention. None of this northern slackness in my Company, my friends.'

Then the door was shut behind him, and the prisoners put their arms about each other, in glee, like children who had just been promised a wonderful present.

18. The Mousetrap and What It Caught

HARALD lounged in the gateway of the great Palace, chuckling to himself in the sunshine. Everything was like a dream, he thought. Three weeks ago, he and Haro and the old man had been in prison, in the depths of despair. Now the old man was no doubt sunning himself and chattering in Greek or Latin to the children of Kristion's sister – and the Vikings were full-blown guardsmen in the Palace of Irene!

Harald would hardly have believed it himself, if he had not his armour and weapons to prove it! There was the fine bronze helmet, with the lion's head moulded on it, and the red horse's plume which swept halfway down his back; the purple cloak of thick Khazar wool, its hem weighted with small silver buttons shaped like acorns; the breastplate of polished silver with Irene's insignia emblazoned on it in rich enamels of red and blue and deep yellow.

As for the weapons – Harald almost wept with pleasure at their rare beauty, and wished the folk along the fjord could have seen them – the long sword with the gold wire round its sharkskin hilt; the short broad dagger with the thin gold inlay along the blade; the javelin of ebony, butted with silver . . . It was all like a dream, as was the great hall into which he looked from time to time.

Pillar after pillar rose like a forest of rich trees, and surmounted by semicircular arch after semicircular arch, until the mind grew confused with the intricacy of the design – and mosaic work everywhere, from floor to the high domed roof! Harald had long since stopped trying to find out who all the figures were in those delicate pictures; for even when he was told, by Kristion, who had taken the Vikings round explaining everything to them before they were sworn in as guards, Harald had not understood what the names meant. Saints, Bishops, Emperors – they meant little to his mind, and so, in the torpor of the summer heat, he had decided to do the only possible thing, and ignore them, merely letting their magnificence shine down on him as he went about his duties.

Then, as he stood there in the bright light, his mind clouded with the memory that came back to him. A week before, he had first made the acquaintance of the great lady, Irene, mother of the Emperor-to-be, and the meeting had not been a pleasant one.

She had stormed into that very hall which lay behind him, a short elderly figure, her wrinkled face painted as brightly as that of a doll, her greying hair dyed an impossible shade of reddish-purple, her clumsy body made enormous by the billowing robes of thick brocade, heavily embroidered in gold and silver thread so that she rustled as she moved, like a forest with the wind blowing through it.

She had stopped before Harald and Haro and with her lips pinched tightly had said, in her coarse high voice, 'So these are the two northern fools who brought that Muslim baggage to Byzantium!'

Then, with a cruel sneer on her face, she had said, 'But have no fears, Northmen, you will never take her back again! When I have finished with her, she will not be worth taking anywhere!'

Kristion had been following the lady Irene in her inspection of the Guard and had winked at Harald when the lady was talking to another man. Harald took some comfort from that wink, for he felt that Kristion meant to imply that Irene was merely threatening Marriba in order to impress her own power upon the Vikings. Nevertheless, Harald had been worried, for Irene seemed viciously selfish in all things. His anxiety for Marriba, however, had soon been driven from his mind by what followed afterwards.

The golden trumpets had blown and then young Constantine had pranced into the great hall, followed by half a Company of his Guards, the men who wore the black plume in their helmets.

Defiantly he had paced to the centre of the hall, and with his hand on his hip had surveyed his mother as she walked the length of the line of her Guards.

At last she had turned and, surveying him with a twisted smile, had said, 'There you are, little one! Your nurses have been looking for you all day! You are really a very bad boy, Constantine, to lead your mother such a dance!' Turning to her Captain, Kristion, she had then said, 'See that the little Emperor is tucked away safely, Captain. If he runs wild with rough companions, there is no knowing to what mischief he may get up!'

Against his will, Kristion had marched to the young Prince and, bowing, had taken him by the arm. Constantine's own Guards had parted to let the great Kristion escort his prisoner away, out of the hall. The young man's eyes had turned in anguish on his mother; his lips had tried to give the order to his own Guards to strike her down, there and then. But somehow, nothing had happened. Nothing, except that the boy had been put into a prison cell specially prepared for him, with all necessary comforts, next to his mother's own bedroom.

'And that,' said Kristion, mopping his broad brow as he told his own Company, 'is the end of Constantine, as far as ruling Byzantium is concerned. He stands no more chance of doing that, than I do of being elected King of the Franks! Not so much, perhaps!'

The Company of Irene's Guard had laughed loud at this, but in each man's heart there was a tiny shred of pity for the young man whose mother was willing to kill him, rather than let him thwart her ambitious claims to the throne of the Eastern Empire.

And so Harald thought of all this, as he stood in the sunshine, at the door of that great hall, that morning. What had happened to Marriba he did not know, and at the moment did not dare inquire, though he and Haro had told each other, whispering at night in their sleeping quarters, that, if the chance arose, they would give the girl what help they could, thoughtless as she had been, both to her father and to themselves.

Then, as Harald bent to pick up a pebble to throw at a white pigeon which was pecking away at the opal eyes of an alabaster statuette in the courtyard, he heard the sound of the golden trumpets once more, and stood to attention, expecting that some member of Irene's family might be entering from the city, through the high gates of black marble.

But another Guardsman, who stood at the corner of the hall, only laughed at him and told him not to stand to attention for a squad of his own Company.

'Where have they been?' asked Harald, quietly.

The other man called from behind his hand, 'Up north, comrade; they've been out a month now, escorting a party of merchants who went to do business with the Khazars, trading our silks, gold, and wine for their furs, honey, and wax. Oh yes, and their slaves – I forgot that! But perhaps it's tactless of me to mention it – since you yourself have only recently shaken off the yoke, as it were!'

Harald made a violent gesture to the man, pretending to be very angry with him, but the other Guard put his finger to his nose and said, 'Speak no ill of the Khazars in this Palace, friend, for the last Emperor, Leo, had a Khazar chieftain as his grandfather, so rumour has it!'

Harald would have asked more of this, for the name Khazar interested him; he knew that they were a great people who inhabited the vast plains far inland, and beyond the Black Sea, a warlike folk who often lived in great skin tents and travelled from place to place at grazing time with their herds, a race of warriors who swept down from time to time on outlying towns, riding their half-wild ponies like demons, to burn and pillage without fear of any man.

But there was no time to ask about all this, for the squad of Guards marched in smartly, despite their long desert journey, followed by the merchants who had come to pay their tribute to Irene – and then the slaves. There were perhaps a score of these, mainly bent and dispirited Tartar-folk, whose dull eyes proclaimed their defeat; but there was one among them who caught Harald's eye, for he was an old friend. He stood as tall as a man and half a man, and was as broad in the back as three men standing together. He held himself erect, and so towered over the small folk of the Steppeland.

Harald started from his post on the steps and called, 'Why, Grummoch, you old rogue! Why, Grummoch!'

The giant shambled forward, pushing the Guard aside carelessly, and ran to Harald, who threw down his javelin and embraced the gigantic fellow.

The squad halted and their Captain did not know what to do; the impatient merchants began to bleat that they had paid good money for this slave and were not going to have him spoiled like this.

But then Kristion appeared, his face stern, his hand on the hilt of his great sword.

'Sooner or later,' he said gravely, 'all the big mice get caught in our mousetrap, my friends. And this is a mouse we shall not let go again. You merchants have provided the great lady Irene with a new Guardsman. He will be the tribute you pay this time. Now you may go about your lawful business; I speak for Irene herself.'

The merchants began to cry out that they had paid an enormous sum for the giant, as much as they normally paid for three grown men, and were not going to let him go like that. Kristion turned on them such a face as made them quail.

'Very well,' he said, 'Irene will accept the rest of your merchandise in the place of this slave. Guard, see that the furs, honey, wax, and other things are delivered to the warehouses immediately.'

Only then did the merchants change their tune. And so Giant Grummoch came to Miklagard and, because of the great heart of Kristion, the Captain, became a Guard alongside his old friends, Harald and Haro – though it was a week before the smiths could beat out a breastplate and a sword to fit him!

19. A New Enemy

GRUMMOCH soon became a great favourite with the Guards, because of his immense strength and his good humour. Nor did he ever take advantage of his size when it came to combat practice – though he always asked for four helpings of anything at mealtimes, and was never refused! Indeed, Kristion sent an order to the cooks that they were to give the giant as many helpings as he asked for, as long as the other men did not go short.

Strangely enough, Irene hated him from the moment she first set eyes upon him, and he her. She had stood before him, taunting him, until Harald saw that the giant's temper was almost outworn. Luckily, Irene seemed to have noticed that too, for she moved away from him and vented the rest of her spite on some other unfortunate Guardsman.

Afterwards, Grummoch said humorously, 'Captain Kristion, keep a good watch over that old vixen, for one night when I feel reckless I may go to her room and gobble her up, crown and all!'

But Kristion had only smiled and passed down the line, without punishing the Guard for what, in another man, might have been construed as disloyalty.

Indeed, few of the men took Grummoch at all seriously. They did not even believe the tale he told of his travels over the last months, though Harald had no doubt that they were true, fantastic as they seemed.

After the shipwreck, Grummoch said, he had swum towards the shore, even though his legs were fastened with the iron gyves. Then, when his strength was fading and the sea was coming into his mouth, he had floated on to a half-submerged rock, where he had stayed that night, barely holding on with his failing muscles. The next morning he was found by a small fishing smack, and taken ashore to a little village still inhabited by Spaniards and not Moors. There he stayed for some days, getting back his strength and helping in whatever ways he could; and at last had started his great journey back towards the north, walking across country, through the mountains, and hoping to reach the land of the Franks.

In the mountains he had fallen in with a gang of robbers who had valued him for potentialities as a warrior, and he had helped them too, in certain ways which he would not divulge; but at last the Emperor of the Franks had sent a large party of soldiers to clear these ruffians out of the mountains and they had taken to the sea, hoping to return when the hue and cry had died down.

But unfortunately, they had been wrecked off Corsica and had lived in the woods like savages for some weeks before being captured by a pirate crew who sold them as slaves to some Bulgars.

After that, Grummoch's tale became very confused, for he had escaped many times and had been caught by this tribe and that, until at last, in a final bid for freedom, he had walked right into a camp of foraging Khazars, who had been delighted with their catch.

And so, many months after his capture, he was exchanged to the Byzantine merchants for forty rolls of silk and five amphora of red wine. And then he came to be a Guard in Irene's Company!

It was a great joy to Harald and Haro to see their giant again, for, to tell the truth of it, they had already begun to feel somewhat lonely, out of place, and cut off, in this swarming palace of olive-skinned men and women – courtiers, officials, soldiers, hangers-on round the immensely powerful Irene.

One evening, when the stars speckled the dark blue sky and the three Guardsmen sat about a small brazier on one of the upper ramparts of the palace, Haro said, 'This is no place for us, my brothers. Here men speak one thing and think another. You cannot trust their eyes, they are dark-brown and sly; they always slide away from one's gaze.'

Grummoch nodded and said in his slow way, 'Yes, and always they seem to smile when they speak, as though they are already making some new plot to deceive one.'

Harald was sitting thoughtfully a little away from them. He rose and came over to the brazier slowly.

'I have been thinking,' he said, 'that now we are together, we should try to do something for Marriba. She was a foolish girl, I know, but then most girls are foolish, I have been led to understand, so she is no rarity. From the rumours which come into this place daily, I understand that Constantine will never be allowed to marry her. Indeed, a water-seller in the street yesterday called out, in my hearing, to a friend of his on the other side of the road, that Irene had sworn to put the girl to the torture.'

Haro started and said, 'How could he know that, a simple water-seller?'

'I took him by the arm,' said Harald, 'and held my sword point ever so slightly inclined towards his heart, as I asked him the same question. He was ready enough to answer me, and said that he had it from one of the cooks who usually took the water from him. She had it from a serving-wench who was in Irene's room at a private feast she gave to some of the counsellors. Irene had been drinking much wine, when suddenly she flung down her crystal goblet, breaking it to a thousand slivers in her anger. Then it was that she had burst out with the threat. Her son, she said, had been tempted to rebel against his mother's gentle guidance by this young Muslim hussy, and the sooner the girl was shown that it was dangerous to anger the Most High, the better.'

Grummoch said in his slow voice, 'Do you know where Marriba may be found, Harald?'

Harald nodded. 'Come over here,' he said. 'Now look where I am pointing. Can you see where the avenue of cypresses meets that tall white building with the pointed tower, away beyond the market square? Marriba lives on the second floor of a house near there, a house with a silver star painted above its archway. The water-seller showed me where it was, for I threatened him with torments for spreading palace rumours.'

Suddenly Haro straightened himself and stood up. 'Could you find your way there in the darkness, Harald?' he said.

Harald nodded his head slowly, 'I could do that, my friend,' he said. 'The same thought had come to me as I sat thinking, but I was not sure then whether you two would be prepared to help the girl.'

Grummoch smiled and answered, 'I would prefer that she were the daughter of the High King of Erin, for she is, or was, my own betrothed; but in cases like this, a man does not inquire about a girl's family or attachments before he gives her the help she needs. I am with you, Harald, come what may.'

'And I,' said Haro simply. 'You did not need to ask.'

Harald drew his friends close to him and whispered, 'Good, then, my brothers. We will start as soon as the Guard at the main gate begins his tour of the outer wall. Then we shall reach the street without anyone knowing.'

Giant Grummoch rubbed his great hands with glee. 'I have spent so much time evading capture of one sort and another, such things as this are second nature to me now, friend Viking! But, one thing troubles me, what shall we do when we find her? We cannot bring her back here.'

'No,' said Haro, 'nor dare we try to take her away from Miklagard, for if we were caught, we should pay the worst sort of penalty as deserters from the Imperial Guard.'

Harald nodded and said, 'I have already thought of that. We shall merely remove her to another place, until such time as we can get her safely away from this city of corruption and intrigue. I had thought that we might get her away to Kristion's sister in the country, but that would place the Captain in an awkward position, since Irene trusts him entirely. So it will be best to put the girl in some little house in a back street, the house of such a man as my water-seller, for example, where she would never be suspected of hiding.'

Haro said, with a strange smile, 'There is one great problem – suppose she refuses to believe us that she is in danger? Suppose she refuses to come with us?'

Grummoch flexed his great arms and said, 'In my time, I have carried two grown calves at once. Surely I can manage a young girl!'

Harald grinned and answered, 'I do not know, giant. A young girl of this sort might well turn out to be difficult, even for such a man as you.'

Just then Haro pointed down over the courtyard; the guard was presenting his javelin and coming up to attention, as they did when they were about to set off on a tour of the outer wall.

'Come,' said Harald, 'now is our chance!'

Removing their bright helmets so that the starlight should not give them away, glistening on the burnished metal, they bent their heads and moved along the wall and so down the first staircase that led to the courtyard.

But before they reached the lower stairway, Harald held up his hand for them to stop. They did so and followed his gaze; he was staring at a small round window in the inner wall of the stairwell. The flicker of candlelight came through the aperture and also the sound of voices – two voices, a woman's and a boy's, the first insistent and domineering, the other high and tremulous, the voice of a coward, or one almost out of his wits with terror.

Harald crept to the window, holding his scabbard tightly lest it should rattle against the wall and give them away. He looked down into a room almost as high and narrow as a water-well. From the many chains and gyves which hung from the walls, he knew what this place was – the torture chamber. But it was not the irons and manacles which caught the Viking's eye – it was the two people in that horrible room – Irene and her weak son, Constantine. The boy lay grovelling among the straw on the stone floor, his legs chained to the wall, his arms stretched out in supplication.

'I will promise to do anything you say, Mother of Glory,' he moaned, 'only do not leave me in this cell another night. I am frightened by the sounds that come in through the window when all the Palace is asleep. They seem to gibber and grunt at me, mocking me . . .'

Irene smiled bitterly and pushed the boy's head back with her sandalled foot.

'I should think they *do* gibber and grunt at you, you fool! That is all the sense you seem to understand, gibberings and grunts!' she said. She paused for a while then and half-turned away from the weeping Prince. Then so softly that Harald had difficulty in hearing her words, she said, 'There are ways of preventing such things from troubling you, brave one. There are ways of stopping unpleasant sounds from reaching one's ears . . . just as there are ways of stopping a man from seeing things which disturb him. You understand me, O Emperor?'

As she spoke, Constantine began to howl with terror, trying again and again to grasp the fringe at the edge of her robe.

'Great Mother, Dear One, Sweetest One,' he cried, 'do not hurt me, I beg you! I will do anything, anything, if you will not let them hurt me!'

Irene looked down on her son in immense contempt, her cruel eyes narrowed, her cruel lips smiling wickedly. 'So,' she said in her deep voice, 'this is the little puppet that thought itself an Emperor of the Roman World! This is the man who would lead an army to glory, is it?'

Harald bit his lip and whispered savagely, 'If I had a little bird bow here now I could rid Byzantium of a devil, a she-devil!

Haro shook his head sadly, 'Constantine is not worth it, my friend,' he said. 'He is as cruel as his mother and would give you no thanks. Consider, had it not been for good Kristion, we should still be rotting in prison because of this coward, Constantine.'

They stopped whispering then, because Irene's voice had begun once more.

'Very well, my little one,' she said, 'perhaps I will forget your wickedness to me this once. Soon I will send the paper to you to sign. You shall declare that you have named me to act as your Regent, and a number of other small things . . . Including your solemn oath not to marry this Muslim wench. Now that I come to consider it, you shall also sign that she is to be put to death, without delay, for

inciting you to break the settled peace of your great City. I will have that drawn up tomorrow. Do you promise to sign it?'

Constantine flung himself face downwards in a spasm of relief. 'Yes, dear mother,' he almost shouted, 'I will sign it a thousand times, if you will set me free.'

Irene gazed upon him again and said, 'There, you are overwrought, little one. Perhaps you are a good boy, after all! Wait patiently until tomorrow when I can get the scribe to make out such a paper, and then, when you have put your mark on it, you shall go free. Or at least, almost free, for I cannot have you wandering outside the Palace, getting into trouble again.'

Harald turned from the window suddenly. 'Come on,' he said, 'it seems that we must act tonight, before that paper may become the law.'

They ran down the lower staircase, and across the courtyard. From the Officers' Mess, they saw the amber light streaming, and heard the sound of merry voices singing a camp song; Kristion's voice was loud and clear, ringing high above all other voices. The three soldiers ran on and passed through the gateway and into the darkness, just as the sentry finished his circuit of the wall and came once more into view.

As they went, keeping to the lonelier streets, Harald said, 'So Constantine is a new enemy! The coward, so to sign away the life of one who loves him, however silly she may be in giving her heart to such a little monster!'

Haro said grimly, 'Perhaps we can get even with him, before our stay in this den of wild beasts is finished.'

Then they came to the place where the avenue of cypresses met the white tower, and Harald suddenly stopped and drew his companions back into the shadow of a column. His eyes were wide open in surprise and bewilderment. 'Look,' he said hoarsely 'we are forestalled!'

The others followed the pointing finger and saw the glitter of breastplates and shields in the light which strayed from the many windows of the square.

All along the narrow street, and across the archway which led to Marriba's lodging, soldiers were posted, men of Irene's own Company, there was no mistaking their helmet plumes and breastplate insignia . . .

Haro struck himself hard upon the chest, as though angry with the part he had played. 'If only we had got here more quickly . . .' he groaned.

But Harald shook his head, 'Irene is making sure,' he whispered. 'She is not one to take chances, my friend. I have no doubt that these men have been stationed here all day long. We must not reproach ourselves. Now there is nothing we can do, except go back to the Palace. Perhaps tomorrow, we may think of something.'

Haro said sharply, 'It will be a bad thing for Marriba if we do not act more quickly than we have done tonight.'

They turned then and walked quickly back along the street, keeping in the shadow of the high houses. Grummoch followed his comrades like an immense shadow, keeping watch that they were not attacked from behind.

20. Unexpected Ally

THE DAY which followed passed on leaden wings. The two Vikings and giant Grummoch were unable to settle down to do anything as it should be done. First they were reprimanded for not making up their beds in the official manner; then they were reported by the head cook for not sweeping out the hall properly, after the morning meal; and before midday, they were threatened with twenty lashes for not burnishing their breastplates so that a man's face could be seen in them clearly, as was the custom among the Imperial Guard.

The sergeant who threatened them glared fiercely down as they sat cross-legged in the shadow of a bathhouse.

'You Northmen,' he stormed, 'are fit for nothing but shovelling cattle fodder! Why I have to train such fools as you, I cannot tell; I must have committed some great sin in a former life and this is my punishment.'

Giant Grummoch lazily took up a javelin and, holding it in his two hands, suddenly snapped the ash shaft with a quick movement. Then, just as lazily, he said in his shrill voice, 'I am sorry the little spear broke, sergeant. I am used to stronger weapons.'

Then he rose to his feet, as heavily as a laden ox, and turned towards the sergeant, his great hands outstretched. The man backed from him, his dark eyes starting in sudden fear.

But Grummoch only smiled, the corners of his broad mouth turning up slightly, and said, 'If you will give me another spear, sergeant, I will see that it does not happen again.'

The sergeant mopped his brow with relief, and trying to regain some of his former composure, said, 'Very well, Guardsman, you shall have another spear. But do not let that accident happen to the new one. You may dismiss!'

Grummoch sat down again, smiling, and pretending to fit the two broken pieces together again.

Haro grinned and said, 'I have not seen a man so frightened for a long time.'

Harald said, 'You saw one last night, when his mother was threatening him with torture.'

But Haro shook his head. 'No,' he said, 'that was not a man – just a small and treacherous beast.'

It was at this moment that a Guard staggered in from the town where he had been on patrol in the big open market, keeping order among the swarming traders. His face was white and fearful. They saw the sweat glistening on his forehead, beneath the peak of his bronze helmet.

'Have you any water, comrades?' he said, suddenly slumping down beside them on the stone pavement.

Grummoch flung his water-bottle to the man, who drank greedily.

'What is the matter, friend?' asked Harald.

The man turned towards him, his mouth quivering. 'Something is wrong,' he said. 'It is as though the scent of death hangs over the city today. Three times I have seen a man stop in the midst of his bargaining and fall to the ground, with the white froth on his lips. It is not good, my friend.'

As he spoke, the bright sky seemed suddenly to cloud, with a heavy sulphurous lowering. The man wiped the sweat from his face and got up slowly.

'It seems that you have a fever, comrade,' said Grummoch. 'You should report to your Captain.'

The man nodded and staggered away, dragging his long javelin on the stones behind him.

When he had gone, Harald said, 'I do not like the look of that. No Guard I have ever seen trailed his javelin in that manner.'

Grummoch said quietly, 'I do not think that we shall ever go on parade with that one again, my friend. He had a strange look about the eyes which I have seen before – but never twice in the eyes of the same man.'

They were about to speak more on this matter when the high snarling trumpet called out that they were to assemble for a surprise inspection in the great courtyard. Instantly men came running from all directions, buckling on their equipment as they ran. The three friends rose and joined their ranks.

Then Irene appeared, strolling slowly through the high arched doorway of the Palace, her painted face set in a grim smile. The Guardsmen stood as straight and as motionless as though they had been carved from stone, though in the intense heat the strain was immense.

Irene moved between the ranks with a painful slowness, as though she meant to test the endurance of her soldiers to the utmost. One young lad in the rear rank suddenly gave a groan and fell face downwards, his shield and spear clattering on to the paved courtyard beside him. His comrades on either side instantly leapt forward to raise him, but Irene's voice cut harshly through the heavy air.

'Let the dog lie,' she said. 'He must suffer for his weakness. My Guards must be men of iron or must die in their weakness.'

She paused a moment and then said to Kristion, 'Have those two who broke the ranks whipped before the sun goes down. Fifty lashes apiece. That should teach them to stand like soldiers when their Empress does them the honour of visiting them.'

Kristion frowned, but could do nothing at that moment. He nodded to a sergeant who marched the two Guardsmen away to the barrack block.

Then Irene was level with the three friends and they saw that she held a small roll of paper in her right hand, decorated with the Imperial seal. They had no doubt that this was the document which Constantine had signed, the death warrant of Marriba.

Irene paused a little while in front of them, smiling as she surveyed them from head to toe. Grummoch felt his legs suddenly quivering, as though the muscles would stand this strain no longer than might make him run forward and strike this woman down.

But she passed on then, and at last returned to the Palace.

When she had gone, Kristion returned to his Company and said, 'Guardsmen, you may dismiss; but hold yourselves in readiness should the Most High require your services before this day is out.'

As the three friends were moving away, he called them and said, 'You heard what the Most High said, about giving those Guardsmen fifty lashes apiece? Well, go and whip them.'

Harald said, 'Do you mean that, Captain?'

Kristion turned a strangely humorous gaze upon the Viking and said, 'I have given my order; but I did not say what you were to whip them with. Use your discretion, Guardsman.'

So it was that the three Northmen surprised the prisoners greatly by tying them up gently and whipping them with a length of helmet ribbon, such as was worn on festive occasions, a thin silk braid. After which, they reported back to Kristion that the prisoners had been well whipped, with a few extra strokes for good measure.

He smiled and said, 'Good; now release them. They are two of my best soldiers – and no doubt, two of your best friends from this day on.'

And so it turned out to be.

Later that afternoon, a provisioner they all knew and trusted – an unusual situation as far as the city traders were concerned – trundled his empty fruit barrow into the courtyard, and spreading his hands in despair bewailed the loss of his goods.

'My lords,' he wailed, 'my business is ruined! All my lovely fruits have been stolen! I was stopped in the street and robbed, I tell you!'

A sergeant who was passing took the man by his arm and shook him, pretending to be angry.

'You rogue,' he said, 'you know well enough that you have sold the fruit intended for us at twice the price to some unsuspecting trader from Khazaria!'

The provisioner shook his head violently and almost wept.

'No, lord, no!' he said vehemently. 'A crowd of ruffians knocked me down – look, here is the bruise – and took my fruit! They said that now the plague has come to the city, it is every man's right to take what he can, while there is anything to take.'

At these words, the chattering groups of soldiers fell silent. The sergeant's smile faded from his sunburnt face.

'Are you sure that the plague has truly come, old friend?' he asked.

The tradesman beat his thin breast in anguish.

'Sure!' he echoed, 'Sure? I should think I am sure! Has not my own brother's mother-in-law passed away with it this very day? Is not my third cousin's youngest child sickening with it this very minute?'

The sergeant flung the man a handful of coins and turned to the assembled soldiers.

'Make ready,' he said abruptly. 'You may be needed in the city at any time now, for riots will break out and shops be broken into when the news spreads.'

Then he marched off to inform the Chamberlain of the grave occasion.

The late afternoon sun had sunk and the first twilight was creeping over the white city, when Kristion strode into the courtyard. His face was set and his eyes narrow. He walked among the men, who stood waiting for any order which he might give, and carefully chose five Guardsmen, telling them to stand to one side. They were the three friends and the two who had been whipped with helmet ribbons that morning. The other Guardsmen stood staring at them, wondering what duty had so suddenly been assigned to them. At that moment, no one envied them, for suddenly the city had become a place of danger, of ill-omen, almost of terror.

Then Kristion stood the five men to attention and addressed them, saying, 'Men, you have been chosen to perform a task of some unpleasantness, but one which you must not shirk if you are loyal to the Most High, Irene, and to your Company. You will march as a squad to a house in the city, led by myself, and there you will do what you are commanded.'

Harald looked him in the eye. 'Captain,' he said quietly, so that only his immediate companions heard his words, 'is the unpleasant duty to do with a certain lady from Jebel Tarik?'

For a moment, Kristion stared back at Harald as though he did not know whether to punish him or not. But at last he nodded slowly.

'I have the Imperial warrant here,' he said, touching the roll of paper with the seal, which they had last seen in Irene's hand that morning.

Then, before the three could frame another question, or even think of what they should do, Kristion formed them up and led them out of the main gate.

The sentry sprang smartly to attention as they passed and raised his javelin, crying, 'May good fortune ever smile on Her!'

Kristion nodded curtly and said, as he returned the salute, 'May She prosper!'

But Harald, who marched nearest to the Captain, noticed that as he spoke those words, his thin lips curled in bitterness.

As the squad marched on through the darkening streets, Harald stole a glance at Haro, who stared back and suddenly made a gesture of running his forefinger across his throat and nodding towards Kristion, who was gazing ahead. But Harald shook his head; Kristion had already been too good a friend to them.

At the end of the first narrow street, they came out into a small square, surrounded by high white buildings and edged with dark trees. At the base of each tree, and huddled in every archway, figures lay wrapped in robes, shrouds, lengths of sacking, anything that could be put to that final and dreadful purpose. In the middle of the square, a great brazier smouldered, throwing off the thick smoke of sulphur and casting a low-lying cloud of yellow vapour, which hung head-high across that forlorn place.

Kristion halted his squad and half-turned to them.

'The plague has struck heavily here,' he began. Then he gave a short gasp and put his hand to his forehead suddenly, knocking off his light ceremonial helmet. The Guardsmen gazed at him in bewilderment and saw the beads of sweat break out on his olive skin, the light froth which gathered at his lips of a sudden, flecking his dark beard. As they watched him, he swung round as though trying to avoid a blow, then staggered away from them and fell, breathing harshly, against the wall.

Harald ran towards him, 'Captain,' he said, 'what ails you?'

Kristion looked at him as though he were a stranger, or as though he could hardly see. Then he shook his head and tried to smile.

'Viking,' he gasped, 'it is the wish of the Most High, Irene, that I strike off the head of the girl, Marriba, tonight. She commanded me to take a squad and see that this was done . . . That is why I chose you and your friends, and those two who owe you something and will obey you . . .'

The Captain's voice failed him for a moment, as Harald said, 'But Kristion, I could never have helped you to do such a thing, you know that.'

The Captain of the Imperial Guard slid down the wall until he rested on his knees on the pavement. He looked up at Harald and smiled.

'I know that well enough, my friend. That is why you are here with me now,' he said weakly.

Then slowly and with fumbling fingers, he untied the purple sash which was his Captain's emblem, and held it out towards Harald.

'Viking,' he said, 'I am a sick man, I know that; I have seen too many smitten with this plague not to know the signs of death. Take this sash and put it on. Then go forward and do as you think is right in this matter.'

Harald took the sash, wondering at the Captain's courage, and slowly wrapped it about his waist.

Kristion, the great Captain, watched him with a still smile, then, raising his right hand in salute he croaked, 'Hail, Captain of the Guard in Byzantium!'

As he finished his greeting, he fell forward on to the stones of the pavement and lay still. Haro ran to pick him up, but Harald waved him away and said, 'There is nothing that we can do, my brother. It is the will of whatever God he prayed to. Let us go quickly and take advantage of this change in our fortune.'

As the others moved away, Harald stooped and patted the Captain Kristion on the shoulder, as though he were alive again and knew what was happening.

Then he hastened on after the four Guards.

21. Marriba's End

AS THEY marched on along the tree-lined avenue, Haro said, 'That was a good man and a true soldier we have left lying in the street, comrades.'

Harald said, 'If all Christians were like that one, there is not a true man who would not be a Christian. Kristion is just such another man as the priest, John, who once held me up in the sea until the Danish longship rescued me. I have often thought about that. I owe my life to a Christian, and soon, perhaps, another will owe her life to one. When I get the opportunity, friend Haro, I shall burn ten candles in a Christian church for Kristion, if his God will accept the offering.'

Haro replied, 'I think that He will, Harald; He seems an understanding God to me, after what I know of Thor and Odin.'

As they talked in this manner, they passed many folk lying in doorways, inert or groaning; and here and there, at the street corners, they glimpsed small groups of men with angry faces, who melted into the dusk as the soldiers came up to them. Over all the city there was the heavy stench of sulphur and of green herbs, which had been flung on to the many braziers and street fires to keep away the plague.

So at last they came to the white tower where Marriba had her lodging. Four Guardsmen stood before the archway which led into her house, looking impatiently to left and to right, as though they were tired of their long vigil.

When Harald marched up to them, they sprang to attention, seeing his Captain's sash.

'Greetings, Captain,' said their sergeant, who stared at the Viking in surprise when he recognized him. 'These are good times for quick promotion.'

Harald sensed the old soldier's resentment and replied, 'That is a question for you to discuss with the Most High. She will no doubt be interested to hear your remarks on her choice of officers.'

The sergeant dropped his eyes and mumbled, 'I meant no offence, Captain.'

Harald stared at him impassively. 'Very well, sergeant,' he said. 'March your men away immediately and report to the Palace. We have come to relieve you.'

Without another word, the sergeant saluted and then turned and called his men together. As they marched away across the square, Grummoch said, 'It was good to me to see the look on that sergeant's face!'

Harald smiled bitterly and said, 'It is the first order I have given, as Captain of the Guard in Byzantium; it may well be my last!'

Then quietly he whispered to Haro to follow him into the house, and told the others to wait outside for him, keeping well in the shadow of the building.

'Do not let anyone come up these stairs,' he told them. 'No, not the Most High herself!'

The soldiers nodded, for already they had come to like this quiet Viking who assumed power so easily without assuming the arrogance which too often goes with it.

On the first landing of the stairway, Harald said, 'Stay here, friend Haro. Come up only if I call you. Do not let anyone follow after me, for what I go to do must be kept a secret.'

Haro said, 'I would hold back the whole of Irene's Company.'

Harald smiled down at him in friendship, then drawing his short sword he flung open the door and entered.

The old woman, Lalla, gave a cry of terror and dragged her skirts over her head, shrinking back among the cushions on the floor. Marriba sat on a small gilded stool in the middle of the room. She did not move as Harald strode across the floor towards her, but smiled quietly, looking past him into space.

'Strike quickly, soldier,' she said, as though she was inviting him to sit down, or to taste some sweetmeat that lay on the little table beside her. 'Strike quickly and cleanly,' she repeated. 'I have been expecting you for three days and I do not wish to wait any longer.'

Harald fell on his knees before her, amazed at her courage, and laid his sword in her lap. Only then did her gaze come back within the four walls of the room, and she looked down at him with a gentle surprise, recognizing him in spite of the great peak of his bronze helmet.

She put her hand on his shoulder for an instant and said, 'Why, have you been given this unpleasant task, then? How cruel of Irene to make you do it.'

But Harald shook his head and said urgently, 'I have come to give you your freedom in another way, Marriba. Come, there is no time to waste, you must do as I say.'

She paused for a moment and said shyly, 'Constantine . . . has he sent no message? Has he not tricked his mother and sent me a message?'

Harald turned his face away, unwilling to look the girl in the eyes when he told her the savage truth of the matter, yet knowing that the truth must be told.

'Lady,' he said as gently as he could, 'Constantine was unfaithful to you; he even signed your death warrant so that he might not be put to any further inconvenience. He is unworthy of you, Marriba; you must forget him and take your chance of freedom.'

She stood up then and said simply, 'Yes, I think I knew it, but I hoped against hope that he might have found strength from somewhere. Very well, Viking, what am I to do?'

Harald took back the sword which she offered him and said, 'First, I would be pleased if you would scream; something rather sharp and frightening, lady; for, after all, I am supposed to be here for a sharp and frightening business!'

Marriba smiled sadly, then she went to the window and screamed. Harald was quite taken aback by the convincing sound which the girl produced. He heard the voices of the soldiers in the street stop suddenly, as though they too had been taken in. Then Harald went to the door and opened it. Haro was standing outside, his own sword out, his eyes wild.

'It is all right, my friend,' said Harald smiling. 'No harm has come to her; you may go back to your post.'

Then, though much against her will, the sword which had been brought to that house for one purpose was used for another; swiftly, Harald cut off the girl's long hair, looking away as each thick tress fell to the floor. Then, with the help of Lalla, who had by now come round, he knotted a small turban on Marriba's head and tucked her long gown about her so that it looked like a tunic.

Afterwards he stood back and said, 'You make a very pleasant-looking boy. You must take care that some silly young girl does not fall in love with you before you reach your father's house at Jebel Tarik once again.'

Marriba suddenly fell upon her knees before Harald, clasping his hands tightly. 'My dear friend,' she said. 'I do not deserve such a protector as you. And am I really going back to my father?'

Harald said grimly, 'If you do not reach your father's house safe, it will be because Haro lies dead on the ground. He will take you back, lady.'

Marriba said slowly, 'But it is so far and we have no money.'

Harald answered quietly, 'Haro has found his way half across the world on more than one occasion; travelling is nothing new to him. He has a sword and a ready tongue; I have no doubt that, before morning, he will have found money, one way or another – though it strikes me that he is more likely to find a boat for the two of you. That is more in his line and would be much more useful than money.'

Harald went to the door and called Haro within. Quickly he told him what they had planned, and as he spoke, Haro nodded solemnly, as though he had expected it all along.

Then Harald turned to go. 'Stay here, my friends,' he said, 'until I have taken my men out of sight of this house. Then make your way down to the harbour by the back streets. One day we may all meet again. Farewell!'

Suddenly Haro clasped him by the hands, and Marriba flung her arms about him.

'We cannot let you go,' said the girl, in tears. 'Come with us, Harald, and I will see that my father makes you a rich man!'

Harald turned his back on them, for he suddenly found that his eyes were becoming damp too. He shook his head.

'No,' he said, 'I have no wish to live out my days in Spain, thank you. Besides, friend Grummoch would feel lonely. Also, I have a hankering to see something more of the world before I settle down. No, I must go my way. Take care of her, Haro; and goodbye, lady.'

As he went back into the street, he was careful to be seen wiping the blade of his sword. But Grummoch was not deceived. A roguish smile played about his thick lips, but he said nothing.

One of the other soldiers said, 'Where is Haro, Captain?'

Harald nodded back up the stairs. 'I have left him to guard the body,' he said. 'The Most High would wish that; she might want to make one of her inspections, you know.'

The two men stared at Harald, a strange light playing in their eyes. 'It is well that we are all in this affair together,' said one of them.

Harald asked, 'What do you mean by that, Guardsman?'

The soldier began to shoulder his long javelin. 'I mean that we are men who can keep a secret, Captain,' he replied. His companion nodded in agreement, smiling. Then they began to march back to the Palace.

When they reached the spot where Kristion had fallen with the plague, Harald stopped and spread his own cloak over the body, and put the purple sash over the Captain's chest.

Then he stepped back and gave Kristion a final salute.

'We shall not see such a man again, my friends,' he said. They did not reply, but looked down on the still Captain with gentle eyes. Then they marched on towards the high Palace walls. Once inside, Harald told the men to wait while he reported that the duty had been carried out successfully.

As he strode across the coloured tiles of the great hall, he almost ran into the Chamberlain, who was bustling out, breathless, his face wet with sweat, his hands shaking with anxiety. Harald saluted him, raising his flat hand out above his head, after the custom of the Imperial Guard.

'Hail, my lord,' he said. 'I bring a message for the Most High.'

The Chamberlain stopped and stared at him as though he were some unusual wild creature brought from foreign parts.

'The Most High?' he said. 'The Most High? Why, Irene is not here. No, she left for Chrysopolis, across the water, half an hour ago. She and the Prince – they think the air will be cleaner there – less danger of plague. And I must be going too, my dear fellow. Really, I must. The boat is waiting for me, down at the quay. You must excuse me.'

He began to totter past Harald, who called after him, 'When you see the Most High, my lord, tell her that we carried out our duty. Marriba will never trouble her again.'

The Chamberlain did not even stop or turn round, but shambled on, nodding, his face streaked with fear. 'Yes, my dear fellow,' he muttered. 'I won't forget . . . No, I won't forget.'

Harald smiled grimly after him, then he too turned and went to where his men stood waiting for him, realizing that now there was no one in authority to whom he could report the death of Kristion.

22. City in Flames

AS HARALD made his way towards the small postern where he had left his friends, his mind was clouded with doubts. Obviously the Palace would soon be left to the care of what remained of the Imperial Guard, since both Irene and her ministers were fleeing from the plague and would undoubtedly be away from Byzantium as long as there was any danger of the disease spreading. Moreover, it was likely that within a few days at the most, death would be so rampant within the city that the Guard would become virtually imprisoned within the Palace walls, for fear of infection.

And that might become inconvenient for at least two reasons; food supplies would be scarce, and the Palace would become the unfailing target for any unrest which arose among the suffering population of the city's poorer districts.

As Harald turned over these thoughts in his mind, an angry red glow was flung across the sky from the northern suburbs of Byzantium. Hardly had this appeared, when a smaller flush spread over the low clouds to the west.

Harald turned in time to see a third area of sky glowing a dull bronze-red. There could be no mistaking such signs. The rebellious elements of the city, having heard, no doubt, that their rulers had deserted them, were taking the law into their own hands, and were setting fire to those parts of the city which were unprotected.

Grummoch met Harald and said, 'This is what I expected, friend. Do we stay and roast, or do we set out on our travels again, to see what else the world holds for a pair of likely fellows?'

Harald turned to catch the eyes of the two soldiers who had moved up close behind him and were waiting for his answer.

'What say you, my friends?' Harald asked them. 'Will you stay in the Palace and risk starving, or will you come for a little walk with us, to see what the world is like outside Miklagard?'

The elder of the soldiers took Harald by the hand. 'Friend,' he said, 'nothing would please us better than to go walking with you; but my friend Justinian and I have wives and children over the water at Pera. It runs in our minds to go now and comfort them.'

Harald said, 'You are wise men, my friends. Go, and one day I hope we may meet again.'

The two men threw their swords and javelins into a corner and ran swiftly towards the great open gate. Harald heard them joking with the Guard who lolled there, telling him that they were only going as far as the next corner, by the sergeant's orders, to see if the night breeze was fanning the fires. Then they disappeared.

'We might try the same trick,' said Grummoch. 'But it would be wise for us to walk in the opposite direction.'

Harald nodded and they walked towards the gate, without their javelins but hiding their swords beneath their tunics.

'Halt!' shouted the Guard, suspiciously. 'Where do you walk, men?'

Grummoch answered, 'We go at the sergeant's orders to see if the fires are being fanned by the night's breeze, Guardsman.'

The man smiled cynically and shook his head. 'You know the rules as well as I do, my little man,' he said. 'Only two allowed out at one time, except by special pass. Have you a pass?'

It was in Grummoch's mind to march up to the man and show him his great ham of a fist and to tell him that this was his pass. But at that moment there sounded a sudden scurry of many feet down the narrow street and a mob of excited townsfolk came into view, yelling and waving sticks and rough weapons.

'Down with Irene, the she-wolf!' they shouted. 'Down with her idiot of a son! They have brought disaster upon us! The Bishops warned us that we risked damnation in supporting Irene! The Bishops are right! Where is Irene? We will slay her and her son! We will burn her Palace of Unrighteousness! Down with Irene! Down with the Guard! They are butchers! They are the hounds of their evil Mistress!'

The Guard at the gate calmly lowered his javelin, which had prevented the passage of Harald and Grummoch. Then

he drew a silver whistle from his belt-pouch and blew a shrill blast upon it.

'You two had better go and get your javelins, my friends,' he said with a cold smile to Harald and Grummoch.

Behind them, in the barrack block, a trumpet began to sound the 'Fall in!' The two men heard the sound of their comrades' feet pattering on the stone courtyard.

They were caught between the mob and the Imperial Guard.

Just then stones began to fly. One struck Grummoch on the chest, but did him no harm; another struck the sentry between the eyes. He fell like a slain ox and lay still.

Grummoch rolled him aside and said, 'Come on, Harald, or we shall be too late!'

Then, with a great roar, he drew his sword from under his tunic and charged at the crowd. Harald came beside him, shouting out with all his strength, 'Up the North! Death to all traitors!'

The mob faded before them, like wisps of smoke before a fierce gust of wind. Suddenly the street was empty and then Grummoch said, 'Come on, lad, or we'll be caught again!'

They turned and ran with all their speed away from the Palace gate, and did not stop for breath until they were once more in the centre of the city.

They stood panting beside a tamarisk tree when Harald said suddenly, 'I have seen the light, friend Grummoch! Look, do you notice a house at the end of that alleyway, with a door shaped like a Frankish shield set on its end? Well, that house was once described to me by an old man, when I was in prison here. It is one of the secret treasure houses of Her Imperial Majesty – one of many, scattered about the city.'

Grummoch ruminated like a great bull. 'I recall what a splendid store of treasure I once had, little Harald, way back in the kingdom of MacMiorog of Dun-an-oir. That treasure I lost – you know how! I would like to reimburse myself for it, somehow, before I die.'

Harald nodded and said, 'Irene owes us a month's pay, Grummoch; and we served her well. After all, did we not dispose of Marriba for her? Come on, let us see what is to be found there!'

The door shaped like a shield opened easily when they set their shoulders to it, and they found themselves faced by a narrow stone passageway, at the far end of which was a small square courtyard, set round on three sides with squat pillars.

Harald ran straightway to a square flagstone in the middle of the courtyard. There was an iron ring set into it.

'This is the place,' he said excitedly. 'The old man described it all – even the iron ring. If we lift that flagstone, we shall find a flight of steps leading directly into the cellar where the gold is stowed.'

Grummoch had taken the ring firmly in his hand when a light shone on them from behind. As they turned in surprise, a man came from behind one of the squat pillars, a long curved sword in his right hand.

'You choose the right moment, my lords,' he said in a sly and silky voice. 'But, alas, you forget that I am the official guardian of what lies below.'

Harald stared him in the eye and said, 'We are Guardsmen of the Company of the Most High. We come at her command, to bring back treasure for her, to pay for anything she might require while she is away from Byzantium.'

The man gazed at Harald for a long while and then began to smile. 'Indeed,' he said. 'Yet only an hour ago a messenger came from the Most High, threatening me with a slow death if as much as a single plate were moved from its place when she got back from Chrysopolis! How do you account for that, then, my good fellows?'

Grummoch shrugged his massive shoulders and walked a pace towards the man, until the point of the curved sword was almost touching his throat. He folded his arms so that the guardian of the treasure should not feel suspicious and then, with a queer little smile on his lips, said, 'Once in Erin, in the kingdom of the High King of Drumnacoigh, there was a treasure house, much bigger than this. And the guardian of that house was a warrior, such as you might be yourself, but with an unusual equipment for the job; he had an eye set in the back of his head, just below where the hair grows thickest.'

The Byzantine guard smiled with malice and said, 'I have heard such stories before, my friend. Do not come any nearer.'

Grummoch smiled and gazed up towards the stars.

'But that is not the strangest part of the story,' he said. 'For this man had a special cap made, with a little hole in the back, so that he could see even when his head was covered – as it must always be in Ireland, for there are to be found small hawks, no bigger than a child's hand, which settle on a man's head and pluck out his hairs and take them to a wizard who lives under the rock of Killymaguish. There the hairs are made into magic potions, and no man whose hair has been so used can ever call his soul his own again.'

The point of the curved sword began to waver. The man said in a slightly less angry voice, 'Yes, that is interesting. We have a story which is similar to that, in Byzantium.'

Grummoch said, 'I will break off my tale to hear yours, friend, for I am a simple man who delights in hearing good tales. Perhaps when I have heard yours, I shall be able to take it back to my chieftain in Ireland and gain the hand of his fairest daughter for telling it.'

He began to laugh then, as though the plan appealed to him. The man with the sword smiled at the simplicity of this great giant and then, with a shrug, said, 'The difference between our stories is that the hawks are very big ones.'

'How big?' asked Grummoch, putting his hands behind his broad back and rocking on his feet as he gazed up at the stars.

'About as broad in the wingspan as this,' said the guardian, stretching out his hands, the lantern in one, the sword in the other.

Grummoch's right foot shot out and the man fell on to his back. The sword clattered away into the dusk. The lantern rolled over the paving stones, sending out a whirligig of light across the courtyard. Grummoch sat on the man, gently but firmly.

'I should have known better than to trust a foreigner,' said the guardian of the Imperial treasure house, sadly.

Grummoch said, 'If you are quiet and do not wriggle so much, I shall not hurt you at all. But if you as much as raise a whisper, I shall leave no more of you intact than would feed a sickly sparrow.'

The man said, 'That is understood, my friend. I am a fatalist. Only I would be grateful if you would sit on another part of me; I have always had a weak chest, and your weight brings on my old cough, which I thought this dry summer had almost cured.'

'With pleasure,' said Grummoch, as he moved lower down. But the guardian groaned so much at this, that Grummoch took off the man's belt and tied his ankles together. Then he tore the man's robe into strips and tied and gagged him.

'You understand, comrade,' he said, 'I could do much more, but I prefer to do less.'

The man nodded, for really he was a reasonable fellow and loved Irene no more than any other man. So Grummoch was able to join Harald, who was by this time down in the treasure cellar, stuffing goblets, plate, and bracelets into a sack which he had found on the floor.

Grummoch brought down the lantern, and when he flashed its beam round the place almost fell back with wonder.

'This is more than I ever dreamed of,' he said, 'and in my time I was not unused to such sights!'

When they had filled the sack, they clambered back up the stairs.

Their surprise did not come until they had passed back down the narrow alleyway and into the street again. Then they saw a sight which almost sent them scuttling back to the courtyard they had left. A mob of over fifty strong was waiting in the square, looking to right and left, waving swords and torches.

Grummoch went first into the street with the treasure sack on his back. The mob saw him and instantly a great howl went up.

'There they are! There are the two who attacked us outside the Palace!' shouted a tall man with a pointed black cap. 'After them, friends! Every blow we strike is a blow against Irene!'

At the end of the street they were in, Harald gasped, 'I cannot go much farther, Grummoch, I have a terrible stitch!'

The savage pattering of sandalled feet sounded behind them, the fierce shouts grew nearer. Stones began to rattle on the walls beside them.

Grummoch grunted hoarsely, 'The deer that cannot run gets eaten!'

Harald gasped out, 'Into that archway, friend. If we stay on the street they will catch us!'

In a moment they had turned into a curved archway. Grummoch swung the heavy door to behind him. They raced along a passageway, across a stone courtyard and then clambered over a wall. They fell straightway into a sloping meadow, where a stream flowed down towards a conduit. The place was surrounded by tall houses with many black windows, but it was night-time and they rolled unashamedly down the slope. At last, standing knee-deep in the covered waterway, they dared to breathe again.

Above them the sounds of pursuit died away, and finally all was still again.

Grummoch said, 'Now let us try to make our way out of this city of evil. I saw a path beyond the conduit when the moon came out last; it leads to a gateway at the bottom end of this field.'

They began to walk slowly along the path, which now shone grey in the moonlight. Just before they reached the broad gateway, Grummoch started back. There was something white, perched on the ledge beside the lintels, and the sound it made was not one which either of these men had heard before.

23. The Inland Sea

THEN Harald burst out laughing at their fear. He moved forward to the white thing and took it up.

'Look,' he said, 'it is nothing but a baby, wrapped in a shawl.'

'And a very young baby at that,' said Grummoch, taking the little creature gently in his big hands and looking down at it. 'I have not seen one as young as this before. What a strange sound they make, my friend.'

Harald stumbled over something in the darkness of the wall. He bent down and then stood upright again with a sigh.

'The child's mother lies there. She is very young. It is sad that plague should be so cruel. She must have placed her baby there for safety before she fell.'

But Grummoch did not seem to hear him; the giant was so occupied with his tiny burden, trying not to jolt the baby, crooking it in the great angle of his arm so as to protect it.

'You must take the treasure sack now, comrade,' he said to Harald. 'I will carry this most precious piece of treasure.'

They went through the gateway and out into a rutted lane, edged with buildings of a more rustic character, as though they belonged to the outermost suburbs of the city.

Behind them, the clustered houses on the hill were illumined in the sullen glow of the many fires which now seemed to rage unchecked within Byzantium. Grummoch nodded back towards them and said, 'I am glad that we are away from that place, Harald. It was no sort of home for men like us.'

Harald answered, 'All the same, friend, we have not done badly. We have come away richer than we were when we first arrived there.'

Grummoch nodded as he shambled on along the uneven path in the dimness of the moonlight.

'Yes,' he said, 'and we have the baby as well. I always wanted a little baby to look after, Harald. It is strange, is it not? Now I remember that when I was a boy, my mother used to set me to look after our youngest child, Caedmac. It was very pleasant in the sunshine to swing him up and down and to listen to his laughter. He was a merry boy, was little Caedmac. I missed him when they sent me away from the village. Now we have a baby of our own.'

Harald did not know how to tell the giant that it would be almost as cruel for them to keep the baby as to leave it in the plague-ridden city; for they did not know where they might find themselves, what dangers they might meet; nor, most important of all, did either of them know how such a small child should be fed.

But the problem was solved for them quite simply. By dawn they walked into a narrow lane, bordered on either side by stunted shrubs and brown rustling reeds, and there they came upon a low hovel, built of wattle-and-daub, with a rushlight burning in the little window. Somewhere in the distance a dog barked at the sky, mournfully and without hope.

Now the baby began to wail again, as though it were desperately hungry. Grummoch looked helplessly at Harald and whispered, 'Perhaps if the Gods are with us, we might find milk for the bairn at this cottage.'

Harald nodded. 'It is worth risking,' he said, 'for we cannot walk much farther with it in this cold morning air. It must be chilled to the marrow, poor creature, as it is.'

Harald went forward and pushed at the cottage door gently, not wishing to frighten whoever might be therein. Yet, as a precaution, he held the hilt of his sword in readiness.

The sight which met his eyes caused him to forget all thoughts of combat, for this was the home of a quiet and gentle-spoken old couple, country folk, unlike the treacherous town-dwellers they had recently become accustomed to, during their weeks in Miklagard.

The white-haired old man was seated at a table, knotting together the strands of a broken fishing-net; the old lady sat at the fireside, stirring the contents of a small cauldron which bubbled on the fire and singing quietly as she stirred. In a far corner of the warm room, a young man was busy packing a small sack with provisions.

The three looked up in surprise as Harald entered, followed by Grummoch, who for the moment kept the baby concealed beneath his cloak.

At last the young man said uncertainly, 'Who are you? What do you want at this hour? We are peaceful folk in this house. What do you want?'

Harald answered them in the Byzantine dialect which he had picked up during his stay in the Palace.

'We are travellers who would ask only that you give this baby something to keep it alive; and then, if you have anything to spare, we would be grateful for a mouthful of that porridge which you stir in the pot, lady, and a draught of milk to wash it down.'

He fumbled in the treasure sack and drew out a small silver bracelet set with garnets. This he held out towards the old lady; but she rose with such a look of disdain that the Viking withdrew his offering in some shame.

She went forward and took the child from Grummoch and crooned to it and took it beside the fire, rocking it and whispering strange little words to it, until it too began to croon back, contentedly.

The old man put down his broken nets and said simply, 'We lost our first boy when he was of such an age. Always my wife has said that the good God would send him back to her; and now she thinks that her dream has come to pass.'

Grummoch gazed at him, wondering.

The young man stood up straight and said, 'You see, strangers, my aunt has dreamt the same dream three times, that men in armour like Gods, and one of them a giant, would come to our cottage one day and would bring back the child which was lost. You are her dream come to life. If you took the child away again, it would break her heart.'

Harald said, 'We shall not break her heart, young man. The child is hers, for its mother is dead and we are not the sort of men to tend such a little one. Lady, the child is yours.'

The old woman gazed up at him speechlessly, but her eyes were wet with tears. Then she began to sing softly to the baby and the old man poured out two dishes of thick gruel for the travellers.

As they ate it, the young man said, 'Where do you travel, lords?'

And Grummoch answered, 'One place is as good as another, for men like us. Where do you suggest, young one?'

The young man grinned and replied, 'I go to join a trading ship, which sails northwards over the Inland Sea to do business with the Khazars. If you fancy such a voyage, I can speak to the captain, who is a good enough fellow, for a Bulgar.'

A little later, the three men left the cottage, where the old woman still wept with joy at the gift which the Gods of her dream had brought out of the dawn. The old man stood at the doorway, calling blessings after them. Harald ran back and pushed the silver bracelet into his hand.

'Keep this for the young child,' he said. 'It may buy him a sword one day.'

The old man gazed at him in wonder. 'A sword?' he said, almost fearfully, 'But what does the child want with a sword? A child wants other things, lord, before he comes to swords. And pray God this one never comes to swords and such like.'

There was nothing Harald could think of in reply to this, for in the northern world the son of a chieftain was always given a sword as soon as he could walk.

Harald shook the old man by the hand and ran after his companions. They walked for a mile down a sunken and rutted lane, which at last opened out to show them the wide marshes surrounding the great Inland Sea. And as the morning broke fully, they came to a jetty where a long ship lay, its red sail already bellying in the strong breeze.

So Harald and Grummoch came to set course again for the north, leaning over the low gunwales and watching the smoking city of Miklagard slowly falling away behind them as the wind freshened.

After a while, Grummoch said to Harald, 'I think you had better wrap my cloak about those golden trinkets in the sack to stop them rattling. The captain of this ship may be a good fellow, for a Bulgar, but his eyes had a strange glint when he heard the sound the sack made as you set it on the deck. I do not trust him too far.'

Harald nodded. 'Nor do I,' he said.

PART FOUR

24. The Empty Land

LATE summer turned to autumn, and the days which followed seemed like a long dream to the two travellers. Sometimes it was a gay dream, as when they all gathered on the half deck of the trading ship and sang songs, or told impossible stories, at which Grummoch excelled. At other times it was a frightening dream, as when Harald woke with a start one night to find a dark figure bending over the treasure sack, trying to untie the hide thong with which it was fastened. When the Viking moved, the man ran off into the darkness at the far end of the ship and Harald did not think it wise to follow him. He did not know which of the crew it might be, though the captain, Pazak, gave him a strange look the following morning, as though he wondered whether Harald suspected anyone in particular.

Yet for the most part, it was a fair enough voyage; the wind held, they put in at friendly villages on the shore of the Inland Sea and got good treatment from the Bulgars there, and never ran short of fresh food and good milk –

though sometimes it was the milk of mares and not of cows or goats, and that took some getting used to.

One evening, Harald stood in the prow of the ship and said to Grummoch, 'Look, straight ahead lies our port, at the mouth of the big river, the Dnieper. I am now anxious to get back to my village by the fjord with this treasure, for I have been away for over a year and soon the winter will be on us, and travelling will be bad.'

Grummoch said, 'Why are you saying this now? What is in your mind, friend Harald? You are a crafty one and seldom speak without some good reason.'

Harald looked behind him before he answered, to see that no one overheard his words. Then he whispered, 'It has come to my mind that when we land at the mouth of the big river, we may find ourselves no longer free men; then Pazak will have gained both ways, by taking our treasure *and* by selling us as slaves. I have no wish to spend the winter so far from my village.'

Grummoch thought for a while and then said, 'You are right. Pazak accepted the few coins we offered him, for our passage, without any argument, and that is a bad sign in a sea captain. They usually ask for twice as much as one offers. Now why should Pazak be so meek? Only because he thinks to gain in the end. Yes, you are right, Harald. So what shall we do, then?'

Harald whispered to him again, and the giant nodded his great head in agreement, smiling broadly all the time.

So it was that in the night, when the ship lay less than a mile off the river mouth, Harald and Grummoch slipped over the side with their treasure and pushed off in the small landing-raft which was towed at the stern. No one saw them go and though they found it hard work to send the raft through the water with the two boards which they took with them, by dawn they ran to the salt marsh flats beside the mouth of the Dnieper, and waded up to the hard ground above.

When the sun had gained its strength and warmed them again, they set off northwards, keeping the broad river in sight on their right hand. Beyond the great river stretched an open land, still green with summer, but vast and empty. Though once when they were walking on a little ridge that ran northwards, they looked down and saw a long line of horsemen making their way beside the river, in the direction of the Inland Sea.

Grummoch shaded his eyes and gazed at them. 'I have seen men like that before, my friend,' he said. 'They are Khazars, riding to meet the trading ship and to buy slaves, no doubt, as well as the wine and fruits Pazak was bringing from Miklagard.'

Harald stared in the direction of the horsemen. They wore high fur caps and carried long lances. They sat slackly on their ponies, like men who almost lived in the saddle, moving with every movement of their steeds.

Harald said, 'I understand the respect in your voice when you mention the Khazars now, Grummoch. They seem a formidable folk.'

Grummoch nodded and smiled grimly. 'Yes, my friend, they are,' he said. 'Come, let us strike northwards as fast as we can; if they were to see us, they might well swim their horses across the river to come up here after us. They are a curious people, and like to know what strangers are doing in their country.'

But the Khazars did not seem to notice them, and at the end of the day they came to a small village of skin huts, set in a little hollow. Dogs ran at them, barking, but an old man with long white hair rose from beside a fire and called the animals away. Then he came forward to meet the two, holding his hand to his forehead as a sign of peace. Grummoch, who had picked up more than a smattering of Bulgar and Khazar dialects when he had been a slave among them, spoke to him, asking for shelter and food. The old man led them courteously to his skin tent and gave them bread and meat and mare's milk. In the morning as they left, he refused to accept any payment for his hospitality, and even sent two of his sons to guide the travellers northwards for some miles, so that they should not lose their way in the marshes which spread out on either side of the great river, from place to place.

These young men said little, but smiled a great deal, and when they had parted, Harald said, 'I do not trust men who smile as much as that, friend Grummoch. I suspect that they may well ride to tell the Khazars where we are. What do you think?'

Grummoch said, 'It would be no unusual thing if they did, I suppose. Perhaps it would be wise if we were to move away from the river, and try to find ourselves horses somewhere. Great herds of them graze on the plains a little farther to the north.'

They left the river then and for three days looked for a horse. But it seemed that these creatures had moved to other grazing grounds, for the travellers saw very few of them, and those few were so sensitive of sight and hearing that it was impossible to get near enough to them to catch one. So when the food which they had brought away from the skin village was exhausted, the two men decided that they must go back to the river, where at least they might be fortunate enough to kill wild fowl and so keep themselves from starving.

One morning, Harald sat down on the river bank and began to laugh. Grummoch stared at him in concern, wondering whether he had lost his reason with hunger. But Harald shook his head and said, 'No, my friend, I am not mad – only very sane, so sane that I think what fools we are to strike off into this empty land with no more provisions than a bag of treasure! What if we throw the treasure into the river and turn our steps southwards again? We should travel lighter and might even be lucky enough to get a ship to take us back to Miklagard. Perhaps things are better there now. At least, there is food to eat there.'

Grummoch was about to agree with him, when round the bend of the river came a long, heavily-laden rowing boat, propelled by six oars. At first the two men thought of running away, but then Harald said, 'Let us wait and see if they mean well; we can always run when we have decided that.'

When the boat drew level with them, a man in a bright steel helmet called to them, 'We are Bulgars, trading in Kiev. We are short of two oarsmen. Will you come with us, friends?'

Grummoch said, 'I have often heard of Kiev. It seems to be a growing town and I would much like to see it. Shall we go with them?'

Harald nodded and said, 'I would go almost anywhere, rather than walk another day across this empty land. It fills my dreams every night. I feel that I shall never see a town again! Let us go with them, by all means.'

They waded out and were picked up. As they boarded the boat, they were careful not to let their treasure sack rattle this time. They were also careful not to let its weight be seen by the rowers who helped them into the boat, but pretended that the sack contained their cloaks and heavy winter jackets.

So they became oarsmen in the Bulgar boat, sitting next to each other on the same bench. The merchant, who had hailed them, was a kindly man, and made no secret of the fact that he was glad to have two such strong fellows in his boat. He fed them well and offered them a place at the oars on the return trip, but Grummoch smilingly refused, saying, 'I have news that my grandmother in Orkney is anxious to talk to me. You see, she sent me on an errand to a neighbour in Ireland ten years ago, to borrow a dozen eggs that she needed, to make a pudding for my uncle, who is in bed with a bad Caledonian cold. I am afraid I was a bad lad, and forgot about the pudding, and now my uncle is getting restive. So I must go back and tell my grandmother, in Iceland, that her neighbour in Ireland had stopped keeping hens.'

The merchant stared at Grummoch, whose face was deadly serious.

'I do not understand,' he said. 'You said your grandmother was in Orkney, and now you say that she is in Iceland.'

Grummoch nodded. 'Yes,' he said. 'That is so. My family move about so quickly that it does not do to be too long away from them. That is why I am anxious to get back as soon as I can. Otherwise, who knows, grandmother might have run all the way to Miklagard with her rheumatics to look for me.'

The merchant shook his head and walked away from Grummoch. After that, he did not invite them to sail with him on the return trip.

But they did not see Kiev. On the eighth day of rowing against the sluggish stream, the merchant allowed them to pull in to the shore to rest and to light fires, for a cold wind had sprung up across the great plains and chilled the oarsmen to the bone.

Some of the men sat about on the shore, while others wandered here and there, looking for anything that would burn. Grummoch and Harald, carrying their sack, as they always did, walked away from the others, to a stretch of low and stunted scrub which they thought they might uproot for fuel. But the work was hard and after a while they sat down, rubbing their chafed hands and wondering whether it was worth while risking the edges of their swords in trying to cut the tough branches.

It was when they were talking of this that they heard sudden shrill cries from the direction of the river. At first they paid little attention to these shouts, thinking that some of the men were playing a game to keep themselves warm. But when they heard the merchant's voice hallooing, they stood up, to look over the scrub and to see what was the matter. They saw two sights which gave them a start; first, they saw that the boat was pulling out as fast as it could go into midstream, and secondly they saw that the hillside above them was lined with men on ponies, men wearing high skin caps and carrying long lances.

Grummoch spread his chafed hands out and said, 'What will be, will be! So that was why they were shouting – they wanted us to get back into the boat.'

But Harald did not answer. He felt too disheartened now to speak. The two men put their swords back into their scabbards, realizing that they could not fight against such odds, and waited for the horsemen to come down the slope and capture them. But for a while nothing happened, and at last Harald said, 'Come on, let us walk along the river again. Perhaps they mean us no harm.'

Grummoch merely grunted and shouldered the sack once more. Then they set off walking and, as they did so, the men on horses kicked their mounts forward and rode alongside them, along the crown of the ridge. When the two friends stopped, so did the Khazars; when they walked on quickly, the Khazars spurred on their ponies to a faster speed.

Grummoch said, 'They are playing with us, shepherding us to their village. I wish I felt strong enough to leap into the river and try swimming across.'

Harald answered, 'That would do no good. Their horses can no doubt swim better than we can, besides, we should be weighed down by the treasure.'

At last they topped a hill and saw below them a sprawling settlement of skin tents, wagons, and thorn fences. Many fires burned there and horses, cows, and dogs seemed to wander wherever they wished, undisturbed by the swarms of children. From the village came up a babble of voices, shouting, laughter, singing, which was made more confusing by the barking of dogs, the lowing of oxen, and the high whinnying of horses.

Harald drew his hand across his brows and said, 'I am not going down there, into that hullabaloo!' He sat down, but did not stay long on the ground, for a horseman suddenly rode up behind him and urged him forward with the butt end of his long lance. Harald rose again ruefully and went down the slope with Grummoch, between the hordes of shouting children and the grazing cattle.

Now the silent horsemen began to shout and laugh, swinging their ponies up and round, and then suddenly galloping off furiously to make a circuit of the settlement, throwing their long lances into the air and catching them as they rode. The children shouted out their applause and the dogs barked as though everything was immensely exciting.

Then the leader of the horsemen prodded the two friends forward towards a big tent of goats' hair and when they were before the open door, jumped from his pony and pushed them inside.

An old man sat on a pile of cushions and sheepskins in the centre of the tent, warming his hands by a smouldering cow-dung fire. He was surrounded by small children and dogs, which rolled about on the carpeted floor of the tent happily together, pretending to fight each other, nibbling, wrestling, while the old man surveyed them gently, quietly amused at their antics.

When the two friends stood before him, however, he waved the children away to the back of the tent, and shooed the dogs after them. Only then did he raise his heavy-lidded eyes and look up at Harald and Grummoch. They saw that his face was incredibly wrinkled and old-looking. His long white moustaches reached almost to his chest and he wore great gold rings in his ears. Beneath his sleeveless jacket of white sheepskin he had on a long robe of heavy red silk stained down the front with wine spots and grease. His fingers, though laden with dull-glinting gold rings, were dirty and their nails cracked and horny.

He surveyed them in silence for a while, smiling mysteriously, and then he said in perfect Norse, 'I began to

think that my men had lost you. They rode the length of the great river again and again after they had heard about you from the two sons of old Kazan. But sooner or later in this land one finds what one seeks. So they found you at last. And now you can put your treasure sack on the floor. It seems a very heavy burden and there is no need for you to carry it any farther. I shall look after it for you.'

Grummoch put the sack down, staring wide-eyed at this strange old man. Harald said, 'How is it, old one, that you speak like a man of the fjords?'

The old man said, 'First, I must ask you not to call me "old one" in front of the children, for here it is a rude term of address. I do not want them to pick up bad habits, for they are my grandchildren and must grow up to address me properly. You must call me "King of the Marshland". As for your question, Viking, it is very easy to answer. I have been in many strange parts in my time, and once spent five years in the north myself, seeking my fortune with the men of Sven Red-eye. But that is all past; I brought back a wife from your folk and she taught me much of your tongue, before, alas, she died. Then later I was lucky enough to buy a slave from some Wends who came this way, trying to get to Miklagard overland. He was a Christian priest and helped me a great deal in the writing of runes, among other things. He died only last year, from overeating when we had our Spring festival. I was sorry to lose him, for he had a most amusing store of tales to tell.'

Harald said, 'You are a courteous man, King of the Marshland; why then do you take our treasure – for I will not try to deceive you as to the contents of that sack?'

The old King nodded slyly and said, 'It would be better not to try to deceive me about anything at all, for I have long ears and sharp eyes, in spite of my age. But I will answer you: I take your treasure sack to keep it safely for you until you return. You see, I mean you no harm. I intend to send you back to your own land, and I ask in return that you should bring a hundred or two of the men from the fjords down here next year, when the rivers have thrown off their winter ice. When you do that, I shall return your treasure to you – but only then. Is that understood?'

Grummoch said, 'What do you want Vikings for, King of the Marshland? Haven't you men of your own?'

The old man nodded and said, 'Yes, I have many men, but they are not good as foot soldiers. Take their ponies from them and they are useless – why, they can hardly walk, my friend, and the task I wish to accomplish needs men who can fight on foot or on horseback.'

Harald said, 'What do you wish to do, King of the Marshland?'

The old man felt inside his red robe and took out a small ivory ball from an inner pocket. This he flung into the air, without watching where it went, and caught it at the side, behind his back, above his head, anywhere, all the time staring into Harald's eyes. At last, when he was tired of playing with the ball, he said, 'I intend to capture the city of Kiev and to become the greatest King that the plains have ever known. And afterwards, I intend to make war on the Franks first, and on the Roman Emperor second. When I have done that, I shall go perhaps to Spain and rule over our Muslim brothers there.'

Harald gasped at the old man's dream of power, but he found wit enough to ask ironically, 'And the north? Will you not conquer the north while you are about it?'

The old man's lips twisted in a sardonic smile and he answered the Viking in the same tone which Harald had used.

'No,' he said, 'I shall spare the north, provided that you come back in the Spring with two hundred berserks and help me on the first stage of my journey.'

Harald bowed before him, with sarcasm, then, and said, 'Very well, King of the Marshland. What will be, will be. We will leave our treasure because we must, and we will go home to the north.'

The old man smiled and said, 'You are a sensible young fellow for a Viking, I must say. I shall send you north on good horses, with a strong escort. We shall have to see to that very soon, for in a month the rivers will be ice-bound. So I shall see that you are taken beyond the great portage, and put on a longship there.'

Harald gasped at the old man's confidence. 'A longship', he said. 'How do you know of a longship so far away?'

The old man closed his eyes and rocked beside the fire with amusement at the Viking's tone of wonder.

'With fast riders like mine, I can keep in touch with most things which happen on the Plains, my friend. There is nothing magic about it. The villagers at the Great Portage are already waiting for Haakon Baconfat to come trading with them before the winter starts. He will take you home, I have no doubt, if you tell him I say he must.'

Harald sat down on the ground with sheer shock then. 'Why,' he said, 'I have known Haakon Baconfat since I was a lad of twelve. He used to make wooden swords for me and teach me to track bears.'

The old man nodded and said, 'Yes, he is a good man with children. It was his sister I married, you know. So in a way, we are relatives.'

Thereafter, Harald felt that nothing in the world would surprise him. He lay back on the cushions beside the cow-dung fire and ate the good meal which a Khazar woman brought for them. Then he drank deeply of the strong barley beer which the old King poured out of a bulging skin bottle. And then he fell fast asleep, too tired and well-fed to bother about anything – even about losing the treasure.

And in the morning, he and Grummoch sat astride two sturdy Khazar ponies, wearing sheepskin jackets and high fur hats, just like their escort. The old King came to the doorway of his black tent and waved them on their journey, saying, 'Go lightly and easily, and come back in the Spring – if you ever want to see the contents of your treasure sack again!'

Grummoch, whose feet hung down to the ground, made such a wry grimace at the old man's words, that all the horsemen shouted with laughter. Then, as the autumnal sun struck across the broad grassland to their right hands, the party set off northwards, skirting Kiev lest they might be ambushed.

25. A Surprise by the Fjord

OLD THORN, the headman of the village by the fjord, sat outside his wooden house in the early winter sunshine, wrapped in his thickest cloak and staring across the cold green water. His old dog, Thorri, snuggled beside him, turning up grateful eyes to his master, who scratched the dog's ear thoughtfully.

Thorn was thinking about the shipload of men who had sailed away from the village over a year and a half before.

'Rascals, the whole lot of them!' he said bad-temperedly to the dog. 'Enjoying themselves in Ireland, no doubt. Living off the fat of the land while we of the village scrape to make ends meet, and winter coming on as well.'

The dog seemed to understand what Thorn was saying, for he put on a sorrowful expression, and lay down with a sigh at the old headman's feet.

'Never mention Harald Sigurdson to me again,' said Thorn, as though addressing the dog. Thorri the dog looked up with wide old eyes as though he meant to say that he would never mention that wicked Harald again.

Thorn's youngest daughter, Little Asa, called him in to eat his breakfast. The old man grumbled and began to rise from his bench, clutching his blackthorn stick tightly.

Just then two men came down the hill above the village, one a man of a normal size, the other as big as a man and half a man. Both were heavily bearded and wore tall fur caps.

Old Thorn stared up at them in surprise, wondering who they might be. Then he called into the room, 'Keep an eye on the pigs at the back of the house, Little Asa. Two strangers come; they may be thieves.'

But the two men did not turn aside to snatch up a pig from behind the little house. Instead they came up to Thorn and the smaller of the men took the headman by the hand and said, 'Greetings, old man! How are you these days?'

Thorn was about to make some sharp reply when he saw the face of the man who spoke, and recognized it, despite the high fur cap and the thick golden beard.

'Why, Harald Sigurdson!' he said. 'Where have you been, you rogue? Where are the others? Where is the good ship we gave you? And who is this great hulking giant?'

Harald laughed at the spate of questions and answered, 'All in good time, Thorn.' Then he called inside the house, 'Little Asa, lay a good meal for us. We have walked for three days through the forest and are hungry! If we hadn't found berries to eat, we should surely have starved to death!'

Little Asa came out and almost fell back in a faint to see the giant Grummoch, who looked an amazingly hairy fellow what with his beard and his thick sheepskin coat and fur cap. But she soon recovered and led them inside, laughing and crying at the same time.

So, over a good meal and a draught of mead, Harald told his story – some of it sad, some of it happy. Until he came to the old King of the Marshland.

At this part of the tale, Thorn rose from his seat and thumped his hand on the oak table-top. 'What!' he stormed, 'after all that, to lose the treasure to that old heathen! I will have you whipped, both of you, for foolish fellows, wastrels and rogues! I will call the villagers together right now and have it done!'

But Harald shouted to him to sit down, and then, from an inner pocket in his sheepskin jacket, he took out a deerskin bag, bulging so tightly that it was almost round. Slowly he untied the hide thong about the neck of the bag and then let fall on to the table a stream of precious stones, of all colours and sizes, until they rolled about the oaken board and even on to the floor. Thorn's eyes almost came out of his head.

'But you said you had lost the treasure!' he said. 'Why, there is enough wealth here for every man of this village to live a life of ease, with ships a-plenty!'

Harald grinned up at him and said, 'When one is among crafty folk, one must stay awake all night. That is what I did, one night, and with my knife prised the stones out of all the gold and silver goblets in the treasure sack. The old King of the Marshland has not nearly so good a bargain as he thought!'

Thorn sat back in his seat, gasping with amazement.

'Well,' he said, 'this is a gift from Odin himself! We must divide this treasure up, so that every man of this village may have his deserts.'

Harald said quietly, 'And we must set one share aside for Haro, who is certain to turn up again, like a bad coin, you can be bound!'

It was at this point that Little Asa said shyly, 'I do not think so, Harald. A seafaring man passed this way a week ago with a wonderful tale of a Viking who had gone to Jebel Tarik and married there a princess called Marriba. I did not dare tell father at the time. I think that Haro has his treasure safely enough where he is.' And no one disagreed with her.

Then suddenly Little Asa said with a smile, 'But what are we to do with this great giant here? He will surely eat us out of house and home! Why on earth did you bring such a one back here with you, Harald?'

Harald laughed aloud at the expression on Grummoch's broad face. He looked like a little boy who has suddenly been scolded for something which he thought was long forgotten.

But Harald came to his rescue and said, 'Have no fear, Little Asa; he will be worth his weight, which is considerable, in gold. You will see that I am right. He is the most wonderful nurse for small babies that ever you saw. Aren't you, Grummoch?'

The giant hung his head and mumbled shamefacedly.

Little Asa rose and patted him on the shoulder as she made her way to the door.

'That is great news,' she said with a smile, 'for all the mothers of our village are beside themselves with extra work in this season, for as you know it is the time when we salt the meat for winter storing. They will be delighted to have such a playmate for their little ones.'

Then she leaned out of the door and began to call, 'Little Sven! Gnorre! Haakon! Knud! Elsa! Come, all of you, quickly! I have a lovely giant for you to play with! Come quickly before he magics himself away with fright! Come on, all of you!'

Grummoch twisted his great hands and said, 'Now I wish I had stayed in Miklagard. At least I had a sword to defend myself with there.'

But Harald said gently, 'Do not worry, friend, our children are kind ones. They will not hurt you.'

Then they all laughed. And such was the manner of the homecoming of Harald Sigurdson.

Viking's Sunset

Contents

About this Book

This is the third and last book about Harald Sigurdson. In *Viking's Dawn*, he was a lad of fifteen, voyaging in the longship *Nameless* to the Hebrides; in *The Road to Miklagard*, he and the giant Grummoch made the long journey down to Constantinople (now known as Istanbul) to join the Palace Guard there. Now, in *Viking's Sunset*, Harald is a mature man and the date is AD 815.

In this book he is a prosperous farmer, with a family of his own, who sails out from Norway on a voyage of revenge and, almost by accident, reaches Iceland and later the southern tip of Greenland, before setting off again, in *Long Snake*, to even stranger places . . .

Here I should halt a moment to say that recorded history tells us that Iceland was discovered by one Naddodd in AD 867, and Greenland in AD 985, by Eric Röde who was flying from Norway to escape a charge of manslaughter.

But I have a theory that recorded history, especially of the early voyages, often lags behind *actual* history. For instance, we don't really know when the early Mediterranean travellers first 'discovered' Britain – though recorded history tells us that the Greek astronomer Pytheas came here in the fourth century BC. I would guess that a cautious scholar like Pytheas would have a pretty good idea, from *unrecorded* travellers' yarns, what he was going to find!

And so I feel justified in letting Harald Sigurdson anticipate Naddodd by a mere fifty-two years. After all, the longships of Harald's time were superb creations, quite capable of the voyages I describe; and the questing spirit of the Northmen was as lively in AD 815 as it was in AD 867.

In my other books I have tried to describe what Vikings were like, but to explain *Viking's Sunset* I must add a little more. The Northmen were immensely brave and hardy; they were also savage and superstitious. They were still pagans when the rest of Europe had long become Christianised. In some ways they were like children – very dangerous children! To the Franks, English and Irish, they seemed like devils, and prayers were offered up in the churches as a protection against them. On the other hand, when the odds were in favour of the English, they treated these Northmen ruthlessly, even flaying them and nailing their skins on church doors, or flinging the ambushed marauders into adder-pits. There were no doubt faults on both sides, for in history no one is ever completely in the right.

What attracts me most about the Northmen is their storytelling. From the Sagas we learn of many fantastic people and their incredible adventures, all told with the great craft and gusto of the Skald. Sometimes, these tales are full of repetition – as children's fairy tales often are – and sometimes they are told so laconically, so briefly, that we almost have to guess what really happened! But almost always they are told with a dry and even a grim sense of humour, for the men of the North were not given to self-pity. They joked even in the face of death; which, after all, was to them only the beginning of a new life in Valhalla, the 'Slaughter Hall'.

In this book I have made an attempt to use the Viking style of storytelling, whenever it seemed right. I have also tried to show what a *berserk* was like, for I think that we must consider these strange creatures if we are to understand many of the things our curious forefathers did.

The bullfighter, dressing up to go into the arena; the boxer, chatting with his seconds before a fight; the racing driver, laughing at a funny story in the 'pits' before the flag goes down, are all brave men: but they are taking a calculated risk, which they assume will bring them money – the more the better!

The *berserk*, stamping himself into a fury, biting his shield-rim, bellowing in the cold air without a stitch on him, had no fortune to gain by his actions. If he saw anything awaiting him at all, it was a grimly-held wall of spear-points, just fifty yards away . . .

Undoubtedly, the *berserk* was crazy; but, as Alan Breck said to Davy Balfour in *Kidnapped*, 'Och, man, but am I no a bonny fechter!' And who can help liking a bonny fechter, however crazy he may be?

One more point: in Minnesota there was discovered a stone inscribed with Viking symbols. This fact struck no chord in my mind until one day an American boy who comes to see me said, 'Didn't you know, some of our archaeologists have found the prow of a longship in one of the lakes?'

Then I did know – not in the historian's way, but in the storyteller's way – just what happened to Harald Sigurdson and his shipload of vikings!

What I 'know' I am telling you in this book; but what Harald Sigurdson found out, he told to no man, for reasons which you will discover.

HENRY TREECE

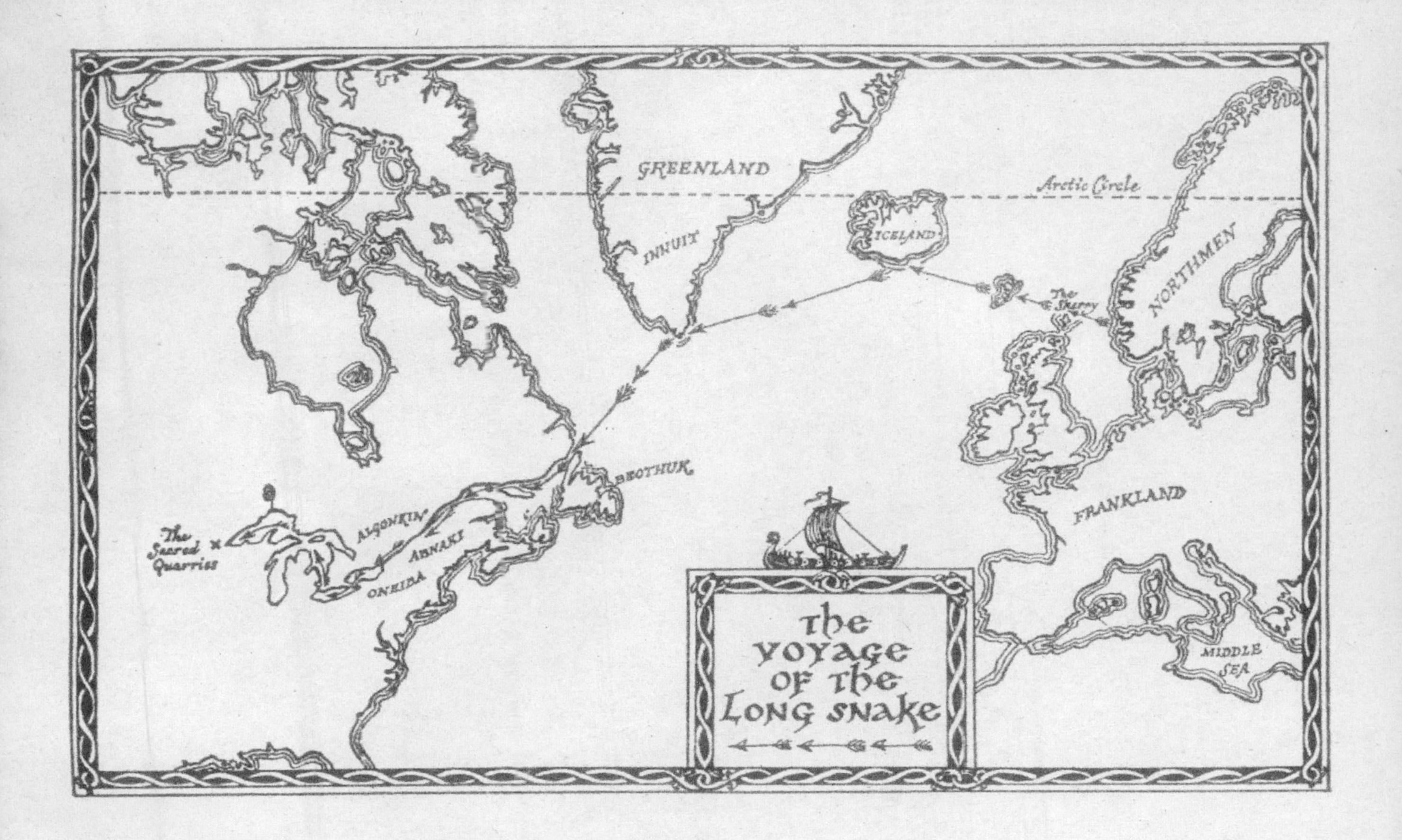
The Voyage of the Long Snake
GREENLAND
Arctic Circle
ICELAND
INNUIT
NORTHMEN
The Skerry
BEOTHUK
FRANKLAND
ALGONKIN
ABNAKI
ONEIDA
The Sacred Quarries
MIDDLE SEA

1. The Barn-Burners

IT WAS spring. Harald Sigurdson and Giant Grummoch were tending a sick cow up above Jagsfjord, with the wind blowing them half off their feet, when a shock-headed thrall came running up the hill to them.

Grummoch heard him and said, 'That is Jango No-breeches. When he runs the world's end is near, for he is the laziest thrall between here and Miklagard.'

Jango called out to them, long before he reached them, 'Come quickly, masters!'

Harald said, 'If the meat is burning, turn the spit and roast the other side. This cow is in calf and it would ill become me to leave her because the meat was burning.'

The thrall began to wring his hands. The wind carried away his words the first time. Then they heard him say, 'The meat is burning with a vengeance, master. But it would ill become me to meddle with it.'

Harald Sigurdson had grown into a stern man, with grey wolf's hair, in the twenty years he had been headman of his village, after the death of Thorn. Now few men dared

stand against him in his anger, save Jomsvikings or Russians from Kiev, and they did not come up the hill every day.

But the thrall would not be silent. He ran to Harald and even took him by the sleeve of his leather jacket, which was a thing few men would have done save Giant Grummoch, who was his blood brother and the second father to Harald's two sons, Svend and Jaroslav.

The thrall said, 'A wise man would come, even if twenty cows lay on the turf in calf, Harald Sigurdson. You have three barns a-burning, and your wife, Asa Thornsdaughter, leaving her broken loom in bitter tears over the wounds of your two sons.'

Harald turned to him now and said, 'I shall whip you for stealing the barley beer we had laid by for the Spring feasting, Jango No-breeches. You have fallen asleep and dreamed a dream. You listen too much to the skalds about the night-fires. Go back and dip your head in a bucket of water.'

The thrall flung himself on to the turf and began to roll about, wailing, for he was of the Irish folk and given to such demonstrations. Grummoch picked him up with one hand and held him out before him like a girl's rag doll, with his two legs dangling.

'Say your message, if there is one, then go home like, a good dog,' he said gruffly, his beard wagging close to the frightened thrall's face.

Jango No-breeches said, 'By Saint Colmkill and the Whitechrist, Haakon Redeye has been here while you were away. What torch has not done, axe has achieved. Down there is no more village left than a man could stow in a longship and carry away – and all charred timber.'

Giant Grummoch put the man down.

The thrall said, 'I bring black news, not white, master. Many have gone to Odin in the last hour. Many have made the long dark journey and hang by their necks from the trees. Haakon Redeye brought eighty berserks with him, and only the young folk and the old were left in the village. How could they stand against eighty berserks with war axes and spears? Your sons were hurt with the others.'

Harald said, 'I do not ask if they are badly hurt, or near to death. I only ask if they carry their wounds on their chests.'

The thrall nodded. 'Aye, master,' he said. 'On their chests and their arms and their heads – but not on their backs.'

Grummoch, who loved the two boys, took up a piece of black bog oak as thick as a man's lower leg, and broke it across his thigh to show his rage.

'In all the Northland,' he said, 'there is only one man who would do such things to old folk and young folk, and that man shall feel his neck snap like this twig before the day is over.'

The thrall said, 'Haakon Redeye has already sailed, master Giant. You must needs mount a swan and fly after him if you would catch him. But let us go down, and save what we can of the village. I am but a simple man and no warrior, but I counsel thus.'

Harald said, 'I am forty years old and looked to sit back in peace in my age. I thought my voyaging was over when I came from Miklagard, but now it seems I must put an edge on my sword again, if I can still lift it.'

The thrall looked at Harald's big muscles and his broad back, but did not speak, for he had learned not to interrupt warriors and shieldmen when they began their boasting.

Harald said, 'By this cow and her calf, I swear that I will harry Haakon Redeye to the edge of the world and will at last set his polished head on my shelf to smile at before this tale is over, for what he has done to me.'

Grummoch, who had picked up the manners of the Northmen in his years beside the fjord, said, 'When I have visited his berserks, they will ask each other why the thunder was so loud, and why the lightning came so suddenly. That is, if they still have heads to ask with.'

Jango No-breeches said, 'Come, come, masters. There will be time to bite the shield-rim and to bellow later, when you have seen what work is to be avenged.'

Then he ran on along the slippery path towards the village and the others followed him, feeling it no shame to be led by a thrall, this time.

2. The Sailing

IT WAS as bad as the thrall had said. Out of thirty-seven houses, only six remained, and no barns.

Harald looked at the old ones and the young ones who lay, no longer fearsome of the axe, and said, 'To call this a bad business is to blow out hot air from the mouth. The only word is in the sword from this day forward. Where is my family?'

The thrall led him to where Asa Thornsdaughter sat, weeping and rocking back and forth. Her two sons lay on a pallet of straw, their wounds covered with moss. Harald lifted the moss before he spoke to her and then said, 'My boys have fought like warriors. Their wounds will heal, Odin be praised, for they are cleanly dressed.'

Asa said through her tears, 'Boys of ten and twelve should not be asked to carry wounds so early on, husband.'

Harald said, 'Asa, loved one, do you expect me to weep like a woman or a thrall when my sons are hurt? The old bear does not love to see his cubs mauled by the wolf – but he knows there is no profit in sitting howling. He knows that for a finger he must take an arm; for a hand, a head. The old bear will go after the wolf and seek his bargain, for Haakon Redeye is outlaw and wolf's-head and will not stand before the Thing to receive sentence. He will not pay the blood money, so he must pay with his head.'

Asa began to cry again, and put her apron over her face so that no one should see the wife of a Viking weeping.

And when the other young men came back to the village, Harald met them and said, 'There has been a slight mishap while you were away in the woods catching hares. The village has been burned down through an oversight of Haakon Redeye, and your families have been entertained by eighty of his berserks. It seems that he was so upset by the nuisance his visit has caused that he has gone away to hang his head in shame.'

A young axe-warrior, given to fits when he was excited, stepped forward and ripped off his own shirt. His chest was covered with scars and so were his arms, from wrist to elbow.

He shook a great axe in his right hand as though it were a little elder stick. 'Before Thor and Odin,' he said, 'I will not rest until I have shamed Haakon's head still further.'

Harald said, 'There you make a mistake, my friend. Haakon's head is not yours for the shaming. I have laid claim to that prize already.'

The young berserk bowed his head, but whispered to his nearest friend that Harald must take his chance when they ran up alongside Haakon Redeye, for in a case like this all men had equal rights, headman or henchmen.

Then they drew out the longship from the creek where it was hidden under bracken and gorse, and they examined its timbers to see if it needed tarring again.

Gudbrod Gudbrodsson said, 'This steerboard side needs caulking, Harald Sigurdson, but there is no time to waste, and we have helmets to bale out the water. They will do as well as any buckets!'

Harald said, 'I will stick my finger in the hole if it comes to it, Gudbrod Gudbrodsson. Throw aboard dried meat, barley bread and two casks of ale, and then we will be off. A man must eat if he is to pay his debts with sword and axe.'

Before he left, he kissed Asa most tenderly and told her that he was leaving twenty men behind to guard them and to set up shelters for them once more.

He told her also that he expected to be back in three days, for his sixty shipmen were capable of repaying all the debts they owed to Haakon Redeye and his eighty.

'A man with vengeance in his sword-edge is the equal of four who have burned a barn,' he said, buckling on his iron friend, Peacegiver.

Asa said, 'Have you got your woollen shirt on, husband? The Spring winds are bitter along the fjords and it would go ill with a war leader to be stricken with a cold.'

Harald said, 'I shall keep warm with exercise soon, my love.'

When he bent over the bed of his two sons, Svend and Jaroslav, the boys smiled up at him and said, 'May Odin speed the prow, father.'

Harald said, 'I am blessed in having a pair of young hawks when many other fathers have only chickens.'

Svend said, 'If we could stand up, we would come with you, whether you agreed or not.'

Jaroslav said, 'I shall weep all the time you are gone, for I put a knife into Haakon's arm before he struck me down with his club. It is not fair that I cannot finish what I have started.'

Harald patted their heads and said, 'Rest awhile, my pretties, then one day you shall have long swords and go after such pirates as Redeye yourselves, while I lie in the straw and think of my cows and the ships I have sailed in.'

Svend said, 'Bring me back Haakon's dagger with the coral handle. And bring back his bronze shield for Jaroslav. It will help us to get better more quickly.'

As Harald went down to the longship, Asa whispered, 'Bring me back something we can put on the shelf and smile at in the feasting times, loved one. Something closer to Haakon Redeye even than his knife and his shield.'

Harald said, 'If I do not do that, I shall do nothing. An ornament is always pleasant in a house, Asa Thornsdaughter. But if the dice fall otherwise than what I think, then get yourself a cross of the Whitechrist and set that up as your ornament to smile at, for then you will know that Thor and Odin are no longer our friends.'

Asa did not watch as they pushed out into the fjord. She hated to see the longships sail away, for sometimes they never came back, and then there was always the misery of remembering how fine they had looked when they set off, with the gay oars rising and falling in unison, and the shipmaster laughing at the prow.

3. Cold Scent

THE DAYS passed as Harald's ship, *Long Snake*, drew in and out of the fjords seeking Haakon Redeye, and each day brought wild-haired villagers running down to the shore, shaking their heads, saying that Haakon had not stayed there, but had passed on north, and north again.

One grey-headed jarl waded into the green waters of Langfjord and shouted, 'They passed this way a day since, the wind in their red and blue sails, ship laden to waterline with plunder. You must needs row harder, Harald Sigurdson, to catch that wolf by the tail. I doubt you'll not find him in Norway. He'll be gone to the far north, to Isafjord Deep, or to Vatnsfjord. He'll be gone to where the white fox runs and the walrus snorts, mark my word.'

So *Long Snake* turned about once more, and headed northwards.

Harald stood by Grummoch, near the steerboardman.

'I swear by the fingers of two hands that I will not give up this chase until Haakon or I lie stark,' he said.

Grummoch said, 'There is not a man aboard who will not sail with you to Iceland, or to Midgard itself, Harald. Ask them and see.'

Then Harald spoke to the Vikings.

'Who will turn back?' he said. 'Who will go back to eat fresh meat and lie snug under the blankets? Let any such man speak now and I will set him ashore with an axe in his hand and money in his pouch to make his way back to the village. Speak now or forever hold your peace.'

Then the seamen turned towards Harald and shook their axes above their heads.

'Who goes back now is a *nithing*,' one called out. 'Do you wish to insult us, Sigurdson?'

Harald answered, 'Thorfinn Thorfinnson, I would as soon insult your namesake, Thor, himself. From now on, I shall ask that question no more. Let us sail onwards, and whosoever comes alive out of this quest, let the skalds name him a hero of the folk.'

Then Thorfinn Thorfinnson began to beat with a hammer on the floorboard to set the rowing time, and all backs bent to the oars. And as they rowed, Thorfinn sang an old song which they all knew:

> *'Makers of widows, wander we must;*
> *Killers 'tween seedtime and salting of kine;*
> *Walking the Whale's Way, sailing the Swan's Path,*
> *Daring the Sun's Track, tricking dark death!*
> *In jaws of the storm, jesting we stand,*

Lashed with hail's fury, hand frozen to line;
Numb head rain-shaken, sharp spume in the nostril,
Salt caking hair – and blood's haven in sight!'

All the men joined in, feeling once more the sharp splash of the water on their faces, breathing deep of the salt-laden air after the long winter ashore.

And many that day blessed Haakon Redeye for giving them the excuse to sail again and to leave the barley field and the pigsty.

Late that night, on a little skerry of stones that hardly poked above the sea's level, they heard a man crying out to them. As they drew nearer the voice, they saw that big white seabirds circled over the rocks, as though to threaten the man who clung there so desperately.

As they came alongside, they saw a man dressed in an old horse-hide clinging to the stones, too weak to draw himself up away from the sea's hands.

Harald called out, 'What man are you?'

And the man answered weakly, 'I am Havlock Ingolfson, master. Haakon Redeye had me flung into the sea because I wanted my share of the plunder now and not when we reached Isafjord Deep. Save me, I beg you.'

Harald said, 'Were you with the men who burned Sigurdson's Steading three days ago?'

The man said, 'Aye, master, and a fine burning we made of it. Take me aboard and I will tell you the story. It will make you smile, I warrant you.'

Then Harald took his axe in his hand and for a while seemed about to leap into the water and put an end to this rogue. But at last he turned away and said to the rowers, 'Why should I hurry his end? Let the Dark Ones who weave our web have their way with him. Set course to northwards again, my seacocks!'

So *Long Snake* passed on, and soon the wretch began to yell out again as the seabirds came back and swirled over him in the dusk.

And at last the men on *Long Snake* heard him crying out no more.

That night they lay out in open sea, three leagues off land, with the top cover down over the roof-slats, and their sheepskins about them.

And as Harald paced the deck, unable to sleep for the thought of his revenge, he thought the mists before the longship parted and a woman wearing a winged helmet and carrying a shield stood upon the prow looking down at him, smiling strangely.

Harald said, 'What have you come to tell me, Shield-maiden? Speak out in clear words for I am afraid of nothing now.'

Then the Shield-maiden spoke and her voice was like the splintering of icicles and sometimes like the swishing that the gannet makes as he falls out of the cold sky.

She said, 'Harald Sigurdson, I have come to bring no message, but only to look on your face, so that I shall know you again.'

Then Harald said, 'Why should you need to know me, Shield-maiden? Are you to bring my doom upon me?'

Then the grey misty shape seemed to laugh, with a sound like the grey seals mourning on some lonely skerry out beyond Iceland.

And at last she said, 'We do not answer the questions of men. We do the bidding of the gods only.'

Harald Sigurdson said, 'Many a time have I heard of you doomsters, yet never have I seen you before, though I have lain helpless in the deep sea off the Western Isles with my body numb and my mind gone from me.'

The woman said, 'We come but once, to be seen by men. And when we come the second time, they do not see us.'

Then Harald said, 'I understand, Shield-maiden. I see that I have done something wrong. I will not ask you what it was, for I think I know now. I should not have left that wretch on the skerry for the seas to drown and the birds to eat.'

Then the Shield-maiden seemed to nod her head and whispered, 'When the winds howl over the lonely nesses and the snow beats across the frozen inlets, you will remember him, remember Havlock Ingolfson, who lived wrong but died right.'

Harald said, 'I will turn the ship round to find him, Shield-maiden.'

But she only laughed and whispered, 'Too late. Too late . . .'

And then, as Harald went forward to see her more clearly, she faded back from the tall prow and into the rocking sea.

So Harald shrugged his shoulders and then went back to the stern shelter and wrapped his blanket about him and fell into a numbed sleep, which lasted him until the dawn.

4. Distant Waters

THE NEXT morning broke clear and cold as crystal. A flurry of kittiwakes swept about the longship; then three stormy petrels came so low that their wings almost touched the mast. A dark cloud built up like a grey fortress on the port quarter, and then a grim wind started up, whipping the salt spume across men's backs as they rowed, as sharp as a whiplash.

Grummoch, who was half as big again as any Northman, got the full force of this, down to the waist, and so ruefully lay down under the lee of the shield-gunwale.

It was as he lay thus that Harald went to him and said, 'Shame would it be on me, not to tell my oath-brother and the foster-father of my children what I have seen in the night.'

Grummoch said, 'This day will test us all. There are berserks here who will weep for a cup of warm milk and a sizzling hunk of pork, before this day is out. What did you see, brother?'

Harald told him of the Shield-maiden and of what she had said.

Then Grummoch raised himself on his big red elbow and said, 'All men must go when the Norns call. Yet I have it in my mind that your dream was more the result of too little food and too much excitement yesterday. I think you will live to be a hundred.'

Harald almost struck his oath-brother then for so tempting the gods; but instead he held down his hand and said after a while, 'The guest who stays longest at the feast sees the most juggling.'

Then he went aft to tell the man at the steerboard to lash his helm to the ship-side, so that they might hold their course to the north.

An hour later the full force of the Spring storm hit them, rocking *Long Snake* as though she were a ship of straw. Few men that day ate; and those that ate scantly kept down their meals. And so it was for three more days and nights, until the men of the longship began to swear that Haakon Redeye was in league with Loki the Wicked, or that Freya, the Goddess, who saw to the bringing forth of life, had turned her back on them and intended them to feed the fishes, and so help bring forth fish-life.

But Harald laughed at them, and did not tell them of his vision of the Shield-maiden. Instead, he told them not to be thrallish-minded, and said that he had sailed through storms ten times worse than this one when he was a young man; though he knew that he lied.

At last, when the long low shape of the land of ice raised itself up over the black sea, most men in *Long Snake* lay on the boards, groaning and asking their friends to slip a knife below their ribs so that they might not have to endure another day of this torment. Wet to the bone, raw at elbow and knee, their stomachs empty of food, these men had hardly the strength to lift sword or axe now.

Harald said to Grummoch, 'These men are in poor case. Not one, save thee and me, could swing a sword or flail an axe.'

Grummoch said, 'Count me out. If a kitten leapt at my throat, I could not save myself. I should be at its mercy!'

Harald smiled to think of the kitten who could spring high enough to reach tall Grummoch's throat, but he said nothing and went forward to where Gudbrod Gudbrodsson lay, making little marks on the planks with his wet finger.

'Friend,' said the shipmaster, 'you know of the inlets and nesses of this place. Where are we to steer?'

Gudbrod Gudbrodsson said without looking up, 'I have heard of these places from my grandfather, who sailed here in a storm when he had not enough money to pay for the killing of Alkai Nobody. But when he told me, he was in his dotage and rambled. I cannot remember what the old sheep said, master. All I know is that he said the place was full of lawless men who had come here to avoid hanging or head-removing. That is all I know.'

Then he went on scribbling over the decks, using his finger as pen, and salt-water as ink, daft with the storm and hunger.

Harald went to the steerboard and unlashed it. Then he scanned the coastline that stretched out before him.

As a cloud of birds came out to meet *Long Snake*, Harald put the helm hard over, towards a place under a hill, where a cloud of dark brown smoke rose.

The longship lay in a sheltered waterway, full of shoals, that afternoon. The Vikings waded ashore, each trying to look fierce, but each cursing the day when Haakon Redeye fetched them out on this blood-quest.

There was a half-rotting whale drawn up on the shore and many men about it, hacking for blubber with great adzes and flensing-knives. They had a huge fire of seaweed beside them, on which iron pots bubbled as they flung the blubber pieces into them. The stench was heavy. Even the birds avoided that place.

Harald went foremost, with Grummoch close behind him.

The men flensing the whale scantly looked up. They were red-eyed fellows, wearing old clothes and their feet bound with sheepskins. Their hair and beards flapped matted and uncombed in the shore wind. Not one carried a true weapon, but only staves tipped with iron.

As the Vikings approached, a short bandy-legged man rose from his business of lifting out the whale's heart and came, red-handed, a pace or two to meet them. His face was set and defiant.

Harald said in Norse, 'Greetings, friend. We seek Haakon Redeye. Can you tell us where he may be?'

The man looked up at the sky. Then he looked to left and to right. Then he spat into the scummy water of the shore puddles.

'He is not here,' he said. 'He is not at Isafjord Deep. Maybe at Ragnafjord, or at Sealflaying fjord. I do not know, and I care less. But not here.'

He spoke in a strange dialect that Harald could hardly understand, as though he had always lived at this place and had learned from seals and walruses and the gulls rather than from men. Harald did not like the looks of him, for his eyes were dark and set close together. Besides, his eyebrows were so sandy-light that who could see them unless he came very close, too close?

All the time he spoke, his score or so of men stood silent about the rotting whale, their adzes in their raw hands, their chapped lips closed, their matted hair blowing in the wind.

Grummoch went forward and said slowly, 'If I took you by the leg, I could fling you over that hill.'

The man said, 'What good would that do you or me? It would not tell you what you want to know, and it would stop me from flensing my whale. Don't talk like a fool. Your body has outgrown your brain.'

Harald said, 'I would give good pieces of money to know where Haakon Redeye is at this moment.'

The man said, 'There are no markets here. No place to use money, friend. We have horses and pigs and sheep. We have fish and whale-blubber. What use is money to us?'

Harald saw that they could neither frighten nor buy this man.

He said, 'Suppose we burn your village down, what then? What would your wives say to that?'

The man said, 'They know better than to raise their voices. They are all lawless women who have sailed with pirates years ago. They have burned villages themselves, and they have built villages. Besides, they never speak unless we give them leave. They are well-trained, unlike the women of Norway and Denmark. If you burn our village, you are welcome to do so. And while you do that, we shall stave in the sides of your longship with our flensing adzes. That is all.'

Grummoch said, 'Suppose we kill you all, here and now?'

The man said, 'If I blow this bone whistle on my belt, fifty more men will come running from behind that hill, and fifty more from the next one. Then they will do such things to you that I have not the words to speak of. Go away and waste no more of our time with your prattle.'

The man then turned back to the whale, and his fellows bent again to their stinking task.

Harald said to Grummoch, 'This fellow is lying. He knows more than he will say – yet his reasoning is good. There is nothing we can do to make him tell us where Haakon Redeye might be.'

Grummoch said, 'It ill becomes warriors to turn back from such a creature. But there is little we can do. Let us go back to the ship.'

As they went, the men about the whale scoffed at them in their hoarse voices, and flung pieces of bone and skin after them. But the Vikings did not turn back, though sometimes they were sorely tempted, especially when the rubbish struck them.

Long Snake set forth again, and rounded the headland and so came into deeper waters, where the grey rock rose high on either side of them. And as they went, they saw fires start up here and there on the hillsides, as though signals were being sent from one part of the place to another.

Thorfinn Thorfinnson said, 'Seems it to me that who catches Redeye must have windows in the back of his head.'

Gudbrod Gudbrodsson said, 'And a sword in each of his eight hands.'

Jamsgar Havvarson said, 'If I had my way, I would wipe this island clear of men and of cattle. Then I would take a spade and dig out the foundations and let it all sink into the sea; for it is a breeding-ground of wickedness.'

Thorfinn Thorfinnson said, 'That comes well from you, who have never dug your own garden in twenty years, but always make your wife do it.'

Jamsgar Havvarson said, 'I do not dig because I have a weak heart and bending down does not suit me. If you had a weak heart, you would understand better. Then you would see what injustice you do me.'

Gudbrod Gudbrodsson said, 'How can a man with a weak heart wield an axe as you do?'

Jamsgar Havvarson said, 'That is a secret told to me in a dream by a witch. I am under oath not to tell anyone else, especially you.'

Thorfinn Thorfinnson said, 'It is as good a way to avoid digging that I have heard of. When I get back home, I shall have such a dream and then I need dig no more. I am no lover of gardening, either!'

Jamsgar Havvarson said, 'You make light of a serious matter. When I have a moment to spare, I shall challenge you to fight and shall cut off your head for those words.'

Harald Sigurdson said, 'If you fools don't stop arguing, I shall fling you all overboard now, and let you swim home to Norway. Then you will see what a weak heart is like.'

Gudbrod Gudbrodsson said, 'It is all one to me. I can walk on the water, didn't you hear? And so can Thorfinn Thorfinnson. We both learned to do it at the same time. We went to a school run by a Russian witch in a cave near the mouth of the Dnieper. We paid good money to learn the trick. I have often wondered when the chance to practise on real water would occur, for up to the present we have only been able to do it on dry land, though we know exactly what to do on water.'

Harald went away then, for he knew that Norsemen would keep up this silly sort of talk for hours at a stretch, until they became so drunk with words that they would draw swords and hit each other, just to prove a point, or leap into the sea for a wager.

5. Haakon Redeye

THAT night they slept again upon the ship, watching the fires burning high on the hilltops, afraid to go ashore lest such lawless men as they had already met surrounded them and killed them as they slept.

They woke at early dawn-time to find *Long Snake* half full of brackish water, from a hole in her side which needed caulking.

And as they lay, half-settled on a sandbank, filling that hole with rope strands and tarring it over, a longship swept out from behind them, down the inlet, and set course to the west.

Seeing their plight, the ship came close to them, within an arrow-flight, and then Harald saw that Haakon Redeye was in the prow, smiling at them in mockery.

'If I had more time,' he said, 'I would stay and help you, Sigurdson. But as it is I am behind time and must go on to visit my old grandmother who lives among the trolls. It is her birthday soon, and I have promised to take her a present. So you will forgive me, I am sure, if I do not stay to help!'

His men lined the side of the longship, grinning above the shields, and waving in derision.

Harald called out, 'Stay and fight like a man. I will meet you on board your own ship, bringing only two men with me. But at least give me the chance of my revenge.'

Haakon Redeye said, 'No thank you, Sigurdson. I have no wish to be struck by such as you. I have just eaten my breakfast, and it would be a waste of good food to go and get killed now. Goodbye!'

So Haakon's longship passed away out of sight, while Harald and his men swore furiously, baling out the water and caulking the hole in *Long Snake*'s side.

And when this was finished two hours later, a party went ashore and filled the empty beer barrels with fresh spring water, while others found a herd of sheep and took eight of them, having frightened away the shepherd boy by waving axes at him.

So they struggled back to their ship with the casks and the carcasses, into which they rubbed salt immediately, so

that the meat would stay reasonably fresh for the voyage they had to make now to the west.

At last, when the sun was sinking and the tarred side seemed to keep out the water, *Long Snake* set forth again in the track of Haakon Redeye.

And Harald said at sunset, 'I don't know where we are going, my comrades, but it would ill become such men as us to turn back now and become the laughing-stock of our women, when we are so close on the heels of the man who has done us such harm.'

They all agreed, cold as they were; and so the chase went on.

6. Westering

EVER afterwards, until it came for them to go through the oaken doorway into Valhalla, where the old warriors sat at the long table smiling and waiting for them, the men of *Long Snake* remembered their journey to the west like a bad black dream.

Sometimes the deep green sea rose above them higher than a tall cliff face, then seemed to hang over them like a dark cloud before it thundered down on to them, smashing them to the boards, smiting the longship like a stick of wood in a waterfall, swirling it round and round again, until the creatures on board lost all sense of direction, all sense of the world, all sense of themselves.

Then they might be in the clear again, rolling and bucking on the great tides, as though they ran some mad sledge race down dreamlike slopes of green death, baling half-dazed with the seawater in their rusty helmets, fighting a losing battle always against a sea that washed as it willed over their sides.

In ten leagues they had lost their mast and sail. In twenty leagues they had lost all knowledge of their names. Speech would not come to their frozen lips. They moved like men in a deep trance that could only end in death.

But by some miracle death did not come, yet.

Again and again he threatened, opening his wide foamy jaws as though to munch up *Long Snake*. And then he withdrew . . .

And once Harald saw Haakon Redeye's longship, rolling far before them on a tide like the side of a green mountain, stumbling like a stallion with an arrow in its heart.

But he told no one. Indeed, for a while he could not recall the name of the man who sailed in her, the man he had set forth to destroy. It was like that, in those days of the journey; men forgot what their task was, the object of their journey, the name of their blood-enemy . . .

And then, when it seemed that even death would be better than such voyaging, the sky cleared and the white birds came down again over the rocking boat, and the tall seas grew smooth as glass for a time – a sheet of glass as broad as the world, as muscular as a giant's flank.

And one evening, towards dusk, *Long Snake* grated beside a skerry, a low heap of rocks set lonely in the vastness of the seas. Then every man who had the power of speech leapt ashore shouting, dragging at the ropes with feeble hands to bring the longship to anchor.

And there, on that lonely skerry, with the darkness coming down over them like a grey cloak, the Vikings broke up a barrel and struck flint to iron and somehow made themselves a fire to sit about.

In the depths of the oceans the men of the *Long Snake* sat on that tiny isle and tried to remember the names of the ten men they had lost in the days of storm-wrack. But before they could bring their brine-sodden brains to bear upon this business, the white birds came down upon them out of the darkness, sweeping them with their wings; and then a man screamed out, 'To the ship! To the ship! This island is sinking!'

Then they knew that the water was up to their knees, and then to their waists. They saw their fire swamped and the little skerry fall into blackness.

And those who still had strength of arm and speed of mind struck out in the wild waves to where the longship wrestled with its ropes.

That night five more men were lost, and over the creaking, leaking, battered longship the seabirds whirled and cried like mocking furies.

Harald said, as he lay by the shield-wall, 'It ill becomes any man to lead his fellows so far out into the hidden seas on so bootless a quest. Once again, Grummoch, I have done wrong.'

Giant Grummoch sprawled, groaning in the scuppers, but turned his great matted head to say, 'Harald Sigurdson, no man may see into the future. No man may choose his fate. His life egg is held in ghostly hands and is outside his reach.'

But others, such as Gudbrod Gudbrodsson, muttered that in the old days it was the duty of a chieftain to let himself be sacrificed when his people fell on evil days. Another man, who lay beside him, said that Harald owed this to his henchmen, who had left their homes to sail with him on his voyage of revenge.

Grummoch shouted above the rising wind to them, telling them that they had left no homes, since there were no homes to leave after Haakon's visitation with fire; and that the revenge they sought was not Harald's alone, but equally their own.

The grumbling stopped then, and Grummoch crawled to the axe chest, where all the weapons were stowed away from the salt water, greased with mutton fat and wrapped about with cloths. He took from this chest his own axe, Death Kiss, which he held before him now and said, 'I am oath-brother to Harald Sigurdson and it is both my duty and my right to stay by his side. Let any three of you come forward now and hold an axe conference with me to settle this argument.'

But no one stirred, then or the next day. And the day after that, as *Long Snake* ran in among a shoal of rocky outcrops, they saw such a thing as took all thought of mutiny from their minds.

Lolling lazily between two pointed rocks, the dark green weed already dragging about it, was the prow of a longship, its bow-post carved in the shape of a dragon's head with teeth of walrus bone.

Beside it on a rock lay an axe, already brown with salt-rust.

Harald gazed over the side and said, 'The man who burned my village has time a-plenty to consider his wickedness now.'

As they ran past Haakon's longship, Gudbrod Gudbrodsson said, 'Mother Sea punished him, Harald; what more is left for us to do?'

Harald said, 'What can we do, but sit here in this ship, our helmets in our hands, to bale out water? Both sail and oars have gone now. Do you expect me to turn *Long Snake* about by magic and guide her back to our fjord?'

As he spoke, a long low coastline jutted jagged over the green horizon, and a wind freshened and drove *Long Snake* onwards towards it.

Harald said, 'That is your answer, Gudbrod Gudbrodsson. We go where the Fates send us; and the Fates send us to a land no man has ever spoken of before.'

And it was in this manner that *Long Snake* at last came to the land which men called Greenland in after years.

7. Innuit

LONG SNAKE landed under the beetling crags in late Spring. By late summer the men who were left, thirty of them, had gathered driftwood from the swirling fjords and had made a new mast and new oars, clumsy but fit for use on the high seas by men whose hands were stronger than most.

Out of stones and driftwood, turfs and the skins of whale, walrus and bear, they made their sleeping bags and hangings, for they were able men with the needle, and each man carried his own sewing case of deerhide filled with needles – of hard-wood, hare's tooth, fishbone. It would ill become a Viking, they said, to have to go home to his wife every time his breeches needed patching!

For food they ate what meat they could come by, even fox, though this did not please some of the younger warriors who had been brought up delicately on a diet of pig and sheep.

Yet one day, in private council, Harald said to Grummoch, 'This goes well enough for men who are born at the outer edge of the world; but I have noticed that a chill wind blows down from the north these last two mornings, and with it comes the smell of snow. Stay we here a month longer and I give it as my opinion that this fjord will become icebound, and what few roots and berries we can find will be hidden with a thick blanket of snow from our eyes and hands.'

Grummoch said, 'Last night I heard the howling of dogs, which I did not like. I went to the brow of the little hill, above the strange humped mounds, and saw a long line of dogs racing away to the west. Not the dogs of our country, but big round-bodied dogs, carrying much fur and running with their tails curled up, in a most undog-like manner.'

'Running in lines?' asked Harald Sigurdson, amazed.

Grummoch nodded his great shaggy head. 'In lines,' he repeated. 'As though they followed a leader. And I will tell you more, Harald oath-brother, though I beg you not to tell the others, lest they call me a madman and pelt me with bones; it seemed to me, in the moonlight, that these dogs ran with two-footed creatures, hardly men, but more like trolls.'

Harald said, 'Describe them, friend, for this is most interesting – more interesting than the lays which Thorfinn skald makes up about the fire at night:

The brown snake glides the green hillocks,
Seeking the red-eyed wolf;
But, finding wolf rock-battered, makes
Its resting-place above the weed-clogged fjord.

That was his last one, meant to tell our story.'

Grummoch snorted. 'It is rubbish,' he said. 'I have known byre-boys to make better songs about the names of their cattle. In Orkney once, I heard a man sing this . . .'

But Harald stopped him and said, 'Another time, oath-brother. That song will wait, but your news must not grow cold. Tell me about the trolls who ran with the dogs last night.'

Grummoch snorted a little, but put on a good face as a Viking should, though angry, and said, 'You will not believe me when I tell you that these trolls seemed hardly taller than my waist, but as thick round as my own body. Their heads were great and round and covered with fur. They made no sound as they ran with the dogs. I think they carried spears, but I am not sure now.'

Harald answered, 'We have fought the men of Frankland and Spain, and also the men of Miklagard. We have outwitted the wild horsemen who ride along the Dnieper. It would ill become us to grow fearful of small trolls with furry heads who run with curly-tailed dogs in the moonlight, think you?'

Grummoch said, 'It depends on their numbers, and on the strength of their magic. However strong a Viking, he must not hope to struggle on if fifty trolls smother him. Nor can any man, Viking or not, as is shown in the saga of Olaf Skragge, lift axe against magic, if it is brewed and cast the right way. It is my counsel that we should lie with our swords at our sides by night, and that we should sleep with one ear open.'

Harald laughed and said, 'Man who sleeps not, fights not. If the trolls come, then we must take our chance; but we must not frighten ourselves to death, lying in wait for them. Look, friend, I counsel that tomorrow we begin to caulk *Long Snake* in readiness for a voyage back home, while the seas are still free of ice. Others can go hunting for meat so that we may feed well on the journey. Then, if we are lucky, we might sail before the wind changes and before the week is out. What say you?'

Grummoch nodded. 'We cannot sail too soon for some of the men. This daily diet of fish and snow-bear meat is making them unwell. Their skin is dry and flaking with the salt, and many of them have such boils on back and buttocks that they will not find the task of rowing a joyful one. Yes, let us go at the first chance.'

When they went back to the men, they found them sitting about the fires, grumbling and wishing they could see their wives and children again.

Thorfinn skald was standing in the firelight, chanting the latest song he had made, to amuse them:

'Danish men have great big feet;
Reindeer meat is good to eat;
Irishmen have long red noses;
What can equal the smell of roses?

I have met a man who can
Swallow the biggest cooking-pan;
I have met a man who knows
A man who knows
A man who knows
A white-eyed king with twenty toes,

And on each toe a white-eyed cat –
And what do you think of that?'

Grummoch said, 'I think very little, friend! Now listen to sense, my fellows. Our leader, Harald Sigurdson, has news that will interest you more than this stuff of Thorfinn's cat!'

So Harald sat by the fire and explained to the Vikings what his plan was, and they all agreed, though some who still bore the scars of their last voyage expressed the hope that this time things would go better.

Thorfinn sulked in a corner, and the young ones called out, 'Pussy! Pussy!' to him, while others mewed like cats.

It was while they all sat listening to Harald, and arguing among themselves, as shipmen always do before a voyage, that Grummoch suddenly looked up and gave a cry of surprise, pointing into the dusk.

All men followed his finger and then they, too, gave cries of surprise, and their thoughts of voyaging faded to the backs of their minds as snow fades when the first sun of Spring breathes down upon the northern hills.

Round them, just beyond the firelight, stood men – but such strange men that none of the Vikings had seen their like.

They were as short as dwarfs and their faces, ringed round with fur, were broad and flat and yellow. The eyes that they looked from were little more than slits in the skin of their faces, and their mouths were broad.

Each one was round in the body and wore the skin of the white snow-bear. Each one carried a short lance tipped with narwhal bone, cruelly barbed.

There were many of these men, perhaps a hundred, and behind them stood dogs, hundreds of dogs, all staring silent and green-eyed at the Vikings round the fire.

Harald said, 'Here are your trolls, Grummoch. I would like to see the hero who could take on this lot, even with his axe – and our weapons are all in the hut, where we cannot reach them easily.'

Grummoch began to rise, lazily, saying, 'I will go amongst them and kill a few dozen of them with my bare hands. Then perhaps they will go away.'

But even as the giant got to his knees, six of the trolls stepped forward noiselessly, and levelled their harpoons at

his breast, without speaking, without a change of expression on their flat, slit-eyed faces.

Grummoch sat down again, thinking twice of his previous offer now.

Then, at last, a wizened troll shuffled forward, his thick legs ragged with hare-skins and deerhide. He carried in his hand a club made of the jawbone of a narwhal, set with the tusk of a walrus so that the weapon looked most formidable.

He went from Viking to Viking, gazing at each one carefully, as though he had not seen their like before.

Close behind him walked four great dogs, with curly tails, and these creatures sniffed at every man the troll halted by.

The Vikings did not move, but sat as still as stones. No one liked that war-club, or those sniffing dogs with fierce eyes and curly tails. But Harald signalled to them with his eyes to remain seated and not to offend the troll or his dogs.

Then, at last, the old troll went back to his many followers and began to talk to them in a strange harsh voice, using many small words and waving his club at each pause.

Someone in the crowd of trolls started to beat on a small drum, and then the trolls began to prance round the fire, slowly, like creatures in a bad dream, waving their harpoons as they went.

At last, when the sweat was standing out on the brow of every viking, the strange dance stopped, and the old troll came forward once again.

He stood in the firelight and tapped his broad chest with the flat of his hand, saying, 'Jaga! Kaga! Jaga! Kaga!'

Grummoch said, 'I think he is telling us his name. Tell him yours, oath-brother.'

So Harald stood up, slowly and gently, so as not to draw the harpoons upon himself. Then he too patted his chest and said, 'Harald Sigurdson! Harald Sigurdson!'

The troll listened, but did not seem to understand. So Harald spoke his name again and again, until it began to sound most foolish and he wondered why the Gods had given it to him.

But at last the old troll seemed to understand, and said, pointing at Harald, 'Rold Sgun! Rold Sgun! Rold Sgun!'

Harald nodded, smiling, making the best of a bad job.

Then the old troll swept his furry hand round to indicate his followers.

'Innuit,' he said. 'Innuit.'

Grummoch whispered, 'He is telling us that the trolls call themselves Innuit, Harald.'

Harald said, 'Aye, that much had occurred even to me, friend. But who makes the next move?'

There was little need to ask, for the question was soon answered. The old troll began to bark like a seal out on a Spring fjord, and immediately the Innuit rushed forward and took the Vikings, binding their arms with thongs of deerhide so swiftly that no man had the chance of defending himself.

Harald said, 'These men, if men they be, move faster then any I have known, even the men of Miklagard – and they are brisk little devils!'

So it was that Harald Sigurdson and the Vikings with him were captured by the Innuit, just when they planned to sail away from Greenland in *Long Snake*.

8. *The Cooking-Place*

NEVER did the Vikings forget their long journey to the north, bound down upon sledges and dragged by dogs; or sitting bundled up in long skin-boats, always nosing northwards round the nesses and along the black fjords.

The Innuit treated them well, pushing blubber into their mouths, whether they wanted it or not; and wrapping them in bear pelts when the early darkness fell.

The old troll, Jaga-Kaga, often came and looked down at them and touched their long hair, comparing it with his own thick grey locks, or the coarse black hair of his younger followers. Then he would nod and go away, shaking his head, puzzled. Once he went round lifting the Vikings' eyelids, and staring into their pale eyes at a close distance, as though he thought they were sightless.

Gudbrod Gudbrodsson said, 'Never did I meet a man who smelt so like a bear before.'

Thorfinn Thorfinnsson said, 'Never did I travel so slowly. These trolls take a week to go the distance we can go in one day, in and out the fjords with their strange boats.'

Always where the Innuit rested for the night, they built little cairns of stones, under which they laid blubber and fish, so that their hunting-fellowship would have something to eat should they need to make the return journey southwards again.

The Vikings, used to salt fish and fire-dried meat, could not stomach so much blubber at first, and many of them were sick when made to eat half-rotten grouse, with the skin still on it, and uncooked.

But being sick did not save them, for immediately the old troll barked like a seal at his followers and they ran forward with more half-rotten grouse, so that their prisoners should not go hungry.

Grummoch said, 'When I get back to Norway, I shall eat no more meat, cooked or uncooked. Nor shall I look a fish in the eye again. But I shall eat only barley bread and drink only fresh milk, straight from the cow's udder.'

Harald said, 'At the edge of the world, it ill becomes a man to speak of what he will do in the future. Mayhap there will be no future but this, for evermore. Only blubber and rotten grouse and skin-boats and stone hovels. Only that!'

'Then,' said Grummoch, 'I hope that these trolls will stick their harpoons in me soon, for I am not the sort of man who likes living with dogs and eating birds with their feathers on.'

Grummoch said this because when they came at last to the great cooking-place of the Innuit, all the Vikings were pushed into a long low hut of stone, together with the dogs, who snapped and snarled almost unceasingly.

The ground was as hard as iron, and now each night there came such a bitter frost that the men were glad of the dogs, who slept on them and kept the cold from them, to some degree.

Then the snow began to fall. The Vikings watched it through the little window-holes. It fell like an immense shower of feathers from the white breast of the swan, until it lay taller than a man, and then the long hut was buried deep.

But the Innuit did not seem to notice this, and carried on hunting and dancing and drum-playing as though it were summer and not the start of a hard winter.

They dug a tunnel to the long hut and passed back and forth, bringing blubber and lamp-oil to fill the little soapstone lamps, which gave a dim and smoky light and made the Vikings cough.

The women of the Innuit came too, to gaze at the white-faced strangers with blue crystal eyes. These women were dressed exactly like the men, in skins, with a fur hood about their heads. But they were quiet-voiced gentle creatures, who simply squatted down among the dogs and smiled at the Northmen, without speaking to them.

One day, as a great delicacy, a party of these Innuit women brought in a stone dish of hot seals' liver and sat down while the Vikings ate it.

This made some of them feel sick, but they did not show their queasiness in case it offended the Innuit women, who went to great pains to see that each Viking had the same amount of food as his fellow.

Grummoch said, 'They think we are dogs. Harald. You notice, they see that each dog gets his fair share, and so they do with us.'

Harald said, 'I do not care what they think we are, if only they would let us move about, outside this hut. I have begun to dream of huts and dogs, every night now. It is becoming unbearable. If they do not do something, I can feel that I shall run berserk, and that would be unlucky for them.'

Grummoch said, 'Yesterday when I was watching through the little window-hole on the side where the snow is thinnest, I saw a young troll strike an older one. They were arguing about hot seals' liver. It was only the lightest blow, but it was a blow, nevertheless.'

Harald said, 'What happened then, oath-brother?'

Grummoch said, 'Ten of the others ran up and stripped off the young one's fur clothes. Then they bound him hand and foot with reindeer thongs and merely laid him out in the snow. He did not cry out, but just lay, smiling. This morning the snow had covered him deeply. He will be seen no more until the Spring thaw, I would say. And this is what would happen if you ran berserk, my friend.'

Harald said, 'If only I had my sword, Peacegiver, I would risk what they did with me after I had struck the first blow. But our swords and axes lie in the weapon-hut near *Long Snake* still. These trolls did not seem interested in them, or in the longship. It is strange.'

Grummoch answered, 'They are a strange little folk. Almost like men, yet not quite men.'

Harald said, 'What did the young one look like, the one they laid in the snow, when they had stripped all the fur covering from him?'

And Grummoch said, 'Just like any other man, save that his skin was yellowish in colour. It seems to me that only their faces are different from those of proper men. It is their thick bundles of clothes that make them look like trolls. Their arms and legs are as well-formed as our own, and their bodies are much sleeker and plumper, since they feed so well, in a desert land that would not seem to provide food for a moderately-sized mouse!'

That night the big dog who was the leader of all the others leapt at Grummoch's throat as he squatted over the fire, for no reason at all. Grummoch was compelled to deal with this dog in a final manner, lest the other dogs followed their leader and killed all the Vikings.

It was not the sort of work which the giant enjoyed. Nor did he like to see the other dogs tearing at the body of their dead leader.

But when it was all over, Harald said to him, 'Now the dogs have elected you as their king, Grummoch. Look how they sit about you with their lolling tongues and bright eyes, as though they are asking you to tell them what they must do next.'

Grummoch said, 'I never hoped to become the king of the dogs. It ill becomes a Viking to talk bark-language, yet who can hold off his fate? And in any case, these dogs might be useful to us, in such a case as we are at present.'

Grummoch got up then and went to the thick wooden door and began to scratch at it, pretending to bite at its edges.

Immediately the pack of dogs jostled each other to do the same, pushing Grummoch aside as though they considered it beneath the dignity of their new king to perform so menial a task.

Claw and tooth worked without ceasing, until at last the fierce dogs had broken through the hide strapping which held the planks together and then the door fell to pieces.

The dogs stood back so that their king could pass down the long snow tunnel that led to the outside world.

Grummoch bent low and crawled through the tunnel. The other Vikings made to follow him, but the dogs turned on them with a snarl, bidding them hold back, for they considered themselves the king's bodyguard and must follow after him.

Thorfinn Thorfinnson said wryly, 'It ill becomes a Viking to stick his nose into business which does not concern him. I am content to wait until my dog-brothers give me leave to pass through.'

Gudbrod Gudbrodsson said, 'If I had my spear, Tickler, I would show these dogs what a Viking can do when he gives his mind to it – but, alas, my own teeth and nails would match but poorly with those of my new furry comrades!'

Jamsgar Havvarson said, 'I do not care now what happens, as long as these dogs do not expect me to run on all fours with them and grow a curly tail.'

Thorfinn Thorfinnson said, 'A curly tail is all you need to complete your equipment, for I have always thought you to resemble a dog rather than anything else.'

Gudbrod Gudbrodsson said, 'The sooner the Innuit lay you two out in the snow, the better; for there are two sorts of men I cannot abide – fools and bad poets.'

Harald Sigurdson said, 'If you three do not hold your peace, I will be compelled to act towards you as Svend Tryvlye acted towards the Lappland giant, and put my toe under your seats with a vengeance.'

Then they were quiet, because Harald Sigurdson was said to have the best kicking-toe in Norway, as he had shown once when attacked without his sword by a bull. That bull had not dared to sit down for a week afterwards, and had attacked no one since. Some men said that this showed how wise a bull he was; others had said that it bore testimony to Harald's kicking-toe.

So the Vikings stopped arguing and followed the last of the dogs down the dark snow tunnel, into the space before the long ice-house of the Innuit.

And there the Innuit were ranged behind their old troll leader, their bone arrows drawn to the head and pointing at the Northmen. The faces of the Innuit were fierce and stiff like stone, so that the Northmen began to think twice about rushing forward any further.

But when Grummoch and the dogs stood in the open, with their breath rising like ghosts out of their mouths because of the cold, the old troll leader held up his hand to his followers and they lowered their vicious little bows. But their faces were still fierce and stiff like stone.

Then the troll leader shuffled forward and patted Grummoch on the chest, as though he were a good dog –

to do which he had to stretch up on tiptoe for there was a great difference in the height of the two men.

Then all the Innuit shuffled forward and did the same, and bent and did the same to the dogs, who now sat with dangling tongues in the snow about Grummoch.

'Odin be praised!' said Gudbrod Gudbrodsson. 'For at last we are accepted as being trustworthy dogs!'

Thorfinn said, 'That is well, unless they expect us to eat bones and pull sledges!'

Harald said, 'Remember the bull I once met on the fells above Jagesgard!'

So they did not start another discussion.

Now the Vikings were invited into the long ice-house of the trolls, among the men and the dogs, and the many women.

This ice-house was buried deep under the snow and all its window-holes were stopped up with rolls of walrus hides. Twenty soapstone lamps burned there, and the place was extremely hot. Nor was the air made sweeter by the stack of seal carcasses and dried fish which stood in one corner. Harald blew down his nostrils for a while, then said to Grummoch, 'Friend, this reminds me of the sweat-baths in Finnmark, but there they do not store fish and blubber as well.'

Grummoch said, 'I care not how this place smells. At least it is better than being in prison in the dog-house. Freedom is a lovely state, Harald. At least a Viking can die with a quiet mind when he knows that he is free.'

Harald said, 'I wish all you fellows would stop talking of dying, as though it is the prize most sought after in life. I want to live, and to see my two sons and my dear wife. Asa, again.'

Grummoch said, 'When I lived in Caledonia on my mother's steading, and before I took service with King MacMiorog of Dun-an-oir, I was a pleasant enough fellow, and thought only of playing upon the flute and kissing the girls at the Wednesday barn-feasts. In those days I never spoke of death, for my mind was set upon making my fortune, and having great adventures. But now that I have had adventures a-plenty, and now that I know that few men make fortunes and keep them, I do not mind contemplating the possibility of death, which under certain circumstances, could become a restful state of being.'

Harald said, 'I shall not argue with you any longer, for this is a fool's topic. I shall only correct you by saying that a state of being belongs to live men, and that dead men are in a state of no-being.'

Never were there such argumentative men as were in the Northlands at that time. They would sit on a rock with the sea rising about them and argue about life and death until they were drowned. Indeed, in the village of Wadnesdon, just south of Kellsfjord, eight Vikings had been burnt to death only that year as they sat about the feast-board arguing about which leg of the table would be burned off first when the fire spread.

Now in the ice-house all was bustle and blubber-eating. The women ran here and there and pushed gobbets of the shiny fat into the mouths of their guests.

And after a while the Innuit men began to take off their heavy fur clothes, because of the great heat, until they wore only a little strip of seal-hide about them. Soon the Vikings did likewise, for this was the hottest place they had ever known.

Then the Innuit men and women admired the wolves and bears and dragons which many of the Northmen had tattooed upon their chests or backs, tracing them with their little yellow fingers in wonder.

Grummoch, who had the great snake of Midgard etched on his broad chest, was an object of especial wonder. He was also very ticklish. So it was that before long most of the young Innuit folk swarmed about him to hear him laughing as he rolled on the floor among the fish bladders and sealskins, trying to escape the roguish fingers.

The dogs became so worried at seeing their new leader treated in such a manner that they began to snarl, and had to be driven back to their dog-house with walrus-hide whips, lest they attacked the Innuit on Grummoch's behalf.

And that evening was a very merry one for all, especially when the Vikings discovered that the Innit had a store of stone jars full of red berry-juice, which had much the same flavour as their own bramble wine back at home above the fjord.

9. *Strange Cargo*

THE NEXT day, since Grummoch had seemed to desert them by sleeping in the ice-house, the dogs disowned him as their king and fought among each other to elect another king.

Grummoch was not sorry about this, for he little looked forward to learning bark-language, which seemed to him a mighty difficult form of speech, especially since it often must be accompanied with waggings of the tail, or suchlike antics, of which he felt himself largely incapable.

Learning the Innuit language was bad enough, in that long winter about the fire with the blubber-lamps smoking and the fish-stack getting riper and riper.

Yet there was this consolation, that the Innuit had very few words, and by and by the Vikings made a fair show at saying what they wished in the Innuit tongue; though they made many errors in pronunciation, of course. Yet the Innuit women were always most patient and repeated words again and again, until even Jamsgar Havvarson, who was slow-witted, had picked up the main words.

Not only did the Vikings learn the Innuit language; they also learned to run with the hunting-fellowship and spear seals and walruses on the frozen sea. Often they would run for mile after mile in the moonlight, for there was no day now at all, to where they had heard there was a family of seals. And then they would help carry back the load to the cooking-place, and be rewarded by the Innuit women with hot seals' liver.

Grummoch said once, 'My next task will be to learn the seal language, which should not be difficult since I have eaten so much seal-meat that I am more than half a seal myself.'

But he did not do that. Instead, he killed a white bear.

This happened quite by accident, since, if Grummoch had known it was going to happen, it wouldn't have happened at all. He was not so great a fool as that.

One day, Grummoch was down in a bear-pit, setting the sharp stakes of whalebone so that when the Innuit had covered the hole with sealskin and snow, a white bear might fall down there and be spiked, since this hole was dug on the white bear tracks.

Suddenly Grummoch was aware that there were no Innuit up above to hand down the whalebone stakes. Then he saw that a great white bear, as tall as himself, was looking down at him, waving its head about on a neck as lithe as a snake.

Grummoch was never a man to refuse battle to anyone, bear or not, but this time he felt at a loss since he had nothing but a whalebone stake to defend himself with. Nevertheless, he told the bear to come on down and to see who was the better man, or the better bear, whichever way the bear chose to regard this challenge. And when the bear did not answer in good Norse, Grummoch tried him with Celtic; and still the bear only stood there and waved his head and showed his curved white teeth as though asking Grummoch to praise their sharpness and whiteness.

'Nay,' said Grummoch, 'you'll get no such praise from me, my lad. If you are such a fool as to stand up there, then I'll come up to you.'

This time Grummoch spoke in the Innuit tongue, for by now most of the Vikings had become so used to hearing this language spoken that they used it constantly, even among themselves, since it would have been impolite to talk in Norse among their hosts, the Innuit trolls.

Well, it seemed that the white bear knew Innuit tongue, however lacking his learning in Norse and Celtic, because as soon as Grummoch made to get out of the hole, the bear began to climb into it, so that the two warriors met halfway and tumbled back into the hole, the bear being rather the heavier of them.

But though Grummoch was underneath, he realized that the narrowness of that hole worked to his advantage, and though he hated to take an unfair part in such a fight, he wasted little time in using his whalebone stake, which served as well as any other sort of sword, at close quarters.

There was much roaring on both sides for a while, during which the Innuit folk came back and stood over the hole to see what was happening down there, and perhaps to shoot a few arrows at the bear if the chance arose.

But Grummoch called on them not to loose forth their arrows in case one of them should go astray and pin him, too, to the ground.

In any case, the outfly of arrows was not needed, for within three minutes Grummoch eased himself from under the slumped bear and climbed up out of the hole.

'I have done my work for the day,' he said to Jaga-Kaga, the troll chieftain. 'Now send your young men down to bring up the bear.'

It took twelve Innuit to raise the great white carcass.

As for Grummoch, his arm and chest were deeply scored by the bear's claws, but otherwise he went scatheless. He laughed about these small scratches as he called them, but fell in a faint on the way back to the cooking-place. It took twelve Innuit to carry him, too; so Grummoch and the bear arrived on sledges at the same time, but it was Grummoch over whom the Innuit women made the greater moan, since they feared the bear's claws might have spoiled the beautiful tattooing on his chest.

After that, Grummoch was given the title of 'Bear Man'. He was also given the choice of any of the young Innuit women as his wife. But he declined this honour, saying that it would ill become a dainty little troll woman to wed such a hulking savage as himself, for he was a man of very bad habits and always went to bed with his boots on.

At this, there was much wailing among the Innuit girls, who now regarded him as something of a hero, but in the end they accepted his decision and instead gave him a necklace of fox's teeth, a sleeping bag of sealskin decorated with little blue beads made of soapstone, and a hatchet of walrus tooth, set in a haft of narwhal bone.

There is no knowing what adventures Grummoch might have had among the Innuit that winter, for the old witch-woman who flung the seal bones to forecast the future had told them all that Grummoch was born to become a chieftain.

'Aye,' whispered Thorfinn Thorfinnson, who hadn't killed a bear, or anything bigger than a small seal, 'a chieftain of dogs, no doubt!'

This was meant to be a joke, but Thorfinn forgot himself and said the words in Innuit tongue, and the dogs heard him. When they had finished chasing him, he had no trousers left, and so the Northmen called him Thorfinn Breechless from that day on.

But Grummoch did not become a chieftain there, for one day, when the snow melted and the ice softened under the warm breath of the new Spring, a great kayak came into the fjord where the cooking-place was. And in it were two Innuit, but of another tribe. They were so thin that it seemed one could see through their skin down to their bones. And they were so weak that they sat in their kayak like dead men until they were lifted out and warmed by the fire in the ice-house.

And after a few hours, when they had gained strength through whale blubber and hot seals' liver, they told how they had been caught by the ice when the winter came on, and could not get back to their own cooking-places, and so had turned about and paddled to the south.

And there, after many many days of paddling, they said, was a great land of rivers and hills and much grass, and such creatures as they had never seen in the Northland, creatures with horns outside their heads and not in their mouths like the walrus.

And besides, there were men, but different Innuit from themselves, although some of their words were the same. They were red men, who grew feathers out of the tops of their heads, and had long noses and wore few clothes.

The two brothers from the kayak said that these red men were very big, almost as big as Grummoch, and most redoubtable fighters with their hatchets.

Gudbrod Gudbrodsson, always looking out to catch someone, said, 'The best hatchets are those made in Norway, for there we have the true iron which will hold an edge. The things you speak of must be toys, fit only for women to chop the kindling or for small boys to tease each other with.'

The man from the kayak said, 'In my boat you will find such axes as the red men use. See for yourselves.'

The Vikings went out to the kayak, which lay in the fjord, and there, in a deerhide wrapping, they found the hatchets, which were of red metal and very sharp. They were set on painted staves and garnished with many-coloured feathers.

Grummoch said, 'These are wonderfully pretty things, but too light for my taste. Yet, if I had a big one like these, there is no knowing what deeds I might perform.'

Harald said, 'You do well enough with a stake of whalebone, oath-brother!'

But Grummoch still said, 'I would like to meet these red men and bargain with them for an axe or two like these.'

Thorfinn Thorfinnson said, 'They might prove to be better bargainers than you, Grummoch Giant, and then where would you be?'

Grummoch said, 'Dead and happy, friend!'

And they could get no more sense out of him. But that night, while the others were admiring the bead necklaces and the copper bracelets that the two brothers had brought back, Grummoch spoke long with Jaga-Kaga, the chieftain of the trolls, urging him to let the Vikings go south and sail *Long Snake* again, towards this land which the brothers had visited.

At first the old man shook his head and wept, saying that he loved the Vikings like his own family now that he had got to know them. But in the end, Grummoch prevailed upon him, and he consented to let them go, provided they would come back and stay with him again.

So the Innuit carried the Vikings southwards on their sledges and there they found *Long Snake*, just as they had left her, and all their weapons in the little hut they had built.

And so they set off in the Spring once more, with a wind behind them to fill out their sealskin sail.

Thorfinn Thorfinnson said, 'If I go back to the Innuit, may Odin claim my head!'

Gudbrod Gudbrodsson said, 'Odin would get small profit out of your head, for it is full of blubber, like your fat stomach!'

Harald Sigurdson said, 'Remember the bull I met on the fells above Jagesgard. Remember my famous kicking-toe!'

Then they were all silent, and did nothing but wave to the weeping Innuit, who stood along the shore nodding their furry heads. Even the dogs seemed sad to see Grummoch and his pack go from the Northland, for they sat in the slushy grass with their noses between their paws, and whined in a way they had never done before.

10. Landfall

SPRING was at its full when *Long Snake* first turned her nose towards new land.

The Vikings had spoken of hardly anything except axes, beadwork, and helmets of feathers since they had set forth from Greenland. Sometimes, it is true, they had remembered Norway; but most often that memory had been pushed from their minds by some other thought, to do with the land they were to find.

Harald said to Grummoch, 'If there is gold in this land, we stand a fair chance of making that fortune which you say few men make.'

And Grummoch had answered, 'Gold was buried in the earth and in the streams to tempt mankind; that is my thought. Whoso takes gold must often take death with it. Consider the case of Thorwald Niklasson of Jomsby, who found a whole box of gold in Frankland and got it back to his own fjord, only to have his throat cut by a little man who hid in a tree, waiting for his longship to make landfall.'

Harald said, 'Nay, lad, I shall consider the case of Grummoch and of Harald Sigurdson, who are brisk enough fellows not to be caught napping by fellows in trees! Besides, Thorwald Niklasson of Jomsby was a beef-headed fool to take gold from a church of the Frankish Whitechrist, for that was holy gold. And the man who cut his throat was sent by the Frankish priests to impress that point upon him.'

Grummoch said, 'It was not the point they impressed upon him, but the edge! And the edge seems to have been very sharp, according to men I know, who saw the situation Thorwald Niklasson was in afterwards.'

Then they sighted land, great stretches of it, and all green.

Jamsgar Havvarson said, 'Hardly ever have my eyes so relished the sight of land, and I am nigh on thirty and have made the sea my trade. But after weeks of sailing – and I grant the winds have been good ones, right from the wide mouth of Freya, bless her! – I am less than anxious to eat another mouthful of raw fish or of blubber, or to drink another cupful of brackish Greenland water or berry beer.'

Gudbrod Gudbrodsson replied, 'A true Viking is a beast without a belly. A true Viking can live for weeks on one breath of salt air. A true Viking thinks more of voyaging than of victuals.'

Then Thorfinn Thorfinnson said, 'Then a true Viking must be a fool, for there is scarcely anything so desirable as good roast pork and barley bread spread thick with butter, and a flagon of well-fermented beer to wash it down with.'

Harald broke into this conversation to say, 'I am a little more than surprised to hear a skald praising so highly the pleasures of eating and drinking. It had been my notion that poets thought only of cloudy heavens where old warriors lay back upon their shields and listened to the Snow Maidens singing endless songs of adventures.'

Thorfinn said, 'A poet must live, Harald.'

Gudbrod said, 'Why?'

Then they drove in towards land.

'I name that long stretch Helleland, that other stretch Markland – and the piece that lies far behind it Vinland – for I am certain that grapes grow there, as they do at Miklagard, it looks so sunny and so rich,' said Harald Sigurdson, pointing.

'And what do you name the boat which is coming towards us over the billows?' asked Grummoch, taking the axe from his belt.

Harald gazed towards a long narrow boat, hardly more than a thin shell, with a high prow and high stern. In it five men paddled swiftly and in rhythm. They were bare to the waist and wore feathers in their black hair. They were now little more than two bowshots from *Long Snake*, for they had moved fast in the trough of the seas and had been hidden for so long.

Harald said, 'I name that the boat of welcome,' but loosened his sword in his belt, all the same.

Now the canoe came so close that any man on *Long Snake* could have thrown his helmet into it with little trouble. And the Vikings saw that the men in it were reddish in the colour of their skin – or, perhaps, a little inclined to the hue of copper.

'These are Innuit of a different sort,' said Gudbrod. 'Try them in the Innuit tongue, Harald, for I doubt they understand good Norse.'

Slowly Harald called out, 'What men are you, friends?' cupping his hand about his mouth.

A red man stood up in the narrow boat. His chest was covered with yellow streaks and his arms were heavy with armbands. He carried a long spear in his right hand, at one end of which was a tuft of feathers, dyed red.

This man threw back his head and in a high nasal voice answered, 'Beothuk! Beothuk! Ha! Ha! Ha!'

Then he poised himself and flung the spear. It struck, quivering, in the dragon prow of *Long Snake*.

'That is a bad omen and a good throw,' said Grummoch. 'These Beothuk seem to be less than friendly, Harald.'

Harald answered, 'Perhaps they are simple folk, like Lapplanders and English. I will talk to them again.'

Once more he cupped his hands and said slowly, 'We are friends from the north.'

The next spear stuck in the mast of *Long Snake*, a hand's breadth from Harald's head.

Grummoch said, 'Aye, simple folk – but good warriors, also like the Lapplanders and the English!'

Now the canoe circled *Long Snake* and then set off again for the shore, the red men laughing as they paddled.

Gudbrod said, 'It seems to me that if all the men of Markland are of one mind, we shall meet with little to laugh about.'

But Jamsgar said, 'Pooh! Look at this spear-point. It is blunted by sticking into our prow. If a piece of oak can ruin a weapon, these cannot be such fearful warriors.'

Grummoch patted him on the shoulder gently so that Jamsgar almost fell to the deck.

'Your ribs are not of oak, my friend,' he said. 'And though this metal may be soft, yet it is hard enough to send you out on the long journey that ends in Valhalla. Bear that in mind.'

Jamsgar said ruefully, 'I shall bear in mind that when Grummoch praises a man with his hand, the man is never the same again. I can scarcely lift my arm now.'

Harald said, 'All the same, we are hungry and thirsty. We shall run ashore for a while at least, in what we call Markland. Mayhap all will be well, after all.'

Long Snake headed for a strip of sandy shore. As the Vikings drew closer, they saw that the shore was thick with red men, and that each of them carried a weapon of some sort – hatchet, spear or club.

Grummoch said to his fellows, 'Have courage, friends, and put on your helmets with the bull's horns, for that may impress these folk.'

Gudbrod said, 'That is scarcely likely, giant. I can see three of the red men wearing bull's horns, too. And what's more, they have eagle's feathers to go with them! We have not eagle's feathers!'

Harald said grimly, sword in hand, 'I have yet to hear that a bunch of feathers can improve a man's swordplay or his strength, and these seem to be without swords, and to be smaller men than we are.'

'Hm!' thought Thorfinn to himself, 'but there are many more of them.'

11. First Meeting

As *LONG SNAKE* ran into the shallows, Harald called out to the Vikings, 'Make no threatening gestures, fellows, but be ready. If they wish for peace, it would ill become such hungry wolves as ourselves to deny it to them. But if they wish for war, then see that each stroke finds its mark, and none of that silly flailing of the axe that Danish men are given to. There are more of them than of us, and every stroke must bite.'

As they leaped overboard, into the waist-high waters, the air was full of the whirring of arrows, and many of the Vikings feared for their lives. But it was noticed that the feathered shafts stuck into the strakes of *Long Snake* and hit no one.

'They are simply testing us,' said Gudbrod Gudbrodsson, who always had an answer for everything.

Thorfinn Thorfinnson said, 'Then I come poorly out of the test, for my legs are shaking like those of a beggar stricken with palsy!'

But Harald and Grummoch merely flung back their matted heads and laughed, as though the flight of arrows was greatly to their taste. Then they turned and went up the beach, side by side, with their men behind them, never once looking back, or showing any fear whatever.

And when they were within ten paces of the thickly knotted line of red men, they halted.

There was an old man, heavily laden with feathers and wearing copper bands the length of his two arms, which stuck out from holes in his long skin robe; and it was to this old man that Harald spoke the first words. He used the Innuit tongue, slowly and with care.

'Greetings,' he said. 'We are men of peace.'

For a long while the red man did not reply, but the younger ones behind him whispered and nudged each other. The Vikings saw that every one had an arrow ready on his bowstring.

Once more Harald said, 'We are men of peace.'

Then the old man who wore the red feathers about his head slapped his chest, and said, in a tongue most like that of the Innuit, but different in some of its lilting, 'We Beothuk are great warriors. Are you great warriors?'

Harald saw then that this question had placed him in a cleft stick, for if he said that the Northmen were great warriors, then the red men might challenge them to fight without delay; and if he said that the Northmen were not great warriors, then the red men might kill them out of contempt. He thought quickly and then said, 'Only the Gods can answer that question. We fight other men when they invite us to do so. We sit about the fire with other men when they invite us, and do not fight them. That is all.'

The red men chattered among themselves, and one great fellow with a barrel chest strutted forward and bowed his plaited head before the man with the feather headdress, speaking to him rapidly with much waving of a great club studded along its edge with shark's teeth.

Grummoch whispered, 'That is the man we have to fear. If he is their champion, I beg you, Harald, to let me meet him. My axe, Death Kiss, is in need of a fleshing.'

Harald said, 'It shall be as you say; but we must wait and see.'

They saw the old chief nod his feathered head. Then the barrel-chested man, who had tribal scars across his broad face, began to address the red men, shouting hoarsely and waving his brawny arms, as though trying to work them to a fury.

At last he turned round and faced Harald.

In a high-pitched tone he said, 'You are dogs. We are men.'

Throfinn Thorfinnson whispered, 'I knew that something ill would come from our living so long in the dog-house among the Innuit. Even the red men can smell dog on us now.'

Gudbrod Gudbrodsson said, 'Lift up your jerkin and show them that you have not a curly tail, my friend.'

Thorfinn Thorfinnson whispered, 'I don't know about that. There is something shaking behind me, and it is not my sword-sheath.'

Then Grummoch stepped forward and flung his axe, Death Kiss, high into the blue air, so that it twisted and twirled as it went up and then came down. He caught it easily in his right hand, his lips set grim, his right foot forward, his great weight upon his left.

'Come forth, man,' he said, 'and let me show how this dog bites.'

The red men were silent then, and lowered their bows, as though anxious not to miss what might happen.

The barrel-chested warrior slapped his thighs, left and right, then began a little jigging dance upon the sand, as though to work up his courage. Then, almost without warning, he gave a high shriek and bounded to the spot where Grummoch waited.

The Viking stood as still as a stone until the red man's blow came down, then thrust out his axe-shaft and caught the club so that many of the shark's teeth broke off and flew into the air.

Once again the angry red man struck, and once more the giant thrust out his axe-shaft, warding off the blow.

Now the red man stood uncertain for a moment, wondering how best to come at Grummoch; and while he stood so, Grummoch suddenly gave a deep bellowing cry, like that of a bull in the last extreme of fury, and leapt forward. The red man held up his already splintered club to stave off the axe-sweep, but Grummoch struck shrewdly that day. One blow he struck, and that blow sheared through the war-club as though it had been made of soft clay. One blow he struck, and that blow came near to shattering the proud chest of the redman warrior.

Save that, in the last inches, Grummoch turned his axeblade with a quick twist of the hand, so that the weapon struck with its flat and not with its edge.

The red man gave a groan, the breath knocked quite from him, and fell backwards, ploughing up the sand with the

force of his fall, for he was a heavy man, and fell sprawling, his arms and legs spread like those of a star-fish.

Grummoch stepped forward grimly, as though he might be about to strike down once more at the dazed red man. Both Vikings and red warriors were silent, their faces grim. The old chief bowed down his head, as though he would not be willing to watch his champion shamed so. But no man raised a weapon to hurt Grummoch as he stood above the warrior.

Then, at the last moment, the giant bent and touched the red man lightly on the forehead with his axe flat, and said for all to hear, 'The luck was with me. Thus I touch you in sign of axe-friendship now. Rise and be my brother.'

Thorfinn said quietly, 'That is easier said than done. The poor fellow's ribs will be too sore for him to get about unaided for a week, I reckon.'

And when the red man made an effort to rise, but could not, Grummoch bent again and picked him up as easily as though he were lifting a child, though the red man was bigger than most men of the Northlands.

And when he did this, the other red men waved their hatchets and began to shout, as though they had gained a victory, not a defeat.

Then the old chief came forward and said, 'This is my son, Wawasha. Though I love him, you must give him death if you so will, for by the laws of our people he may not accept life from any man. If you do not kill him, then expect no thanks from him ever. It is your choice.'

And Grummoch said, 'Wawasha is a brave warrior. I, Grummoch, man of the Northlands, love brave warriors and do not wish to kill them. Let Wawasha be my brother and also the brother of my oath-brother, Harald Sigurdson. I do not wish a red warrior to thank me for sparing him; I only wish that he shall become my brother and that our bravery shall go forward together.'

Then Wawasha, who had regained some of his breath, though his face was still deathly pale, smiled ruefully and said, 'Let it be so.'

And, as Grummoch and Harald and Wawasha made a little circle, each holding the other's hand in friendship, the Beothuk people began to shout and to dance on the sand where they stood, waving their feathered hatchets and nodding their black heads up and down like the heads of horses.

Gudbrod Gudbrodsson said, 'One brother is worth ten enemies.'

Jamsgar Havvarson said, 'Aye, but a brother at dawn may be an enemy at sunset.'

'Oh, go on with you,' said Thorfinn Thorfinnson. 'You are like an old Lappland butterwoman at a Spring Fair – full of strange omens, with a black cat on your head.'

Jamsgar Havvarson who was a simple soul felt on his head then, and said, 'I have no black cat on my head, only my hair.'

Gudbrod Gudbrodsson said, 'Hold tightly to it, friend, for if you can see what I see, these Beothuk seem fond of collecting other men's hair. Look at the scalps which hang from their belts.'

Jamsgar Havvarson said, 'I shall put my hat on then, for I have no wish to lose my hair, full of Innuit lice though it may be. I value my hair. It is very pretty when it is well combed and made into plaits. Indeed, along the fjord, there are women who say that they have never seen hair like it.'

Thorfinn Thorfinnson said, 'Indeed, they speak the truth, for it sticks out like the hay in a rick; it is coarse like that of a sow; and it is thin like that of an old donkey. In truth, friend, keep your hat on for if such a treasure were lost, its like would never be found again in all the Northland.'

Jamsgar nodded gravely. 'I shall do that, friend,' he said.

Then they followed the red men up the shore to a green place among the trees, from which the blue smoke was rising into the still air.

12. Beothuk

THE VIKINGS found life among the Beothuk much to their liking, especially after their long stay in the ice-bound land of Innuit and their bitter journeys over the seacrests.

The old chief, Gichita, allowed Harald and Grummoch to sit with him and his son, Wawasha, nearest the fire, and even gave them feather headdresses as a sign that they were accepted into the tribe as warriors. These were fur caps, into which hawk and eagle feathers were set at front and rear. The one which Grummoch wore was edged with small silver buttons which clinked as he moved. Harald's headdress had a band of white beads upon a broad blue cloth background.

When Gichita made the presentation of these headdresses, he said, 'Great warriors should wear the signs of their fame.'

Gichita's young daughter, Neneoshaweg, taught the Vikings how to dress their hair in Beothuk style, drawing it down at the back in a long tail and pulling it through a tube of bone, so that it stayed there when they ran through the thick woodland.

'This is less trouble than plaiting our hair, oath-brother,' said Grummoch to Harald. 'The only thing is that this tube of bone bounces between my shoulders when I move, and that is worrying. I keep turning round, thinking that someone has tapped me on the back.'

Harald answered, 'That is a thought which you can cease to worry over. If ever you are tapped between the shoulderblades here, there will be little point in turning round. The damage will be done by then!'

But in spite of this grim jest, life among the Beothuk was pleasant for a while. The Vikings made presents to Gichita of iron swords and axes, which had belonged to the men who were lost on that perilous trip from Iceland to Greenland; and in return Gichita gave them feathered hatchets of stone and elk-bone, and also hunting knives, beaten from copper and from cold iron, their blades set in the horn of great stags or elks.

And soon the Vikings took to wearing the warrior-paint across their faces, in broad bands, sometimes blue from a woodland plant, and sometimes yellow, made from a clay which the Beothuk dug from a damp glade near the settlement.

Gudbrod Gudbrodsson said one day, 'This face-covering becomes you well, Thorfinn Thorfinnson.'

Thorfinn bowed his head solemnly, after the manner of the Beothuk. 'I am pleased to hear you say that, my friend,' he answered.

Gudbrod nodded. 'Aye,' he said, 'it becomes you well because it covers your ugliness so that you seem less like an ape from Jebel Tarik and more like a man, though a very strange man at that!'

Thorfinn gave a snort and walked away to where the musicians were playing on their drums and bone flutes and one-stringed harps.

And there, in the glade, to the monotonous rhythms, Grummoch danced the Bear Dance, which he had once learned in Lappland, bending his great body and shuffling one foot after the other, his thick arms hanging down before him.

This pleased the Beothuk, who knew well enough what the dance symbolized; and soon they, too, were imitating him, for this dance was greatly to their taste.

The Vikings were welcome in other ways, for they were great tellers of stories about the evening fires and before they went to lie down in their hide sleeping bags under the skin awnings in the glade.

The story which Harald told was most admired by all, and he was asked to tell it again, and again, until the Beothuk knew every word of it.

'Once, years ago,' he began, 'the great goddess Freya had two sons – one, Balder the Handsome, the other Hoder the Blind. Fine was it to see Balder riding his white horse through the skies,' (here he had to stop and explain what a horse was, for the Beothuk had never seen one) 'and sad was it to watch poor Hoder stumbling among the forest roots, helpless. For Balder was a man among men, much like Wawasha here, while Hoder was of little use save to eat meat by the warm fire and to snuggle into his sheepskin bed at night.'

When Harald spoke these words, a strange silence fell upon the listening Beothuk, who all looked towards a pale youth sitting at the back of the circle.

'Freya was so pleased with her warrior son,' Harald went on, 'that during one Spring feasting she called upon birds, beasts, and trees of the woodland to swear a great oath never to harm Balder. She even made the thunderclouds and the rushing waters swear this oath, too, which they did willingly, for Balder was such a favourite in the Northern world.

'And when earth, water, fire and iron had sworn never to hurt Balder, Odin thought it was time for the feast-jesting to begin, and called upon all the warriors and champions to hew or to shoot at him, to prove whether the oaths had been sworn well. And they had, for swords, axes and arrows fell harmless from the young Viking's body, and he smiled as the champions thrust at him with spears, for they slid away from him, though he wore no armour.

'It was while this feasting was going on, the horn-cup passing from hand to hand, that Loki the Mischief-maker came to Freya and asked if there was nothing in the whole wide world that could hurt this splendid fellow. And Freya, drinking with the men, answered carelessly that there was one thing – a plant called the mistletoe, which grew eastwards of the hall of Valhalla, and was too weak and too young to be the cause of any fear.

'So that night Loki put on his dark cloak and crept out of the noisy hall, and went to the grove where the mistletoe grew. And there he cut down a twig of the plant and shaped it into a little javelin with his sharp knife, Evil-doer. Then he returned, the twig hidden beneath his dark cloak, and went to Balder's brother, Hoder, who stood silently among the shouters, at the edge of the circle.

'"Why do you not join in the merrymaking, Hoder?" asked Loki.

'"Because I cannot see where my brother stands, and because I have no weapon with which to strike at him," answered the blind one.

'Loki said, "Such things are not beyond the wit of man or god to set right. Let me lead you forward through the hall and set you close to Balder, so that you may throw this stick at him, in token that you too have tested him. For it ill becomes a brother to hang back at a time like this, when everyone, even the kitchen-thralls, have honoured him by striking at his weapon-proof body."

'So blind Hoder let Loki take him to a spot before the laughing Balder, and set the mistletoe spear in his weak hand, and guided his hand, so that the shaft flew towards Balder's heart.

'All men gave way when Hoder made his cast, for he was of the kingly blood and was not to be denied anything.

'But when the little shaft struck Balder, it sank deep into his heart, and the handsome warrior-god fell forward on his face, trying to drag out the strange weapon which had brought his death upon him. But it had bitten too shrewdly, and Balder died on the floor of the feast hall with his friends weeping over him.

'Loki slid quickly away into the darkness. No man blamed Hoder, for it was seen what a trick had been played upon him by Loki. So Balder's brief hour of triumph was over.

'Then, among weeping, the shield-men carried Balder's body down to the fjord and laid it aboard his longship,

Ringhorn, the hugest of all ships ever built along the fjords. And with him on the funeral pile lay Nanna, his wife, who had died of grief that night. And at his feet lay Balder's great white stallion, Reksgor, with all his golden trappings.

'And so, at last, after some difficulties, the longship was sent blazing across the fjord, where at last it sank. Both gods and men wept sorely, feeling that something had gone from their lives.'

When Harald had finished, there was a great silence about the camp-fire of the Beothuk, for this tale moved them every bit as much as it moved the listening Vikings, many of whom let the salt tears fall upon their chests without shame.

To lighten this silence, Grummoch said, 'Gichita, this is an old tale. Do not weep. You have a son every bit as handsome and as warrior-like as Balder. Wawasha is such a one.'

Then Gichita rose and pointed to the pale-faced youth who sat at the edge of the fire-circle.

'Yes,' he said, 'and I have, also, a son who greatly resembles poor Hoder, except that his hands and not his eyes are useless. Come forth, Heome, and let our stranger-brothers see your hands.'

13. Heome

THE BRAVES about the fire moved back, so that Heome might obey his father and stand before Harald and Grummoch. This he did only after his father, Gichita, had spoken three times, and then with a bad grace, which showed in the expression on his pale face.

Standing in the firelight, under the low spruce boughs, he said bitterly, 'Here are my hands, white strangers. Feast your pale eyes upon them and laugh in your hearts. A brown bear of the forest tore them when I was but a lad. Look on them and smile!'

He held out his wasted arms and the Vikings saw that the hands were puckered and useless.

Gichita said with bowed head, 'This happened when Heome was in his twelth year, at the time when the boys are initiated as braves. It is my sadness that Heome failed in his testing-time.'

Harald was about to find something to say which might give pleasure to the young man, but before his tongue could move, Heome gave a bitter laugh and said for all the warriors to hear, 'You sent me to the woods, my father. You commanded me to do that which has cost me my hands. On you rests the blame! On you rests the wretchedness of my crippled hands!'

Gichita bowed his head and covered his fierce old face in the blanket of buffalo-hide. But Wawasha, the great warrior, leaped up in the firelight, with the red glow upon his copper armbands and in the feathers on his head, and reached out his hands towards Heome.

'Brother,' he said, 'speak no more in that manner. Our father is old and should not be so tormented. He sent you to the woods because that is the custom of our people, not because he wished you harm. You are the flesh of his flesh; he would not wish that flesh to be hurt, brother!'

Heome turned in the firelight and spat in his brother's face. The gathered braves drew in their breath.

Heome said, 'Since I was twelve the women have fed me with bone spoons, and morsels in their fingers. Is that a life for a man? You tell me not to hurt my father; I tell you that I hate my father, for what he has done to me. I tell you that Gichita has lost my love.'

Then Heome began to weep, and the sound of his weeping in that twilit forest was worse than the sound of his anger, for it was the sound of a damned creature who had lost all hope and had nothing to live for.

Even the birds of the forest took up his weeping cry and echoed it along the avenues and glades, and for a while all the wild woodland was astir with the deep sadness of this red man's bitterness.

Harald rose and, thinking of his own wounded sons, said, 'All men have their sufferings.'

But he got no further, for Heome swung round upon him and said, 'Be quiet, dog, when your betters speak! One day I will see you burned in the slow fires for a meddling hound!'

And then he turned and strode away into the darkness beyond the firelight. The braves drew away so he might pass by unhindered.

Then Wawasha said, 'That is my only brother, whom I love more than I love my own right hand, and who hates me.'

And the old man, Gichita, said, 'I would suffer my own old hands to be smitten from me, if Heome could have back the use of his.'

After that, the singing and dancing, the story-telling, were over, for this quarrel about the fire cast a gloom upon all who were there.

In their own tent, Harald said to Grummoch, 'One day, Loki will come and teach crippled Hoder how to kill his brother Balder.'

Grummoch nodded. 'That thought ran in my own mind, too,' he said. 'Yet what can we do to prevent such a thing? We are strangers here, and a stranger does well to stay outside the door when his hosts quarrel within.'

Harald answered, 'Perhaps I did ill to tell that old Norse tale by the fire this evening.'

But Grummoch shook his head.

'The damage had been done long years before we sailed from Norway, oath-brother,' he said. 'You cannot blame yourself for Heome's misery.'

Harald thought for a while, then nodded his head, meaning that Grummoch was right.

'Yet,' he said, 'if the chance comes, I will see to it that Heome is accepted by his tribesfolk as a warrior. Then perhaps his thoughts of vengeance may be turned aside.'

That chance came sooner than Harald, or anyone else, expected.

14. Grey Wolf

THE HUNTERS ran through the forest, silently as shadows. The Vikings, who ran in a separate party, led by Harald, made rather more noise, not being used to this sort of thing.

From ahead of them, the Vikings heard that the Beothuk had sighted their quarry by the high owl-cries which this folk made when excited.

Gudbrod Gudbrodsson said, 'When our folks see their enemy, they do not hoot like a flight of night-birds. They go in and finish him, silently.'

Thorfinn Thorfinnson said, 'That is because we are a modest folk, and brought up not to boast of our deeds. My uncle, Svend Threeswords, from under the hill near Gulpjefjord, once killed fifteen Danes in the night, as they slept in the heather, with one little knife. He wiped it and went home for his porridge and never a word did he say to my Aunt Besje, until she asked about the stains upon his arms. Then he said he had been picking blackberries. Another time he hung on a frayed rope above a deep gorge, when he was gathering samphire, for fourteen hours, and at the end of it, when a shepherd came and saw him and offered to drag him up, said, "Please yourself, fellow, I am prepared to go on dangling here until tomorrow. It is no effort when once one has got the hang of it." He was a modest man, you understand?'

Jamsgar Havvarson said, in his simple way, 'Yes, it is true that we Northmen are anxious to avoid all praise. When my father sailed into Frankland and burned eight churches of the Whitechrist, the Pope offered him great reward for acting so valiantly, and promised him bed and board for life in the stoutest jail in Rome, if my father ever visited that city. But he did not go to claim his lifetime's lodgings. Other men would have jumped at the chance, but my father, who was a simple fellow, chose to stay at home with his goat Nessi and his four cows, whose names I now forget, rather than have his fame bruited abroad in Rome.'

'Indeed,' said Thorfinn, nudging Gudbrod, 'we are a modest folk. Let us hope that our modesty is well repaid by the gods.'

It was while they were thus talking and running that Harald almost stumbled over Heome, who lay under a juniper bush, exhausted at trying to keep up with the other Beothuk hunters.

Grummoch picked the young fellow up and slung him over his shoulder.

'Come, friend,' he said, 'you may not be able to kill a bear, but there is no reason why you should be left behind if there is anything to see.'

After a while, Heome tried to kick at Grummoch, in his anger at being so shamed, but the giant affected not to notice this display of temper, and so they went on. At last Heome made no further effort to resist.

And towards midday, when the sounds of the Beothuk had died away in the distance, the Vikings came to a glade in which was a heap of stone slabs, almost overgrown by lichen and creeping plants. In that heap was a doorway, so that it looked like a little house.

Harald went forward to look into the doorway, but drew back as though he had been slapped across the face. Then all who were close by smelled the bitter scent of wolf.

Harald called out, 'There are two grown wolves in this lair. One is a dog-wolf, the other is a she-wolf with a litter of cubs.'

He had scarcely given this news when the great grey dog-wolf swept through the opening, his tail swirling in anger, and stood before the door, as though to guard it. All men noticed how strong in the jaw he seemed and how long in the teeth.

Gudbrod said, 'I had rather tackle that one with an axe than with a skillet-spoon; the weapon which my grandmother used against the English when they came to visit up the fjord one Spring.'

Thorfinn said, 'This is the grandfather of all wolves. I have seen nothing like him in the Northland.'

Harald would have backed away, respecting the dog-wolf's right to protect his wife and children, but the great grey creature suddenly gave a low growl and flung himself at the Viking, who stood not more than three paces away.

Harald saw the beast springing and knew that it would be foolish and also cowardly to try to avoid him. Therefore, he drew his hunting-knife and, leaning over so that the wild creature should not strike him in head or chest, held the keen blade in such a way that the grey wolf swept along it in the course of his flight through the air.

And when the wolf landed, howling with mortal agony, Harald turned on him and, apologizing, struck him just behind the skull, so that his end should be swift. The great grey wolf lay still, silent now, and giving forth only the slightest tremor of the hind legs.

Jamsgar Havvarson said reflectively, 'No blow was struck more shrewdly, not even among the Lapps, who are very able with the small knife. If I were a king, Sigurdson here should have a gold armring for this brave deed.'

Thorfinn Thorfinnson said, 'If you were a king, no one would have a gold ring but you, and that you would keep in an oak chest buried in the ground, while you went in rags. I know your sort of king.'

But before this wrangling could go further, Grummoch went forward and whispered in Harald's ear. Harald nodded, as though in agreement.

Then he turned and spoke to Heome, who now stood trembling at the edge of the glade.

'Heome, son of Gichita,' he said, 'all the world knows that you are a brave fellow, only prevented by your wounded hands from showing your valour. To prove this valour to your folk, I give you this wolf. We can say that you grappled with it, and had it nigh dead, when one of my men ran forward and gave it the end-stroke. How would that please you?'

For a while, Heome's dark eyes went from Harald to the wolf and back. Then he said, his pale lips twitching, 'Such a deed would make my people respect me at last. They would accept me as a man for killing a wolf barehanded. But what of these white men here – would they not speak of the wolf-killing and let fall the secret?'

Harald said, 'I promise you, there is no fear of that. These men are my friends and followers, who have sailed with me through many bitter storms, over many salt seas. They would not betray our secret; would you, Vikings?'

The Vikings, standing in the glade, shook their axes and promised never to speak of this affair again.

And so the party turned back, bearing the dead dog-wolf. Grummoch carried it, for it was full-grown and heavy, until they came within sight of Gichita's tepee, and then he passed it to Heome, who struggled along with his load to his father's skin house.

And there he laid it down before the old chief, and explained how he came to kill the fierce beast. The Vikings stood behind him, their arms folded, nodding at every word.

At first Gichita looked doubtful but when he saw that Harald and Grummoch were nodding, too, he called the elders of the Beothuk Council, and solemnly they declared that Heome was now a brave and a full man.

The squaws skinned the wolf and made a head-covering for Heome from the pelt. His new name was 'Wolf-slayer'.

When Wawasha returned, carrying deer upon a pole, he saw Heome strutting about among the squaws in his new finery, and asked what had happened. And when Harald told him that Heome had now proved himself a warrior, Wawasha ran to his brother and clasped him in his arms, almost weeping with pleasure that this should be so.

But the Vikings observed that Heome shrugged off his brother's embraces, his lips curling proudly, so that Wawasha was somewhat hurt.

Grummoch said in a whisper, 'Perhaps we have not done as well as we thought, oath-brother.'

Harald said thoughtfully, 'Perhaps. But that rests with the gods. We have sworn to keep the secret, and from now on the incident is closed.'

But there were many among the Vikings during that feast-night who regretted that they had taken the oath in the glade that day, for they could not abide a proud coward, being warriors themselves.

15. Journey Inland

NOW THE Spring was at its height, and all the trees were full and green. Young deer and foxes ran in abundance through the glades. Birds nested in every tree. Hawk and eagle hovered in the blue sky, seeking prey for their young.

And, at last, Gichita called his folk together and said, 'Now is the time when we leave our cooking-place in the forest and move to the great plains where there is meat and hide enough to feed all the world and to clothe them through the winter. Make ready, for this is the journey-season and we must not miss the fine weather, if we wish our canoes to sail smoothly through the waters of river and lake.'

During the next two days, the braves patched and greased their long skin canoes, and carried them down to the water. There they loaded them with all that would be needed for the Spring journey – meal and dried meat, the carcasses of young deer, wine-skins of buffalo-hide, and all the weapons of the chase.

Long Snake still lay at anchor by the shore, and the Vikings prepared her, too, for the long voyage inland, little knowing what they were to find there.

On the day before they were due to sail, Wawasha came aboard and said, 'Gichita, my father, will lead this sailing, and the new warrior, Heome, will sit in the canoe with him to guide the folk. Let me sail with you, stranger-brothers, in this great canoe of wood. It is something I have wished to do ever since I saw you come to the shore.'

Harald took him by his strong brown hand and said, 'Willingly, Wawasha. I would wish for nothing else. You are the first red Viking!'

Then all the Northmen began to laugh, and Gudbrod Gudbrodsson gave Wawasha an iron helmet set with bull's horns, and decorated at the front with a strip of copper inlaid with red garnets.

This gift pleased Wawasha greatly, and he swore that he would always wear it, heavy though it was, as a sign of their brotherhood.

And when the hunting-party set off, Wawasha stood in the prow of *Long Snake*, with Harald and Grummoch, looking so proud that the Vikings swore they had never seen a better man, no, not even along the fjords back in Northland.

'If only he carried a proper axe of iron, instead of that little woodpecker!' said Thorfinn.

Gudbrod said, 'Have no fears, that little woodpecker could do as much damage as your great wood-cleaver! Think, my clever friend, Wawasha has only to go Pick! Pick! and a man is no more. Whereas you have to swing your lump of iron set on a tree-trunk twice round your head before you can strike a blow – and then you are exhausted!'

Thorfinn said, 'Why, I do declare, you are more than half a red man yourself by now. Why do you not put on a hide shirt with fringes at the edge?'

Gudbrod said, 'I have been thinking that myself, friend. They are very warm, and are much more serviceable than the old woollen jerkin I am wearing at the moment.'

Thorfinn said, 'Oh, go and paint your face, you savage!'

But in his heart, Thorfinn also admired the Beothuk, and especially Wawasha, who would one day be a great war-leader as fine as any man of the Northland.

Only two things bothered the mind of Harald Sigurdson; one was the dream that now came to him almost every night, of his wife and two sons, who stood on a hilltop above the fjord, holding out their hands to him and asking with their eyes when he would come back to their village. The other was the behaviour of the new warrior, Heome, who lost no opportunity of pointing out his great prowess to all he met.

On the first day of the sailing towards the west, Harald drew Grummoch aside into the sheltered place at the stern of the longship and said, 'Grummoch, there are two questions I wish to ask you, old axe-friend.'

Grummoch scratched his tawny head and said, 'Ask on, Harald my oath-brother; provided that you do not want to know where winds come from, or what makes the moon round like a plate. I do not know the answers to those questions, I will be frank with you. Though I fancy I could answer you almost any other question!'

For a jest, Harald almost asked him where the tides started, but he did not, for he was at heart serious now. He asked instead, 'Would it not be wiser for us to turn our ship round and sail towards the rising sun, towards our homes, and not towards the sinking sun?'

Grummoch said, 'That also had been in my mind, for we have been a long time from our homes. But consider – we are fewer than we were when we set out from the fjord. Until we can persuade some of the Beothuk to sail with us, we would make a poor showing back across the broad waters. Besides, it is the duty of every Northman who comes as far as this to take back treasure to his village, and we have not found treasure yet. It is my hope that if we go with the Beothuk inland, we may chance upon gold or silver, or precious stones, which can be carried easily in

Long Snake. Then we should return home with the knowledge that the long voyage had not been wasted. Does that answer your first question, friend?'

Harald nodded, yet in his heart was still the great yearning to set eyes once again upon his dear wife, Asa Thornsdaughter, and upon his two sons, Svend and Jaroslav.

'What is your second question, Harald?' asked Grummoch, scratching his side idly, as though he were a great prophet, to whom the answering of questions came as easily as swatting flies.

Harald said, 'I am worried in my mind about Heome. He was once weak and despised among his folk, because of his powerless hands; but we have given him manhood, hoping to give him pride in himself. Yet all that has happened is that he has gained contempt for all. Now he lords it above the warriors, and even speaks to his warrior brother, Wawasha, as though he is a dog beneath him. One day, I fear, he will betray his brother and perhaps try to kill him, so that he, Heome, will become chief of the Beothuk when Gichita dies. Moreover, it is in my mind that Heome will try to do away with us, for we know his secret, having made him what he is now.'

Grummoch yawned and said, 'Heome is still nothing more than a gnat that bites, such as these which follow the ship. They are irritating, but nothing more. When one wishes to be rid of them, it is an easy matter to waft them away. And if one settles on a man's arm and tries to bite, it is an easy matter to slap them into nothingness with one pat of the hand. So it is with Heome. He calls himself

Heome the Wolf; I call him Heome the Gnat. If Heome the Gnat offends me, I shall pat him with my hand, and he will be nothing but a memory.'

Harald nodded, thoughtfully. 'Brave words, friend,' he answered. 'But brave words are not always wise words. I have often watched the face of Heome, and have seen in it a strange sort of power, as though when the time came, he might well be a man to reckon with, and not a mere gnat. We must not underestimate him, Grummoch. He could do us an injury.'

Grummoch began to hum a tuneless little ditty, then he said, 'We will take that chance when it comes, Harald. When I think of the men I put paid to in Ireland, in the time of King MacMiorog, I laugh at the thought of dealing with little Heome.'

Harald replied, 'The men you met, years ago when you were young and lusty, were simple warriors, whose only strength was in their axe or their sword. Once you had overcome axe and sword, those men were finished. But Heome is not an axeman or a swordman; he has no hands to hold such simple weapons. His weapon is in his mind, and that is the craftiest weapon of all – for it will attack in unsuspected ways, in a bear-pit, a falling tree, an avalanche, a hole in the bottom of a boat, poison in a drinking-cup, a cord round the neck while one is sleeping.'

Grummoch answered, 'We are all in the hands of Odin, oath-brother. What will come, will come; and there is no doing anything about it. Why, you might as well worry about that misty Shield-maiden who came to you when we left Haakon's man, Havlock Ingolfson, on the skerry to drown.'

Harald answered sadly, 'You speak truer than you know, friend! I *do* worry about her, every other day. I am not a child to be put off with sweet words; I know that I did wrong that night in leaving the poor wretch to drown on the lonely skerry, and I know that Odin will punish me for it, in one way or another, before he has done with me. It may even be that he has already chosen Heome the Gnat to be my death-giver.'

Grummoch laughed aloud at this, and made Harald drink a horn of red berry-juice, to put him in a better frame of mind.

But though this remedy worked for an hour, it did not last the day out, and towards evening he was sad again. He would not even join the other Vikings at axe-throwing, a pastime which whiled away the tedious hours for them.

They set up a cord, no thicker than a man's small finger and drawn tight between two sticks. Then they went back ten paces and aimed their axes at it, trying to cut the cord in the centre. Harald was usually the first to do this; but now he shrugged his friends away when they asked him to join them.

Gudbrod Gudbrodsson said, 'Friend Harald is in a black mood tonight.'

Jamsgar Havvarson said, 'I think he has a stomach ache which is bothering him. That is the only thing I know which can make a man look so thoughtful.'

16. Long Sailing

THEY crossed a narrow stretch of water on the first two days, and then camped for a night under beetling mountains, with the wolves howling above them as the moon rose, pale and full.

This was a green land, but lonely.

'Who lives here?' asked Harald of Wawasha.

Wawasha spread his great hands and shrugged his brown shoulders.

'Few men,' he said. 'Tribes who do not give themselves names, but hunt only in small parties. They are not men like us; they wear fur about them, like bears, and come from far far North. The Moon is their Goddess and they feed rather on the fat than on the flesh of the creatures they kill. They are not men to be afraid of, for when they see us coming with our feathers and our axes, they run away into the forests.'

Grummoch said, 'Are there any men you are afraid of, Wawasha?'

Wawasha said, 'A Beothuk brave is afraid of no man, giant. But there are some men we treat with caution; men such as the Algonkin, who live a moon's distance up the great river we shall enter before long. They are fierce warriors, and there are many of them. They do not love the Beothuk, because once, many generations ago, some of our young men landed on their shore and chopped down their sacred tree, not knowing what they did, but only wishing to build a shelter for themselves against the storms that come on towards the close of the hunting season, when we make our way back to our own cooking-place.'

Harald asked, 'What of the Algonkin? Do they come out to fight with you, friend?'

Wawasha nodded. 'Some years they lie waiting for us to come up the great river; then there is bloodshed. But some years they stand on the shore and watch us go past, hoping that the river will kill us – for there are many hazards there, rapids, waterfalls, rocks and landslides.'

Grummoch asked, 'Why then do you go every year inland, when there is food enough to be got from your own forests?'

Wawasha said, 'We go for many reasons. First, because the great God, Gichguma, commanded us to go, at the beginning of the world; secondly, because our tribe have always gone, just as most other tribes have gone; and lastly because we must visit the great quarries beside the lake, where the sacred stone is dug out of the ground. Nowhere in all the world can this sacred stone be found, but in this place. Without it, we could not make our peace-pipes or the necklaces which protect us from thunder and lightning.'

He put his hand within his light robe and drew out a long necklace of red stone. Each bead was carved in the shape of a man's head, and was threaded on a thin string of buckskin.

Harald handled this necklace gently. 'This stone is hard, Wawasha,' he said. 'How could it be made into such fine shapes, then?'

Wawasha drew the necklace away from the viking's fingers, quietly, as though it might lose its magic if it were handled too long by another.

'When it is first dug,' he said, 'it is as soft as clay; and it is then that we shape it with our knives. But later it grows hard and keeps its shape, as you have felt. This necklace was made by the father of my father's father, and that was many lives ago. It is still unbroken, as you see. It is very strong medicine, too, for not one who has worn it was ever harmed by thunder or lightning.'

Grummoch said, 'I must have one of those, then Thor can do his worst!'

Thorfinn Thorfinnson, who had been listening, said, 'It is foolish to speak so, Grummoch Giant. Thor may well be listening, and may decide to strike you down before you can dig such a necklace. Then where would you be?'

The giant shrugged his massive shoulders. 'Burnt to crackling under a tree, I expect,' he said. 'What worry is that to you, Thorfinn Thorfinnson?'

The other said, 'It is a great worry, for I might be standing beside you, and then I, too, would be burned to crackling under a tree.'

Gudbrod Gudbrodsson said, 'Then you would be cooked in good company. That would be better than being cooked with Jamsgar Havvarson, who is a skinny man and would not cook well.'

Wawasha listened to the Vikings as they wrangled, but he had learned now that this was their manner, and that ill seldom came from such arguments, unless the Vikings had been drinking berry-juice, or held axes in their hands when the discussion started. But this night, none of them held axes, and few of them had more than a sip of the red juice from the stone gourds.

The next day they started before dawn, and made their way along the shore, the braves in the canoes paddling slowly, in their accustomed manner, at a pace which they could keep up all day without resting, if they needed to do so.

The longship sailed among them, an east wind in her great sail, like a mother goose among her many goslings, for in truth the canoes of the Beothuk floated as thick as seeds upon the broad waters.

17. Algonkin

THE NEW moon had come and gone when *Long Snake* and the many Beothuk canoes left the broad waters, and ran into the narrow mouth of the river. Now the voyagers could see the shore on either side, not more than three bowshots away.

It was growing dusk when Wawasha first sniffed the air, like a questing hound, and then whispered, 'I smell danger, friends.'

The red men in the canoes were holding up their heads as Wawasha had done, and now among them passed a slight stirring, a shimmering of concern. The canoes seemed to bunch together, rubbing side by side, as though they were living creatures, deer perhaps, who had caught the sudden acrid whiff of wolf-scent.

Harald whispered, 'Are they Algonkin, Wawasha?'

The Beothuk warrior nodded. 'Algonkin and Abnaki, my nose tells me. I had not thought to smell Algonkin yet awhile; and most years the Abnaki folk move towards the coast, not inland. To smell them both together is bad. Abnaki alone mean little harm, but when they are with others they grow brave and dream that they are a great people once again.'

Now Gichita's canoe pulled alongside *Long Snake*, and the old chief whispered hoarsely to his son, 'I have seen lights on both sides of the river, Wawasha. The men in the forests there are waiting for us, and care not if we see their fires. That means they are strong. What do you counsel, my son? are we to go forward, or to turn back and make the journey later in the year, when these tribes have moved away?'

Wawasha said, 'The Beothuk folk have never yet turned back from Algonkin, still less from Abnaki, who are eaters of squirrels and drinkers of muddy water! We have our white brothers with us now, and that should make us a match for such warriors as lie in wait for us tonight. I counsel you, father, to let the canoes containing the squaws and the young children draw behind *Long Snake*, and we will go forward like true warriors.'

Heome sat in the prow of his father's canoe, his hands shaking, his pale lips trembling.

'Let us go back, father,' he said, his voice thin and afraid. 'My brother, Wawasha, thinks only of the glory he will gain, perhaps. But I think of our people. What will it profit us, even though Wawasha hangs ten scalps in his tent, if the pick of our warriors are left dead upon these shores?'

Gichita did not turn to answer his younger son, but still gazed up into Wawasha's face, as though waiting for his final word.

Now the warriors swung their canoes alongside that of their chief, waiting tensely for the words which were to be spoken.

Wawasha said, 'Never in my life have I turned away from battle. Nor shall I turn away tonight. If you, my father, listen to Heome's words and go back down the river, I shall still go forward with the white warriors in *Long Snake*, for this quarrel with the Algonkin must have an ending. If we run away from them now, never again shall we be allowed to pass on up the river to dig the sacred stone. All the folk of woodland and plains will speak of us with laughter and call us dogs and eaters of carrion. That is my answer!'

Gichita bowed his head and said, 'So be it, my son. That is the answer I expected you to make, and the answer I wanted to hear.'

But Heome gave a low cry, like that of a woman who is suddenly afraid, and flung himself down in the canoe, covering his head with his buffalo robe.

Gudbrod Gudbrodsson said quietly, 'How can such a father have such a son? I am baffled by the ways of Odin Manmaker.'

Thorfinn Thorfinnson said, 'Odin Manmaker made thee and me; but he cannot be blamed for red men. They are the children of some other god.'

Darkness had fallen and the moon stood like a silver sickle in the night sky, casting down little light. All about him, Harald Sigurdson heard the small sounds of men unwrapping arrows, or stringing bows, drawing knives from sheaths, feeling for war-axes. The canoes lay still upon the darkly gleaming waters for a while, the men in them as nervous as hounds before the hunt.

Then Gichita whispered, 'Onward! May Thunder-voice bring us victory!'

Grummoch muttered, 'I'll set my trust in axe Death Kiss! This Thunder-voice may not come when I call him – but I know where Death Kiss is!'

Harald Sigurdson said, 'I have sword Peacegiver in my right hand, so I am content. When the blow-trading begins, brother, see that we stand back to back, then we shall know that the odds are fair ones, even if these Algonkin come at us ten to one!'

And all along the deck of *Long Snake* Vikings spoke so to their war-brothers, in the old manner, arranging how they would meet their enemies. Thorfinn stood with Gudbrod; Jamsgar stood with a tall youth from Jomsberg, named Knud Ulfson. This youth was fond of needlework, and wore his yellow hair in four thick plaits, bound round with copper wire.

Yet no one in *Long Snake* thought it wise to offend him, for he came of a family of fifteen berserks, and had himself taken the heads of three Saxons before he was fourteen.

Then Gichita hooted like a night-owl, and the canoes swept on.

For a while nothing happened, and there were those on the dark water that night who began to think that this was a false alarm, when suddenly from either side of them in the thick woodlands, rose the war-yells of the Algonkin, like the yapping of foxes in wintertime; and then came the bear-grunts which were the battlecries of the Abnaki.

For a moment or two the air seemed to murmur with arrows. Harald felt a shaft pass under his right arm, and then heard it slap against the oaken side of *Long Snake*.

'That was a close call,' he muttered to Grummoch, who was humming a little tune which always came to his lips when there was fighting to be had.

'Aye,' said the giant, shuffling his great shoulders, 'and doubtless there will be others before this night is out!'

Then from all about them, the Vikings heard the horrible death chant of the Algonkin:

> *'Where is my enemy? Where is my enemy?*
> *Catch him quick!*
> *Where is my enemy? Where is my enemy?*
> *Catch him quick!*
> *Chop off his hands! Chop off his head!*
> *Where is my enemy? Where is my enemy?*
> *Catch him quick!'*

Thorfinn Thorfinnson said, 'It ill becomes a stranger in these parts, like myself, to speak harshly of the local skalds, but I have it in my mind that this song of theirs would better become children at a hopping-game than grown men about the noble business of battle. When this affair is over and we have a little leisure to think of gentle things, I shall set my mind to making a decent battle song that we may use when such occasions arise.'

But Thorfinn Thorfinnson never carried out his promise, for suddenly the *Long Snake* echoed with the swift passing of slippered feet and into every man's nostrils came the smell of the rancid bear-fat with which the red men coated their bodies before an affray, so that their enemies might not gain a fast grip about them.

Thorfinn was the first to fall, with a lance-point between his shoulder-blades. Yet even so he twisted and with his last strength took with him the Algonkin who had made the deadly thrust.

After which, Gudbrod, his henchman, set his back against the mast and had enough to worry about thereafter.

Harald and Grummoch, their eyes now grown used to the dusk, began their terrible battle-laugh. They were too big to escape the notice of the red men who swarmed upon the decks, and therefore they decided to go down into the red pit like the warriors they were.

That laughter echoed over the churned waters of the river, and struck terror into many hearts that night.

Harald struck out with Peacegiver.

'One!' he said, laughing.

Grummoch struck out with Death Kiss.

'One,' he said, laughing.

A sly lithe shape twisted under Harald's arm. The Viking shortened his weapon and drove it upwards as the tomahawk bit. He heard a deep and gurgling groan.

'Two and a scratch,' he said, changing his sword to his left hand.

Grummoch swept Death Kiss in a wide scything motion about him, for the black shadows were thick on his side. Only he knew how many times that sharp edge took its meal; yet it was for every man to hear the cries which followed.

'Three and no scratch!' he said grimly, and began to laugh as though he owned the skies.

Harald said, 'Go slower. I cannot keep up with you, oath-brother! It is not fair!'

Then they both began to laugh as though they rode with the Valkyries across the darkened North sky under the stars.

Behind them Jamsgar Havvarson felt his sword carried away from him when he had buried it deep, and now he fought on with bare hands, warding off blows with his forearms and then grappling and throttling. At his feet lay four braves of the Abnaki, before a shrewd thrust of the knife laid him low.

He said with his last breath, 'Knud Ulfson, I must be a little out of practice. If I do not wake from this sleep, go to my wife and daughters beside the fjord and give them my regards.'

Then he died, and Knud Ulfson felt the great pulse begin to beat in his temple like a war-drum. This was a sign he knew, but always forgot, once it started. It was the berserk sign.

While Grummoch smashed down with the back-point of his axe and called out, 'Eight!', and Harald, hardly able to stand now, replied with 'Six!', Knud Ulfson began the song which his family had always sung on occasions like this; for they were all berserks:

'Alas, my friend has gone away!
Away from the field and the fjord!
He leaves kine and kin,
Bread and board,
He leaves his wine-cup empty upon the bench.
Just it is only that I go
To where he is, and visit him!

But to get there I must pass
Through a dark low doorway
Guarded by trolls!
No troll shall prevent Knud Ulfson
From visiting his friend!
So, go you, troll!
Go you, troll!
Go, troll!
To death!'

He marked the beat of his song with great blows, and at each blow a red man fell back, sometimes silent, sometimes howling, until at last none came near Knud Ulfson, for he had built about himself a barricade of Algonkin and Abnaki.

Grummoch called out, 'Twelve. But this axe-edge is not now what it was, and some blows have to be struck twice! I must sharpen it in the morning. This will never do!'

Harald leaned hard against him, his chest and arms streaming with the hot red wine of war.

'Nine,' he said, and sank to the deck.

Grummoch felt him go, and stepped back so that he straddled him, swinging Death Kiss.

In the canoe below *Long Snake*, Wawasha straddled his old father in the same way. Heome lay huddled beneath a heap of blankets, hardly daring to breathe lest he be discovered.

And so at last those who were left of the attackers scrambled for their lives over the side of the longship and fell into the water when they could not see their canoes, and paddled as quickly as their wounds would let them towards the wooded shores.

No longer did they yap like winter foxes, or grunt like forest bears. All their breath was needed for the paddles.

And when they had gone, Wawasha called up to the longship, 'Let us follow them, now, my friends, and finish this affair as it should be finished, by burning their boats and their villages. They must have cause to remember us for ever!'

But Grummoch, who did not know yet how badly his oath-brother was hurt, said back, 'Go you, with your braves, and light the little fires yourselves. It would ill become a Northman to sail with his decks uncleared and we have much tidying up to do. But call for us if you are hard pressed and we will come then.'

Wawasha said no more, but set off with all the warboats he could gather. And shortly the woodland shores on either side of the river glowed with flame.

Wawasha lost no men in that village-burning, for the Algonkin and the Abnaki had vanished from the land as though they had never been.

The only living creature Wawasha found was a small brown papoose, forgotten in the headlong escape, who lay propped against a war-drum, smiling and sucking its thumb.

Wawasha took up this child, for like all his folk he regarded small ones as sacred and not to be harmed – unlike the early Vikings who made what they called 'a clean sweep' of any town they captured. And Wawasha carried the baby boy back with him in the prow of his warboat, fondling it with red hands, clucking and singing to it, to keep it from becoming afraid in the darkness.

And this child he gave to a young squaw whose husband had fallen in the first of the fighting that night. She called the boy by a name which meant 'Gift from the Gods', and was always happy with him, and he with her.

For a baby boy does not consider whether he is Algonkin or Beothuk; he sets store only by milk and mother-warmth. And gentle songs murmured in his ear when the fire glow dies at evening time.

18. Dawn and Brother-Trench

WHEN the morning light came again, so that the red men and the white men could see about them, they knew that they had paid well for that night's victory. Ten canoes had been sunk, and each one had held four braves. True, some of the braves were still there, but not in such wise as they might go hunting again, or singing again, or eating again.

The Algonkin were masters of axe and scalping-knife.

Gichita mourned, his robe over his head, while Wawasha, his forearms tied up with strips of cloth, tried to console him. The chief's legs had been cut across by a single blow of the war-axe and he could not rise; though the old squaw who attended him, putting herbs and mosses over the wounds, said that all would be well before the moon came to its full again.

Heome, once more despised because of his fear, sat alone, staring across the river waters, deep in his own despair, speaking to no one.

On *Long Snake* Harald and Grummoch took stock of their losses. Harald had a lump on the side of his head almost as big as a man's fist.

The giant said good-humouredly, 'Praise be to Odin, he gave thee a good hard Northern skull, oath-brother!'

Harald nodded, but did not speak. Instead, he pointed to Jamsgar Havvarson and Thorfinn Thorfinnson, who lay with their faces to the heavens, as though in a white sleep.

Grummoch said, 'Gudbrod Gudbrodsson will be lonely now. There were not such a pair this side of Valhalla while they lived. But look at the red men who lie beside them. They did not waste their time, those two.'

Then they saw the warrior Gudbrod, standing by the mast, the bodies of Algonkin and Abnaki heaped about him, and at first they thought he was sorrowing for the death of his friends, his head sunk on his breast.

But it was not sorrow which dragged his head down so, nor was he thinking of his dead friends, or of anything at all. Two Algonkin arrows held him upright to the mast, so that he did not fall with the rest.

Knud Ulfson sat by the shield-gunwales, binding his arm-wounds with rags and singing, his eyes wild still:

'When the young bucks go from the herd,
Old stag fights on; he knows
No rest from conflict. He
Now runs across the hills,
Sharp-horned and fiery-eyed,
Seeking the killers, his chest
Flecked with the froth of his anger.

The stag, Knud Ulfson, says
That now the young bucks have gone
From the herd, he will run to the end
Of the world, seeking the killers!'

Harald went over and patted him gently on the scarred shoulder.

'The killers have been paid, berserk,' he said. 'Their villages have been destroyed as though they had never been.'

But Knud Ulfson only looked up at him with empty eyes and half-open mouth, as though he did not understand the words his war-leader was speaking. Then he went back to his chanting, seeming to forget the very existence of Harald.

Grummoch said, 'There is little profit in talking to him yet. These berserks live in a closed world of conflict and brotherhood. It will be long before Knud Ulfson's ears will be open to the voices of men, for he is in the battle-trance yet, and I doubt whether he could see his hand before his face. That is the way of berserks.'

Harald said sadly, 'And look, we have lost four others. This is a dear price to pay for crushing the Algonkin and Abnaki on behalf of our red friends, the Beothuk.'

Grummoch said, pointing to a great man who hung half over the longship's prow, 'The enemy have paid dearly too, it seems.'

The two friends dragged the giant red man back into the ship and looked down at him.

From head to foot, he was garbed as only the greatest of chieftains could be. He wore an immense war bonnet of eagles' feathers, their tips dyed brown and garnished with red strands of hair, their bases fluffed out with the white down from the breast of the goose. About his throat was a necklace of a hundred bears' claws, each one set in silver and hanging from a thin hide string. His arms above the elbow were heavy with bands of copper, beaten and embossed with the sign of the great-winged thunderbird. His apron and breechclouts were smothered so with beads of red, and blue and yellow, that it would have been hard to get a lance-point between them. The shoes upon his feet bore the pattern of the rising sun, worked in thin strands of gold wire, against a sky of azure beads as small as an ant's head.

His face, caked with yellow clay, was still proud, even in the fearful sort of death the Northern axe had brought to him. He still held his feathered tomahawk in his right hand, as though prepared for anything on the long dark journey that lay before him.

Wawasha climbed over the side of the longship and gazed down at the dead red man.

'That is War Eagle,' he said. 'He was the greatest of all the Algonkin chieftains. Once he was my father's young friend, until they quarrelled over a squaw. Then they swore to kill each other. But my father, Gichita, still loved him, and would be hurt to the heart to know that War Eagle had died on your ship, from which his spirit may not rise to the Last Hunting Grounds. We must not tell him, for he has troubles enough.'

Then Wawasha bent and touched the Algonkin first on the right cheek, then on the left; then on the right breast, then on the left. And at last he knelt before the dead War Eagle and spoke softly to him, so that no one could hear, closing his proud eagle's eyes with gentle fingers.

And when he had done that, the Vikings stripped the Algonkin of his fine clothes and then tied a piece of iron to his feet. They heaved him over the side of *Long Snake*, away from the canoe of Gichita, so that the old man should not be further troubled in his mind.

Later that day, they made a funeral pyre on the shore, beneath the heavy green boughs of the spruce trees, and so sent the dead Vikings to Valhalla. The red men put their dead into the branches of the trees, seeing that each man's weapon lay across his lap, so that he should awake, ready for battle or hunting, when he came to the journey's end.

And that day, when the sun stood at its highest point in the blue sky, Gichita commanded that his son, Wawasha, should take Harald and Grummoch as his true blood-brothers.

A slit was made in the arm of each man by the medicine man, who bore bison horns on his headdress for the occasion, and their blood was intermingled as it flowed, so that some of Wawasha's seemed to enter the wounds of Harald and Grummoch. Then, holding hands, they were all three laid in a shallow trench, which the braves had dug in the soft ground above the shore; and then the turfs were lightly placed above them, so that they could not be seen.

This was the sign that as brothers they must live, and as brothers go into the earth together at the last call.

And when this was done, the Beothuk sang songs and danced, to the high wailing of the bone flute and the deep throbbing of the skin drum.

Only Heome showed no gladness, but sat alone among the squaws and the children, pale-faced and glowering.

19. The Lakes of the Gods

THEN came a long season of labour. Sometimes, to avoid the rushing, buffeting river, the red men took little streams that ran slower and curled round among overhanging tree-boughs. Once a creature like a great cat leapt down into a canoe, upsetting the braves into the water. They swam around the cat and struck it with tomahawks until it no longer showed its teeth at them or at anyone. The squaws and children in the other boats clapped their hands and laughed at this, and each cried out for the great skin to wear as a robe.

At other times they were faced by a wall of rock, down which the water thundered, white as ice; and then they had to pull ashore and carry their canoes on their shoulders up the slope and away from the waterfall. These were the hard times, for *Long Snake* was a mite too heavy to be hoisted upon shoulders and carried! It was then that the braves cut down tree trunks and made rollers to go under the longship, and so, tugging on hide ropes, all the men and women helped the Vikings to drag *Long Snake* up to the higher reaches of the river.

'We have known such portages in Russia,' said Harald. 'There was one such when we came back from Miklagard in the ships of Haakon Baconfat.'

'Hm,' said Grummoch, shielding his eyes and gazing at the immensely high wall of rock down which the river-water gushed. 'But it was not such a portage as this. There cannot be such another portage as this in all the world!'

But they got to the top in the end, hands chafed raw, backs almost breaking, the blood singing in their heads. And at the top they made camp for that night, too tired to go any further up the great river.

Once, when they were resting so, at the edge of a pinewood, the women tapping quietly on small skin drums while the older children danced about the fires, Heome leaped up and began to wave his arms about, his pale face bitter with anger.

'Why is it, my father,' he asked old Gichita, 'that these white strangers of the long wooden boat sit beside you and my brother Wawasha, at the fire, while I am given a place among the children? Have I not proved that I am a man, like the others?'

Gichita smiled sadly, his yellow face wrinkling in the firelight, and said gently, 'Heome, my son, I cannot overthrow the customs of our people by asking for what I desire or for what you desire. All men of the tribe know that I love both my sons with an equal love, as a father should. I care not if one is big and strong, the other small and weak. Among the bear folk the great father plays with the crippled cub just as he plays with the strong ones, who may grow to overthrow him one day.'

Heome said bitterly, in the firelight, 'Might not the crippled one overthrow him, too, by tricks the old bear did not think of?'

But Gichita, whose legs were troubling him, spoke on in some pain and said, 'It is true that you brought back a wolf which you killed in the forests near our home-place; but since then, we have met the Algonkin and the Abnaki, and men have said that then you did not act like a warrior, like the son of a chieftain. They say that while they were fighting, you lay among the deerhides in the boat, covering your face with your blanket, as though you were not there. That is why you sit where you do, about the fire; and there is nothing I can do, Heome, until your chance comes again to prove yourself. Then, my son, you too shall sit beside me with the others; and you, too, shall take the oath of blood-brotherhood with the great white warriors here, and shall lie with them under the turf.'

Heome gave a high shrill cry and said, 'I would rather die, Gichita, than stoop to claim brotherhood with these strangers, who are white wolves and nothing more ... white wolves who come with us for what they can get, not from any love of our people!'

Harald and Grummoch sat silent at the fire, staring at Heome, who would not meet their eyes; but others of the Vikings were not so calm. Some said that they had lost good men, fighting a battle which was none of their business. Others said that if they had had their way, *Long Snake* would now be halfway home to the Northland.

But in the end Wawasha quietened them all by getting up and performing the Eagle Dance, spreading his arms wide, making a wide and leaping circle, as though the bird he represented was hovering above the fire, and all the time calling out, 'Ku-e-e-e!'

The women about the far fires took up this call – 'Ku-e-e-e! Ku-e-e-e!' until the woodlands echoed and re-echoed with the sound.

Then, as the drumsticks of green ash and hickory pattered out the delicate cross-beats of this dance, Wawasha stopped, poised high on his toes, raised his arms, quivering, as though they were truly wings, and let his fingertips touch lightly above his head.

In the dead silence of the climax of this dance, Heome rose and spat into the fire, contemptuously.

But no one regarded him, their eyes were fixed on the young warrior who would one day become their chieftain.

Suddenly, when Wawasha was at his full height, the drums beat out a loud and concerted *twang!* as though a gigantic bowstring had been released.

Then, in the silence which followed, Wawasha gave a high scream, 'Ku-e-e-e-ok!', fluttered wildly in a circle, always sinking lower and lower towards the ground as he moved round the fires, until at length he fell to the turf, one wing still beating in spasms.

At last this arm sank, too, and the drumming became softer and softer, until it was little more than a whisper, dying away with the dying of the bird.

The women's eyes glistened with tears. The children crept closer to them, snuggling their heads within the buckskin blouses of their mothers. Only the braves still stared at the motionless figure of Wawasha, their copper faces blank and impassive, expressing their admiration by silence.

Gichita bowed his old head and spoke a prayer to the Eagle God:

> *'Thunderbirdman! O Thunderbirdman!*
> *We worship you!*
> *We of the Beothuk look to you for aid!*
> *See that we journey well, O Thunderbirdman!*
> *See that we reach our cooking-place safely!*
> *That is all we ask, O Thunderbirdman!'*

Then Wawasha rose and went to his father, smiling.

'Did the dance go well, Father Gichita?' he asked.

The old man nodded. 'It went well, my son,' he said. 'I feel in my heart now that we shall live to see the Great Lakes and the sacred stone quarries!'

But Harald whispered to Grummoch, 'I should feel happier if that mad wolf, Heome, were tied up safely with a chain about his neck, so that we could always know what he was up to. Last night I dreamed that he was standing on the waters of the river, speaking with the Shield-maiden who once came to visit me out of the mist, after I left Havlock Ingolfson to drown on the rocky skerry in the mist. In my dream, it seemed that Heome and the Shield-maiden came to some agreement for they took each other by the hand, and smiled a great deal. The strange thing is that Heome's crippled hand seemed to come alive again, to have movement in its fingers, as he reached forth to clasp the white hand of the Shield-maiden.'

Grummoch said, 'Dreams are not always to be trusted. I once dreamed I had a new sword and axe, studded with rubies from Miklagard. I tell you, those weapons were as clear to my mind as anything I have ever seen. Even in my dream, I felt that if I touched them on the edge, they would cut my hand. Yet, what happened? When I awoke and felt under my bench, where they were supposed to lie – they were not there! Nor have I ever been given them! Nay, Harald, dreams are not to be trusted. Think no more of Heome the Wolf. If he becomes too dangerous, I will suggest to Knud Ulfson, the berserk, that he takes friend Heome into the woods and shows him the path to Valhalla – with a little knife. No doubt, it would be a task which Knud would enjoy, for he thinks of little else but that sort of thing. We cannot get him to row or to pull on ropes! He should do *something* for his living!'

Harald turned away without answering, for he felt that it would ill become a fighter like Knud Ulfson to kill the crippled son of Gichita, however venomous he became.

However, Knud Ulfson was put to another task the next day, which was greatly to his taste, and which came as a complete surprise to him and to everyone else.

He was out strolling through the woods alongside the river, when all others were rowing upstream, when a red man dropped out of a tree and struck at him with a war-club.

Now Knud Ulfson was not a man to refuse battle to anyone, so he let the club sweep over his bent back, and then he kicked the red man's feet from under him.

What he did with his axe then, neither he nor anyone else recalled. The red man who lay at his feet never knew, anyway.

And when Knud had sung a little song about his own skill as a warrior, he stripped the brave of his headdress and buckskin waistcoat embroidered with red and yellow beads, and then put them on, for he liked finery, having so long lived a pretty poor life on this long voyage.

When at length he caught up with *Long Snake*, which was fighting against the swirling waters of the rapids, many of the Vikings cried out that here was a white-skinned red man – until they saw his long yellow plaits and recognized him.

Wawasha smiled grimly and said, 'You wear the clothes of a chieftain's son. That is Oneida beadwork. It is very pretty.'

Knud Ulfson preened himself and shook out his great feathered headdress, then answered, 'The man who wore them did not deserve them. Who wears such finery should fight with more skill.'

Nor would he say more than that. But Wawasha said to Harald, 'If your man has killed a son of the Oneida, then we had best move swiftly, for they are a revengeful people, and will not sit by their fires singing peace songs when once they know what has happened.'

After that *Long Snake* and all the canoes went forward, by day and by night, until they thought they were out of Oneida territory.

Once, however, they were forced to rest the night, in a little basin, overhung by spruce trees, for Gichita's right leg had swollen badly and was red and inflamed. An old woman of the Beothuk, who had great art in dressing wounds, said that the swelling would not go down unless

Gichita lay the whole of one night with the skin of the green snake wrapped about his leg.

Though the old man shook his head and said that he did not wish to hold up the journey, especially in such a perilous place, the young braves refused for once to obey him and laid down their paddles. Some of them went off into the woods and after much searching came back with three little green snakes, which were skinned that night and the skins bound round the wound while they still held their moisture.

That night a party of red men wearing heavy bearskin robes came down to the basin and sat beside the canoes, their war-axes ready on their knees, their faces flat and motionless, their dark eyes like slits in a deerhide.

And when Wawasha awoke and looked around for the guards he had placed about the camp, the leader of the men in bearskins said, 'Do not blame your guards, friend. We crept upon them and tied them to trees. They are not harmed, nor will you be harmed, if you are men of sense.'

'Who are you?' asked Wawasha. 'I do not know your language, yet I understand a word here and there.'

The other said, 'We are Swamp Cree, my friend, and have lost our tracks through this woodland. To us, every tree seems like its fellow. We are not used to wandering through forests.'

Wawasha nodded. 'What do you want, men of the Swamp Cree?'

The man said, 'We want to go to the pipestone quarries beside the Big Lake, but we do not know the way. Our way lies further north and we have lost it. Let us travel with you, and all will be well.'

Wawasha said, 'It is not wise to speak threateningly to us Beothuk, my friend. We have gods travelling with us in their great ship of wood. If they woke and heard you speak too proudly, they might decide to lessen you in height by the length of a head, or in number by a few dozen.'

The Swamp Cree gazed back at Wawasha, their lips drawn down in a smile of disbelief. Wawasha whistled three times then, and Grummoch, who was a light sleeper, leaped on shore and strode to where the Swamp Cree squatted, their axes across their knees.

He stood the height of a man and half a man, and was as broad as three men. He wore an iron helmet, at the sides of which sprouted out the black horns of a bull. About his body he wore a rusty iron hauberk. His axe was so heavy that few men could swing it.

And when Grummoch strode among them, the Swamp Cree drew back, gasping, though too brave to show fear.

Grummoch said, 'What! Have the bears come to break their fast with us, or on us, Wawasha, my brother?'

Wawasha said, for all to hear, 'It is for them to decide. If they choose the first, there is deer-meat for them; if they choose the second, there is death.'

Grummoch nodded lazily, and began to swing his great axe, Death Kiss, in the pale dawn air, as though this were a matter of little importance. The axe made a whistling sound as it swung and the Swamp Cree watched with admiration.

At last their chief said, smiling wryly, 'This fellow is not one I would care to offend, unless I had my ten brothers with me!'

Grummoch stopped swinging his axe and said, 'I beg you, go and fetch your ten brothers. I will sit here on this stone until they come. I do not run away from a challenge.'

But the Swamp Cree shook his grizzled head and answered, 'In the north, we are a great folk, and are respected by all, even by the Big Innuit. We wish to remain so, which might not be if we had the ill luck to let your axe fall on our necks too often. Look you, white god, let us travel with you, and we will fight with you if the need arises. Is that a bargain?'

Wawasha nodded, so Grummoch agreed, too, for in truth he had not wanted to fight so early in the morning, before he had eaten his breakfast.

Then Harald and the other Vikings came and sat down with the Beothuk and the Swamp Cree, about a great fire, while Gichita watched, smiling, for his swelling had now gone down and his leg had lost its redness, just as the old woman had promised.

Then the chief of the Swamp Cree took from his inner tunic a long hollow rod of black wood, to the end of which he fitted a carved red stone bowl. And into this bowl he sifted grains and shreds of a dried herb. And when this was done, he set fire to the herb and sucked at the black rod of wood. Smoke came out of his mouth.

Knud Ulfson said, 'By Thor, but this is strange magic! Never have I seen smoke in a man's mouth before. Does it not burn his inner cheeks, Wawasha?'

Wawasha said, 'No man has been burned by it yet. Though it is not a custom my folk are given to. Yet they blow the smoke out of their mouths when they are required to do so by other tribes who use the pipe; for it is a sign of peace.'

Then the chief of the Swamp Cree passed the smoking pipe to Grummoch and signed that he should do as he had already done.

The giant gave a great suck at the hollow rod, and then began to cough as though he would die, for he had forgotten to blow out the smoke and had swallowed it, as he would have done a draught of mead.

Now all the red men laughed, and one of the Swamp Cree even dared to go forward and slap Grummoch on the back. Though he made a wry face as he did so, for Grummoch's back in its iron coat was as hard as a barn door made of solid oak.

So, among laughter, the pipe was passed back and forth among the leaders. Knud Ulfson took it and blew out the longest stream of all.

'This is child's play,' he shouted. 'Why, I dare eat the pipe, fire and all!'

But Harald stopped him with a black look, for the berserk was liable to do anything he said he would, regardless of the wisdom or foolishness of his promise.

At last the pipe went back into the robe of the leader of the Swamp Cree, whose name was Lanook; and so the two parties of red men travelled as one from that time, the Beothuk and the Swamp Cree.

Until at last, one bright morning, they sailed round a bend in the river and then stopped, stricken with awe by the sight that met their eyes.

Before them lay the waters of the Big Lake, so broad that it might have been a sea, for it was impossible to see to its furthermost shore. Waves rippled across the deep green waters, and great trees floated on it, like longships, here and there.

Harald said, 'I have travelled through Finnmark, and know the lakes there; but to this one, they are nothing but puddles left by the rain!'

Grummoch asked Wawasha, 'Are these waters indeed those of a lake, or those of the sea? I can scarcely believe that a lake could be so immense.'

Wawasha said, 'This is a lake, my friend. The Lake of the Gods. But it is not the end of our journey, for we must pass through this lake, and then into another, and yet another until we come to the greatest of them all – and then we shall reach the gathering-place of the tribes. That is the end of our journey.'

20. The Gathering-Place of the Tribes

NOW IN the full summer when the eagle flung himself across the sky for the sheer fury of living, and the sun seemed to burn brighter with every day, the Beothuk and the Swamp Cree set up their buffalo-hide tepees, each one the height of three men standing on each other's shoulders. These skin houses were painted with bright colours, and had their smoke-holes facing towards the east, for the wind which most commonly blew across the Plains came from the west.

Along the shores of the greatest lake, and stretching inland beyond all woods and across the wide prairies, tribes had set up their tepees, until it seemed that all the red men in the world had gathered there to hunt the horned buffalo and to dig the red stone from the sacred quarries.

Harald and the Vikings stood on the deck of *Long Snake* and looked outwards, at the multitude of tepees and the great clouds of dust and smoke that rose above the plain. They shut their eyes and listened to the myriad sounds of a great community – the shouting of men, the lowing of cattle, the squealing of children, the yelping of dogs, the singing of women, the sound of axe on wood, the drumming, the fluting, the pounding of feet . . .

Grummoch said, 'Never did I expect to see and hear such a vast multitude. In Caledonia, when the geese gather to fly away for the winter, we children used to think that nowhere in all the world could so many creatures mass together and move away. But if all the geese that have lived since the beginning of time could gather and fly, there would not be such a number as these red folk.'

Harald said, dreamily, 'If one could carry this great host back to the Northland, and set spears and real iron axes in their hands, what might one not do! The warlord who led such a host might conquer England, Frankland, Miklagard, Spain, oh, everywhere! Such a lord would be the greatest the world had ever known, brothers!'

Knud Ulfson said, 'My father once led a war-party of Irishmen and Danes and Icelanders on a foray against the Franks. But the result was that they cut each other's throats, and my father was left in Frankland with a leaking boat and only the rusty sword he carried, to gain his fortune. It took him three years to walk back home. Nay, I for one would not wish to be the warlord of such a varied folk as these red men, who seem more apt at cutting throats than most folk I have met.'

When the Vikings went to the great tepee of Gichita, they found that he was holding a council with the chieftains of the other red folk. He lay back in his litter, for his legs still troubled him so much that he could not stand on them for long at a time, surrounded by the stoutest of his warriors.

The other chieftains passed a stone peace pipe round the fire, grunting and nodding, their black eyes expressionless, even when the white Vikings arrived and ranged themselves behind Gichita.

Harald gazed round the great circle with astonishment. He had not thought that men could be so different, one from the other. In that crowd were small men, as yellow and flat-faced as the Innuit, and wearing bearskins with the hide outermost; tall brown men, who hardly wore anything at all, save a bead loincloth and copper armbands and a small sheaf of arrows slung before their chests; sturdy men with beaded waistcoats and moccasins, high headdresses of eagles' feathers, and carrying feathered lances and fur-trimmed bucklers; men of all sorts, of all tribes. Gichita spoke to them in a simple language, helped out by signs of the hands and the head. They answered by nodding, or by making gestures with hand and arm.

Wawasha whispered to Harald, 'We are the last folk to arrive, and so must give an explanation of our journey. That is why Gichita, my father, is addressing them. It is the custom. The language he speaks is the "first language", as we call it; it is the tongue the first red men brought with them when they came, a thousand men's lives ago, over the northern ice with their packs on their backs, to settle here in woodland and forest, in desert and by seashore. All red men know this "first language" and use it when they speak together, at this time of the year. It is the language of peace and of brotherhood. Later, when we leave the red stone quarries and go back to our own cooking-places, we shall speak our own tongue, Beothuk and Algonkin and Oneida, not the "first language".'

Harald said, 'Does that mean that when you all leave this place, you will kill each other again?'

Wawasha nodded. 'That is the old custom,' he said. 'We all move out from the quarries on the same day, when the first breath of winter begins to blow, and make our way homewards. It is the old law that for three days, no man may fight with another. After that, when the red folk are well away from the sacred place, they may please themselves.'

Grummoch said, 'This is not an unusual notion. The folk south of Miklagard who make their yearly journey to Jerusalem, where their sacred place is, do likewise; and so do the Franks and the Avars and the Saxons, when they go to Rome, I have heard. It is a convenient arrangement, and results in less shedding of blood than might be the case if there were no such law.'

Wawasha smiled grimly and said, 'Even so, there are those who drink the maize beer about their fires at night and forget the old law. Then they dance until they have forgotten what they are about, and their next idea is to raid the tepees of any tribe they hate.'

Knud Ulfson said, 'That I can understand, coming from a family of berserks myself. The joy of life lies not in sitting about a hearth-stone, listening to the tales of old women, but in swapping blows with other men, and laying one's enemies at one's feet. That is the true joy of life.'

Harald Sigurdson looked at him sternly and said, 'I have a wife and two sons, who live beside the fjord and wait for me to return one day. It is my intention to go back to them, and so I will have no more of this berserk talk, Knud

Ulfson. What your family did is one thing; what I command you to do is another. So have the goodness to keep away from maize beer and dancing while we are with these red men. And keep your axe where it belongs, on the thong at your side. If ever I see you putting on that daft berserk look, I shall save the red men the trouble and will silence you myself. Remember that!'

Knud Ulfson did not like those words; but he knew that Harald Sigurdson never spoke unless he meant what he said. Indeed, along the fjord there was a fire-saying which went:

'Thunder threatens but may not strike;
Rain threatens but may blow over;
Wolf snarls but may not bite;
When Harald snarls, your life is over.'

So Knud bowed his head and turned away, anxious not to see the snarl appear on the face of Sigurdson.

That night there was much singing and dancing, to the many talking-drums and the wood and bone flutes. In the firelight a long line of red men from the far south stood, mother-naked, whirling great bullroarers about their heads, until the purple dusk was alive with the whirring, thrumming, murmuring of these instruments. Beyond the firelight a group of red men from the western shores danced in a ring, their backs garnished with a circle of painted feathers to represent the sun. The sound of their feet beat out a rhythm which seemed to throb through the earth itself and then crept upwards into everyone's bones.

Harald, wandering among the many groups of red men, noticed Knud Ulfson drinking deep from a great earthen jar, held to his lips by a smiling red man whose face was decorated with bars of white ochre. Knud was shuddering as he drank, and Harald knew this to be a bad sign.

Gently he took the jar from the berserk and handed it back politely to the red man, who stared up at him half dazed. Then Harald took Knud by the neck and led him to a high totem pole which was set firmly in the earth, and there he tied Knud Ulfson by the hands, to the pole, with thongs of wet deerhide, until the morning.

When he came to set Knud free, he saw that the berserk had gnawed the painted wood like a savage dog. But when Knud looked into Harald's eyes, he bent his head as though ashamed of himself.

Harald said, 'If I see you drinking maize beer again, I shall bring peace to you suddenly. Is that understood, berserk?'

Knud Ulfson said, 'It is understood, shipmaster. I will abide by it – though I feel that such laws are unmanly and unreasonable.'

Harald gave him a smack that almost laid him flat, and said, 'While I am the master of *Long Snake*, I will not be told what I am to do by any seal-brained berserk from the fjords. Now get you gone and sleep off your madness.'

Later in the day, Grummoch came to Harald and said, 'It ill becomes a Viking to set great store by trifles – but today I have seen a strange sight.'

Grummoch waited for Harald to ask him what the strange sight might be, for that was the manner of

Northmen when they had interesting news to disclose. But Harald merely sat and smiled at him, until the giant could stand this scrutiny no longer and said, 'There is danger brewing, Harald Sigurdson. Mark my words, and I do not speak lightly.'

Then Harald said, 'What is the danger, Little One? I am always anxious to hear of danger, for it gives spice to my meat.'

Grummoch said with a frown, 'This danger may not be to your taste, oath-brother. Heome has sworn a brotherhood with that fool, Knud Ulfson. He has caused Knud to forget his oath to you, in his battle-madness. Heome has said to him that Knud shall be his hands and his arms, and in return for what he is to do, Knud shall be named the greatest berserk of all the red men. I heard all this in the forest when I bent behind a bush to fasten up my shoestrings.'

Harald was silent for a while, and then at length he asked, 'And what does Heome wish daft Knud to do, then, oath-brother?'

Grummoch answered, 'He has asked him to destroy his own brother, Wawasha, and his old father, Gichita. That is all.'

Harald said, 'And that is quite enough. We must keep a steady eye on those two fools now, for such a pact could mean our own end, too.'

'That is what I thought,' said Grummoch, slyly, 'but I did not like to suggest it, being but a simple giant, as you remind me so often, and you such a man of cleverness and great affairs.'

Harald gave him a grim look, but said nothing.

21. Strange Partners

THEN followed a time of fishing, when the many red folk dragged nets through the shallow pools, or rode in their birchbark boats over the lake waters with their sharp fish-spears poised. Sometimes this happened at nightfall, when the fish little suspected their attackers; and then the rolling lake seemed like a place of magic, with the bobbing torches and the men in their white-clayed buffalo-robes, standing, ghostwise, in their boats, their many-pronged hardwood lances held at the ready.

And after that, the buffalo hunting.

In and out of the great shag-haired herds ran the lithest of the hunters, the wind in their impassive faces, their lances thrusting hither and thither among the heaving stupid beasts.

Often, after such a raid, the plains were dotted thickly with immense brown bodies, just as though it were a battlefield of giants, and the giants had come off the worst of the encounter.

Though sometimes the red men suffered, too, as when a woodland tribe, little accustomed to this hunting sport, allowed itself to be caught in a narrow sandstone gully,

when the furious frightened herd crashed through in terror, pursued by other men and dogs. That day the Seminole, a simple swamp folk, who seldom made the long journey to the sacred quarries because of the distance, mourned their many crushed dead. Hardly one of them could be recognized, so harshly had the hooves treated them.

Grummoch had great taste for this sport, being swift of foot and strong of the lance-thrust. During that time, he alone killed two score of the lumbering creatures, moving amongst them as he would do in a battle with men, striking to left and to right, then jumping clear of the wildly tossing heads, the fiercely threshing hooves, the agonized twisting of the great bodies which could crush a man.

Among the many red men, Grummoch became known as 'Bull Killer', and at least four of the tribes sent deputations to him, asking him to hunt with them and to live in their lodges.

Always Grummoch shook his own great shaggy head with courtesy and said, 'I have lord and lodge already. It ill becomes a man to change his chieftain.'

Harald was likewise held in great respect by the red folk, for in a shallow valley, darkened by overhanging thorn bushes, he had stumbled on a nest of poisonous snakes, and had trodden each one of them into the ground fearlessly, before they had had time to sink their fangs in his legs or feet.

For this he was named 'Snake Destroyer', and given snakeskin armbands by the troop of Ojibwe who had watched this strange encounter.

And always, when the Vikings gained fame in this manner, Wawasha and his father Gichita called the Beothuk together about the fires and ordered dancing and drumming. The drums of all shapes and colours were seldom silent in that encampment.

And always, when such feastings took place, Heome Nohands went away to the lakeside and wept, beyond the power of man to soothe, praying bitterly to his private gods that the strangers who had belittled him, by being so strong themselves, should suffer. Yet now he had learned to smile when he spoke to his brother, and Harald, and Grummoch, so covering the bitter heart-thoughts that he held against them. And in his dreams, he saw the three of them drowning in the lake, or crushed under a fall of rocks in the quarries, or trampled down by the wild buffalo on the plains. Always he saw them dead and out of the way, so that he alone could gain the love of his tribe, and of his father, Gichita, without having to kill him . . .

Then, at last, when the moon was at her full, the great medicine man of all the red folk sent round the chopping-axe of staghorn among the multitude of tepees, as a sign that the sacred red pipestone was ready to be quarried, and each tribe made its own plans to go to the quarries, unarmed, save with staghorn picks, and to dig what they needed in the coming year, for the making of pipes and beads and images, armbands for the young squaws and earrings for the young braves. This was an order which had never been disobeyed since the red folk came across the far northern ice with their bundles on their backs, thousands of lifetimes ago.

Before dawn the following day, the men of Gichita's tribe, together with the Swamp Cree and the Vikings, rose silently and broke their fast, but carried neither food nor water with them; for it was the law that the diggers of the sacred stone should neither eat nor drink until they had returned to their lodges in the evening.

Grummoch tore at a great hunk of buffalo-meat, saying, 'Well, if I may not eat until sunset, I will make good use of my teeth now!'

Wawasha smiled and slapped him on the back. 'We have a saying,' he said, 'that big eaters make small diggers. See that your pick sinks deeper than any other man's today, for you have eaten more than anyone else of the tribe!'

Grummoch pretended to look offended and answered, 'If that is how you feel, then I will carry a buffalo with me, on my shoulder, to nibble on the way! A fellow must keep his strength up, my friend!'

The sacred stone quarries lay two leagues away from the lake, and Wawasha was anxious that his folk should get there to find a good digging-spot before all the other red folk took the best places. He hurried them along as much as he dared, seeing that every man had his staghorn pick and a buckskin bag into which he would put his diggings.

Between the tepees he met Harald and said, 'I have been searching for my brother, Heome, but cannot find him. He is not in his tent. That is strange, for every year he has gone with the others, and, though he cannot dig, he has spoken the prayers of our people as his part of the ceremony.'

Harald said, just as solemnly, 'My man, Knud Ulfson, is nowhere to be found, either. That, too, is strange; for always he has been at my back, since we left the Northlands. Do you think they may have gone together to the quarries, unwilling to wait for us?'

Wawasha thought for a while, his chin in his copper-coloured hand, and then he said, 'They may indeed have gone together, and mean to wait for us. But, if so, they have gone alone, for none of our tribe is missing, and two lone dogs like that will drag down few deer, it seems to me.'

Then the two men said no more, but began the long run towards the stone quarries before the other tribes should wake.

For some time they saw no one since they had set off at such an early hour, and at last their way ran beside a swampy stream, in a little gully, where the grass grew rank and stinking from the brackish water and the dead creatures which had gone there with arrows in their sides, or sinking from some disease, such as that fever which comes of eating the Juraba plant.

It was not a pleasant place to find oneself in, as all the vikings agreed. Here trolls might lurk, they said to each other. As for the Beothuk, they blew down their nostrils frequently, so that the spirit of the place might not enter their hearts and poison them.

But the Swamp Cree were accustomed to such places, and they trotted on, smiling, as though there was nothing in the tangled roots and slithering creatures to trouble a man.

In a thorn bush which stood above them, on the skyline, a bird suddenly screeched. The running party stopped and looked up. It was a swamp hawk, its feathers tattered and torn, as though it had suffered many conflicts with the other birds of the plains and marshes.

Wawasha said, 'Those birds are usually brave. It is not often that one hears them cry out when a man approaches. Perhaps it is an omen, my friends.'

Harald, who ran beside him, said, 'It ill becomes a man to stop in his running because an old bird suddenly feels the sadness of its life.'

But Wawasha said, 'We of the red folk learn to listen to the words of the creatures. And this creature tells me that it is disturbed in its heart. I would say that it has been made afraid this morning, by others than us.'

They ran on then, but Harald thought of Knud Ulfson, who was such a man as might trouble more than a mere bird, when he was in a mood to do so.

A little later, one of the Swamp Cree ran up to Wawasha and showed him a copper armband, thick with swamp mud.

'This I found beside the waters, chieftain's son,' he said.

Wawasha answered, 'This belongs to my brother, Heome. We must go carefully, my friends, from this point onwards. The gods have spoken to us twice; once through a bird, once through an armband. It would be foolish to shut our ears and our eyes to such signs.'

Grummoch said, 'They are two and we are many. For my part, I would as well run singing at the top of my voice. Who can harm us, when all folk go to the quarries without knife, or sword, or axe?'

Wawasha said nothing, but from then on he ran cautiously, sometimes watching the ground for spoors; sometimes swinging his fine head from side to side, like a questing beast.

But nothing happened, and at last they came out of the long valley where the swamp water stank and the flies buzzed, to see ahead of them on the top of the slope, a high and circular mound of clay. It stood against the blue sky like a smoothly-polished helmet, and looked to be big enough for forty men to stand upon in comfort, without jostling each other.

'That is an ancient burial mound,' said Wawasha. 'It was there before the first of the red folk came, and our tales say that it will still be there when the last of us have gone away from the land.'

Harald said, 'In England, in the south, there is a circle of great stones, about which men say the same thing. It was there before the Romans came, and it will be there when Odin decides to crumble the world in his two great hands. There are some such monuments which are meant to teach man that he is but a little thing, with a life hardly longer than that of a spring fly.'

They said no more, but set their course towards the ancient burial heap, beyond which lay steps, cut in the rock, leading down to the sacred quarries.

When at last they arrived at the tumulus, most of the men were glad, for they had somehow expected to be delayed, with one thing or another.

And so they scrambled up the smooth slopes with relief, at last standing on the summit and gazing below them, for a distance greater than ten men could shoot with one arrow after another.

Harald almost gasped with sheer amazement at the size and beauty of the great quarry, for he had never seen its like, in all his journeyings across the world.

It lay, like an immense hole scooped from the earth by the greatest hand of the greatest god the earth had ever known. A city ten times as great as Miklagard might have been placed within it, and then have left space for Rome. It was deep, deep, deep – deeper than the waters of the Jimjefjord, which, as all Northmen know, has no bottom. And its sides were sheer, save for the yellow bushes which sprouted here and there like the tufts of beard on an old man's cheeks. Its stone was of many colours – red, yellow, black, blue. The Vikings cried aloud and said that this must be the end of the world, for they had seen no place like it, nor had heard of any in all the sagas they knew.

Wawasha pointed to a place a hundred paces away.

'That is the only way down,' he said. 'There are steps there which were cut when my grandfather's great-grandfathers first came here, when the sun was young and so small that a man could hold it in his hand without being burned. That is the place we must go to. All the tribes use those steps. We call them "The Steps to Life and Death". Let us go down! None of the other tribes will be here for another hour yet!'

As he spoke, they all stood on the mound top, against the blue morning sky, their buckskin bags and staghorn picks in their hands.

And as he spoke, Wawasha suddenly let fall his pick and bag and gave a strange sobbing cry, then half-turned and flung his arms out wide. Harald and Grummoch, who stood on either side of him, caught him in their arms and gazed at him in amazement. Then they saw that a little arrow, hardly longer than a man's hand, stuck deep in his head, just above the right eye. There was little comfort to be had from asking Wawasha any questions, for his jaw had dropped and his eyes had rolled back sightless. In that one moment he had died, and now lay as heavily as three men, his great arms hanging useless before him.

Harald turned to Grummoch and was about to speak some words of astonishment, when from the lip of the sacred quarry, men began to run towards them, men of the Algonkin, the Abnaki, the Oneida, all swinging spears or tomahawks, all painted with the white and yellow war-ochre. And at the head of this pack of warrior-hounds ran Heome and Kuud Ulfson, shouting like berserks, calling down death on all the men who stood on that ancient mound, their hands grasping short picks of staghorn, their hearts full of foreboding.

Grummoch gasped, 'By Thor, we are ambushed! Form a ring about the head of the mound, and strike with what you have! This is the warning that the swamp hawk spoke to us, though we had not ears to hear it then!'

And so the red men and the white men gathered, close to each other, like buffalo waiting for the slaughter.

22. The Fight on the Mound

NOW, WITH the yapping of foxes and the deep and terrible grunting of bears, the attacking red men came in, striking low with their tomahawks, thrusting up viciously with feathered lances.

Grummoch, who stood well to the forefront, his tawny hair flying in the high breeze on the tumulus, shouted out, 'Come forth without delay, all who wish to try their skulls against this little horn pick! The play has just begun, catch me while the mood is on me to strike once only and cleanly; later, my blows may grow careless, then meeting will give little pleasure to either side!'

The Vikings around him laughed and cried out, 'Where are the famous Algonkin now?'

A tall young brave of the Algonkin, wearing a high fur hat stuck round with hawk's feathers dyed yellow, called back, 'We are here, pale murder-wolves! Have no fear, we shall come at you as soon as there is room to move!'

The Swamp Cree set their brown faces grimly and struck slowly and surely, each man grunting out the number of those who fell before his staghorn pick. But they were hampered by their heavy furs, and the attacking Abnaki on that side of the mound gave them small chance to strip off their clothes and to move freely.

The Swamp Cree suffered bitter losses that bright morning, used as they were to a different manner of combat. But the Beothuk sucked in their breath and dilated their nostrils with contempt for their enemies; and soon the Algonkin learned that the little pick of staghorn, used with craft, can equal the copper-headed tomahawk, while its point lasts and its stave remains whole.

Harald, facing the Algonkin with the high fur cap, fending blows, striking blows by turn, saw from the edge of his eye a young Viking named Olaf Miklofsson take a stroke from an Abnaki axe on the shaft of his pick, then kick upwards into his opponent's chest with such force that the man fell backwards, to be lanced through by the oncoming Indians. Almost immediately afterwards, Olaf Miklofsson was struck on the neckbone by an Abnaki who had pushed his way among the Swamp Cree and was standing in the midst of the men on the burial mound.

Harald shouted out, 'Stand back to back, you red men, then they cannot come amongst us so!'

The great Algonkin who faced him bellowed out that the white men were cowards, and drove at Harald's shoulder with his long-bladed axe.

Harald said, 'A little more to the left would have been better, friend!' And swaying from the blow he slashed sideways so that the sharp-pointed pick entered the Algonkin's side, between the lower ribs.

The warrior fell sideways, dragging with him Harald's pick, its shaft now slippery with sweat and other things. Harald bent swiftly and snatched the long-bladed war-axe from the dying brave's hand.

'Exchange is no robbery, friend!' he said grimly, and then turned to ward off the blows of another red man.

Grummoch saw this happen and said, 'When I go back home to the fjord, I shall tell all I meet that Harald Sigurdson is so crafty a bargainer that he even sets up his market stall on the battlefield!'

This was meant to be a taunt, but Harald took it otherwise, as is the right way among warriors at such a time; and he answered, 'It would well become Grummoch of the rusty hair to call a higher price for his blows. He is letting them go too cheaply, and half his enemies are escaping with little more than a broken arm or a cracked head!'

Grummoch was indeed so sorely pressed that often he had to let his opponents stagger away without the endknock which he was used to giving on all occasions, wherever possible.

Indeed, at the moment when Harald spoke, three red men were about the giant, stabbing with lances, almost cutting each other in their haste to be at the giant.

Harald stepped forward and sliced down at two of them before they knew where he was. The third, seeing that now he stood against two of the white warriors, swung about and rolled down the hillock into safety for the time being.

The Vikings laughed and slapped each other on the shoulders. Then Grummoch stopped and chose for himself the best and the longest of the lances dropped by the fallen red men.

'Now we are well-armed for such as will come against us,' he said. 'And thank you, oath-brother, for that bit of advice about bargaining. I have never before needed to trade my weapons in battle, and the wisdom of your words came at a good time.'

Harald said, 'I am always pleased to advise a friend on such occasions.'

Then, in the little lull that followed, Grummoch pointed over the black heads of the swaying red men and said, 'Look at the edge of the crowd. Heome and Knud Ulfson are there; I wondered when we should see them again!'

Heome was beating on a shallow drum with his nerveless hands, since he could not hold a drumstick. The rhythms he was evoking from the stretched deerhide came over the littered ground like the mutterings of death.

Knud Ulfson had torn off every stitch of clothing, and was nodding his head back and forth in time to the drum, like a war-stallion that can hardly be restrained from plunging, blind, into the thick of the fighting. His plaits, which were usually yellow, were now stained red, and flopped stiffly behind him. His right hand clutched a long iron axe that he had brought from the ship. On his left arm was a round buckler, such as the red men carry; a thing of wood, covered with buffalo hide and edged about with the down of the winter goose.

Grummoch said bitterly, 'It ill becomes a Viking to strike against his kith and kin. Yonder youth is drunk with more than maize beer this time. Now he is thirsty for honour among the Algonkin! I think he looks to be their war chief when this affair is over!'

Harald said grimly, 'At the end of this morning, Knud Ulfson will lie stark upon this mound. That I promise you, and I do not speak hastily in these matters.'

Grummoch, whose arms were red to the elbows, and whose broad face was streaked with blood and sweat, yelled out then, 'Knud Ulfson, I bear an invitation to a party! Come up here like a man and let us dance together, my friend!'

Knud gazed about him, blank-eyed as a blind man, and called back into the blue air, 'I am Loki now, the red one. Crippled Hoder beats the drum for me, because proud Balder is dead! I come to no man's bidding!'

Harald said, 'The poor fool is quite mad, as mad as the red man who has brought this battle about!'

Then, raising his voice, he shouted to Knud, 'Ulfson, little man, Harald Sigurdson commands you! Come up the hill and show him what you still know of axe-usage, for, remember, it was Harald who taught you all you know, in the pasture-field behind the village middens!'

Knud Ulfson gave a little shuffle of the feet, as though he might be about to fall down, then he waved his bloody head from side to side, mincingly, like a girl who is petulant, and cares not who sees it.

And at last he called out in a high, unnatural voice, 'Harald Sigurdson is a man! I will not harm Harald Sigurdson, who taught me all I know of the axe-play! Let Harald Sigurdson come down the hill and stand by my side as my brother and he and I will fight for Heome together! Two true berserks among a pack of mangy wolves!'

Harald Sigurdson replied, 'I take only men as my brothers, Ulfson Maidenhair! I fight only for men, and Heome Tenderhand is not my man! Come forth, Ulfson, and learn what it is to face a man!'

Then the red men on the hillock began to laugh in mockery, though they stood knee high among the bodies of their dearest brothers, and their own strength was failing as the sun climbed higher in the blue sky.

Knud Ulfson heard this laughter and began to grit his teeth so savagely that pieces of them broke off. He began to bite his lips with such abandon that his own blood ran down his long chin, giving him a red beard. He began to swing his long-shafted iron axe so perilously that all the red men stood away from him, knowing in their own savage way that he was now beyond speech and reasoning.

Then Knud began to cry out, to the beat of Heome's little drum, which stuttered with the berserk's stuttering words, as though the two young men were in unison of thought and feeling:

'Knud Ulfson speaks to all the world!
And this is what Knud Ulfson says:
Neither the white bear of the wasteland,
Nor the white ghost in the darkened hall;
Neither blood, nor bone, flesh, nor entrails,
Neither belly-wound nor eye-wound,
Liver-wound nor armpit wound –
Causes him fear, causes him delay
In answering challenge!
Knud Ulfson has outstared the breeding wolf;

He has snatched the snake from its mossy shelter;
He has held the bear's paw in his right hand.
Knud Ulfson will not waver from Harald's blade,
Will not avoid Harald's thrust,
Will not shrink when Harald strikes;
For though Harald is great,
Knud Ulfson is greater;
Though Harald kills Knud,
They will go together to Valhalla!'

When Grummoch heard these words, even he shuddered, for he knew that now Knud had reached the outermost boundary of berserk madness, the point at which a Viking's mind deserts him and he runs upon the spears gladly, laughing and joking, knowing not what he feels or says. Such men die without knowing they are dead; but always they take with them any who stand within reach of their blows. Such men make no effort to defend themselves, but set their heart only on delivering blows . . .

Grummoch muttered from the corner of his spittle-flecked mouth, 'I stand beside you, Harald. When he comes in, I will strike his legs from under him with the shaft of my lance, then we will send him packing as he sprawls upon the ground!'

But Harald did not answer. His face was set and hard, like a face carved from wood. He slowly set himself, left foot forward, to meet the berserk's charge. His motions were deliberate. It was as though he stood before a king and prepared to make his bow. It was as though he stood before a lady and prepared to dance with her, in some high

hall at the winter feasting. It was as though he was a statue carved in ivory; a statue of a man preparing to stand before death himself.

Then Knud Ulfson began to scream, high and in the rhythm of the little drum. Heome pounded the hollow gourd, beating out the pulses of the berserk's inner heart.

Then suddenly Heome himself twirled round thrice, shouted high in the barking of a dog, and ceased his drumming.

Knud Ulfson flung back his blood-stiffened plaits and charged, his lips drawn upwards so that his white teeth could be seen, clenched in a smile of death.

The red men on either side parted before him, their axes now lowered, their eyes wide with wonder and fear.

Grummoch made to stand before Harald, but Sigurdson gave such a bull-like bellow that the giant fell to one side, his lance-point almost in the ground. And thus he learned that Harald Sigurdson wished to meet his fate alone, and with no aid from any man – not even from his dearest oath-brother, and the foster-father of his children, Svend and Jaroslav.

23. Settlement

THERE are the moments in a man's life when he welcomes other folk about him, so that they may comfort him, bring him food, or presents, or the simple pleasure of kindly words. But there are other moments, which come but infrequently in a man's life, when he needs no other but himself to be beside him. These are the moments when food, and presents, and kindly words count as nothing; for the man stands before death himself, who is not concerned with food and presents and kindly words.

Before death, man stands alone, and no one may comfort him. Nor does he need comfort, for he is now aware that only he may pass through the low door into the darkness; that none may go with him, however much food, however many presents, however many kindly words they bear.

The man at the brink of death stands quite alone.

Harald Sigurdson stood quite alone that morning, upon the blood-slippery clay of the ancient burial mound, that had been there before the first red men carried their skin-wrapped packages across the frozen seas to the north. The hot sun beat down upon him, from a world outside man's knowledge; the hot sun burning down, thoughtlessly, upon another world of ants, some wearing feathers, some wearing iron helmets; ants, without sense in their movements, power in their minds; ants who must die one day, from sun, or frost, from hunger, or the letting out of blood; from the deep salt sea, where great creatures moved mindless among the weed . . .

And as Harald Sigurdson stood, watching Knud Ulfson with eyes as keen as a hawk's, as through a crystal glass, sharp and clear – though the world of men about Knud was grey and misty and blind – Harald suddenly remembered poor Havlock Ingolfson, crying out as he drowned upon the lonely rocky skerry off the coast of Norway, with the bitter sea in his mouth, and the mocking seabirds screeching over him.

And when Knud was no more than a full lance-thrust away from him, Harald remembered the Shield-maiden, who had told him he had done wrong to leave the wretch, Havlock Ingolfson, to drown so miserably, he who had sailed the length and breadth of the world's seas in a cockleshell of a longship. She had said she would come twice, and now Harald felt that she was near, perhaps at the edge of the red stone quarry, or behind him, laughing, her white-golden hair in thick plaits, hanging to her waist, her broad shoulders held back, waiting for him to die and to go with her to Valhalla, where Thorfinn Thorfinnson waited with a new jest, and Gudbrod Gudbrodsson burnished his poor breastplate with an old piece of iron that he had found in a kitchen-midden in some village they had sacked in their earlier wicked days . . .

Harald wished that Thorfinn and Gudbrod were there to see him now. He did not think of Asa, or his two young sons, Svend Sigurdson and Jaroslav Sigurdson. Nor did he think of poor Jamsgar Havvarson, who was a good fighter, but who had doubts about Thor and Odin, and wished sometimes that he had followed the Whitechrist.

Harald did not think of many things that morning, upon the slippery burial mound of the first stone-men, who painted their caves with pictures of bulls, and wore bones in their hair.

He did not hear the cry of the hawk and the carrion crow and the thunderbird above him. He did not hear Grummoch's weeping. He did not hear Knud Ulfson say suddenly, as he halted in his wild rush before his shipmaster, the man who had taught him the usage of the axe, 'Harald Sigurdson, I am a fool who has come to his senses. I obey you in all things. I love you in all things. I am your man. Let us now fight as brothers!'

Harald did not hear these words. *For he too was a berserk . . .*

His long-bladed Algonkin axe came down, precisely as a drawn line, without fear, without feeling; without mercy, or without hatred.

And Knud Ulfson died with a smile on his silly northern face, his plaits a yard apart from each other, his silly hands, smooth with no rowing, fingers wide, and weaponless.

For he had flung his weapons away at the foot of the hillock, when his grey-misted mind had cleared and had shown him Harald again as his true master.

And so, with a handful of men on either side left, the fight upon the burial mound ended, even as the thunderbird shrieked, calling a close to the dawn.

Those who had stood behind Heome and the dead berserk that morning now turned like whipped hounds and ran westwards, over the hot rock and the withered scrub, so that none of the tribes coming later to the great quarry should meet them and know that they had broken the peace which had always reigned over that sacred place . . .

For all this had happened while other men were in their beds, and still dreaming of the day before them.

24. The Judgement of Gichita

OLD GICHITA sat, towards midday, under a buffalo-hide awning, scratching the ears of his favourite dog, Weuk-weuk, and watching two young boys wrestling on the sandy soil before him, the rays of the sun glinting upon their copper-coloured backs as they strove to show their chieftain what warriors they would become.

The old braves and the grey-haired men of the Council stood or squatted behind Gichita, silently watching the contest, sometimes sipping from the water gourds at their sides, for the day was warm, though the chieftain had had his awning moved up on to the clifftop, high above the great lake, so that he and his folk might enjoy what breeze there was. Far below them, the sheer cliff face flattened out and dark trees grew down to the green water's edge. The longship lay at anchor, a bowshot out, her sail furled, her timbers dry and faded by the sunlight.

And as the boys wrestled and the old men nodded, waking only to whisk the flies away from them, a squaw suddenly stood up and wailed in a high and nasal tone, 'Aiee! Aiee! But ill-fortune comes, Gichita!'

The old man turned, angry with the woman for breaking the warm silence. At first he could not see to what she was pointing, for there was a dust blowing across his sight, being old; and the heat of the day had drawn moisture out of the land to form a faint haze up there on the heights.

But at last he saw clearly the nature of the misfortune to which the woman referred. A handful of men were coming slowly along the shoulder of the hill. Gichita recalled that two score of men had gone forth that morning at dawn; but here were not more than six returning.

And as they came still closer, Gichita saw that of that six three only were red men, of his own folk, and the others were white strangers. His eyes picked out the giant Grummoch, who seemed to be half leading, half carrying Heome. Harald, the Viking leader, was helping another white man to carry someone, who hung limp between them. The others walked slowly, like men who had come a long distance and were nigh exhausted.

Gichita called sharply for the two boys to stop wrestling. They did so, and crept, afraid, behind the awning. The old dog, Weuk-weuk, did the same, sensing that his master was troubled in his heart and wished not to be worried.

And then Gichita saw that the red man who was being carried by the two white ones was his own warrior son, Wawasha; and he knew from the way Wawasha's arm hung down that the brave was dead.

The squaws knew this also, and fell to their knees and covered their heads with dust. The older braves pulled their blankets over their eyes and shuffled away, so as not to be near Gichita when the greatest of his grief came upon him.

And so Harald and Grummoch returned, with dead Wawasha and gibbering Heome. And with them were only one other Viking, and two sorely wounded Beothuk braves, besides Wawasha and Heome. The others lay stark in the sun upon the ancient burial mound, the birds already squabbling over them, the carrion-foxes sniffing about the base of the hill.

And Harald laid down the body of Wawasha before his father and, swaying with tiredness of mind and body, told the story of that bloody day above the sacred stone quarries.

And old Gichita listened, rocking backwards and forwards on his buffalo-hide pallet, moaning like a sick animal at his great loss. Now the drums of the women, the flat death-drums, began to murmur behind Harald's words, keeping up an undertone of grief in the sunlight.

And Harald said, 'Gichita, blood-father, our sadness is great, both yours and mine; for we have both lost a man we loved. Yet there is no profit in tears or in wailing, for they will not bring back laughter to dead lips, or sight to dead eyes. Wawasha is dead. The gods have taken him. There is no more to say.'

Harald stood for a while, leaning on his sword, Peacegiver, which he had taken up as they passed through the encampment on their way to the heights above the lake.

His face was drawn and haggard, filthy with blood and dust. His great arms were gashed, his clothing half cut from him. His hair hung damp and matted about his ears.

Grummoch sank to his knees now, his tawny head bowed with tiredness, his hands hanging before him as though they were asleep.

Heome stood between the two Beothuk braves, his thin lips twitching, the muscles of his pale face working as though they were ripples on the surface of a lake. His weak body was shaken from time to time with spasms, as though he were already an old man, ready for death.

And when the long silence had grown as heavy as a great weight of logs or of buffalo-meat, Gichita held up his hands for the squaws to begin their drumming again, for he was about to make his pronouncement, to speak his words of judgement, which a chief must speak.

At first his voice was flat and dead, like the sound of the night wind rustling among dry sedges; and then it gained more life, more fullness as he went on.

'Members of the Council, my braves, my white guests – blood has been shed. Tears will not bring it back. Vengeance will not bring it back. Nothing will ever bring it back. The warriors who have died, both red and white, will not come back and walk amongst us ever again, though we weep, though we cry for revenge. Wawasha will never sit by my side again . . .'

The squaws began to wail at these words, and the old men of the Beothuk Council bowed their heads and murmured. Heome suddenly shook his wild head and began to beat upon the little drum that hung from his neck still, striking the skin with the heel of his hands, in unison with the other drums, as though he, too, mourned the dead.

Gichita stared at him as though he had never seen him before. And then he said, 'On whom should we call for revenge? Who is there worth the dead who lie on the hill for the wolves to carry away, now? There is only Heome; only Heome, who smiles and plays his little drum before you now, mourning his dead brother and all the braves who lie upon the hill. Those of you who have lost friends, or sons, have the blood right, if you choose to take it, the right to take vengeance on the man-thing who shudders before you. Those of you who wish may take the war-axe and let it speak to the head of Heome, poor Heome, who wished to be a brave but was denied by the gods. Take your vengeance now, old men; take it upon Heome, if that will satisfy you, if that will repay you for the strong sons you have lost.'

Harald looked up for a moment and saw the headman of the Council shaking his grizzled head, and heard him say, 'We of the Beothuk Council are beyond such acts of blood, Gichita. Though Heome died a score of times, that would not repay us for our lost sons.'

Harald saw the smile creep across the pale face of Heome, saw his great eyes suddenly blaze with a flat amber light, the look that comes into the eyes of a wolf when it slides safely away from its hunters and runs for freedom.

Harald gave a snort, to clear his nostrils of the foulness of the air, and, sick at heart with the memory of his dead friends, moved away from the group about the awning, to the edge of the tall cliff.

He saw the lake below, and the clustered pine trees that bordered the lake. He saw *Long Snake* lolling on the waves, never more to be manned by Northmen, and then the tears began to run down his cheeks. As he stood there, with the breeze lifting his tangled bloody hair, he named his friends again, silently, as though in homage – Gudbrod Gudbrodsson, Thorfinn Thorfinnson, Jamsgar Havvarson, Wawasha, and all the others.

For a fleeting instant, he even thought of the name of poor wretched Havlock Ingolfson who had screamed with the birds on the salt-caked skerry that night so long ago,

deserted by Haakon Redeye, deserted by Harald Sigurdson, deserted even by Odin . . . Only the Shield-maiden had spoken up for poor Havlock Ingolfson . . .

Then Harald heard Gichita say, 'My braves, you are generous. You will not kill my only son, Heome, and for that I, an old man, am grateful, for, poor thing that he is, he is all I have left now, the only blood I have.'

For an instant, Harald almost fell upon his knees before the old chief and offered to serve him as his son, all his life. But then he recalled Asa Thornsdaughter and his two sons, Svend and Jaroslav . . . One day, one day, perhaps, he might get back to them again, beside the fjord . . . One day, before the boys had grown to be men and had quite forgotten him . . .

Then Heome spoke, and his voice was thin and trembling, like that of a bird, light and bodiless, fluttering above the heads of men, almost above their understanding.

'Heome, son of Gichita, brother to brave Wawasha, speaks to you. Listen and be silent, for Heome's voice is the voice of the gods, the voice of the raindrops, the voice of the little drum. In the pattering of my drum, hear ye now the voices of the rain, the torrents, the falling of leaves. Hear ye now the message that the first gods tried to bring to man but could not speak, for lack of tongues and hands. Heome lacks hands, too. He is like the gods, he is the gods! But Heome has a voice and a little drum, and the magic of the gods is in that drum. Hark!'

Then he gave such a blow on the taut skin that it split across, like a gaping mouth. But Heome did not notice that, and went on beating at the soundless gourd, his stiff hands moving in a frenzy.

'Hark ye! Hark ye!' he intoned now. 'In the thunder of my drum speaks the voice of the great mountains, the enormous forests. Out of my drum comes the call of the Wendigo, the horned beast that quests for the bodies and souls of men through the snow wastes and down along the lakesides. Those of you who would live, listen to that voice, for I am the Wendigo, the questing beast, the . . .'

Then Gichita, the old chief, drew his withered hand across his eyes, and groaned with anguish. To the brave who stood beside him, he said in a broken voice, 'Take the poor fool and bind his hands and feet. The gods have stolen his senses away and they will not return. Heome has killed his brother and now his heart will never be whole. From now on he shall live with the squaws and the young children, for he is no fit companion of men. It had been better to have killed him, my braves, in vengeance.'

Harald heard these words, suffering that the old man should have been caused to speak them. Then suddenly he heard other words, which he did not understand, until it was too late. They were the words of crazed Heome.

'Viking dog,' he screamed, 'on *your* shoulders lies the blame! Until you came, we were a folk of peace!'

Then suddenly Heome was running forward with a slithering, scurrying rush, the red dust rising about his legs, his shrivelled hands whirling like those of a scarecrow. And he was upon Harald before the Viking knew it, before he could prepare.

Then Harald heard the high cry of alarm from the braves under the buffalo-skin awning, and saw Grummoch rise and put his great hands before his staring eyes.

And then, cackling like a night-hawk, Heome flung his arms about Harald and toppled him to the crumbling edge of the cliff above the great lake.

The two fell from sight, one screaming, one silent.

When the giant Grummoch reached the cliff edge, all he saw was a rivulet of stones that raced madly down in a shroud of red dust.

25. Long Snake's Last Voyage

GRUMMOCH and the one remaining Viking made their way down the slope towards the lake, followed by those of the braves who could still perform such feats.

The Viking, a small man called Thorgeif, from Lakkesfjord, no great hand with axe, but a fine sailor, said, 'If Harald's fall was broken by a bed of moss, such as grows down here in the dampness, he might yet be alive.'

Grummoch did not answer, so great was his grief.

Thorgeif said again, 'Or if he fell into the boughs of a tree, they would save his life, perhaps.'

Then Grummoch turned upon the man and swore at him, harshly, not meaning to hurt him, but too full of grief to hold his tongue. Then Thorgeif was silent, and ran with the sweat coursing down his face and his thin jaws set.

And at last they found Harald Sigurdson, not on a bed of moss, or in the boughs of a tree, but on the toothed edge of a rock shoulder, lying like a broken doll, but still breathing.

At his feet lay Heome, smiling but dead, the broken drum still about his neck, and the sword Peacegiver through him.

Thorgeif said in his simple way, 'Harald must have rammed this message home even as they fell. There was never such a fighter before.'

Then Harald, from the rock from which Grummoch dared not try to move him, said in a whisper, 'I have struck many shrewd blows, Thorgeif Rammson of Lakkesfjord, where the flax grows better than anywhere else in the Northland, but this was my masterpiece. It had to be done swiftly, or the wolf might have gone scot-free to trouble others.'

Grummoch laved Harald's head with water from the lake.

'Lie easy, brother,' he said, 'and do not talk.'

Harald smiled and nodded gently. But in a short while he whispered again, 'That was a good blow, was it not, Grummoch? Did you ever see a better blow? And all done in the air! Where is Thorfinn? He should make a song about it. Where is Thorfinn?'

While Thorgeif knelt down and began to weep, Grummoch told Harald that Thorfinn was in the woods, looking for a hare for dinner, though the words almost choked him to speak.

Harald said, smiling, 'He was always a great fellow for his stomach, that Thorfinn . . . I remember, out on the seal-skerries beyond Isafjord, one autumn . . . I remember . . . I remember . . .'

But Harald Sigurdson did not say what he remembered, for those things suddenly seemed to be of little importance to him.

Then, with the grave-faced red men about him, he whispered again at last, 'Asa Thornsdaughter, and my two sons, Svend and Jaroslav, are waiting above the fjord to see *Long Snake* come in to haven, Grummoch. I have just seen them, and they send their dear love, my friend.'

Now the giant Grummoch turned away his tangled tawny head and let the salt tears run as they pleased. He heard Harald say, 'On the way home, let us pick up poor Havlock Ingolfson from the skerry. He will be mighty cold, Grummoch . . . mighty cold now, after a winter in the icy seas.'

Old Gichita was carried on his litter to Harald's side, and touched the Viking, with fingers as gentle as those of a woman, upon the ruined forehead.

'Go easy, my son,' he said, 'you have nothing to fear. You are a man. The gods know that and wait for you.'

And though he spoke in the red men's tongue, Harald heard him and understood him and opened his eyes for the last time and said, 'Red Father, I go easy and my hand is in the hand of my brother, Wawasha. He stands beside me now, smiling that we are together again.'

Then Harald gave a little shiver and shook his head a time or two. At that moment, a skein of geese flew over the pine woods, the air whistling in their pinions.

Harald's voice came from far away and his eyes were closed now.

'The Shield-maiden has come with her swans,' he said. 'Do you not hear them?'

Grummoch bent over him and clasped his cold hand. Then all the braves bowed down their feathered heads as they passed the rock on which the Viking lay, in their last homage.

And at last, when it seemed that the world had stopped in its courses through the sky, Gichita lifted up his head and wiped his eyes.

'The three of them shall go together,' he said. 'At last Heome shall be with warriors.'

And so *Long Snake* was brought to shore by the braves, and her deck piled high with the resinous wood of the fir tree; and Harald was laid with his sword, Peacegiver, in his right hand, and with Wawasha on the one side of him and Heome on the other.

In Wawasha's hand the red men placed a war-axe; but Heome's hands were still stiff and useless, even now, and they were forced to lay his axe upon his chest, beside the broken war-drum.

As the sun was sinking below the far hills, the red men flung tarry torches among the dried wood, and then set *Long Snake* off on her voyage, with the wind of evening in her parched sail.

She was twenty bowshots away when the red flames leaped the length of her mast and ate up the wood and the hide of the sail; she was thirty bowshots away when the flames ravened down to her waterline.

And then, still flaring like a great furnace, *Long Snake* slipped below the surface of the lake, just as the distant sun fell from sight behind the hills.

Thorgeif said softly to Grummoch, 'I have sailed with Harald Sigurdson since he was a lad – by North Sea, White Sea and Middle Sea. But I never thought to see him sail away and leave me in a strange land, among foreign men.'

Grummoch turned from the lake and put his great arm about Thorgeif's shoulders.

'We shall have each other to speak Norse to in the evening time,' he said slowly. 'A man must be thankful even for small mercies in this world.'

Then, to cover their grief, they walked together, chanting an old feast-hall ditty from Jomsburg, about a man who put his arm round a bear in the darkness, thinking it was his sweetheart.

But before they reached the bright fires of the Beothuk encampment, they were silent again. For a while there would be nothing worth saying. They knew that well enough.

A PUFFIN BOOK

Extra! Extra!

READ ALL ABOUT IT!

HENRY TREECE

THE VIKING SAGA

1911 *Henry Treece is born 22 December at Wednesbury, Staffordshire. He goes to the high school there, and then wins a scholarship to Birmingham University*

1933 *Graduates from Birmingham University after studying English, History and Spanish. During this time he begins writing poetry*

1934 *Starts teaching English, working in several schools. When war breaks out, he joins the Royal Air Force and works in Bomber Command intelligence*

1939 *Marries Mary Woodman and settles in Lincolnshire where he becomes a teacher at Barton-upon-Humber Grammar School*

1940 *His first book of poetry is published by Faber and Faber, to be followed by four more*

1952 *His first historical novel for adults,* The Dark Island, *is published*

1954 *His first book for children,* Legions of the Eagle, *is published. Over the next twelve years he writes many children's books, mostly historical novels set in times when people faced great changes in society*

1955 Viking's Dawn, *the first in the Viking Saga trilogy, is published*

1957 The Road to Miklagard, *the second part of the trilogy, is published*

1959 *Retires from teaching*

1960 Viking's Sunset, *the final part of the Viking trilogy, is published*

1966 *Dies 10 June, aged fifty-four*

1967 The Dream-Time, *his last novel for children is published posthumously, with a postscript by renowned children's historical fiction writer, Rosemary Sutcliff*

INTERESTING FACTS

Henry Treece was good at boxing. He was the captain of one of the teams at his university.

One of Henry Treece's sons, Richard, played in several rock bands, including Help Yourself.

Henry Treece did not like violence, and thought war was dreadful. However, he respected a brave fighter. In one of his books, a character says, 'He wished that all people, the men and women and horses and owls and dogs could agree to speak the same words. Then all things would be easy, to speak and to be understood. Perhaps no one would fight then.'

Over his lifetime, Henry Treece wrote and published more than seventy books of poetry and historical novels.

WHERE DID THE STORY COME FROM?

Henry Treece was very interested in poems and stories, and the Vikings were fine poets and storytellers. One source for The Viking Saga *is the large body of literature the Vikings left us. These were first told orally, but in the thirteenth century, after the Latin alphabet had arrived in Scandinavia, Icelandic monks wrote them down.*

The sagas are long tales of heroes and their deeds. Egil's Saga *and* Laxdaela Saga *are famous examples. The Eddas are poetry and other literary forms. The story of the death of Balder, which Harald tells his Beothuk friends, comes from the Völuspà, the first of twenty-nine Eddic poems in the* Codex Regius. *This collection gives us the Norse story of the world, from the beginning until the twilight of the gods.*

As well as Viking sources, other people wrote about the Vikings. Ahmed ibn Fadlan was an Arab traveller and writer, who was sent on a diplomatic mission by the Caliph of Baghdad to the ruler of the Bulgars. He described the people he met, and gave a detailed and impressive account of a Viking ship burial and the cremation of a Russian chief on the banks of the Volga River in AD 922.

There is a wealth of archaeologists' finds from Scandinavia, Iceland and Greenland, and the Vikings also left their mark while travelling through Russia and down to what is Istanbul today. They traded – and fought – everywhere they went. Henry Treece would have been fascinated by the news of the discovery of a Viking settlement at L'Anse aux Meadows on the island of Newfoundland, Canada. The first major dig took place from 1961. It can be no coincidence that Harald Sigurdson and the crew of Long Snake *landed in north-west Newfoundland, and met the Beothuks who lived there!*

GUESS WHO?

'Gnorre Nithing, you have given our ship her name. She shall be the Nameless. *She shall wander as you have done, Gnorre, an outlaw of the seas. Perhaps all men's hands will be against her, as they are against you. But though she may be nothing at her launching, she may prove to be something at her beaching when she returns. Then we will give her another name, you and I.'*

B

'I have news that my grandmother in Orkney is anxious to talk to me. You see, she sent me on an errand to a neighbour in Ireland ten years ago, to borrow a dozen eggs that she needed, to make a pudding for my uncle, who is in bed with a bad Caledonian cold. I am afraid I was a bad lad, and forgot about the

pudding and now my uncle is getting restive. So I must go back and tell my grandmother, in Iceland, that her neighbour in Ireland had stopped keeping hens.'

C

'You are real men, I can see that; and warriors, I can see that also, from the scars you bear. I observe, moreover, that you come from the north - by your accent and by your fondness for bears' claw necklaces!'

D

'The language he speaks is the "first language", as we call it; it is the tongue the first red men brought with them when they came, a thousand men's lives ago, over the northern ice with their packs on their backs, to settle here in woodland and forest, in desert and by seashore.'

E

'If one could carry this great host back to the Northland, and set spears and real iron axes in their hands, what might one not do! The warlord who led such a host might conquer England, Frankland, Miklagard, Spain, oh, everywhere! Such a lord would be the greatest the world had ever known, brothers!'

ANSWERS: A) *Thorkell Fairhair* B) *Grummoch the giant*
C) *Kristion* D) *Wawasha* E) *Harald Sigurdson*

WORDS GLORIOUS WORDS!

*Here are some **words** and **meanings** from the story. You can also look them up in the **dictionary** or online for fuller explanations!*

Aeolian harp *a musical instrument with strings that sound when the wind blows through them. Aeolus was the Greek god of the winds*

amphora *a Greek container for liquid, with two handles*

bog oak *wood that has been preserved in a peat bog. It is black, and very hard*

bruited *spread about, in the sense of passing on news, gossip or rumour*

caulking *filling up the seams in a boat or ship with waterproof material*

corselet *armour that protects the body*

dhow *a ship used by Arab sailors. It has a lateen rig – a triangular sale held at an angle of 45° to the mast*

dun *a fortress or fortified place, a royal residence*

eke-name *a nickname. 'Eke' means 'also'*

flensing *cutting up a whale or a seal*

gorget *a piece of armour designed to protect the throat*

gunwale *upper edge of a ship's side*

gyve *a shackle or fetter, particularly for the legs*

jarl *a powerful chieftain, who owned land. Only the king had a higher rank*

Jomsvikings *a group of Viking mercenaries, who would fight for anyone who could afford them*

Norns *The giant goddesses who looked after the fates of men and gods. There were three Norns: Fate, Obligation and Being*

palsy *a medical condition in which someone is paralysed and has fits of uncontrollable shaking*

pannikin *a small cup*

ropewalk *a long piece of ground where rope is made*

samite *a silk fabric, sometimes with gold threads woven into it*

skirling *making a noise like a bagpipe*

skerry *a reef or a small rocky island*

Thing *a public meeting of freemen in a particular area, sometimes a whole kingdom. Those attending discussed matters of importance. The Thing was also a court, when a jury would decide whether the accused should be fined or outlawed*

thrall *a slave*

Ultima Thule *the end of the world. 'Ultima' is Latin for 'the last', 'furthest'*

Valhalla *the hall of the slain. In Norse mythology, the souls of warriors who died in battle were taken to this hall, which belonged to the god Odin*

White Sea *an inlet of the Barents Sea, on the north coast of Russia*

wolf's head *an outlaw, someone who should be hunted down like a wolf*

QUIZ

What was the name of the magician from Lapland who could raise the wind with a piece of string?

a) *Gnorre Nithing*

b) *Bjorn*

c) *Horic*

d) *Sigurd*

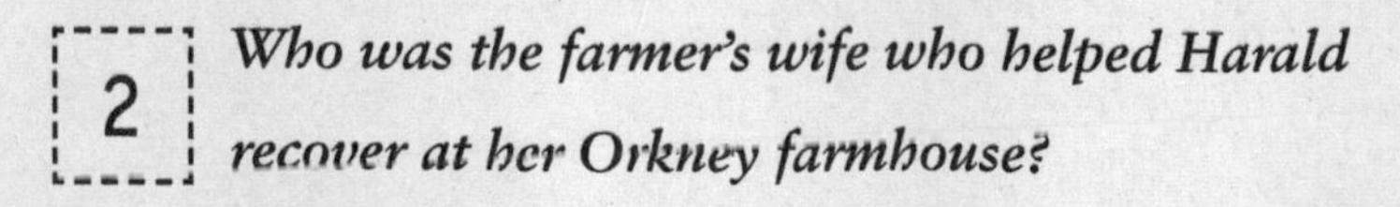

Who was the farmer's wife who helped Harald recover at her Orkney farmhouse?

a) *Astrid*

b) *Asa*

c) *Solvig*

d) *Ada*

3

Where was the Nameless *shipwrecked?*

a) *Ronaldsay*

b) *Leire's Dun*

c) *Dun Laoghaire*

d) *Leth Cuinn*

4

In what kind of boat did Harald and his companions escape?

a) *a coracle*

b) *a curragh*

c) *a knörr*

d) *a rowing boat*

5

Who was the prince with whom Harald sailed to Ireland?

a) *Arkill*

b) *Thorkell*

c) *Arnott*

d) *Tarquin*

6

Who was the king whose treasure they wanted to raid?

a) *MacMiorog*

b) *MacGillicuddy*

c) *Macbeth*

d) *MacIntosh*

7

What was the name of his town?

a) *Dundrum*

b) *Dunedin*

c) *Dun-an-oir*

d) *Dun na mBarc*

What was the name of the town where Harald and his companions served as slaves?

a) *Jebel Tarik*

b) *Jedburgh*

c) *Jericho*

d) *Djibouti*

9

What was the name of the Captain of the Guard in Miklagard?

a) *Kieran*

b) *Kristopher*

c) *Kyril*

d) *Kristion*

10 ***Which empress did they serve?***

a) *Irene*

b) *Zoe*

c) *Theodora*

d) *Iris*

11 ***The men of which people captured Harald and Grummoch on their way home from Miklagard?***

a) *Cossacks*

b) *Wends*

c) *Bulgars*

d) *Kathars*

12 ***What was the name of the man Harald left on the skerry?***

a) *Haakon Redeye*

b) *Haakon Baconfat*

c) *Knud Ulfson*

d) *Havlock Ingolfsson*

13

Who were the people Harald met when he left Greenland and travelled west?

a) *the Algonkin*

b) *the Abnaki*

c) *the Beothuk*

d) *the Oneida*

Who was killed with an arrow made from mistletoe?

a) *Loki*

b) *Hoder*

c) *Odin*

d) *Balder*

What were Harald and his friends going to dig out of the ground by the great lake?

a) *iron*

b) *red stone*

c) *gold*

d) *clay*

ANSWERS: 1) *c* 2) *b* 3) *b* 4) *b* 5) *a* 6) *a* 7) *c* 8) *a* 9) *d* 10) *a* 11) *d* 12) *d* 13) *c* 14) *d* 15) *b*

IN THIS YEAR

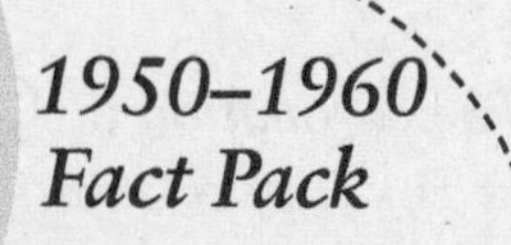

What else was happening in the world when Henry Treece's Viking books were first published?

Walt Disney's Cinderella *and* Alice in Wonderland *are released in 1950 and 1951 respectively, and become* huge hits.

The Korean War *begins in 1950 and continues until 1953. It starts as a civil war between North and South Korea, then develops into an* international conflict *between the democratic and communist powers of the US and the USSR. It becomes one of the most* brutal *wars ever fought.*

Climber Edmund Hillary *and Sherpa mountaineer* Tenzing Norgay *scale Mount Everest and become the first to reach its summit on 29 May 1953.*

The coronation of Queen Elizabeth II *takes place in 1953. In celebration, people are given extra food rations – four ounces of margarine and one extra pound of sugar.*

The polio vaccine *is launched in 1955 and the world has been using it ever since.*

The first McDonald's *opens in Illinois, USA, in 1955.*

The Sound of Music *opens on Broadway, New York, USA, in 1959.*

In 1960 the British Prime Minister Harold Macmillan *gives the* 'Wind of Change' *speech in Cape Town, in which he announces his government's intention to grant independence to the territories in South Africa currently under British rule.*

MAKE AND DO

*The **Short-twig** – a **Secret Code!***

*When Vikings wrote things down, they used **runes**. These were designed to be scratched or cut or carved on wood or stone or metal. The alphabet was called the Futhark, after the first letters. There were several versions of this runic alphabet. The runes in use in Norway at the time of* The Viking Saga *were called 'Short-twig'.*

TO WRITE RUNES, YOU WILL NEED:

- *Paper (or a blackboard, a slate, a small plank – anything hard with a smooth surface)*
- *Pen (or pencil or chalk)*

Here are the letters:

a b c d þ e f g h i k l m n o p q

ç r t u v w x y y z æ ø

Can you work out what your name would be using Short-twig runes? You may have to use the rune with the nearest sound for some letters. The fifth rune, which looks a bit like the letter 'p', is a 'th' sound.

Use this for writing important and secret information. Share it with your friends, and use it as a secret code!

DID YOU KNOW?

Miklagard is the Viking name for Byzantium, which was later called Constantinople – today we call it Istanbul!

The earliest pictures of Stone Age boats have been found in North Norway. They are cut into rocks.

The Vikings invented the keel, which makes a ship more stable, and allows the sailors to control its direction. They also invented a steering oar, which was attached to the starboard side of the ship. Their ships had a shallow draught – they did not sit deep in the water – so they could sail up rivers as well as out to sea.

The mast of a Viking ship was placed exactly in the middle. This meant the ship could be sailed

forwards or backwards, depending on what was needed.

The great longships in which raiders travelled the seas, were called 'drakkar' *(dragon ships). The standard size was about 28 metres long, and about 4.5 metres broad, taking fifty or sixty crewmen. Ships for trading, which were wider and shorter, were called* 'knörr'.

The remains of a Viking settlement was discovered in 1960 at L'Anse aux Meadows (say 'Lancy Meadows' – it comes from the French for 'Jellyfish Cove') in north-west Newfoundland, Canada. There were three large houses, and several smaller buildings. They appear to date from around AD *1000. Viking sagas from Iceland mention 'Vinland' – could this site be Vinland? In 2012 further evidence of Vikings was found, at Tanfield Valley on Baffin Island and two other islands in the Canadian territory of Nunavut. These remains appear to be older than the settlement at L'Anse aux Meadows.*

In 2014, remains of a Viking ship were found in Tennessee by archaeologists from the University of Memphis, USA, excavating at the point where the Wolf River meets the Mississippi. It was a knörr, *a merchant ship. A broken sword was also found.*

Vikings travelled down south-flowing rivers to Byzantium, carrying their ships past obstacles or over land between rivers. These Vikings were called 'Rus', from a Finnish word meaning 'Swedes', and the land was called 'Russia' after them. They overpowered the Slavic tribes they met, and set up trading posts, which became towns such as Novgorod and Kiev.

So many Vikings travelled to Byzantium, and they were such good fighters, that in the tenth century a special unit of the Imperial Army was set up for them. It was called the Varangian Guard, The Varangian Guards served as the Emperor's personal bodyguards.

The red pipestone prized by the Beothuks and other indigenous peoples is quarried from hills in what is today south-west Minnesota, USA. When Europeans came to the North American continent, they heard about the soft rock that could easily be carved, and saw such things as pipe bowls made from it, but it wasn't until the nineteenth century that they actually found out where the rock was obtained.

PUFFIN WRITING TIPS

Two heads are better than one! Find a ***writing buddy*** *with whom to discuss and develop ideas!*

Change your scenery, *and go see something you've never seen before.*